After the Flood

a dystopian novel of hope

After the Flood

After the Flood

a dystopian novel of hope

Shane Joseph

Hidden Brook Press

 Hidden Brook Press
www.HiddenBrookPress.com
writers@HiddenBrookPress.com

After the Flood
a dystopian novel of hope
by Shane Joseph

Layout and Design – Richard M. Grove
Cover Design – Joanna Joseph

Typeset in Garamond

Printed and bound in Canada

Library and Archives Canada Cataloguing in Publication

Joseph, Shane, 1955-
    After the flood : a dystopian novel of hope / Shane Joseph.

ISBN 978-1-897475-67-6

    I. Title.

PS8619.O846A6 2010   C813'.6   C2010-907502-1

To Jonathan, Inez, Richard and Lizz.
Yours is the world after the Flood
– please keep it safe.

Part 1

Genesis

The Lord said, "I will wipe mankind whom I have created from the face of the earth—man and animals and creatures that move along the ground, and birds in the air—for I am grieved that I made them."

—Genesis 6:7

Prologue

May 12, 2012

W*HEN THE TWO BLACK-SUITED MEN CAME to our door, I knew it was time to leave. They were Witnesses, one tall and black, the other short and white, prowling the neighbourhood with increased frequency. They looked confident as they stood on the doorstep with the rain pelting down behind them, shaking the water off their trench coats and umbrellas.*

I interrupted their usual opening spiel. "Same answer this week, I'm afraid—we have religion in this home," I said.

"Yes, brother," the black man said. "But the kingdom of God is now at hand. In fact, it's down on Kingston Road, not a half mile from here."

"That close, eh? I thought we would have more time."

"Are you ready to receive?"

"We have received. My folks are packed to leave. I suggest you do the same."

"God be with you, brother," the short one said. "Many have joined us today—the culmination of our work is at hand. It's a day of great fulfillment!"

"Good. You'd better be off then. And don't leave it too late either," I said, shutting the door on them. Their smugness bothered me. Through the window I saw their companions swarming across my neighbour's waterlogged lawn. My van, packed with our belongings, stood in the driveway. Dad's boat was on the trailer in the backyard, but it would have to stay where it was—we were not going to be slowed down. In hindsight, the boat may have taken us farther.

"Time to go folks—the flooding has reached Kingston Road," I said, rushing down to the basement. Dad was packing his fishing rods; he had four of them already on the roof of the van. The damp patches in the basement floor had widened since my last visit half an hour ago. "Dad, come on, there will be plenty of time for fishing later." I threw his raincoat across his shoulders and gently led him upstairs.

"I'm not so sure about that anymore," he said shaking his head and muttering under his breath. "Hope there isn't too much water damage to the house. You think my tool shed will be okay?"

"Sure," I lied. I was worried about the shed too. About everything. But there was no use in showing it.

"Help me get the baby's things in the van, Sam." Adele slowly made her way from the bedrooms upstairs; she was six months pregnant and beginning to look a little weak in the mornings. Cole, carrying a small suitcase, shut the door behind them. They had abandoned their waterlogged apartment downtown to stay with us these past two weeks. Cole was good for Adele, caring, respectful and kind; he had been that way ever since they'd met in high school.

"Not much more we can take, I'm afraid, the van's packed—even the roof."

"But we have to take the baby's things, no?"

"Sure we have to," I said, helping her down the stairs. It was nice embracing my kid sister. We didn't do that much anymore.

"Not taking your jazz collection?"

"No, there's no room. It'll be safe 'til we return."

"Samson Arthurs! You never let it out of your sight."

"It'll be okay. Where's Mum?"

"Watching TV again."

When I went into my parents' bedroom, Mum was indeed watching TV and wiping her eyes. Tissues littered the floor.

"Why do we have to leave, son?" she said, staring into one of those riveting news broadcasts that ran non-stop now. I went over and switched off the TV.

"Come on, Ma. It's time."

"But the house—thirty-five years of our lives are in this house."

"We'll come back when the emergency is over, Ma. And we'll fix the damage, if there is any."

"You promise?"

I didn't say anything but gently coaxed her out to the van. Dad, Cole and Adele were already inside, squished amidst the food containers, clothing and memorabilia threatening to burst the van at its seams. I checked the tarpaulin over the ski rack and it looked like it would hold, even though the wind was beginning to pick up. I was soaked by the time I slid into the driver's seat. When we left our street and joined the stream of cars headed north for the highway, I didn't realize that would be the last time I would see the old house on Saddler Street, where I had lived my entire life.

Chapter 1

WHEN I LOOK AT THE "OLD GUARD" encircling our family mausoleum, I remember my father's words about his friends. "They never age," he said. "They just fade away."

Nathan Goldman stands tall and erect, but his thinning gray hair and emaciated body betray his frailty. "Damn awful weather for a funeral!" he coughs, gritting his teeth against the wind. He takes a cigar out of his pocket, then changes his mind and puts it back. I recognize the threadbare coat from ten years ago. It's hard to believe that he is the richest man in Tolemac and that he was my father's staunchest ally.

"I hope Samson is at peace, wherever he is," says my mother-in-law Kamala, standing to his right, stifling a tear. She is a beautiful woman in her late fifties. She has the grace of a dancer and yoga practitioner melded with a keen brain and a gentle heart. It's hard to imagine she is chief justice of our city-state. She loved my father from a distance; I have always known that, although she will never admit it to me.

Belva White Dove, in her flowing orange and black kaftan, leads the funeral ceremony. Optimistic and in control, her matronly jowls are subdued today, yet her voice retains its high melodious pitch during the hymns. Head schoolmistress at the Tolemac Academy of Learning and newly-appointed spiritual leader of our church, she looks the same as when she taught me in high school.

It is raining; a thin May drizzle that quickly turns the ground into mud and makes the grass ooze. In Samson's youth, the ground absorbed more rainwater than it does today. In fact, it does not rain much anymore except during the winter. Today's rain is a rarity. A connection to the Old World Samson emerged from. Belva preaches a medley of animal medicine chants and biblical verses. My father would have loved the psalm she has chosen: "The Lord is my light and my salvation—whom shall I fear? Though an army may beseech me, my heart shall not fear. Do not turn me over to the desire of my foes . . ." She then leads us in an Old-World hymn, "Nearer My God to Thee," an anachronism on this twenty-fifth day of May 2046.

Umbrellas go up as the drizzle thickens to steady rain. I am impressed by the loyal following that has entered the gates of the mausoleum. Politicians from the Humanitarian and Capitalist realms, the church congregation, the river transport people, and the general populace of Tolemac, from as far away as the New Settlements—they are all here. Even John Williams is here. Poor, dumb, stupid John; dumb from the day I can remember; stupid from the day of his childhood accident when he swallowed construction glue that gave him a brain haemorrhage, tore out his insides and nearly killed him. John is unaccustomed to the rain. It drips off his well-tailored dark suit and cape and makes him look like a wet sparrow—an orphaned, lonely, wet sparrow. I allow the rain to fall on me too, without seeking the protection of a raincoat or umbrella. I want to get a sense of what it is like to be well and properly wet, as Samson had been during the Flood, when for days on end, all he could hope for was a bit of earth to hug that was not shaking or under water.

"Are you holding up?" Sonya inches up to me.

"I'm okay." I take her hand in mine. Sharing an umbrella with her mother, she has so much of Kamala's poise and dark eyes. She will age as beautifully as her mother. We have quarrelled a lot over this last year and only recently discovered the mystical bond that unites a husband and wife. Our children, Joey and Hannah, dressed in dark clothing and holding small umbrellas, stand respectfully beside their mother. Hannah, the serious one, takes after me with her blond curls, and looks like she is pondering a deep mystery. Joey has the dark hair and complexion of his mother.

"David..." Belva is next to me now. "Would you like to say something before we end the service?"

"No." What was there to say? There is not even a body in the coffin. This is just a ceremony to remind ourselves that my father has been finally pronounced officially "dead" and will now lie in peace next to my mother's remains in the family tomb and that we can get on with our lives, which have been on hold since he went missing.

"Are you sure? It's customary . . ."

"Yes, I am sure. You are doing a wonderful job. Please wrap it up for us."

After a few final words, the tomb is closed and people are lined up to shake my hand and to offer condolences. The President of the Federation of Humanitarian States—the FHS—passes by, having come up all the way from Oceania. Congressman Gordon, sole representative from the Capitalist realm, and his entourage follow closely behind. Gordon shakes our hands sincerely, spending meaningful moments with each family member.

"Don't forget to call me, David," he says, taking my hand. I stare into his kindly eyes. "We have to continue our work," he reminds me firmly.

The general population follows the politicians. I feel the sincerity in their hugs, even a tinge of remorse. They merely watched during Samson's persecution. Umbrellas and boots jostle around, drenching me with water and mud. I have never understood why they built the cemetery by the waterfront and not up on Sunset Hill. Something about it being one of the first places built, as there were many dead to bury before the post-Flood rebuilding began, and the fact that the buried could reside close to their less fortunate family members submerged forever in the waters surrounding Tolemac.

With the ceremony over, the people disperse towards their homes. Some go up Sunset Hill while others head down into the city core. And others walk over to the public transport terminal to take the forty-five minute monorail ride out to the New Settlements. Congressman Gordon's and the President of the FHS's respective entourages return to the helicopter terminal at the port. I take the uphill exit and pause just outside the cemetery gate for Sonya and the kids to catch up. I look upon downtown Tolemac hugging the harbour, about half a mile away. The crypts and mausoleums make the cemetery resemble a damp, miniature city within a city. Samson once told me that in the pre-Flood days, they buried people. But that will not work now with the water levels where they are, so we house our dead in these miniature marble houses.

I'm looking forward to going home. There is something I need to do once I get out of these wet clothes. Suddenly a voice from behind me calls, "David!"

It's Peter Lowry. My anger mounts at the sight of him.

"I'm surprised to see you out today."

"Things are out of control, David. This place needs fixing again."

"You've left it a bit late, haven't you?" I wave my hand carelessly towards our little city tumbling down the hill. The ocean, once a lake, surrounds it on all sides; there is no other land in sight—there never has been as far as I can remember. Rows of neatly arranged white houses run downhill indicating nothing but tranquility. But whenever the wind shifts, the smell of smouldering rubber wafts down from the Williams's house up on Sunset Hill, reminding us how John Williams found himself orphaned, and of the "fixing" that is needed.

"We must repair the damage," Peter continues. "I'm sorry for what's happened."

"You are?"

"David, if you hate me, I understand. But sometimes we only see things in retrospect. Can we meet tomorrow—say at eight o'clock at the youth centre?"

I can't believe my old opponent is talking of meeting at our old teenage hangout, which became my failed campaign's headquarters, just six months ago. I hear myself agreeing, "Okay!" It's the only sensible thing to say. He nods, turns on his heel and heads downhill. Sonya and the kids are at my side, and we begin our walk through the fading light. The rain is coming down harder now and I am soaked, but reluctant to share their umbrellas. I hope the rain will quench my anger, sense of loss, and helplessness and the thousand other emotions this funeral has evoked in me.

When we get home, I sit on the steps outside the house under the overhang, while Sonya, with an understanding glance, takes the kids inside. I am on the lower step and can see underneath the house. Even though our home on Lilydale Crescent is part way up Sunset, it's built on stilts because of the flooding that occurs from time to time. So we fill the hollow bottom with flowerbeds. And if the flowers wash away when the rain comes down really hard, we plant again after the waters recede. Samson instilled this practice in us, a practice that most early Tolemacians copied, for it gave them a reason to go on. "We shall overcome," he would say. "Despite the elements." Today, the daisies are peeping up yellow and bright—defiant against the rain falling outside and creeping in little rivulets under the house. I am wet and shivering. Yet, I do not want to go inside just yet.

"This place needs fixing again," Peter had said. Sure, more than anything it needs trust, sharing and tolerance again. It needs a swing back from the Capitalist forces that had enticed it, and still do, hovering just outside its physical and virtual political boundaries. And a change in laws, too—oh, those laws! And most important, we have to save the young people, the next generation, at any cost. During the Flood—trust, sharing and tolerance had gushed forth from the survivors and sustained them. But now, in times of relative calm and prosperity, we are falling back on our slothful, selfish human ways again. Peter had looked to me, expecting that I could magically fix all this. Just as the people who built Tolemac had looked to Samson's leadership after the Flood. Can I run away from this duty any longer? Would my father's spirit be disappointed in me if I did? He had waited patiently for me to get onto the public stage, yet it was I who held back for so long. My reluctance to go inside the house resembles that earlier hesitancy. But if I do not go inside I will soon catch pneumonia. Just like the destruction that is sure to engulf Tolemac if we—all of us—do not act quickly and be forever on guard. What was that old Canadian anthem—"O Canada, we stand on guard for thee!" No one did, and the Old World collapsed through a combination of human greed, seismic events and God's resulting punishment. This New World is ours to lose again. It all seems so overwhelming. Can I cry and have someone "take this cup away from me?" But tears elude me.

After another ten minutes, with the darkness of night fully descended on Tolemac, I pull my dripping coat about me and drag myself indoors.

Joey is on the Communicator as I come out from the shower, shedding my wet clothes. I am feeling only slightly better for being dry again. "Dad, they are talking about Grandpa in Oceania."

"Yes, I saw that." I see a pre-recorded clip on the screen. It has been repeated four times today already and I have seen each replay.

"He's hogged your Communicator, all day. He's not even using the one in his room," Hannah says.

"So what—and you've messed up your password again," Joey shouts back.

"I did not. You are being mean to me—again!"

Joey and Hannah are normally not this crabby, but I guess today is an unusual day.

"He was the best grandpa in the world," says Hannah.

"I'll straighten out your password tonight, honey," I say. Instinctively, I grab and hug her. Her golden curls smell of apple, but she does not giggle like she would normally. I start to feel better, just with her touch.

"Thank you, Daddy!" Then she goes into her room down the hall with her head bowed. Other than her recent outburst, she has been silent for most of today. She has still not seen Samson's ghost, which is comforting. Like her mother, seven-year-old Hannah often sees ghosts.

Sonya brings me a cup of hot ginchanecea tea. I take it gratefully. "Joey, it's time to get off the Communicator now," she says. "We agreed to turn in early today." Normally, Joey would protest, but on this occasion he gets up and follows his mother. The animated screen continues to pipe in various messages over the Infoway, our only link with the outside world all these years, until the helicopters arrived. Oh, there had been boats of course, but those we always took for granted.

Sonya turns to me and there is concern in her dark eyes. "Is this going to be another all-nighter? A good night's sleep will do you good, you know."

"I have a few things to tidy up here. Don't wait up for me." I sip my tea. The gloom is lifting rapidly now. "I won't be wading over my losses tonight, I promise."

When the sounds from the rest of the family subside in the rear of the house, I go into the study and pull out Samson's journal from my desk drawer. Over this last month, I have intended to read the journal many times, but always held back in case he was found alive. Reading a live person's personal secrets is spying and we were taught not to pry. But he is dead now, at least officially.

Although I've finished with the grieving part, there is still a piece of this story that needs closure. And the answers, I believe, are in his journal. It contains the story of those stoic souls who built our city and our lives after the Flood— their joys and their tragedies. I pray I will find those answers tonight, so that we can move on to the next phase of our lives.

I open the journal.

The picture on the inside flap shows Samson fresh out of university, towering above his parents, arms wrapped around both of them; dressed in a denim shirt and jeans, his wavy blond hair is blowing in the wind, and his sister

Adele, in ponytails, is looking admiringly up at him. When the Flood occurred, he was twenty-seven years old, an engineering graduate from the University of Toronto. He was also the youngest member on the board of governors of his local United Church, a group he argued with constantly because of their outdated ways of running a religious institution. The endless church committees and bureaucracy drove him crazy. That is why Tolemac, a city state of fifty thousand residents, has an Executive Committee of only eight board members and our Church of the New Covenant, a board of seven. And Samson would have preferred the Executive Committee to be even smaller—"Heaven is run by the Father, Son and the Holy Ghost. Why do we need so many to run this place?"

But the journal will tell his story better. Earlier today, just before leaving for the funeral, I read the first three pages out of curiosity, the part about how they left their old home in what was then known as Toronto. But my emotions got the better of me and I couldn't continue. Now I force myself back to where I stopped . . .

Chapter 2

May 13, 2012

WE'VE SPENT THE ENTIRE NIGHT *in this van. This ride was not like our regular rides down to Florida where we stopped off at motels along the way. The motels are shut down; no one is hanging around, everyone is moving, or trying to. The ground-level motels will become deathtraps when the waters come.*

Dad's complaining about his arthritis. He often has to get out and stretch his legs. That's no problem because the traffic moves about one mile an hour. I put in two extra tanks of gas—but it may not last the way we idle. Most gas stations are closed, and any that are still functioning are sold out of gas.

When I switch off the engine, people toot from behind—as if we were getting anywhere fast! At one point, just outside Port Hope, I pulled to the side of the road and let the traffic go by—it was bumper to bumper with cursing, swearing, young people singing and dancing and getting drunk; old people sleeping or praying; children bawling, being suckled by mothers who wished they had more breasts to go around. The music from the young people hit many falsetto notes, accentuating their underlying hysteria. The waters of Lake Ontario in the distance looked angry, swollen, and the railway tracks and beach cottages were under water. I am writing in this journal during these stops— not sure how much time I'll have further down the road.

Adele passed the crackers around continuously—cheese and crackers—I'll always associate them with a rising panic in my stomach now. Mum refused to eat today and has gone into one of her "moods."

A bunch of leather-jacketed, swastika-bearing bikers—brash, superior in their ability to get ahead—swerved in and out of the line of crawling traffic just out outside Pickering. Just outside Oshawa, we ground to a complete halt and the word of mouth filtering back through open windows was that one of the bikers had run out of gas (duh!) and his buddies were holding up traffic, demanding fuel from other vehicles. A slow growl of discontent in the line increased to a roar in no time and then, magically, the line started moving again. When we passed the offending site in Oshawa, we saw the bikes all piled up in a ditch, and a couple of the bikers nursing their wounds. Well, at least some power hierarchies are being toppled in this calamity.

A man tapped on the window and pleaded for water. His hair was blowing wild all over his face, despite the constant drizzle falling outside. Water—what an irony—we are drowning in the stuff and yet there is none that's drinkable! Cole put the side window down, ushering a blast of moist warm air into the van, and gave the man a glassful of water from our supply of six plastic jugs, the first one now empty. Mum scowled at him. "At this rate, we'll be feeding the masses and starving ourselves to death," she said. Then she burst into tears, "Why am I talking like this—why have I become so selfish?"

"You have strong lifeline, sweetheart," Dad said from the front passenger seat. "Here, Sam—let me out again—this leg is killing me. I'm also finding it difficult to breathe."

"What's got into you?" Mum was being feisty again. "The windows are wide open. And the breeze from this window will blow the van over. And you can't breathe?"

"Settle down, everyone." I had to act firmly to reduce the crankiness permeating the van. "Save your energy. We have a long ride ahead."

I pulled over to the parking lane to let Dad out again. I'd pick him up ten minutes later and fifty yards ahead.

The journal record of the exodus ends here with a more recent note by Samson to refer to the "Flood Broadcasts" for further details. I know what that means—most Tolemacians have heard these broadcasts. They are still played in schools as part of history lessons. They are a collection of radio broadcasts from the period—don't ask me how Samson got them or why he kept them. He claimed to have received the recordings from various sources in the New World over the past thirty-three years. He then pieced them together into a collage of digitized data stored on the local server of his home Communicator, along with his favourite pre-Flood movies.

Paul Manfield was the local announcer on those Flood Broadcasts. Long dead now, he possessed the calmest voice I've ever heard. I'm pretty sure that even if the broadcasting station had been on fire, Paul would not have deviated from his deeply modulated tone, which soothed people as much as it drove them crazy with the news he delivered.

I dial up Samson's home Communicator. He'd included his password and digital signature in that final email he sent me. Finding the Flood Broadcasts from his personal portal contents is easy. I hit the play button, and lean back, closing my eyes, letting Paul Manfield take me back to our genesis.

"Good morning everybody, this is Paul Manfield reporting live from KPCL Radio in Toronto on this the twenty-first day of April 2012. There are sunny skies over our beautiful city this morning. But not for long, I am told. Before we get into our regular news program, we have some late-breaking information from the weather bureau. A disturbance is brewing in the Hudson Bay area that could see some early melting and flooding in the surrounding areas of northern Canada, with heavy rain further south, reaching us here in Toronto. Elsewhere, the weather patterns are also unsettled. An earthquake watch is in effect over the entire west coast of the United States and Canada following last week's explosion of a nuclear device by suspected terrorists in the San Andreas Fault area. The North American Perimeter Guard is out on full alert and KPCL will keep you posted with regular updates. In fact, we have moved the weather reports to the front of our coverage this week to deal with these uncertain conditions. Oh, well—it's spring anyway, and what do they say about spring, folks? 'April showers . . .'"

I spin the data meter forward to the next track. It was recorded three weeks later.

"Good morning, Toronto! It's Paul Manfield on the morning show! And what a roller-coaster time this is for all of us. Mothers, have you got your galoshes out for the kids? And don't forget the raincoats—you can throw away the umbrellas because the wind will get them anyway. Stay away from the downtown area this morning. Heavy flooding has shut down everything south of Front Street. The Gardiner Expressway is out of commission, too, and there are questions regarding its stability due to the heavy floodwaters. So, folks, don't go anywhere down there today or for the next little while.

"We have some more news from the west. Not very good, I'm afraid. Another earthquake measuring 8.5 on the Richter scale has rocked the state of Oregon and is spreading down to southern California and all the way up to northern British Columbia. In fact, parts of coastal B.C. are now split off from the mainland. Emergency crews using boats and small fishing craft are helping people to get back inland. Our weather specialist advises people in the affected areas to move inland by as much as two hundred kilometres as the whole west coast, in fact all coastal areas, are very fragile right now.

"And when it rains, it pours . . . pardon the pun folks, but I'm trying to keep my spirits up and hopefully, yours, too. In Europe, massive flooding is occurring in parts of northern Russia and from the North Sea into Great Britain and parts of northern Europe. When will this all end? The Pope has called for prayers at this time, which he is referring to as the 'Rapture' as foretold in the Bible . . ."

The last radio segment is followed by a film clip of the mass evacuation, taken at the time when Samson and his family hit the exodus trail. The strings of cars stuck on big highways, located in the region formerly known as North America, were familiar from similar clips I had seen in school. There was honking as people stuck their heads out of car windows, wondering why traffic was not moving. There were even funny parts, of people fighting and jostling with one another to get ahead in the traffic jams. People did that in those days—fight and jostle to get ahead. The footage taken later into the exodus did not show any more honking or fighting—instead, people looked resigned, and they even clapped when the line of traffic moved a few yards. But the vehicles did not get very far—parts of the highways were washed over and many bridges had collapsed. Subsequent video showed people abandoning their cars, which were stacked bumper to bumper, and walking on the car roofs as the flood water surged knee-high around the stalled vehicles.

"We got out and walked just east of Trenton," Samson told me when he first got around to recounting the story of the Flood. I recall being about ten years old at the time and we had worked all afternoon to complete building the storage shed in our backyard. Samson and I were sitting out in the gathering dusk and he looked rather pleased with himself that day. I guess it was because his post-Flood home was finally complete with the building of the shed. It was time to talk about the past, now that all signs of it were finally buried. "We headed north, through the smaller highways and country roads. There was always mud, I remember. And the ground was constantly shaking—tremors."

"How many of you were together?" I asked him.

"There was Ma and Dad, my pregnant sister, Adele, and husband, Cole. We met the Lightfoots along the way. Belva was a teenager then and they tagged along with us. Thank God, we were heading into summer or else we would have all perished."

"But some of you did?"

"Yes." Samson looked tired suddenly and it wasn't only because of the physical labour we had just performed. His ruddy face screwed up in a frown. "Dad was seventy, and his heart gave out on the third day of our march. He never said a word, just dropped dead alongside us. Adele went into premature labour and had a miscarriage when she saw Dad go. We had to stop."

"Did anyone help?"

"Everyone was trying to help themselves. I couldn't blame them. There was scarcely any food around. The road was always full of people walking . . . walking. Cars were pushed off to the sides when they ran out of gas, or got stuck in the mud."

"What happened then?"

"On the third day, I rustled enough dry wood to build a funeral pyre and cremated Dad, as well as Adele's foetus. I could not risk burying them because, if the water levels rose, wild animals would dig them up. Then something amazing started to happen."

"What?"

"People huddled around the pyre to get warm and dry. They began to talk among themselves and take stock. They forgot fleeing for a moment. Dad's death seemed to have brought them together. It was like that afterwards, whenever someone passed away on the march, we would stop for the cremation, to talk and pray together."

"When did you reach Tolemac?"

"Adele was haemorrhaging badly and we had to stop a second time. Belva's family tried to help with their native medicine. Her father was a medicine man on their reserve before it went under water."

"But Aunt Adele survived, did she not? She got to Tolemac."

"I think Tolemac found her. I began to carry her on my back after awhile. She was always my kid sister and I was not going to leave her behind." Samson swallowed. "Then Mum started to falter and I had to carry them both. I would carry Adele for a while, and then I would set her down and carry Mum while Cole hauled our belongings. Cole and I took bets on how long I'd carry each one. It kept our spirits up and Adele and I laughed a lot, even though I stumbled a few times. It was like when we were kids."

"How did you get to Tolemac?"

"I told you—it found us. We were on our last legs and had camped out for the night. There were makeshift tents all over and people were sharing food. Belva's brothers had even managed to kill a deer in the woods and divide it among all of us refugees.

"The next morning I woke up early and went up the hill in front of us. It was more than a hill; it was almost like a good ski run. I climbed to the top and looked down. We were in a valley and this hill offered us protection from the flood waters. I felt that we would be safe and told the others."

"That was Sunset Hill?"

"Yes. We set up our tents on the top of the hill and I guess Tolemac grew up around us."

"Jeez!"

"I wish it had ended there," Samson said, leaning back. "Adele was frequently in need of blood and we called for the helicopter ambulances that were circling around. We had a big HELP sign tied on a tree looking skywards. They were very busy and couldn't help everyone. And then Ma went AWOL on us."

"What!"

"Yes. Her body was found several days later at the site where Dad had been cremated. She had walked back against the tide of evacuees for two whole days before she got there."

"How did you find her?"

"I had a picture of her set up on the roadside with a sign asking for information. Somebody came over to let us know. By the time I got to her, she was dead."

"But her ashes are in our mausoleum?"

"Yes, I carried her back. I had cremated Dad and lost his remains, but I wasn't going to leave Ma behind. We'd lost too many family members by then."

"How come you never told us all of this before?"

I could see the strain in his face and I bit my tongue, wishing I'd never asked the question.

"It was a story of dying. I'd much rather talk about the birth of Tolemac and the good things we have been able to achieve so far. It's easier to be busy and keep going. Nobody wants to stop and talk about the dying."

And true to Samson's hunch, when the flooding eased, the waters came to rest halfway in the valley, leaving them safe up on Sunset Hill.

I skim through the next broadcasts. How does one sit through repeated news of some lands rising from the ocean and other lands disappearing below it? Of the millions of people dead, vanished without a trace from one day to the next. Of the many who did not make it because a road was blocked or a car engine seized and its occupants subsequently swept away as the waters rushed inland. Or of the stubborn ones, who refused to leave their homes and perished, praying or getting drunk indoors. Or the ones who could not bear the changes and turned around like Lot's wife, or Grandma?

I switch off the Communicator, having had my fill of the Flood Broadcasts for this evening, engaging though they always are.

Chapter 3

*J*ULY *1, 2012— FORMERLY KNOWN AS* "C*ANADA* D*AY*"*—we arrived at the place that was to become our new home.*

How do you come to terms with the familiar past being suddenly wiped out? You cannot go back to it because it's under water. These last few days, I have reminisced about the great neighbourhood barbecues and pool parties we celebrated in what is now the "Old World" before the Flood, yearning for some of that familiarity. Yet now that I look back, those times were not without their flaws. The neighbours, who were great fun to be with at hockey games and such, were middle class and inscrutable. But I had considered that normal. When they had all suddenly disappeared, it dawned on me that in the twenty-seven years I had lived on Saddler Street in Toronto, I had never seen inside the lives of my neighbours. Yes, we kids had all grown up playing street hockey, and had graduated into the teen years experimenting with our bodies and wrestling with studies, consumer choices and career paths. And those years had culminated in the big wedding that Dad threw for Adele and Cole, where half of Saddler had been in attendance. Yet, never in all those years had any of my parents' baby-boomer buddies— who played golf on their days off, went to church on Sundays, painted their houses in the spring, mowed their lawns in the summer and went to lakeside cottages on most weekends—ever revealed their lives to each other. They'd never talked of their inner desires or revealed their flaws openly. There was only polite chatter and tasteful banter between them in all their exchanges. Oh yes, there had been the time when Mr. Smith ran away with his next door neighbour's wife, Mrs. Roberts. And the time that Mr. Olsen was busted for running a kiddie-porn business out of his basement—and all the time he was such a great coach in the softball league. Occasionally, a house would go up for sale and the neighbours would mutter "poor so and so, didn't get along with the wife—divorce." Or a prayer request would go up in the church because "so-and-so's wife or husband is ill in hospital, please pray for them." We never went beyond the thresholds of each other's houses to help, unless formally invited. After all, we had been a "civilized society." Still, it had been a predictable and comfortable old world, one now lost forever.

And now we were among strangers—strangers who knew only one certainty—that tomorrow was never guaranteed. As we woke every morning, someone was in pain. We heard it, as there were no insulated walls separating us anymore, just makeshift tents. Every grunt, burp, fart or gasp of sexual gratification bound us together. And we went uninvited to help one another, because it was expected now—help from any stranger, no formalities.

My fellow refugees are an odd but interesting bunch, thrown together up on Sunset Hill. There is Nathan Goldman—a tall scrawny Jew, a Wall Street investment specialist, who had seen his portfolio go down the tubes. "But I've got some stashed away for a rainy day," he said cheerfully the day we first met, as he helped a gang of us volunteers dig the cesspit we so desperately needed for the bodily waste that was piling up behind bushes all around us. Pinstripe trousers folded up to the knees and caked with mud, and suspenders over a very soiled undershirt were all that remained of his past occupation.

Burly Burgess Williams is an RCMP officer who was separated from his law enforcement unit in the Flood. Burgess is obsessed with making sure that everyone is battened down at night with their belongings secured, for fear some of the refugees might steal, given the sorry state we are in with little food and supplies. He arranges hunting parties with the Lightfoots and erects fences around the tents that are cropping up daily and now stretching almost down to the water at the base of Sunset Hill. I feel safe having Burgess around. In the evening, he'd be pumping his weights (don't ask me how he carted those around with him). Then he would challenge anyone to an arm wrestling match. I took him on many times and he is strong. And it is great to pit oneself against a predictable human for a change, rather than against the forces of nature that have gotten so out of control. In the forty matches we had in the first three weeks (before I lost count), he had the edge on me. Burgess and his newly-wedded wife, Cynthia, are expecting their first baby; I guess that's why he seems so obsessed with protecting his own kind.

Then there is our happy-go-lucky hunter, Billy White Dove, a native Indian from

Belva's reserve who claims to have lost his entire family in the Flood and who likes to brew his own alcohol with any fermentable material available. He prays most evenings, and when he prays he never drinks. But there are times when he decides to get drunk instead, and then he doesn't pray. When I asked him why, he said that he needed "balance," that was all! When he chooses the path of alcohol, he is usually drunk by eight o'clock at night, but when he is sobered up by day he is a great hunter and trapper. He is also attracted to the budding Belva Lightfoot—whose situation reminds me of Anne Frank—there are not many choice pickings, being cooped up here on Sunset Hill and Billy is looking like quite the catch, despite his drinking habit.

We went looking for water, eventually. Food we could do without, water—no. Nathan, Burgess, young Billy White Dove, and Asif Murtaza the Muslim guy with the boat, formed our hunting party. The waters surrounding us were polluted, we were sure of that, judging from the number of carcasses beaching every day and the assorted garbage accompanying them—clothing, food containers, family albums, even money. "Filthy lucre" was an apt expression for the money, and nobody cared to take it because what could we buy with it anyway? There were U.S. dollars and Canadian dollars and, among some of the immigrant families we cremated, even Hong Kong dollars and East Caribbean dollars. The really damaged notes were often burned with the bodies. The day we went looking for water, we decided to go inland; the coastal areas were of no use. We walked for about an hour, crossing Sunset and going down into the valley on the other side. Something struck me as we descended—the trees had taken on a luminosity that was unreal. Everything was glowing. "It's untouched by death," Nathan said, "the dying is on the other side." "Maybe—," replied Burgess, "maybe it's been like that always— we've just been exposed to so much death and destruction. It's just nice to see something alive again." But even he looked curious. When Burgess stuck his pickaxe into the earth, it was soft and yielded easily. "There is water here, I know it," he said, and kept digging. Before long, we were all at it with our motley collection of tools. "There has to be water here," Burgess kept repeating, mopping his sweating brow. We were infused with his enthusiasm and I bet the boys that the last to quit would be the first to drink. The earth got moist and wobbly as we went deeper. A couple of hours later, Nathan had to sit down—that's when he told me that he'd suffered from a rheumatic heart as a kid. Burgess puffed his way to a halt, too, and then it was only Billy, Asif and me. Billy yelped suddenly and the next thing we knew he was sinking. We all grabbed him and tried pulling him out. "Quicksand!" someone yelled. "Water," another yelled. "Allah, be praised!" And then Billy was yanked out like a cork from a bottle; bursting in his wake was a huge spring. It gushed about ten feet in the air, wetting everyone to the bone, before settling into a widening pool around us. We let it wash the smoke, the sweat and the smell of death off our bodies. Later that evening, we formed a human bucket brigade to get the water back to our families. No one knew where this water came from; its unspoiled underground source had been spared the ravages of the earthquakes. That night, as we sang our way home, I fell on my knees on the top of Sunset Hill, looked down on the makeshift tents below us and thanked God for leading us to this fountain of life.

Our joy was short-lived that night for old Mrs. Arabella Parks died just as we were bedding down. We heard wailing from her tent, which was at the lower reaches of the hill. Elfrida, Mrs. Parks's spinster daughter, caused the commotion and when we all converged on the Parks's tent, she was bent over the old lady, a rosary clutched in her hand, sobbing and shrieking over the stiffening corpse. We quickly found out from Frida that Arabella had been suffering from diabetes and without the proper medication had slumped into a coma and passed away a few hours ago. Frida had prayed all afternoon, hoping for her mother to come out of the coma.

"Why didn't you tell us earlier?" Nathan asked.

"What could you have done anyway—there haven't been any helicopter drops for days now?" Frida sobbed, her eyes red and puffy.

"I guess not."

I pulled out my pocket Bible that never left me and we prayed for the old lady's soul. The tent smelt of mould and the air was heavy. Then we took Arabella down to the water's edge, where Rocky Sabbattini was on the night shift, burning the bodies washing over.

"One more," I said, laying down the deadening weight of the old lady draped in her bed sheet. Frida sank in a heap by her mother's corpse and looked like she was going to go next.

"We'll get it done tonight—it's busy here." Rocky said. He'd owned a pizza parlour and was from upstate New York. I think he'd been watching too many Sylvester Stallone movies. He even talked like Stallone.

"It's starting to smell again." And I thought I was getting immune to death but the smell was still hard to get over.

"There are only three of us tonight."

"I guess I'll stay then. Unless Adele needs me." It was drying the bodies that caused

the smell. But we couldn't burn them until they were dry, as we did not have much fuel to get them going.

I was not to stay because Burgess came running down the hill just then. "Sam, come quick—the baby, I think it's arrived." For a big policeman he was surprisingly white with fright, quite useless in these matters.

We rushed back uphill again, leaving Frida and Rocky to do the needful for old Mrs. Parks.

Cindy Williams was rolling around in her sleeping bag, gasping. The bag was distended like it was about to burst and I realized that was because of her bloated stomach. I was not thinking anymore—grabbing my pocketknife, I ripped the sleeping bag open, releasing her cramped legs and torso. Her ankles were swollen. I spread her legs, and ripped off her soaked panties, without thinking of decency. At times like this it's better not to think, for when you do, you realize your sphincter is about to give way and you've sweated through what was once a shirt. There was only one thought in my mind. We had lost Adele's child, we were not going to lose this one. By God, we were not going to!

"Get boiling water and lots of cloth," I shouted.

The baby was in breach position—the heel of one of its legs sticking out between Cindy's legs, wriggling, struggling for life. I willed it to live—it had to—we were all willing ourselves to stay alive. Come out and join the gang, kiddo! The baby seemed to understand and its heel withdrew inside again, temporarily. The hot water arrived and I plunged my hands into it with the knife and all—it was agonizing but I was past care—the child was all I cared about now. It's a strange feeling sticking a hand into a woman's distended vagina but I managed to get the child by the bum and flip him—he was co-operating—he wanted to be born that was for sure. I had read of this stuff in books, never really practised it—wasn't licensed to.

"Heave—bear down—whatever, push the baby out," I was urging Cindy and I could see the strain in her face as she tried to comply. Ethan Williams shot out like a bullet on the third try.

Burgess yelped—with joy this time. "Well, I'll be damned—you're a bloody doctor, too!" There was gratitude in his face and relief on Cindy's. I grabbed the child who was bawling—not waiting for the customary slap on the back. As I bathed the muck off its shuddering body, I suddenly realized there was about a yard of umbilical cord sticking out. Then Adele, pale and haggard, was beside me with a pair of scissors—don't know how the heck she had dragged herself out of her camp bed. There was a steely determination on her face as she released the child from the cord and gently pulled the placenta out of the mother's body, something I would have never thought to do. Then we were jumping and howling with joy—for the first time since we'd arrived on the hill, Adele looked triumphant. I hope she is on the mend.

"My baby—give him to me," said Cindy, who had a greedy look on her face. As I handed the infant over, I was struck by his gaze, which was focused on me. Little Ethan's eyes followed me all the way to his mother—it was creepy—it was almost as if a nemesis was staring back at me. Had I released some evil into our midst or was the child resentful of my bringing him into this crazy world? I shrugged the feeling off—this was a moment of joy—we had plucked life from the jaws of death—for once, life had won— that's how this night should be remembered. I wondered if maybe I had been too immersed in death to appreciate life when I saw it.

I was too drained that night to help Rocky down at the cremations; Nathan kindly stepped in. I used the remaining cooking grease from our communal dinner pots to salve my raw hands. Laying down to sleep that night, I realized how different my neighbours were now—they were living, dying and being born in front of my eyes and asking, crying to be part of that experience. Yet I had lived thirty years on Saddler Street in old Toronto and had never shared so much with so many in all that time.

*   *   *

Then the earthquakes began. Gargantuan rumbles—as many as three or four times a day and increasing in intensity. The quakes sent the tents and contents tumbling, and people had to sleep out in the open. When they woke in the morning, the settlers saw mushroom clouds in the distance and a crimson sky. The name "Sunset Hill" was coined at this time because of the permanent sunset on the horizon. There were often jarring sounds, too, as if pieces of the earth's crust were adrift. Sometimes a loud bump signalled that a piece of land had come to rest close by. The settlers on Sunset Hill watched as many of the travellers on the exodus trail turned back. They heard stories that the way ahead, about forty miles north, was flooded. There was no way forward and now there was no way back—all the land, including the spot where Samson had cremated his father, was now under water. The jarring and heaving was also lifting Sunset Hill. What had once been a sizeable ski hill became a small mountain after the land settled again and the earthquakes and aftershocks abated.

*   *   *

July 15, 2012

"Therefore we will not fear, though the earth give way
And the mountains fall into the heart of the sea."
—Psalm 46:2

That verse sustained us. Each morning we rose and looked towards the east—the sun was covered in cloud or ashes or smoke—we did not know which. But there was an orange glow in the sky, too. The world was on fire. Fire and brimstone at the "end of days" we had been promised—we could see it now. I wondered if those Jehovah's Witnesses were still having fun or if they were as scared as we were. Some of the stranded became hysterical, the rich ones particularly. Except for Nathan. That's when I knew he was special, a chosen one like me. Chosen to lead this lost flock back from the abyss. The trick I discovered as those days trembled on Sunset Hill was not to think too far ahead. "Live for the day," Christ had said, and it was a very comforting solution— it put the fear at bay. I got a charge of energy, too, with so many people relying on me. I tried talking about this philosophy at night with the other survivors and some started practising it. Soon they were giving testament to the theory.

For instance, we never fought anymore when the food drops came. The ones who fought had been taken by the Flood and those of us who remained knew that God would provide—hadn't he thus far? In exchange, we were supposed to live by His laws, but were we?

"How can you go about your business as if nothing has happened?" Frida asked me one day when I went over to her tent with Nathan to see how she was doing. She wasn't very well—hadn't eaten in about a week and was looking haggard. I threw the flaps of her tent open to let in fresh air, at least the smell of the smoke fires were preferable to the stale smell of Frida cooped inside all week.

"He says he's special," Nathan piped up.

"Shut up, Nathan." I poured a cup of instant soup, my last pouch from the helicopter drop of three days ago. I pulled out a piece of fried venison saved from the Lightfoots' open-air, universal barbecue and stirred it in the soup. "Here Frida—you've got to have this. No sense in us all dying."

"Maybe we were all intended to die," Frida said.

"No." She was annoying and I felt my blood boil over. "If we were all meant to go, this would have been all over. The strong and repentant are being spared. Culled from the rest."

"He says we are chosen to build the New World. He's a great guy to be around at a time like this," Nathan said. I knew he was not joking anymore.

I fed Frida the soup, holding the ladle firm every time she seemed to lose interest. Finally, she knew there was no way out and drank all her soup.

"I'll check on you again, tomorrow," I said as we pulled the wrap down on her tent. "I want you down at the soup kitchen by Thursday—we need lots of help there."

"Thanks Samson," I heard her whimper as we departed.

Frida showed up at the soup kitchen on Thursday.

*　　*　　*

July 28, 2012

Food is getting scarce again. The helicopters that flew over sporadically and dropped rations, clothing and tents, have started to thin out. Where they came from or which government they belonged to is not clear, nor does anyone care. No one is in a mood to eat much these days, but everyone prays. People who had forgotten how to, or who hadn't attended a church in recent memory, have begun to pray in earnest and have discovered a new faith within. I gather the congregation at dawn every day now and we pray for the strength to live through another day. And, at sunset, with the horizon blazing a bright crimson, the survivors thank God again for sparing them and promise to live by His laws.

*   *   *

August 10, 2012

We cremated Adele today. It broke my heart to see her go, but she couldn't hold on any longer. We tried to get her the blood she needed but it just wasn't available. I even asked the attractive nurse, Agnes, in the temporary hospital, if I could give Adele my blood, or if they could identify someone else who could give her their blood, but Adele has a rare blood group. I should have gotten her spare supply stored at Toronto East General before the exodus, but how could I have kept it from getting contaminated? Blame, that's all one can do now. No, I've got to stay above the blame. There are too many people losing their minds and wandering about this place because they are blaming themselves. Poor heartbroken Cole is like that now. I need to watch him. He's all I've got left of family. I can't write anymore tonight, I am just so . . . tired.

I remembered the last snippet of conversation between Samson and me the day we built the shed.

"What happened to Uncle Cole?" I had asked that evening many years ago as we put away our tools.

"He had a mental breakdown soon afterwards. A lot of people couldn't put up with the strain at the time. Drowned himself in Lake Ontario—we never recovered his body." Samson walked back into the house, and I knew that was all I was going to get out of him on the Flood for a long time to come.

Chapter 4

August 15, 2012

VLADIMIR PATIMKIN IS A FIFTEEN-YEAR-OLD bucktoothed and lanky kid, camped with his family just across from us on Sunset Hill. Ignoring his mother's request that he carry his one suitcase of clothes and personal belongings, Vladimir had swapped them for a laptop computer, inseparable from him since he was four years old. Thus he has spent these ugly days up on Sunset fiddling with his laptop and its wireless Internet connection, finding assorted means of charging his laptop's battery, even adapting batteries of other devices, such as broken vehicles or cell phones. He is quite the technical genius. Last night there was a big commotion, when Vladimir came running out to tell us that the Internet was still working. This was the best piece of news since Adele died. I was glad that for once he had disobeyed his mother's wishes.

I recall the rest of this part of history that I learned in school, and now teach.

Slowly the news filtered in through Vladimir's Internet connection, and the Patimkin tent became "news central," where people would gather at odd times in the day for the latest update. They were marooned. The nearest human settlement was east of what was formerly Ottawa, about a hundred kilometres away, but separated by water. They were calling this place Oceania for want of a better word. It was a collection of pieces of land and people that had floated in from Western New York State, Northern Ontario and parts of Atlantic Canada. Across the way, other parts of Eastern New York State, Southern Ontario and pieces of Ohio and Pennsylvania had coalesced into a land mass being called New Eden. Email messages were sent to try and attract attention. Initially, replies were slow and sketchy, as people were trying to sort themselves out and figure out which country or state they belonged to. Broadcast email was subsequently sent everywhere. Response times were erratic, as no one really knew who was in charge of the Internet, yet it seemed to run on with a life of its own. Apparently, its inventors had envisaged such a phenomenon when they created it in the late twentieth century and it was now fulfilling that vision. Investments in satellite technology had also helped, with information transmissions skipping to this medium whenever they hit a block along the more robust land cables, many of which had been severed during the earthquakes and flooding.

Eventually, offers of help started to trickle in from other communities, stranded as they were themselves. Food and medical supplies started arriving by boat to supplement the diminishing airdrops. Burgess organized a local militia to maintain a modicum of order and to prevent dishonesty among the constantly arriving streams of newcomers. The Lightfoots and Billy White Dove organized daily hunting parties for deer, moose and other wildlife to keep the settlers provisioned when the helicopters were too busy elsewhere. Fishing was initially discouraged as everyone feared the toxins floating in the waters.

Human activity slowly resumed. A handful of veterans made a trip to Oceania, led by Burgess and Nathan; essential goods were purchased and early trading ties established. When the first boat returned a week later, Nathan reported, "Oceania has lots of land and people and lots of infrastructure still in fairly good condition. They are willing and able to help us rebuild." Soon, more trips were arranged and the relief operation got underway in earnest. Samson organized the building of sturdier housing from the supplies that Nathan was able to procure from these early excursions "abroad." A makeshift hospital went up, and a call went out for anyone with medical training. Among those responding was a young Australian nurse on an exchange to Toronto when the Flood hit—Agnes, soon to be my mother.

A few months into the rebuilding effort, the prime minister of Canada and the president of the United States, in two separate addresses over the Internet on the same day, advised that their respective countries had forever changed in composition. Federal, provincial and state governments were useless and nearly bankrupt in this new reality and, therefore, the three levels of government were pooling their resources to focus only on areas such as urgent medical aid, trade governance, monetary policy and defence, which included keeping communication lines open, via the Internet only. Local communities were urged to set up their own governance structures and be self-sufficient as the helicopter drops of food and other aid were prohibitively expensive and would soon cease. A medical co-operative was started by a group of enterprising doctors and medical centres run by this co-operative started to open in key cities. Local communities were urged to subscribe to these services. Where direct facilities were not affordable, virtual medical consultation was made available via Internet links—that's how Tolemac got its first specialist medical services. They did however build psychiatric wards in most states, due to the high rates of neurosis and shell shock that people were dealing with at the time, which expanded many years later into our psychiatric centre at Tolemac General Hospital.

And build back they did. After the hospital came the graveyard. They stopped the cremations because the smell of burning bodies was driving people crazy, and instead housed the dead inside crypts in "mausoleum city." Schools and shops started to spring up as people began to reclaim their lives and ply trades again. There was a desperate need to be "normal." There were about five thousand people in that first census they took on Sunset Hill. The city fathers decided to name their place of refuge "Tolemac," for Camelot in reverse. They felt that God had led them to this magical place, safe from the ravages around them; a place with undulating fields, surrounded by water, with its characteristic mountain that looked down upon the land on all sides. Samson particularly liked the name (and given that Camelot was one of his favourite Old-World movies, I'm sure he had a big say in the naming of our city). He explained that the people at the time believed the Flood had washed their sins away and given them another chance so that this new Camelot could reverse the history of its fabled cousin that went into decline due to man's greed and sin. I guess people needed to believe in fairy tales at the time.

July 1, 2013

Despite what scientists say about a seismic shift in our planet that has led to this cataclysm, I am convinced now that we have paid such a huge toll due to our own constant slide into complacency and sin. That was our slow but seismic shift—into sin. And I, too, paid that heavy ransom by witnessing my entire family perish. I hope I have paid enough, that we've all paid enough. I am not alone in this belief; most of the settlers on the Hill feel they have been spared, not so much because they have not sinned—we all have in some shape or form—but because we were aware of sin and tried to steer away from temptation as best as we could, before the Flood. When the Executive Committee was first formed, we passed laws making Bible study mandatory in school, irrespective of religious persuasion, and outlawed alcohol consumption and recreational drug use. We allowed tobacco as some people were addicted to it and we did not want to add any more stress to their lives. But we need more laws, against adultery and stealing for instance, and those will come in the days ahead—laws that will make this survivor nation live by God's commandments again. There is so much to do, so much infrastructure – physical, moral and societal – to build, now that we have regressed so many years. I wonder if there will be enough time in my life to even catch up to what we had. That being said, we felt good after those first laws were passed; it was as if we had appeased an angry God.

Sure enough, more laws came. The laws against stealing and civil disobedience were pretty straightforward. The law of transparency was innovative. All income earned by each citizen was to be made publicly available via Communicator bulletin boards and the tax collection scheme of pre-Flood days was abolished. Instead, every citizen was to contribute 10 percent of his earnings to the social safety net. This could be in cash or kind. Therefore, voluntary contributions of time to public service were also acceptable towards this tithe. Ownership of property and the accumulation of wealth were not discouraged—lessons from the fall of Communism in the pre-Flood era were recognized. But it became each citizen's duty to practise "from each according to his ability, to each according to his need."

The invasiveness of these laws into citizens' lives was balanced by the privacy laws. The privacy laws deemed it unlawful for any person or body to spy into the personal records of another citizen or body, other than those records made publicly available on Communicator bulletin boards. Thus our personal email and voice records, Communicator channels and other forms of communication were free from being tapped. The Communications Centre that was set up early in Tolemac's history was able to carry out the tenets of the privacy law. Samson quipped one day that "the Executive has been more foresighted in its passing of laws in the first fifteen years of its life than pre-Flood nations in the two thousand plus years of their existence."

When Sonya and I were married, our vows enshrined the morality laws and Samson, who presided over the ceremony, insisted that we honour the post-Flood tradition of facing our wedding gathering and repeating these vows individually to each attendee, asking that they be witness to the new, righteous life we were going to lead together as husband and wife. Thus the sexual act, which had gotten out of hand in pre-Flood times, was given its appropriate place. It was mainly for procreation, and the morality laws helped to keep our carnal instincts from drifting into sin outside the bounds of marriage.

I asked Kamala, just before Sonya and I were married, how the Executive enforced the chastity law. Kamala was taking tea with us at the time, as we prepared for the wedding. She placed her cup down deliberately, and looked at Sonya and me.

"Breaking that law is very hard to prove in this instance. Finding three witnesses for every charge is difficult, unless the accused confesses willingly."

"Three months of public humiliation by getting them to clean parks or sewers is a bit stiff," I said.

"We've had very few people break the law."

"Or very few who confess or get found out?"

"Maybe. But in the end, the people of Tolemac welcomed the legislation; it lent structure and relieved them of having to decide between what was moral and what was not."

"It's still a tough penalty for a primal urge that we are all born with."

"Well, there was a lot of abuse of that primal urge, as you call it, and many were sick because of it. AIDS had wiped out half of Africa before the Flood. There had to be another alternative. We found it in the teachings of the Bible and decided to go back to this tried and tested formula again."

But it was not always easy to comply with this law. Sonya and I had difficulty restraining ourselves beyond the permissible kissing and cuddling during our courtship and engagement, which was mercifully short. She was more conscious than I was of our moral code and would instill caution in me. "Now, now, honey, let's not get carried away. There will be our whole lives ahead of us after the wedding."

But after the wedding, our first night together was an anticlimax—the expectation and anticipation overrode the event. We were clumsy and self-conscious. After I had shed her virginity and hurt her in the process, spewing blood all over the bed sheets—we figured that following the law made sense—sex was mainly for procreation. However, as our married life progressed, the awakened sexual beast in me became addicted to the twice-weekly ritual, disturbed only during Sonya's pregnancies and menstrual periods. She was less enamoured of the whole thing and submitted sometimes only to please me. One night she murmured, "The law was good at telling us 'what' to do, but not very good at telling us 'how.' " I guess she had a point. There were also times, particularly on nights we had indulged in sex, when I would have a recurring dream, of standing in front of a door beyond which I knew there was a great treasure. I just did not have the key.

*　*　*

Thus history taught us that Samson and the rest of the "tent dwellers" stuck on Sunset Hill went on to build our city state and to practise the great experiment in social democracy called "Humanitarianism" that other like-minded city states such as Boston, Brunswick, Saska-Manitoba, Hampshire and Oceania emulated. These Humanitarian states were all bound together by a co-operative for shared services such as health care; while the more entrepreneurial states, like New Eden, Alberta, Michigan, the Floridas and Mexico, carried on their unfettered experiments in free enterprise or "Capitalism." In those early days, the pragmatic people moved to or stayed within the Humanitarian states, while the ambitious and opportunistic ones gravitated to the Capitalist states in pursuit of wealth and prosperity, with the inherent risks they posed.

In the beginning, attempts were made to bring the Capitalists and Humanitarians together under common trading laws, but ideologies clashed and talks always failed, leading to Samson's cynicism about dealing with the Capitalists. Rivalries began as the Capitalists called abroad for all those seeking "life, liberty and the pursuit of wealth" to come to their shores. The Humanitarians countered with calls for those looking for "freedom, security and community." Thus began waves of immigration as people moved to where their motivations led. Whole families splintered along this ideological divide. When the ebbs and flows subsided and population levels stabilized again, borders, particularly on the Humanitarian side were tightened, as anyone coming over could be deemed to be "nothing else but a Capitalist!" The Capitalists, however, pursued a different strategy by always keeping an open invitation to those with exceptional talents who wanted to make it big in their realm. The only border between each block that remains open today is for students and short-term visitors. Thus the polarization between Capitalism and Humanitarianism was complete in what was once the North American Free-Trade Zone.

Within a few of years of the Flood, the two countries formerly known as Canada and the United States of America dissolved, and two new entities emerged: the Federation of Humanitarian States (FHS), and the League of Capitalist Nations (LCN). With these new groupings, member states like Tolemac have much more autonomy than their predecessors had in pre-Flood times. Most Humanitarian states subscribe to large publicly run co-operatives that provide medical, legal and banking services. (They have a unified Dollar of the Americas.) The Capitalist states do not buy into this philosophy and, instead, encourage competition in all these sectors. The North American Defence Fund (NADF) is the only privately run co-operative that both Humanitarian and Capitalist realms subscribe to. The threat of another Flood and the threat of invasion from the more turbulent states formerly known as Asia and South America—now regrouped and reorganized under totalitarian regimes—are too real. The NADF took over all remaining defence assets of the former countries, Canada and the U.S.A., to set itself up as the new defender of North American-perimeter security.

July 4, 2016

It was like someone cut an umbilical cord when our two old countries ceased to exist. We had always been either Canadians or Americans—but now we were neither. We were a new hybrid, the ones in Tolemac keen to share and find strength from each other. As if to divert attention from the end of these two great nations, Belva Lightfoot and Billy White Dove decided to get married on that same day. They were a rather mismatched couple, just like Canada and the U.S.A. had been.

The folks in Capitalist states like New Eden and Alberta are looking to reap profits from this new landscape where all they see is opportunity for growth. C'est la vie; each to his own.

"Why don't you go to New Eden?" I asked Nathan, for he was always moaning about us not fully exploiting opportunities, like the new skinless potato they had discovered in the last round of genetic engineering.

"It's not about the money—it's about wringing maximum value from all of our resources—don't you get it?" he replied.

"You'll make a great Capitalist. You think like one. You could own lots of land and things," I goaded. "More than those farms you've bought on the other side of Sunset."

He fished in his pocket for a cigar, the cigar he had extinguished halfway and neatly put back in his pocket half an hour ago. "Those Capitalist guys still don't get it, Sam. Ownership is an illusion. This land and its resources belong to the Man upstairs and we are merely tenants. He's just given us a renewed lease not to screw it up again. "

Chapter 5

WHILE I ADMIRED SAMSON, I confided in my mother. She was quiet, reserved and retiring, but a hard worker in her own way. I never really knew much about her background. Post- Flood adults, especially those who had lost a lot, did not talk about their lives. It was generally known that her entire family had perished back in Australia during the Flood, and that she had decided to remain in Tolemac and make it home. With the help of a word uttered here and there, especially by the ladies in the church congregation, and as a kid snooping around, I was able to piece together portions of her life.

It is sad that when people depart this world, they leave behind images that coalesce only around significant events. I can picture my mother now as someone constantly hauling water from the communal tap (in those early days before indoor plumbing was restored) for washing and cooking; someone who fussed that I needed to take a bath at least twice a week, even though water was hard to come by; who sat by my bedside the time I got the mumps and groaned and moaned all night because my jaws were swollen. She always supervised my homework and would often fall asleep on the rocker while I struggled on the computer wondering when Samson would come home to take me bike riding. She quietly took charge when her grandson, Joey, was born; Hannah followed three years later and Sonya and I fumbled as new parents going under water fast. Joey was a colicky baby, but every time he lay at my mother's breast he slept peacefully, giving Sonya and me a much-needed rest. My mother was a quiet but mysterious angel, who would listen patiently when I needed to sound off. I also remember the time I saw Samson sneak his hand into hers during one of the more recent "March of the Lamps" ceremonies down at the Waterfront Park, just after Hannah was born. I remember that incident because, instead of a glow of happiness on her face, I saw tears—as if she had been missing something all her life and had just found it, a bit late. In her final years, she became acerbic and I often wondered what had caused that.

There has to be something in Samson's journal that talks about Mum, and I hunt for his reflections about her. I find only three: one at the very beginning, one in the middle on the day Billy White Dove went missing, and one almost at the end. There is nothing else. It's as if post-Flood males had taken the women for granted in their frenzy to return to normalcy.

December 24, 2012—Went to midnight mass with Agnes—our first "date."

That's all it said. Samson and my mother were always so "proper," conducting themselves as respectful leaders of our emergent society. But there had to be something else hidden under the surface. Of course, it was too late by the time I found out. I recall the first time I began probing Mum for answers; only a couple of years ago did she begin to open up.

My mother was in the kitchen that day, baking those famous cookies of hers, a weekly ritual she undertook for her grandchildren. After her baking, she would head down to Tolemac General Hospital, for the late evening shift from 6 p.m. to midnight, and then walk back uphill to the family home, which was perched on the summit of Sunset Hill overlooking the city.

While she was baking, I came up behind her bent frame and put my arms around her. She was a small woman just over five feet, and of slender build. Her greying blond hair was sweat-streaked at the back of her neck from the heat of the electric oven. Somehow I missed the raw energy of the old wood stove that still sat like an old carbon-scarred relic at the farther end of the kitchen. It was mid-June and the temperature outside was already around 40 degrees Celsius.

"Hi, Mum."

"Hello, son!" She turned around and her liquid blue eyes got me as usual. They always seemed to melt in front of me, her head to the side, as if contemplating an amusing picture.

"Everything okay?"

"As well as they can be. Just the old aches and pains from time to time. Old age you know." She had a funny accent—part of her Australian heritage, she claimed. I found it very musical.

"You shouldn't be doing those graveyard shifts at the hospital anymore. Get one of the younger ones to do them."

"It's the nights that are the hardest for the sick. That's when they need us the most."

"It's time you and Dad took a holiday out of Tolemac." I had never seen them going away together on a vacation. In fact, they had never taken a break, period. There was always some activity or other in the community that needed attending to. "I hear that they have opened a beach with resort facilities in Oceania. When the weather gets warmer in a couple of months, you should go."

She stared out of the window for a while. Then she went over to the cupboard and took out an old, unlabelled bottle. This was her bottle of "bootleg" brandy. Alcohol was not openly for sale in Tolemac, being a dry state. Brandy was used only sparingly in the hospital for therapeutic reasons. My mother had always maintained that she drank a periodic "tot," as it was good for her weak heart, and her doctor concurred. Samson usually frowned on alcohol, calling it the Devil's brew, but he tolerated it in Mum's case, due to her conviction of its medicinal qualities. Her work at the hospital kept her in a regular supply of the Devil's brew.

"I always dreamed of going on holiday with your father, but we were always too busy."

"What was it like, Mum, when you two first met?"

"Our first date?" Then she smiled and immediately had tears in her eyes, too. "I remember our first date. It was wonderful," she said looking out the window again.

"Tell me about it."

"It was midnight mass on our first Christmas following the Flood. People were very sad at that time, and some were wondering whether Christmas should even be celebrated. But your father was insistent that we not deprive ourselves of any more good things."

"That ancient pagan tradition of dressing up the tree and decorating the crib?"

"Well, it was never a pagan tradition to us. When we were children in our former world, Christmas was a very happy time—out on the beach in Australia, with lots to do in the home and so much food around, so much that we threw a lot away and people were so overweight after the Season."

She continued, and I let her ramble on, the alcohol was making her talkative. "That night, there was no beach of course, it was just wet, and smoke from the cremations was still strong. I guess I will never get that smell out of me. I had seen your father several times before that occasion. They were building our city at that time and he was always where the action was. Whether it was a rousing speech to get everyone to build the sea wall, or to make contributions towards the school construction, or calling for volunteers to help at the makeshift hospital tents, he was always on a platform, pleading, not ashamed to invoke tears in us, although he never shed them himself.

"I was secretly afraid of him. He seemed too powerful for me. As more disasters began to strike us at that time, he seemed to get stronger, as if he was God's messenger sent to deliver us in our hour of need. One day, as I was making the rounds of the tents—I remember I had just put Mrs. Squire's mother away for the night—she had suffered a collapsed lung—and there was this tall man, awkwardly standing by the nurses' post. I noticed Samson as I made my way over. He looked different. I thought he was ill or something. He was not on a platform anymore, and he looked strangely human.

"I asked him if there was anything I could do for him. He stood there silently, putting his hands in his pockets and pulling them out again, nodding his head to say that he was indeed, in good health."

"'Do you want to see the head nurse, then,' I said, not sure if I was senior enough for this hotshot civic leader we had just elected."

"'No, it's you I came to see,' he said."

"'Me?' "

"'Yes. I wondered if you would come with me to midnight mass tonight?' "

"I must have blushed deeply. For I remember turning my back on him and busying myself with some papers that had fallen off the nurse's table into the mud."

"'Those papers are upside down, Agnes,' he said and we both laughed. When I turned around he had a serious look on his face."

"'We must be there,' he said. 'Our people need hope now.' When I looked at him, there was no big politician on a platform; there was a scared young man, willing himself to carry on and keep living. 'I'm sorry about your sister,' was all I could say. I must have fallen in love with him that night. He was the thread of hope we all needed at the time, a man who felt his fear and was working with it."

She rose and went over to the oven and took the cookies out. They were burned. "I ramble too much. These will have to be redone. Please tell my darlings Hannah and Joey that I'll bake them a fresh batch tomorrow."

But I wasn't interested in cookies at that moment. "Tell me what happened then."

"I went with him to mass that night. It was one of our limited social gatherings. We either went to mass or gathered to bury someone."

"And?"

"It was the most joyous Christmas service ever. The carols were never more joyous, our voices never more melodious. I hit high notes I have never hit since. Later that night we walked by the waterfront and our voices echoed across the water as we laughed and tried to remember a better time—the days before the Flood. He told me about the girls he had dated, there were only three before me. I think he was telling the truth. They had all disappeared since the Flood."

"Did he tell you other things about himself—his interests, hobbies . . . ?"

"Yes. Work, study, caring for his parents and younger sister. He played occasional basketball and hockey, and was on his church board. But that was all—just a wholesome, caring, committed man. That night Samson asked me to marry him and I accepted."

"But you hardly knew him?"

"I knew enough. I knew that tomorrow was never guaranteed, that joy was of the moment. And I was in a state of joy. That's where I wanted to be, always."

"And Samson?"

"He was the planner, the builder. I was his foundation. And he would build on me just as he would build on Tolemac. We were perfect for each other."

"You are still perfect for each other?"

"I wished there had been more children. I let him down there. And then, I guess, we got busy."

"It's not your fault—you had me despite the odds."

"When I think of it, it was more like he had you. He breathed life into you. I produced you weak and vulnerable to the world." The hardened look was creeping back into her face, and the limpid gaze had all but gone.

"You can't go on living in guilt over that. You have been a wonderful mother."

"I thought you were gone the first night you were born, when I saw you sitting in the cup of Samson's hand. There were no incubators in those days."

My mother said that to this day Tolemacians suffer from a mild form of paranoia —never sure if all they've built will be taken away from them again. There was a preoccupation with having children to beef up the population and babies were born in increasing numbers following the Flood. I was born prematurely within the first year of my parents' marriage. My mother carried me for only seven months and I weighed a kilo at birth.

I remember that story well, as she recounted it.

"We put you by the wood stove in the kitchen throughout those winter months—that became your bedroom. I rubbed ointment on your little bony body to insulate you from the cold, and Samson laid his hands on you each night, willing God to enter and give you strength. And every night the town folk would come by to enquire how you were doing. At times there were line-ups outside the door and it was quite overwhelming. Somehow your birth was more important than others—you were born but not yet born— just like Tolemac was, I guess. Then after your third month, when you had gained weight and were about four kilos, the doctor from Oceania visited and pronounced that you were healthy and would live."

"The two of you went through hell to keep me alive," I said. I wanted her to pat herself on the back and not look so down.

"When Samson heard what the doctor said, he cradled you in his arms and ran through the streets of Tolemac holding you aloft shouting, 'Praise God, He has delivered us!' Many people joined him on the dirt track we called Main Street that evening. I think the event was a turning point, for we felt we could believe again. Life could be snatched from the jaws of death."

My mother couldn't have any children after I was born. I heard about many miscarriages. Artificial insemination, cloning and other lab reproduction techniques from the Old World were banned in the Humanitarian realm, so there was no help on that score. They must have stopped trying eventually, for Samson got increasingly involved in his work and so did she. As he had said to me that day we built our shed, "It's easier to keep busy. Nobody wants to stop and think."

47

Chapter 6

FROM THIS POINT ON, Samson's journal gets sketchy—sparse in places and detailed in others, as if he did not have the time to write. And I have to use my own memory to fill in the gaps of growing up in Tolemac.

My earliest recollections were playing in the yard, which was always damp. Every time a hammer banged or a handsaw began scraping, toads jumped between the building materials that forever lay around our yards. My next-door neighbour, Ethan Williams, a year older than me, would climb into my backyard from his house below and go hunting toads which did their darnedest to escape him. His little brother, John, crawled about in diapers, inspecting the dead toads lined up on the back steps of the Williams's house, sometimes putting then in his mouth as he was just cutting his teeth. Suddenly, their mother Cynthia would burst on the scene and scream at them and Ethan would take off down the road, evading his punishment until later, while John was snatched and taken indoors. The swearing Cynthia would glare at me, as if I was the instigator of these vile acts of cruelty. John's habit of putting things in his mouth finally led him to swallow the construction glue left open in the Williams's backyard. He nearly died that time, and had to be rushed to Oceania. When he came home a month later, they told us that he would never speak again and would have slow mental growth. I must have been about four years old at the time.

I also remember going down to the Waterside Park when it was first built. There was a lot of construction going on at the waterfront and many boats came and went as trading with the outside world got underway in earnest. Burgess was very optimistic about his new venture—the port. There was a hotel, called the Waterfront, being built. The dock had been extended and two new piers were taking shape. Children were not allowed inside the construction sites; for as they dug to build the piers, more skeletons from the Flood were unearthed. I saw these skeletons when I was old enough to visit the Flood Memorial Museum in Oceania many years later. A piece of marshy land was filled over and converted to the Waterside Park. Standing in it, one could look into the distant horizon over the water. Samson said that the Capitalists were on the other side and we should be careful who we traded with. Being a child, I did not understand what he meant at the time.

One of the interesting things that I remember, from when I was about six, is the children standing by the water's edge, communing with spirits. Every day, this handful of children in our community would urge their parents to take them to the Waterside Park. At first, the parents acquiesced, and the children ran down to the water's edge and stared into the lake-ocean that surrounded them. They looked transfixed and began talking to themselves. The parents became alarmed by this behaviour and tried to keep them indoors after that, but the children cried and made a lot of noise, saying they wanted to go to the park to "talk to their ancestors." Samson's explanation was that these children were suffering from post-Flood trauma transferred through parental genes. Mum said that it was the children's ability to be in harmony with their environment, physical and spiritual, and this "sixth sense" should be encouraged. Belva White Dove had an interesting spin when we asked her about this in class one day, many years later: "The children of the new generation are more psychic and are able to commune with the spirit world. There are many troubled spirits living over the water who were drowned in the Flood. These children can put their ancestors' spirits at ease and send them on to their next phase." Belva always had deep answers.

One day, I went down to the park and watched the children. They were between the ages of five and seven, with even a few toddlers among them. I tried looking at the water to see if I'd see any "ghosts," but did not see any. When I turned to walk back, however, I felt a chill on my spine. I spun around but there was nothing; maybe it was my imagination. But as I left the park that day I had a feeling that some other presence had been there with the children. I concluded that I must be fairly intuitive even though I couldn't see any ghosts, and this intuition has guided me in my life. Hannah talks to ghosts now and I feel her talent had simply skipped a generation on my side of the family.

City Hall eventually passed a motion to build a wall around the park to prevent any of these psychic children from coming to harm if they accidentally fell in the water. But just before the construction crews got going on the project, the children suddenly lost interest. They stopped coming to the park and their numbers dwindled. As a result, City Hall gave up on the idea of the wall and shifted their focus to more pressing things. I was curious to find out what had happened, especially as I was one of the "sixth-sense challenged." There was a girl, a couple of years younger than me, who came to the park regularly and was one of the last to cease coming. Her name was Sonya, and she was particularly striking in the way she looked into the water and sang into it. She was dark-skinned and her mother was a widowed judge. I remember my first conversation with Sonya. She was leaving the park, walking in front of her mother, ruminating on a water lily in her hand.

"Are there no more ghosts, then?" I asked, coming up behind her, offering her some flowers that I had gathered as a peace offering and hoping she would talk.

She looked at me curiously, a little annoyed. Then she continued on her way, skipping and humming under her breath.

I kept pace with the girl, determined to get an answer. Out of one corner of my eye, I saw Samson, who had brought me to the park, walking over to talk to Sonya's mother, who immediately brightened and smoothed her clothes on sight of him.

"Please tell me," I insisted. "I won't tell anyone."

"You won't tell those people who are building the wall?" Sonya said, her eyes large and enquiring.

"No, I promise!"

"The 'ancestors' are leaving now. They thanked us for talking to them."

"You actually talked to them?"

"Sure, silly. Can't you see them?"

"No, I can't."

"Then you must be handicapped or something. You better see the doctor."

That was all we spoke that first time. But she evoked such curiosity in me, and it has lasted my entire life. I married her the moment we were out of school and had finished our tertiary education. Our parents were pleased, too, because that's what Tolemacians did; they married young and had lots of children, if possible.

January 10, 2019

I had to mend Kamala's sewer today. She had no handyman around the house ever since her husband met with that fatal accident down at the waterfront last year. Poor man! He operated the grain elevators and had one elevator land on him as a result of another of Nathan's creative ventures—stringing a grain elevator over Sunset to the farmlands on the other side! Kamala is also worried about her daughter, who spends hours in her room talking to her dead father. I couldn't get there till late evening, as I had to run a few errands for Mrs. Appegio after my shift at City Hall. The little girl Sonya had locked herself in her room, Kamala informed me. I set about trying to fix the plumbing. The sewer had backed up, flooding the toilet with gunk. I spent an hour cleaning all of it up and Kamala was embarrassed. "It's no problem, I've seen worse," I reassured her. She hadn't seen the dead bodies we piled up routinely in those early days—the staring eyes of people wondering why they had been selected to die by drowning or just by fear. Nor had she seen the dying in the hospital tents. A little shit from a backed-up sewer was a cakewalk in comparison. But she was embarrassed nevertheless. After cleaning the floor, I set about fixing the flush, and that took another forty-five minutes. When I was wrapping up my tools, I heard a slight step behind me; the little girl had emerged from her room and was watching me. "How are you doing?" I said. "Fine". "Just 'fine'?" "Actually, very well," she smiled and looked just like her mother, talked like her too, same composure. "I've been talking to my father." "What did he say?" "He's asked me to look after mummy and says that he accepts his passing now." "Wow, that's heavy stuff for a kid like you to be talking about." "No, it's not. Can I use the bathroom now?" I got out of the way—she had a persuasive way of making me blush!

Kamala thanked me profusely for my work. "It's good to have a man about the house when these calamities occur," she said, and her eyes had a glazed look of enchantment that made me slightly uncomfortable. Yet, she is an attractive woman, a stoic soul in our society, and someone deserving our respect. She also appears to be very lonely.

Time had gone by very fast that evening. When I got home I realized that I was late for dinner; missed it completely, in fact, and today of all days—it was our seventh wedding anniversary!

* * *

But there were happy times, too, growing up in Tolemac. I remember the first "March of the Lamps." It was soon after the psychic children stopped communing with their ancestors. There was a pre-Flood celebration called "All Souls Day," which is still celebrated by some members of our church congregation. A gathering of women went down Sunset Hill that evening in early November, holding lamps in their hands. People looked out of their makeshift houses, watching these women resolutely make their way downhill to the Waterside Park. There, they began singing hymns and praying for the dear departed. Despite the balmy temperatures and the rain that fell, they carried on undeterred. It was as if they had made a connection with some other realm, or were trying to emulate what the little psychic children had achieved. The next year, around that time, my mother, Belva, Kamala and the ladies from the Women's Association, started planning a more elaborate ceremony and invited all members of Tolemac to participate, irrespective of their religious beliefs. That occasion is still etched in my mind—the lamps came from all over Tolemac—from Sunset Hill, and from the other side, too, where new houses were springing up daily. Strings of light snaked downhill along each of the two main roads, Dundas and Ontario, leading to the waterfront. They met on Main and turned left, heading into the Waterside Park. The procession, led mainly by the women, with their children hanging on, wove down into the park to celebrate the souls of the dead. Some men joined in belatedly. The prayers in the park reached a crescendo and could be heard all around Tolemac.

Samson had been busy at a co-operative construction site that day and came home late (in those days he volunteered most evenings to build homes for people). Upon hearing the loud praying and singing, he quickly dusted himself off, got our bicycles out and took me downhill to see what was going on. I had to get on his shoulders to see above the crowd. There, on a makeshift stage, the women were singing, swaying from side to side, a lamp in each one's hand. Gathered in the shadows around them was the whole of Tolemac—about ten thousand people. The women's voices carried over the water and echoed back like the voices of our ancestors speaking. It was eerily fascinating. Samson's face glowed and he said proudly, "The women have outdone us this time. They have indeed unified this community. God Bless them!" The March of the Lamps has endured as an annual event on All Souls' Day.

Our Church of the New Covenant got its name soon after that ceremony. Samson changed his sermons, too, to be more generic and to accommodate the many shades of pre-Flood Christian faiths that were represented, as well as the few Muslims, Buddhists and Hindus, since these faiths were not sizeable enough to have their own houses of prayer. Samson took me to other religious temples, too, on courtesy visits, like the nearby Jewish synagogue, and they all had a common theme. They used the Flood as a reference point to launch their teachings. It seemed that no one was able to make sense of the Old World that had become so complicated with its wars of aggression, corporate greed, terrorism, drug dealing, cyber crime, poverty, starvation and deadly diseases such as AIDS, SARS and Avian Flu. Religious leaders were desperately trying to make sense of the New World, so that it would not get as complicated as the Old one.

There were other joyous occasions, too, like Market Saturday, down on Ontario Street. As early as I can remember, goods destined for the waterfront, or produce grown in the fields of Tolemac, were offered for sale to the locals before they were exported. As kids, it was great to get lost among the adults as they haggled over the stalls, bargaining for clothing, grains, vegetables, meats, electronic goods and other household commodities. The boats coming in from other Humanitarian states unloaded their produce not far from the market stalls and the noise level was often high. It was as if there were two levels of activity taking place: the haggling by the adults, and the games of hide–and-seek played by the kids, who dove in and out among the stalls. We knew we were always safe as long as we stayed where the crowds and the stalls were; if we got separated, we just sat tight—our parents would find us anyway. Loudspeakers blared occasionally to say that so-and-so's kid was at such-and-such stall waiting to be collected. The hidden pleasures around the food stalls where we would sneak a drink or a piece of candy – so much nicer acquired this way than purchased at the store – was my only real exposure to the world of sin. But it felt good then, when we were growing up.

*   *   *

"Dammit—don't pass inside the penalty zone—just shoot!" Burgess's yelling from the bleachers still rings in my years as Ethan bulldozed his way past the defenders, one of them being me, to shoot a hoop, and then turn around triumphantly to his father, as if to say, "I can do it!"

That was a few years later when we entered our double-digit years but weren't quite teenagers yet. The school had expanded to house a basketball court and our parents were teaching us to play this sport, invented in the former Canada. I couldn't quite understand why there was so much body contact, when all one had to do was pass the ball between one's team members and drop it into the basket at the opponent's end of the court. We had four teams in our league then. But Ethan made it a point to use his superior weight to edge us away all the time. His team always won the league. I didn't much like basketball!

October 15, 2023

When Nathan proposed the hockey rink, I thought he was nuts.

"It's too warm!"

"We could get the turbines from the grain elevator when it shuts down at night and use them to crank out some ice."

"Then you are going to have to build that rink right in the port."

"We could clear a bit of land just on the north end—let's hit up Burgess for a short-term sublease—and shine all the flood lamps from the port on it."

There was no stopping his madcap scheme, but the more I thought about it, the more I liked it. Yes, we were going to do the impossible, again!

The next day I put out a call for volunteers. I got nearly two hundred responses.

Burgess was generous with the land he had recently leased to build the port. Within a week, working evenings after our day jobs, we flattened a circle out to the side of the turbines so we did not have to move them. It took us a few hours to generate the ice. Flood lamps were created from any form of lighting we could find, including kerosene torches used in the countryside. Hockey sticks and other pre-Flood equipment and memorabilia appeared out of nowhere—even masks and pads for the goaltenders—we were good to go!

The whole of Tolemac attended that first game. What was most interesting was the number of people who got on the ice after the game, to skate. These people, who were my age, hadn't skated since the Flood. Their kids looked on dejectedly. I knew instantly what our next project was going to be—teaching the kids to skate!

That first makeshift rink and its success led to the subsequent "conscription" of children to learn to skate and play hockey. It was a great novelty for many of us, who had never donned a pair of skates in our lives, our parents having been occupied with other, more important things. Burgess subsequently donated the rink to the city. Four years later the new, regulation-sized hockey rink was opened on Tolemac's fifteenth anniversary, and the adults celebrated more than the children. All these older men, Samson among them, were whooping it up and having a great time, recalling old times as they jostled each other on the ice. Unlike in pre-Flood times, alcohol was not allowed, and the game started with a prayer, which Samson, as custodian of the church, conducted. His prayer went something like this: "Lord, we are gathered today to engage our bodies and minds in a sport that united a once-great nation and fostered goodwill between nations. Give us the wisdom and spirit to play hard, win or lose graciously and leave having learned something from our competition and each other." But what followed was different: body checking, fans yelling, even a few fisticuffs when things got really heated up. An elevated noise level jarred my nerves and lasted for many hours in the arena after the game ended. The gentle people of Tolemac needed hockey as a release from their daunting new environment. Ethan, and even little John, loved this sport and were soon playing on our school team. I remember Burgess in the stands shouting, always yelling advice at them that they scarcely paid attention to. I didn't like hockey any more than basketball. There had to be a better way than head-on competition.

October 15, 2027

David came home from school early today. It was one of those days that I had stayed indoors to do the church accounts. The lad looked bedraggled and sad. I haven't spent much time with him of late. I put away my files and talked to him. It transpired that he had been dropped from the basketball team—he was number nine in line. The coach had offered him a place on the bench and a chance to learn from watching the other players.

He hasn't made much headway in his hockey either. David is a sensitive boy; he would not rebel against being sidelined or go head-to-head with the coach over it, like Ethan and the others. He wants me to be proud of him. Which kid doesn't want his father's pride? But I have to make him feel he has to do more to earn his spurs. As for being dropped from the team, he will probably keep his head down, be polite, agree to go along and suffer in silence.

Maybe Agnes and I have overprotected him in our zeal not to have him endure the shocks and ravages of our post-Flood society. We always made sure one of us was around (Agnes mainly) when he was growing up so that he didn't go wandering off with those Williams boys, especially Ethan. David was always the bookish kind, particularly fond of studying the history of our society, and always asking me intelligent questions.

One day, I found a school essay he had kept lying around on the topic of "Competition"—the lad abhors competition and says it must be renamed co-opetition. Never heard such a word! He claims that contact sports, such as basketball and hockey, should be banned, while the arts, such as writing, reading, painting, music and drama, should be promoted instead. After all, he claims, if the purpose of basketball is to score hoops, why not get both sides to aim for the same goal and score more hoops than they currently do in a game where each side is out to thwart the other? I think he is being bullied too much by Ethan Williams, and is trying to find his own star in more non-competitive arenas.

Maybe he'll make a good college professor one day. But there are times when I just wish he had a little more gumption.

Gumption! I knew Samson was disappointed in my not being his replica—but gumption! That was rankling! I excelled in the classroom, and he conceded that. I read books at an early age, even though there weren't too many to go around in those early days. The Bible was my first real book; I still read it. Then the Internet got serious about book publishing and we could subscribe to selected writings either in instalments or in whole-book form. There was a handy portable machine, invented before the Flood, that could download a book from the Internet and read it back to you in voice format. I used this machine, which Samson bought me on my fifth birthday, for when he was out on civic work and unable to give bedtime readings.

There were interesting subjects at school, too, as we entered our teens. New World Ethics, New World Geography and New World Economics—subjects I teach now. In addition, there were a heap of older subjects: Math, English, Religion and History. I asked my teacher why the title "New World" was added to rather "Old World" subjects like Ethics, Geography and Economics.

"Because it's different," said Mr. Taylor, our New-World subject teacher. "The whole world has turned upside down from how we knew it."

I have to pause a minute and picture Mr. Taylor. He was fifty at the time of the Flood, a career schoolteacher, who taught in the public school system of the old world. In addition to teaching, he was always learning, and you never saw him without papers or a book in his hand. He lost everything in the Flood, including his family and his house. His wife and children were in one of those large shopping centres called malls, when the roof caved in due to water seepage. None of them survived. Yet, he was one of those who immediately started to chart the New World. On the Internet, he led a virtual team of pioneer cartographers, gathered from all over the old North American continent, some from the now almost-vanished Europe and others from New Zealand, and they spent hours arguing about the contours of the New World. He would then come to class, and his new lesson would be an update of the previous one, because new information had come to light.

And new information was always becoming known to Mr. Taylor. I will never forget the conversation I once had with him in my senior high-school year. I had stayed back after class for help with my schoolwork and Mr. Taylor was immersed in the classroom Communicator, pouring over his maps. He was messy; papers were strewn everywhere; his scanty, grey hair fell over his collar, and his giant glasses magnified his eyes. Yet, when he turned that gargantuan look on you, it was kindly, even sad at times.

"I have a question for you Mr. Taylor."

Taking his immersion on the Communicator to mean a "yes," I carried on. "Why do we Tolemacians trade only with other Humanitarian states? Isn't trade supposed to be free?"

"Of course, it is," he said, continuing to frown at the map on the screen in front of him. "We could trade with New Eden if we wished."

"Then why don't we? They have better things than us—I mean consumer stuff like clothes, electronics, even Communicators and things."

"But do we want to? That is the question," he said, folding his glasses and putting them into his shirt pocket. He rubbed his eyes and yawned.

"But, why not? Aren't we supposed to trade with people who have the best economics for producing certain goods?"

"That's the old Adam Smith model, David. That model is obsolete now. What does your new textbook say about trading principles?"

The textbook in question bears an acknowledgement to Mr. Taylor and other experts like him for their research contributions. The text was used widely among schools in the Humanitarian States. I said, "That we trade with people who do not seek to beat us at all costs."

"Win-win deals. Good! And—?"

"That one must have value to trade."

"And 'value' as defined by whom?"

"The customer—the people we are trading with, in this case."

"Ah, ha! A wise observation! You will see this clearly illustrated at the end of term when you take my 'Trading Game' test." He turned back to his papers and got busy again. It was as if he did not want to stop and look at the world for fear he'd remember what he'd lost. At least, that was my theory, now that I understood what Samson meant by 'keeping busy.' "

Mr. Taylor's theory came home to me when we took the Trading Game test at the end of term. He assembled the entire class in the church hall that day; we needed lots of floor space for the exercise, and our classrooms were too small. The church benches were cleared away and on the floor lay a giant map of Mr. Taylor's creation: Tolemac, Oceania, New Eden and its colonies, Saska-Manitoba, Alberta, even the Californias were on it, and to scale, as we had seen them in our New World geography books. He then split us into population blocks; each student to represent approximately thirty thousand people. He selectively placed us on each of the land masses. I got on to the map as the single occupant of Tolemac, representing its population at the time. Ethan, Peter Lowry and the Brady twins stood in for the much larger New Eden (they also happened to be buddies on the school hockey team and I wondered if Mr. Taylor had deliberately done this). Sammy White Dove, Jose Garcia and a couple of others were placed on Oceania, and so on it went. The Californias, being scarcely populated islands, were grouped together and given to fat Charles Baldwin who forever slept in class. He promptly spread out on the floor with his feet touching the coastline of Arizona and his head reaching down to the Hawaiian Islands. "I have to cover my land area, end to end," Charles said, yawning, and Mr. Taylor smiled.

Two students were appointed "rovers." They represented the Defence and Medical Funds, respectively. Periodically, each rover would tour our city states to collect contributions, which had to be made regardless of our trading success, if we wanted the benefit of these shared services.

Next, Mr. Taylor brought out our "assets." They were brightly coloured wooden blocks, each representing resources such as farm produce, manufactured goods, mineral resources, labour and services. He also distributed fake Dollars of the Americas that stood for cash reserves: "These are your natural, manufactured and fiscal resources that you can trade with. Trade with anyone you wish, Capitalists and Humanitarians alike, although this does not happen in real life, and you will see why today." He looked at me when he said this, winking. "The only little twist here, as in real life, is that the Humanitarian states have their own trading rules, and the Capitalist states have theirs."

"This is complicated," said Charles. "Can't we have just one set of rules?"

"You wish!" said Mr. Taylor. "But there are no common sets of rules—not yet anyway. There used to be such rules before the Flood—the World Trade Organization, the International Labour Organization, NAFTA, GATT and so on, but these institutions' rules were violated all the time. So, after the Flood, people with common ground and understanding, blocks like the Humanitarians and the Capitalists, made up their own rules. They are less likely to break these— at least the Humanitarians are." He then handed out two different coloured sets of sheets, each set representing the respective trading rules of the Capitalist and Humanitarian realms. We were not allowed to see the other realm's trading rules.

I was given three wooden blocks, immediately recognizable as familiar sights in Tolemac: one for farm produce, which we had in abundance, given our twice yearly harvest brought on by the post-Flood climatic change and advances in genetic engineering; one for the port facility, now a central transhipment point for the many ships plying routes in the North Atlantic; and one for our microchip facility that powered Communicators around our New World and employed nearly everyone who was not in farming or working down at the port. But my three blocks were paltry next to those of Ethan and his gang. They were prancing about the larger land mass of New Eden surrounded by a pile of blocks representing diamonds, gold, oil, various manufacturing categories and services. Charles had a single block in his hand: for fisheries. The kids in Oceania were better off, having assets such as manufacturing, natural resources and educational facilities.

Ethan was a bulky, pimply teenager at this point, with fake tattoos on his arms, a shadow of a moustache always present and jet-black hair falling to his shoulders. He started a non-rhyming rant among his teammates that went something like "Rah, rah—let's get 'em guys." Being the solitary person on Tolemac, I had no one to launch a counter-rant with.

Mr. Taylor blew his whistle and announced: "Before you begin, remember the purpose of the game is to maximize your assets by trading. You have one hour to complete your activity and then we will take score. In between your trading, I will give you periodic information regarding farm and industrial output so that you know what you have to trade with. I will also draw occasional 'chance cards' that signal new developments, such as crop failures, bankruptcies, new trading alliances and so on—the unexpected stuff that happens in a normal world. So, take your cues accordingly. Let's go!" He blew the whistle, long and hard this time, and we got underway.

The next hour went by in a blaze of activity except for Charles Baldwin who had a hard time selling his fish. The East Coast states had polluted waters and did not have a fishing industry as such, but fish had gone out of fashion as a food category there, so his sales to them were somewhat limited. Mr. Taylor drew a chance card that announced New Eden's opening of a new microchip factory. Ethan jumped on this opportunity and told me that he did not need to buy my microchips anymore now that he had his own facility. Then he proposed buying mine and merging it with his. I declined. I opened my port to Charles's boats, but, as his sales in Oceania and New Eden were weak, he couldn't pay the bills and I ended up keeping one of his boats as payment. But then I didn't know what to do with it; it had become a useless asset.

The Oceania folks were by far the best to trade with as they used my port as an entry point for access to Saska-Manitoba, Tolemac and other southern states. They also bought my microchips for their Communicator manufacturing plant. They had established export markets beyond North America and were trading with people as far as New Zealand. Ethan and his buddies launched a "price war" for microchips undercutting my price, but I knew that Jose Garcia, who represented Oceania, did not like Ethan, and despite the latter's low prices, opted to deal with me instead. This made Ethan angry and he whispered to the rover from the Defence Fund. I found out later that he was trying to get a special project approved by the Defence Fund, a project to raid Tolemac and capture its port. But the Defence Fund, dependant on subscriptions from all member states—Capitalist and Humanitarian alike—declined, as it was against its rules of association.

"I'll pay you more. I'll pay you their subscriptions, too," Ethan called out to the Defence rover, Paul Samuel. But Paul declined and roved on to collect his subscriptions from Oceania. So Ethan and his crew opted out of the Medical Fund, ticking off its rover, Garry Appegio, and started to save up more money. They had a fierce debate among themselves at that point—Peter Lowry, the moderate among the New Edeners, resisted until Ethan's dominant personality soon won over. I envied Ethan's ability to opt out without care for the consequences. I found the two roving funds draining me each time they came around on the quarter of the hour and I had to redouble my efforts at earning trading dollars to keep meeting their payments. To make things worse, the next information sheet on farm output distributed by Mr. Taylor had Tolemac producing 10 percent less on their recent harvest. I was in pretty bad shape for the quarter.

After awhile, Ethan and his buddies gave up on focusing on Tolemac and started to trade with Alberta, further west of us—another Capitalist state. In addition to agriculture, Alberta had lots of labour, for many Californians had migrated there following the Flood, and that's all they were able to offer New Eden, which well suited Ethan in his desire to be top dog. At the forty-five minute mark, one of the three people sitting on the Alberta land mass physically moved over to New Eden to signify the emigration of migrant workers.

"Charles Baldwin, what are you doing to keep your state afloat?" Mr. Taylor passed by, nudging a drowsy Charles who had lost interest in the game.

"Well, there's nothing much you can do if you have nothing to trade, is there?" Charles shot back.

"But you have to try, my boy—get creative!" an uncompromising Mr. Taylor said.

Soon after, I saw Charles in conversation with one of the Brady twins (I could never distinguish Jeremy from Jermaine at a distance, because they were identical and dressed the same way, too), who ran back to Ethan and started whispering hurriedly. There were a few more hushed conversations before money exchanged hands. Then a proud Ethan exclaimed, "We have just signed a treaty with the Californias. They will become a part of New Eden, in exchange for goods and services provided by us. All their assets have been folded into the greater state of New Eden."

"But that's not fair," I protested to Mr. Taylor. "It's not in the rules. Acquisition of states is not allowed."

"That's in the Humanitarian book of rules. In the Capitalist book, anything goes," said Mr. Taylor.

I was nervous looking at Ethan's gleaming eyes; he was planning a more diabolical strategy. He was circling Tolemac, by buying over the Californias and subjugating Alberta. He was poised for a takeover. All that lay between Tolemac and the encroaching "Western Capitalist front" appeared to be sleepy Saska-Manitoba, and it only had the incumbent Natalie Sacik defending it. Saska-Manitoba's main asset was farm produce, not much to bargain with. My only hope seemed to be Oceania, which, despite being slightly smaller in size than New Eden, dealt equitably. Sammy, Jose and I could hold off those goons from New Eden; I figured there was strength in numbers. So I went over to Sammy and suggested an alliance. Jose looked at his rules sheet, and said that we could have an alliance based on trade, but we would have to remain autonomous in terms of governance; those were the Humanitarian rules. Paul Samuel of Defence came by on his fourth and final round and we asked him how he could protect our boundaries from the New Edeners. He read off his Defence rules and said that he was responsible for perimeter security for all subscribers. He was there to defend us against the Africans, Asians, Europeans and South Americans, but not to sponsor or defend us against intra-jurisdictional disputes. He did remind us though that New Eden was still a subscriber and any aggressive behaviour by a member would result in its expulsion from the Defence Fund.

"But that won't help," Jose said. "With the Californias and Alberta in their pockets, New Eden could still attack us. And the Defence Fund will be ineffective and bankrupt without three of its key members."

"They've trapped us!"

But Mr. Taylor's final whistle blew at that time and we were mercifully spared trying to resolve that problem.

When we took the final tally, this was the outcome:

Californias (Capitalist)—no more assets, now a dependency of New Eden;

Alberta (Capitalist)—still holding its own, about the same materially, but having lost a third of its population to New Eden;

New Eden (Capitalist)—wealthier because of its increased manufacturing industry and the opening up of its trading markets with Indo-China. Also, New Eden had increased its leverage and power within the Americas;

Oceania (Humanitarian)—moderately wealthier, with its population still intact, and some new trading agreements with the Middle East and New Zealand;

Tolemac (Humanitarian)—weakened, having cash-flow issues; and

Saska-Manitoba (Humanitarian)—near bankruptcy, too little demand for its farm produce due to the abundance of such in Alberta, its neighbour. Its only export market is Oceania.

I think I had got Mr. Taylor's message. It was obvious that the New World was getting as complicated as the Old one. Understandably—because there were human beings still living in it!

That Trading Game played out in real life, too. Graduating from high school, Ethan Williams went to university in New Eden and got absorbed into the business world there. Jermaine, of the Brady twins, also left for New Eden, leaving his identical twin behind. I was always surprised by this move. Paul Samuel moved to Oceania and joined the NADF. The rest of us dispersed ourselves among the growing population of Tolemac. I became the professor Samson had wanted me to be, at my old school, the Tolemac Academy of Learning.

Chapter 7

October 20, 2029

BILLY WHITE DOVE DISAPPEARED TODAY. And this wasn't as a result of his usual binge, after which he would be found among the migrant workers in the farms on the other side of Sunset, snoring away the previous night's booze. Belva rushed over to our home, looking harried, which was unusual. At thirty-five, she was getting bigger and rounder. She had two children, Sammy and Rose, and probably would have more if Billy had taken the time to procreate, instead of killing his seed with alcohol. What I admired most about Belva was her determination to be in charge, despite all the obstacles. The Flood had trained her well. If she hadn't kept her cool and lived a spiritual life, her family would have disintegrated long ago because of Billy's drinking.

"He's gone again, Sam. This time, I think he's gone for good."

"Don't say that, dear—" Agnes blurted, trying to mollify the situation. Agnes was distracted and irritable that evening. In fact, we'd been arguing before our visitor arrived. Now, she was relieved to focus her energy on Belva. "He's probably gone out with his friends," Agnes said.

"Oh no, he's gone for sure this time." Belva kept shaking her head. Her face remained impassive.

"I'll go look for him." I said. "He's probably sleeping it off somewhere. Did you check to see if he's been arrested?" That was the safest bet—Burgess's anti-drinking patrols were out in force around this time, as it was monthly pay time for the migrant workers.

"Checked it—no one has seen him."

"Stay here and catch up on the news with Agnes. I'll be back." I pulled on a jacket and headed out into the cool evening.

Getting over Sunset Hill to the migrant worker quarters on my bicycle took about half an hour as I am no longer a twenty-year-old. Providing accommodation for these itinerants was another of Nathan's bright ideas, now that he owned most of the farmland this side of Sunset. "It's our competitive edge. We'll never be short of workers for the abundant harvests we've been getting lately," was his rationale. And he was right; we had a steady demand for workers and were in no short supply of them due to this perk. Short-term labourers pay for these facilities in other states. The only problem with migrant workers was their transient nature; it wasn't very comforting, not knowing where they really came from—Humanitarian or Capitalist realms. And they brought a lot of bad practices with them, too.

Squat white buildings sprawled down the hill at the edge of the farms, looking ghostly in the night. Children ran about playing hide-and-seek or flying kites in the gathering darkness, while teenagers held hands and cuddled in corners. Loud chatter and the smells of cooking emanated from inside dwellings, and there was the sound of salsa music. Occasionally, a domestic quarrel broke out and voices rose, including those of children and older parents. Dirty overalls hung from clotheslines. Tomorrow they would be worn again until the end of the week when they disappeared into the communal laundromat.

It made me reflect on the long hours the men and women spent working in the fields, while the grandparents looked after the young and prepared the meals. Migrant families went to bed late, but at dawn they came hurtling downhill on their bicycles to work the farms in the valley below. In between the toil, they also took time to sow their seed in plenty, for the number of children among them put the highly procreative Tolemacians to shame. Very soon, we would have to build special schools for these children who have lower than average academic skills. When the growing season ended, we could make sure that they all returned where they came from, or we could be generous and offer them permanent residency. This was another big decision for the Executive Committee in the days ahead. Still, these children have a better life here than in those awful "colonies" of the Capitalist states.

I saw Juan Gomez, Billy's buddy, hanging about the convenience store where the workers lined up every evening to play Communicator games on three crumbling machines. Often some got bored and sold their spot in the line-up for a cigarette or relief on the next morning's shift. I had seen this happen when I held a weekly church service here a few years ago, hoping to give these people something more uplifting in their lives. I stopped the service after three months when attendance dwindled. They clearly preferred to play Communicator games after doing all that back-breaking, brain-numbing work in the fields.

"Hey, Juan, how's it going?"

"Mr. Samson! Nice to see ju! What brings ju to our humble hole?"

"Seen Billy?"

"Yah—early today. Said something about going away. Permanently."

"Like where?"

"Don't know. Found his missing brother and sister, he said."

"That can't be. They were lost a long time ago!"

"Nah, nah—remember he used to get drunk and sit by the water till ju folks come to fetch him home?"

Another haunt of Billy's, after a binge, was the Waterside Park. He could often be found looking longingly across the water in the direction of New Eden. No one had ever figured out why. That was a place I'd often check before Burgess's men got there and arrested Billy for the night. Billy was a peaceful drunk, singing songs or crying or laughing to himself while under the influence, never hurting a soul, not even Belva or the children.

"Went over to Brady's to get a loan so he could catch the boat," Juan said.

My blood boiled at the mention of Brady. "Was Billy drunk?"

"No. Very sober this time, Mr. Samson."

"Oh, come on. You guys running that still of yours again?"

"Oh, no Mr. Samson. We are real clean here now."

I wished I could see Juan's eyes in the gathering dusk, but I needed to get to Billy. And remind Burgess to mount another raid on these hovels where illegal alcohol stills churned out their deadly brew amidst the smells of cooking and strains of salsa. At least, the migrants kept the stuff within their community and did not try to peddle it outside for fear of deportation. The control we had on how long they stayed with us was all the enforcement needed.

"You stay out of trouble now, Juan," I said, remounting my bicycle. "And make sure you read your Bible, daily."

"Yes sir, Mr. Samson. Sure will."

I managed to catch a water taxi out to Brady's Island Bar, a rackety shack sitting on an old oil platform that had floated down in the Flood and come to rest about three kilometres offshore from Tolemac, just outside the two-mile limit of our civic boundary. The taxi driver, a regular at our church, looked at me in surprise.

'Brady's, Mr. Arthurs?"

"This is not a drinking visit, I assure you" I said, and remained silent for the length of the twenty-minute ride.

From the outside, Brady's Island Bar was a shanty on top of a crumbling mass of metal that refused to sink. The roof blew down at least once during the rainy season, but Brady, an ex-sailor, would have it up and running again in a week. The money made from this outpost was certainly not reflected in his lifestyle, or in the décor of his cash cow. A foot ladder trailed down to the water from the deck, the main entrance. I wonder how many drunken sailors had fallen off the ladder on their way back from Brady's. They usually came in groups off Tolemac-bound boats. Afterward, they stayed on their boats until they were sober enough to go on shore in Tolemac and not get arrested. The heavier-drinking patrons were those leaving Tolemac, to go where abstinence no longer mattered.

Tobacco smoke filled the shack. Men sat around wooden tables, with glasses and bottles all over and peanut shells littering the floor. The air reeked of sweat, smoke, sea and the strong smell of alcohol. Behind the bar, Brady was doing brisk business. Some of the sailors, who recognized me, averted their eyes. Ironically, Brady lived in Tolemac with his twin sons Jeremy and Jermaine, but plied his trade in this rat hole, where our laws could not reach him. We still have so many loopholes in our legal system. All we could do was shun him and his family. So Brady moved his home to the outskirts of Tolemac behind the docklands, after his wife left him in disgust five years ago, and went to live in Oceania.

It was said that Brady decided to stay in Tolemac and thumb his nose at us because of what his wife had done. She and a band of her women friends burst in on him one day, in bed with a woman from one of the migrant labour camps. The woman was deported; Brady, charged with adultery, had to perform three months of manual labour down at the city's garbage dump. Mrs. Brady visited every day and hurled insults at him as he worked the kilns. She left for Oceania two days before his sentence ended, leaving the twins behind. He opened his island bar a few months later.

"What will it be, Arthurs?" Brady wheezed, then coughed.

"*Water. Seen Billy?*"

"*This a police investigation, or what? Why didn't you send Burgess?*"

"*Juan told me Billy came here, so cut out the excuses. Where's Billy?*"

Brady scratched his pot belly. He was wearing a singlet, and body hair sprouted all over him, sticking through the narrow cotton strands of the garment. The shock of red hair on his head was unruly and tangled. When he grinned, he revealed irregular and tobacco-stained teeth. He poured a shot glass of spirits and pushed it over to me.

"*Come on Arthurs—this is a free country—I think. It's you fellas who are passing all those laws and shutting us poor folks from making a living.*"

"*Where's Billy?*"

"*Gone to New Eden. To his folks. He wasn't getting any from the wife—you guys have ruined our women, with your morals and laws and such. They don't even screw anymore! So, join me in a drink. Let's celebrate Billy's escape from your Bible thumping.*" *He looked triumphant, as if he had socked me in the face. "Hey guys," he shouted to the patrons within earshot. "Let's celebrate. To Billy's freedom!" He raised the bottle and took a couple of long swigs. Wiping a hand across his mouth, he took on a feisty look. I kept my calm; I was outnumbered here. "You don't want our hospitality, eh? What the hell do you want, Arthurs?"*

"*I hope he returns the money you loaned him. Billy barely settles his bar tabs,*" *I said.*

"*Let's say, it was a small investment.*"

I pushed the glass back to him, untouched. "He'll be a cheap supply-chain runner for you. But one day we will shut you down, Brady."

"*And one day I'll have branches of Brady's Island Bar surrounding your little island Arthurs—just you wait. You and your Executive Committee are too dammed high and mighty! Who gave you the right?*"

"*God gave us the right, Brady—to survive. You could have done better this time around.*"

"*This is all I know, Arthurs. Sailing ships and waiting bars. And it has worked out for me. Perhaps God could have taught me a new skill, if He was so bloody concerned.*"

"*Hasn't it occurred to you that your business does well because we are dry in Tolemac?*"

"*That's the beauty, ain't it, Arthurs? Go on, make Tolemac wet and drive me out of business! I dare you!*"

"*Good night, Brady. One day—we will see.*"

* * *

When I got home, Belva had left. Agnes's mood seemed to have progressively worsened. She was pacing.

"Why didn't you call?" she said. "We gave up waiting for you and I asked Belva to go home." She quit pacing and sat down at the table. "Belva's stoic. Thank God, for stoic women in our society."

"It took a while to track Billy down. He wasn't around his usual haunts. He's gone to New Eden," I said. I didn't want to open a conversation on the stoicism of women.

"Why on earth would he go there?"

"Says he's found his missing relatives."

"His family is here—Belva and the kids. He's just a . . . no-good . . . cop-out!" I noticed that Agnes had a tot of brandy in her glass.

"You are stressed again."

"Every night of late. Thanks for noticing!"

"We had an agreement. The people of Tolemac need—"

"Sam, I am sick of these agreements! How much can we give and give and give? I also represent 'the people of Tolemac'. "

"Agnes, you've had a long day. I don't want to start another argument at this time."

"There never is a right time." She downed her drink and headed off toward the bedrooms. She will sleep in her own room tonight, as she has of late. I was glad that David was at a night-study class and wasn't around to hear this altercation. And there have been many, recently.

As I write this entry down—a very long piece, after a very long time—I wonder if we have indeed built a utopia out of the Flood's destruction. Yes, we have laws and law-abiding people now, and have caught up materially to where we were before the cataclysm. And we believe in God and do not have crime, and we believe in sharing. Yet when I think of the hidden costs of creating this new life, the burden on our personal lives and the encroaching threat of greed manifested in ideas such as Brady's proposed ring of island bars, I wonder if the battle is over yet. Perhaps it was never intended to .end

Brady's unsavoury comments about "Bible thumping" and "women not screwing anymore," lewd though they were, bother me for another reason. They bother me because scoundrels like Brady have not earned the right to the truth.

Part 2

Descent

"I saw something else under the sun. In the place of judgment—wickedness was there. In the place of justice—wickedness was there."

—Ecclesiastes 3:16

Chapter 8

DAVID PAUSED ON THE STEPS OF CITY HALL. Was he doing the right thing? He couldn't put Samson off any more. He made sure to sign the guest book and date it. It was mandatory for candidates intending to run for election to attend at least three months of Executive Committee meetings as observers.

The Executive Committee of Tolemac held their meetings at City Hall, next door to the Church of the New Covenant. City Hall was an extension of the church, a rather nondescript wood and brick building that could pass for a bank or library. The Spartan furnishings inside the Committee chamber were symbolic of the Tolemacian lifestyle. Having studied former civilizations and their excesses—Rome, Washington and Ottawa—the people of Tolemac made certain their governance chambers looked conservative. Except for the Trillium flag (Tolemac's emblem) hoisted in a corner, a bowl of fresh cut flowers sitting on a round metal table surrounded by metal chairs, the Committee chamber was empty: no pictures, no trophies. It was all very functional.

The Committee was gathering in the chamber. David paused at the entrance, then took the side stairway before anyone noticed him, making it up to the gallery. This was a good place to watch the proceedings, unseen. But he was surprised to see that he had company on the empty balcony.

"Leo, what are you doing here?"

The youth, who was opening his mobile Communicator and getting ready to record the proceedings, looked up and blushed.

"Mr. Arthurs? Are you attending the mandatories?"

David's hesitation caused Leo's face to light up: "Wow, that's great! Really great, Mr. Arthurs!"

"Now, don't get your hopes up. I've got to get elected first. What are you doing here?"

"I asked my father if I could record the proceedings of the trade issue for our school project."

"That's impressive. Giving up an afternoon to see the elders debate our future." Leo Patimkin was a bright social science student, although he struggled with math and the physical sciences. In Leo's buck- toothed expression and lanky frame, David saw a reflection of Leo's famous father, Vladimir, who sat in the chamber below. Vladimir ran the Communications Centre, Tolemac's de facto information gateway to the outside world.

"Don't hold your breath on the trade issue, Leo. Samson has warned me that they sometimes drift from the agenda."

David studied the members of the Executive as they took their seats at the round table. Burgess Williams, looking more like an ex-prizefighter than a defence secretary, with his cane leaning up against a chair, was shifting through some papers and whispering in his usually conspiratorial manner to Vladimir Patimkin. Murtaza, head of the river transport teamsters, with a steaming cup of tea beside him, had his eyes closed in prayer; he still prayed six times a day according to his religion. Nathan Goldman, holder of the finance portfolio, was arguing loudly with chief justice Kamala Sunderam about something called "incentive funding." He kept banging his hands on the table trying to propound another of his pet theories. David overheard his mother-in-law say, "Nat, why don't you table the issue, if you feel so strongly about it?" Dr. Morden, head of the Tolemac General Hospital, was his usual urbane self, focused on reviewing the agenda. He looked disinterested in the side conversations and kept checking his watch; he was also the only black member in the group, tracing his ancestry to the first free slaves who crossed over from the former U.S.A. into Canada through what was then known as the Underground Railroad. Most Tolemacians were so mixed these days, it was rare to find a pure black or white person.

When everyone settled down, Samson opened the proceedings with a verse from the Bible. His steely grey hair was cut long at the shoulder. He also sported a beard, which emphasized his sense of authority over the group. Samson read his adapted version of Jeremiah's prayer: "We know, O Lord that a man's life is not his own. It is not for man to direct his steps. Help us in our deliberations today and guide us to make the right decisions for the people of Tolemac who have been entrusted to our care." There was a reverent silence, except for a rustling of papers from Burgess.

"We have two items on the agenda today," Samson said. "Let's aim for consensus, as usual. The first item, to be tabled by Burgess, concerns our defence funding. The other item is about the ongoing refugee situation, which I will cover; there is a new development."

"Mr. Chairman, I have another," Nathan said, as he cleared his throat.

"Yes?"

"It's the subject of incentive funding."

"Nat, we've covered this one before. It never moves beyond the 'idea' stage."

"And yet we must resolve it! Are we for it or against it?"

"Is there someone who will second that agenda item then?"

"I will," Kamala said.

Samson looked surprised. "All right, it's on the agenda. Anything else?"

There were no other items. Burgess rose to present his case.

"As you all probably know, we need to increase our defence contribution this year. Our payments have been static over the last three years and the population of Tolemac has increased by over ten percent during that time."

"I don't see any return for our money," Nathan said.

Burgess reddened. "You are not supposed to. The fact that you have a stable community, free from outside threat, is the return on your investment."

"How do we know that there is any outside threat to begin with? It's all hearsay and fear mongering."

"You know that Oceania was attacked recently."

"I think that was an inside job. Just to scare everyone into paying. If we have honest citizens here—which I believe we do—why can't we 'pay as we go'?"

"The North American Defence Fund, the NADF, needs a stable source of funding to keep its fleet and personnel up to date."

"Or is it to pay its workers a healthy bonus at the end of the year?"

"I resent that!" Burgess erupted.

"Now, now gentlemen," Samson interrupted. "Nothing personal here. I would like to entertain other thoughts from the floor on this issue." It was a known fact that the NADF was well-funded and paid its employees above prevailing labour rates in an attempt to be free of internal corruption. In his part-time job as Tolemac's representative to NADF, Burgess earned a good and stable retainer. That was very clear from public servants' salaries published on local Infoway bulletin boards under Tolemac's "transparency" laws. His other source of income, as head of the port of Tolemac, had combined to make Burgess a wealthy man as he neared retirement.

Asif Murtaza, who had woken up from his prayers, raised his hand. "Mr. Chairman, if there is any extra funding to be allocated, I think we need to put it towards strengthening the sea wall. We could have another breach and lose valuable waterside property. As it is, I have to constantly reinforce the moorings for our boats."

"And I'd like to increase processing capacity and beef up our firewalls at the Communications Centre. I submitted my annual budget, but did not anticipate the usage, or the hacker attacks that beat my predictions every year," Vladimir said.

Burgess didn't agree and kept bringing up statistics to support his case. "Don't forget, it's not only the threat of a physical attack, what about the drugs that are now creeping into Oceania?"

"Serve them right for allowing trade with the Capitalists . . ." Nathan interjected, chuckling. "And if you ask me, you're better off stopping that damned drunkard Brady. I'm told he's planning to open a third island bar soon."

"It's a question of where to apply our limited funding, Burgess," Kamala said. "To protect against nature or our fellow humans."

Burgess replied. "Nature has been docile these many years, but humans do not forget their bad habits when the danger is past. It's the humans we have to guard against now."

"Mr. Chairman," Nathan waded in once more. "This issue is probably related to my issue of 'incentive funding.' I was waiting my turn, but let me table that issue now. If we constantly pour money into areas that show no improvement, it amounts to welfare. And welfare impaired the former Canada from reaching her true greatness."

"You are not advocating free market forces are you, Nat?" Samson was showing his impatience.

Up in the gallery, Leo whispered to David, "The Committee is all over the place."

"I warned you!" David replied, biting his lip.

Nathan had collected himself again. "No, I'm not advocating unbridled capitalism. Lord knows what that's done to those guys across the water. But I think that that there should be concrete deliverables attached to all monies doled out, including welfare and defence payments. And if these are not met, then the funding should be withheld or diverted to more deserving causes. I have finally gotten down to writing my long-promised paper on incentive funding and welfare reform, coined WorkOUT—it's a take on an Old World term from the former Canada, called Workfare. And I'd like your permission to table it at an upcoming meeting."

"We'll look forward to your paper, Nat, when it's ready. You've promised it every time but we always end up in these fruitless debates. Until your paper is ready for review, Nat, I suggest you keep further discussion on this subject out of this forum," Samson said.

"I will, Mr. Chairman, trust me, I will." Nathan grinned.

"That's dumb," Leo said. "Nathan shouldn't have tabled a half-baked topic like that yet."

"Not so dumb," David murmured. "He has been talking about WorkOUT for years. This is his way of keeping it top of mind for the Committee."

The Executive returned to the defence issue and debated back and forth until Samson called a vote, which David later discovered happened very rarely: the Executive usually reached consensus on most issues. The voting ended in a tie, due to one member, Izzy Garcia, being absent. Samson, who had the tie-breaking vote, abstained, saying that he would like all funding matters of this nature—those that were not in the annual budget—to be studied against other priorities, before firm decisions were made.

"You are making a mistake, Sam," Burgess said, sitting down and dropping his papers on the table with a loud thud. "Defence is something that you can't quantify like that. An outside attack is a disaster waiting to happen. Often it does not happen. But you will kick yourself if it does and you were not prepared."

"You will have my vote the moment we have all funding re-evaluated. But not before."

Kamala volunteered to do a review of all ad-hoc funding requests and present it to the Committee within the next three months.

"Next, we have this issue of refugees," Samson announced.

"It's an old issue," Burgess replied.

"I thought we had minimized the problem after we gave the migrant workers citizenship?" It was Dr. Morden speaking up for the first time.

"It does not go away— they still trickle in," Samson said, shaking his head. "A sick man, his wife and son—the Stones—arrived by boat yesterday, smuggled in the hold. They have no proper immigration papers or money. We have housed them temporarily at the Waterfront Hotel."

"New Edeners?" Kamala asked.

"Yes. The man is sick. The same old story, condemned from work, to be banished to their 'colonies,' or whatever they call those wretched places."

"Well, we can't take them all in," Nathan said. "You want to know how the population in this place is growing—that's how! Perhaps, New Eden should pay for our shortfall to the Defence Fund!"

"Come now, Nat, you know that is not strictly true," Samson said. "Our people have crossed over to their side, too, especially, the younger ones."

"I will go and visit them this afternoon and do what I can to assist," Kamala said.

"Thank you, Kam. I have made arrangements for them to move into the vacant caretaker's cabin beside the church. The Waterfront Hotel can only put them up for so long."

"But what is the long-term solution?" Nathan said.

"Why don't we enter into a reciprocal agreement with the Capitalists?" Dr. Morden said. "Trade each other's refugees back to each other?"

"That's all right for our people," Samson said. "Ours are economic refugees anyway, spurred on by greed. It will serve them well to get back to reality in Tolemac. But we will be handing back their refugees to the colonies and a premature death. Besides, I don't trust the New Edeners. Their interest lasts only as long as self-gain is plainly in sight."

Kamala said, "Maybe the answer is to do everything we can to keep our citizens inside our respective borders."

"I agree," Samson said.

"But how do you keep the barbarians from entering the gate?" Nathan said.

"Help New Eden and the other Capitalists introduce humanitarian programs to catch their fallen. They could use our welfare model," Kamala replied.

"Try talking to them!" Samson said. "All they are interested in is profits. Social welfare is too mushy."

"Maybe my WorkOUT plan will interest them this time," Nathan said. "Samson, are you willing to open discussions with New Eden again?"

"There hasn't been a lack of trying. We just can't agree on anything."

"Maybe you need to have insiders on the other side who share your views to give you some help. You've always gone at this alone."

"I haven't gone at it alone. I've involved successive presidents of Oceania and Saska-Manitoba, I've appealed to successive presidents of the Capitalist realm . . ."

"But it's always been from the outside in; you've got to enlist some of their own people. We need a few Capitalists in our court."

"Come gentlemen," Kamala interrupted. "I'm sure this issue needs a lot more reflection and discussion. We will not solve it today."

Pausing and clearing his throat, Samson said, "I am going to talk to this family and others like them who have arrived recently and come up with a better proposal for the New Edeners. In the meantime, I need an agreement in principle from this committee, that the Stone family and other refugees can remain in Tolemac until we have found a safe alternative. Our track record to date has been spotty—sometimes we've turned them away, sometimes we've taken them in—we need to be consistent."

With Kamala's strong seconding of the motion, Samson got his wish and the entire Committee voted in favour, with Burgess abstaining. Nathan shook his head, despite supporting the decision. "I hope this doesn't signal to the Capitalist states that Tolemac is open to their rejects."

When the meeting adjourned, David glanced over at his young companion. Leo was lost in thought as he shut down his Communicator.

"Pity they didn't cover the trade issue, Leo."

"They have a lot of problems to deal with, Mr. Arthurs. I thought Tolemac was a utopian society, but it doesn't appear to be when you sit inside here."

"The Committee is a focal point, remember that. It looks a lot worse sitting in here."

"Are you gonna run, Mr. Arthurs?"

"I'm still considering my options."

"We need people like you, Mr. Arthurs. I think the older Committee members have been around too long. They are getting irritated with one another."

Chapter 9

Later that afternoon, David accompanied Samson down to the Waterfront Hotel.

"Did the meeting benefit you?" Samson asked.

"Burgess is getting crankier these days."

"We all are. He's been going sour since Cynthia died. Hope Ethan's return in the summer will turn him around."

"Ethan's returning?" David felt his hands get clammy at the news.

"Yes, Burgess mentioned it just before the meeting. He needs help in running the port. Besides John is no company for him; more of a burden. You worried?"

"No." David's answer was too quick. Yet, to be faced again with his childhood nemesis wasn't something to look forward to.

"I am worried," said Samson. "Burgess wants Ethan to run for election, too. He'll be competing with you."

"I haven't said I was running yet."

"Well, don't let Ethan's return put you off."

"If I decide not to run, it won't be because of Ethan." But by the look on his father's face, David knew that Samson wasn't convinced.

The Waterfront Hotel was built adjacent to the port, to house sailors ferrying Tolemac's exports and imports between neighbouring Oceania and other Humanitarian states. It was a sprawling red brick building, three floors tall, running east and west along the waterfront from a central reception block. Its windows dripped precipitation from a combination of the building's ventilation and the sea spray. The port was a busy place with boats arriving and departing frequently. The few land vehicles in Tolemac all converged here. The noise irritated David.

It was impressive, however, to turn around and see the ski-lift-turned-produce-conveyor straddling Sunset Hill and ferrying grain, fruit and vegetables from the farms of Tolemac located on the other side of the island to the port. Today, the conveyor was active, for it was the first of Tolemac's two harvests of the year. Bags, evenly placed along its belt, moved swiftly downhill to be deposited into larger containers that were being manoeuvred into position by forklifts. This produce conveyor was recently voted the most energy efficient, low-tech system in the entire Humanitarian realm.

The smell of salt was strong. It had steadily increased every year. When the land between the ocean and Lake Ontario had collapsed in the Flood, salt began seeping inland. Now the waves were like the ones that had crashed in oceans from pre-Flood days. Seagulls, calm and serene, circled for scraps of food that Tolemacians generously fed them. On weekends, David spent hours with Sonya, Joey and Hannah, feeding these creatures that linked his new world with the one swallowed up thirty-three years ago.

As they neared the hotel, a car started up and took off with a high revving of its engine. This was one of the few sports cars in Tolemac and David instantly recognized Joe Sabbattini at the wheel. Joe was the only child of the hotel's proprietor, Rocky Sabbattini, the ex-pizza parlour owner from the Bronx. Joe was a handsome young man, given all the good things in life by his indulgent father. Joe was also very popular with the girls at school.

"Quite the showman, isn't he?" Samson said, waving after the speeding youth, who looked surprised at this tall, bearded civic leader curtsying in the middle of the street.

"Afternoon, Sam, David!" Rocky Sabbattini greeted them from the hotel's roof. He was always fixing his roof from the ravages of salt and water.

"That patch we put in didn't help, eh?" Samson enquired.

"It lasted okay. But now the other side is giving trouble."

"I'll see if I can come down this evening and give you a hand. Got some visiting to do right now."

"Sure could do with the help. Thanks! Your visitors are in room two-thirteen," Rocky waved them on.

They walked down the damp, silent passageway of the second floor. The walls looked like they would melt anytime. The transient guests—the sailors and dockworkers—would be at work at the port right now. Rocky was putting on a gallant show to keep the place afloat, David surmised. But the property was too near the water. At the same time, Tolemacians didn't want sailor types getting close to the established residential areas of the city. Sailors were loud and they picked up unsavoury habits from other ports. Older Tolemacians were wary of them, just like they had been of the migrant workers a generation ago.

"Thanks for coming along with me today—civic duties are part of the job," Samson said. "The better part, especially when the politics wear you down."

As they neared room 213, David felt his energy vibrations go off kilter like they did at the sounds in the port. There were raised, angry voices behind the door.

Something banged, and a man raised his voice. The sound of a Communicator increased suddenly, drowning out the man's voice. Samson knocked on the door. He heard a woman's voice. It joined the man's voice, and both seemed to compete with the noise of the Communicator. After about a minute the door opened and a boy, about ten years old, stood there—the noise behind him amplifying tenfold. He had freckles, rumpled red hair and watery blue eyes that looked old and knowing. He was dressed in a pair of faded jeans and a crumpled shirt with a Capitalist zipper on it. Humanitarians wore buttons. He fixed the visitors with an enquiring gaze, then looked over his shoulder and stepped slowly away from the door.

David noticed the woman first. She was in her early forties. Red, tousled hair hung down over her shoulders. She had a strong curvaceous body, and an upright posture that made her medium height look taller than it was. She was wearing a sleeveless undershirt that pressed hard against her full breasts, and as she gesticulated agitatedly at the man, there were traces of hair under her arms. On her, the hair did not seem unattractive—in fact, it heightened her sexuality. Samson sucked in his breath behind David. Tolemacian women are well groomed, almost sterile in their looks, a throwback to their North American heritage before the Flood. This woman's earthiness was a new experience for both of them. David glanced over at the man on the bed. He was thin, blond and emaciated, with a coverlet thrown half over him, half on the floor. He was shouting at the woman and waving a bottle in his hand. They were oblivious of the visitors.

"This dammed stuff—doesn't work! Don't you get it? I can't put up with the pain!" Then the man screamed—a hoarse, strangled scream that drowned everything out. His straggly blond hair was damp with sweat and a droopy moustache heightened the intensity of his misery.

"That's all we have. Maybe we need to change your prescription," the woman countered, shrugging helplessly, her large brown eyes full of repressed anger. Although her features were contorted, her face must have once been beautiful. Then the woman saw the newcomers and froze. The man caught on, too.

Samson cleared his throat politely. "Good afternoon! Mr. and Mrs. Stone? I am Samson Arthurs, from the City. This is my son David. Sorry for interrupting. Your boy let us in."

The woman quickly grabbed a jacket from a nearby chair. "Oh, hi! Sorry we are a bit disorganized here," she apologized, straightening her hair and slipping into the jacket, zipping it quickly. Then she went over and started to tidy the bed around the man, who, spent from his last outburst, had slumped into a stupor, mumbling under his breath. "Doug, lie back now. You must rest. Give the medication time to take effect," she said.

She spoke over her shoulder as she tended the man. "I'm Delia Stone. You must have met our Joshua at the door. This is my husband Doug. He has to get some rest. I will be with you shortly." She eased the man onto his pillow. He was suddenly compliant. The boy returned to his Communicator viewing, and turned down the volume, which allowed everyone to speak without having to raise their voices anymore.

"This may be a bit late on our part, but we wanted to welcome you to Tolemac," Samson said. "And that includes all of you," he said, sweeping the newcomers in with a gesture of his hands. The man and boy were self-absorbed in their respective pursuits and did not acknowledge Samson's words.

"Thank you. Please sit down here," Delia pointed towards the pokey kitchenette that led off the main bedroom. Rocky Sabbattini had generously given them a mini-suite, normally reserved for long-stay guests. "The manager has left us some tea, can I get you some?"

"No thanks, we were passing by. We wanted to make sure that you were all right."

"I can't thank your people enough, Mr. Arthurs—"

"Oh, no bother at all! Kamala Sunderam, our local judge and—", seeing the look of concern cross her face, Samson quickly added, "Oh, don't worry, she's only on a humanitarian mission this time. Kamala will drop by this afternoon to check on anything else you may need. In the meantime, please feel at home here."

"Mr. Arthurs, the people of Tolemac have been more than generous so far. We have little or no money—"

"That is not important. In Tolemac we look after each other. As our Lord said, 'To each according to his needs, from each according to his ability.' "

"Watch out for the catch." The man stirred from the bed in the other room. The Communicator volume increased simultaneously. "Joshua, turn that bloody thing down!" Doug Stone yelled.

The woman blushed and looked into Samson's eyes, defenceless.

"It's all right," Samson winked. "Your husband is ill and under stress. We understand."

"Thank you!" She threw a grateful look at her visitors.

The woman certainly redeemed all the bad things David had heard about New Edeners. Despite her sexuality radiating strongly across the table, she bore an authentic vulnerability.

"I have made arrangements for your family to move into a cottage beside our church," Samson said.

"But we can't afford it."

"There's the catch!" Doug was almost singing in the bedroom. "I told you. They get you by the rent!"

Samson cut in, "You don't have to pay anything. You can't stay at this hotel. It's not a place for a family in the long term."

"But I don't understand?" Delia said. There was a hint of suspicion in her eyes.

"You came here to seek refuge. Yes?"

"Yes. I thought this was our only chance. We had heard of others—"

"I told you it was a bad idea," Doug continued. The Communicator volume rose again and stayed up despite his loud curses aimed at the boy.

Samson walked over to Delia and laid his hand on her shoulder. "You must trust us, Mrs. Stone. You have been led to a place of refuge. We will look after you." Then he went into the bedroom and towered over Doug, who shrank instinctively in the bed. "Doug, you are free to leave if you don't like our offer. And end up in the colonies for all I care. But if you choose to stay, then you play by our rules. And the first rule is do not bite the hand that feeds you. Got it?"

They stared each other down for a long time. Doug finally cast his head down and stared out of the window.

"Good. We should be going now," Samson said, returning to the kitchenette. "That's a mighty fine boy you have there, Delia. Make sure he comes to Sunday school. And I hope you can all make it to service this Sunday."

The woman let out a sigh. "Thank you! It's a relief to be able to trust someone."

David suppressed a smile as they made their way to the door again. Joshua followed them outside. "I heard you guys teach meditation in your Sunday school?"

"Yes we do, Joshua," David said. "In fact, I teach the meditation class—would you like to join?"

"Great!" he whispered before tiptoeing inside again and reluctantly closing the door behind him.

*   *   *

The following Sunday, Delia and Joshua Stone attended service at the Church of the New Covenant. Delia was dressed in jeans and a white zippered shirt, which was open to where her cleavage swelled out. A black headband swept her red hair back and accentuated her high cheekbones. She wore makeup, and the tired lines around her eyes were now gone. She and Joshua walked confidently up to the front row and sat across the aisle from the Arthurs family. Agnes wanted to know who they were, and whispered to David across from Hannah and Joey. As David explained, the kids rolled their eyes. Sonya peeped over at the new arrivals, an inquiring frown on her face.

The church congregation was a microcosm of Tolemacian society. Although many churches dotted the island—not all of them Christian—the Church of the

New Covenant was the oldest and largest, standing downtown, on the corner of Main and Ontario streets. The faces of the fifty-plus group were devout, even stern; religion had sustained them during the Flood and they could never forget that. The younger adults like David, born post-Flood, were more open and distracted; the teens talkative and questioning and the preteens serious, almost like their grandparents. The congregation was a fusion of complexions and colours. David recalled Samson's pictures of pre-Flood church congregations; they were either white or black or of some ethnic majority. Civil wars were fought over colour in the Old World. Today, many in the church were between those extreme racial categories. Hannah and Joey exemplified that fusion, with a Caucasian father and an East Indian mother.

Everyone came to attention the moment Samson opened the service. He was dressed in a dark jacket and cape; steel-grey hair was slicked over his shoulders, and his beard was neatly combed. It was his beard that was most prominent, for when he got animated during his sermon it came free and waved about at the audience before slumping back into shape when the service ended. Today's reading was from I Corinthians, verses 10-13, and Samson's sermon was based on it.

"Temptation is not new," he said. "It is a part of the fabric of our lives, what we define as human. So don't fear it—recognize it. But the Book also says that God is faithful and will not tempt us beyond what we can bear. So do not fear the problem of drugs in Oceania, we can battle it. Do not fear the threat of commercialism—we can sidestep it. God will provide the way. He did provide the way to us thirty-three years ago, when the world, as we then knew it, was ending. It didn't end for us who had faith. Today we have a new world—one full of promise. But one in which we must be forever on guard, for temptation oozes out from those dim recesses within us and overtakes us before we know it."

Samson's beard was loose now and the passion in his voice was greater than usual. David glanced across at Delia. She appeared transfixed, as if she were drinking in all of Samson's words. There was a look of serenity about her—maybe it was because the fragrance of the Josticks was particularly strong today. Occasionally, she would close her eyes and open them again, all the while looking at the animated figure in the pulpit. Samson avoided her gaze, never once looking in her direction, keeping his eyes and words centred towards the middle of the hall.

After the service, Joshua came to the meditation class. He hung about the door at the beginning, uncertain. David went over and escorted him in, introducing him to Joey and Hannah. Within no time, Hannah was taking Joshua around to see the other kids and literally thrusting him into their midst. Joshua would be her new trophy friend for the next little while. When all the students were gathered and the socializing was over, they covered the reading lesson on classroom Communicators. Joshua kept nervously looking up from his screen and Hannah would wink at him each time. After the reading, the children took up their yoga postures in a circle on the floor and counted down into the meditative state. The regulars relaxed easily and their breathing synchronized. Joshua's breathing was laboured—he was very nervous. He kept fidgeting and David was certain the lad never really got to the meditative level of relaxation. After the class, David took him aside, reassured him that it would take awhile before he mastered the technique, and offered to spend one-on-one time with him the following Sunday. Joshua nodded and was quiet.

But he never returned to the class, although he did attend Sunday services with his mother on a few more occasions after that.

The Stones didn't stay long after the classes ended on that first Sunday. By the time the picnic tables were set up for the traditional Sunday lunch—a joyous affair that usually led to the sharing of stories from the week before—the Stones had long departed for home.

"Delia had to attend to Doug's needs," Samson informed David, in between mouthfuls of chicken from the barbecue stand that was the Sabbattini family's contribution to the weekly community event. The younger children were running in between the tables playing "island hopper," an imaginary game of travelling between the islands of the New World. The older kids were helping their parents serve—a job every child had to do after the age of ten. Hannah, at seven, was still revelling in her freedom, while Joey who had just crossed ten, served. The older, teen Bible study club had spilled out on to the lawn and an animated discussion was taking place. David was soon dragged into answering a question about whether Jesus had indeed travelled to the Americas between his twelfth and thirtieth years, when the Gospels had no record of him. Before he got sucked in to giving his opinion, David looked around for the rest of his family. Agnes was over by the salad bar that she normally supervised. Sonya was over by the toddler's area, helping the children in the wading pool and Kamala was with the older ladies, probably planning the next picnic or the annual "March of the Lamps." It felt great to be part of a community, one that was engaged and happy. Everyone was pulled into serving, in some way or another, as part of keeping this city state alive and together. David wondered if the Stones had ever had a sense of community back in New Eden. Maybe not—maybe that was why it was easy for them to pick up and leave.

*　　*　　*

The Stones eventually moved into the vacant caretaker's cottage next door to the church. It was a wooden structure on stilts with a combined living-dining room, single bedroom, kitchen and shower. The outhouse was located at the other end of the church compound by the city sewer. Due to its raised foundation, this type of cottage did not have an indoor toilet. Still, it was a comfortable home if one were prepared to make it so. Since their approval as refugees by the Executive Committee, Samson had enrolled the Stones in the "Dependents Program," which was reserved for residents of Tolemac and other Humanitarian states who had lost the ability to earn a livelihood, through a personal or family catastrophe.

Whenever he visited the church, David often saw Doug sitting on the porch, covered in blankets, dozing or reading a book, sometimes staring into space, a bedpan and pitcher of water by his side. Delia was usually in the vicinity, tending the flowers that ran around the cottage, or reading to her husband. It soon became known that Doug suffered from a rare blood disease that kept him anaemic, and gave him bouts of excruciating pain. Dr. Morden had visited and ordered medication from Tolemac General.

May gave way to June and the summer heat started to make its presence felt. In Tolemac, the summers came early and lasted well into late November. David hoped to see the snow Samson had often talked about, especially around Christmastime, but Tolemac got mostly rain and grey skies in December. The temperature would dip to about ten degrees Celsius in February, when the storms came, and then start to get warmer again. It snowed only in the Arctic regions, but David hadn't been up north in his entire life. Large tracts of water separated what had once been the great land mass of North America, making travel difficult. In fact, there were days when he felt too insulated in Tolemac, despite the electronic Infoway connecting them to the outside world.

One Saturday evening in June, while the rest of his family was flying kites down at the Waterside Park, David went to the church to prepare for the following day's Sunday school class. He looked in on the Stone's cottage. Doug was asleep in his chair; a book had fallen from his hand and struck the pitcher of water, wetting the ground at his side. Delia was nowhere to be seen. David tiptoed over to Doug, picked up the book and placed it on the doorstep to dry in the dying rays of the sun. That's when he heard the gasping coming through the open window directly over his head.

It was a woman's sound and it drew him towards the window—it sounded like a mixture of pleasure and pain. He paused, not wanting to wake the sleeping man, yet compulsion propelled him forward. He reached for the windowsill and pulled himself up to eye level. What he saw nearly made him let go of his grasp.

Delia was rolling around in bed, her nightdress over her waist, one hand between her legs, the other squeezing the nipple of her right breast. Her face was flushed, and she was biting into the pillows as if trying to quell her deep gasping. Then with a thrust of her hand deep between her thighs, she let out a stifled scream.

The last image froze in his mind as David slid off the window to the ground. Glancing nervously at Doug, who was still fast asleep, David slunk off back to the main road with pounding chest, fearing discovery at any time.

He hurried down Dundas Street, onto Kennedy Road and sat down on a street bench. He needed to collect his thoughts and make sense of what he had witnessed. The familiar street scenes of Tolemac faded into the background, yet he tried to grab onto them just to keep himself grounded. Frida Parks passed by and waved. David waved back at her mechanically, and hoped that she would not stop to make conversation. She kept walking, but looked back at him with a puzzled frown. He heard the sound of music. Without even looking up, he knew it was Mrs. Wang, setting up for her weekend open-air ballroom dancing class in Martyrs Square at the corner of Kennedy and Dundas. Ballroom dancing was an

Old World practice the Wang family had followed for ages in Shanghai, before immigrating to the former Canada. Mrs. Wang held her morning dance classes, and couples from all parts of the city joined in—the classes were her free contribution to the community. David also spotted Nathan, mat in hand, heading for his Tai Chi lesson down at the Waterfront Park, which in the septuagenarian's own words, "Keeps the arthritis at bay." But none of this comforting predictability helped to distract David, whose mind raced with thoughts of Doug and Delia Stone.

He had read about the carnal acts that men and women had committed in the Old World and masturbation had been one of them. It was a part of the old order that was eventually destroyed. Self pleasure. Me first! The Old Testament in the Bible had been full of it; the Old World up until the Flood had been full of it. But the Flood was supposed to have cleansed them all. That's what Samson had taught him. That's what the education system and the moral code of Tolemac had taught him. That's what he and Sonya had discovered as a married couple, hard though it was at first; it had left them with so many unanswered questions. But following the law gave them guideposts and shut out questions. He knew of no other way. He couldn't understand the new phenomenon he had just witnessed. Who were these people? Was Tolemac inviting unknown forces and desires into its midst? He knew he had to talk to Samson or to someone— get it off his chest, resolve it. The image, even though it had been short, was too vivid—and disturbing. She had seemed to enjoy the act, too. It also gave him a strange tingling and he grudgingly acknowledged that he had been terribly aroused. Was there a secret longing for carnality still lingering in the human genetic code? He decided that he could not discuss this with Samson; it was too personal and embarrassing.

He must have been sitting there for a long time. The music from Mrs. Wang's class had stopped. He realized that he had to get back to the church and attend to his chores.

He dragged his feet back to the church and let himself in through the side door on the other side of the Stone house. He went into the children's classroom and checked his notes for the next day's service; he fed questions for his students into the server. The work cleared his head. He reminded himself to ask Vladimir about finding a way of getting this server hooked up to take a remote download from his home. So far, Vladimir was reluctant to hook up the church server to Tolemac's communications network. The communications chief's reluctance was fuelled by Samson's fear of information pollution. "You don't want to corrupt the minds of the children," Samson had said when the subject was first raised. Tolemac's information network had been compromised a few times already, despite Vladimir's valiant efforts to beef up the firewall.

David spent about half an hour setting things up for the next day's class. When he was done, he shut everything off and made his way out the side door again. About to exit, he heard the front door of the church close (that door was left unlocked for any soul in need of quiet time) and footsteps pattered up the central aisle. Normally, he would not have paid attention, for there were people coming and going all the time. In fact, Samson encouraged solitary moments as a good exercise for the soul. But something made him turn and look.

Delia was kneeling down in the front pew, her face silhouetted in the candlelight surrounding the main altar. She did not see him and David hung back in the shadows. She began praying and her features were locked in pain and uncertainty. He couldn't hear her prayers and didn't want to get any closer; he had snooped enough already. All he could see were tears pouring down her cheeks as she prayed with an earnestness that shook him and made him forgive her earlier actions.

Chapter 10

June 15th 2045

DELIA STONE *INTERESTS AND DISTURBS ME. A red haired angel, or a maven of men, come to disrupt the comfortable role I have accepted and settled for here in Tolemac? Her luxurious hair glows and pulses with life, her poise is confident in the face of adversity, her sexuality is in my face whenever I visit. And I have visited her many times in this past month, sometimes on false pretexts, just to see her.*

I imagine her next to me in the early hours of the morning, when I turn over in an empty bed and hear a tired Agnes snoring quietly in the next room, desiring Delia's flesh against mine. What am I saying? Lust – am I caving into it? After years of denial, I feel drawn to its suction.

The day I visited her at the Waterfront Hotel to finalize their moving arrangements, she showed me the welts on her body where Doug had squeezed her. Quite naturally she hoisted her skirt to just under her panty line and showed me the red hand prints, turning purple, on her firm thighs. I wanted to reach out and stroke her bruised flesh, comfort her, go even higher up her leg. I restrained myself and averted my eyes.

"Why do you put up with him?" I asked. I kept my voice lowered for Doug was in the other room, sleeping no doubt, but still present.

"He has lost something. The ability to have sex like a normal man. Those medications. I have lost something too."

"We have all lost something. We lost something in order to survive," I replied, grabbing for the safe alternative.

She looked at me, her brown eyes piercing, inviting. "I was born after the Flood. All I know is that we have to grab at anything, or else we are left behind."

From a chair, she lifted a holster belt with a cylinder attached to it. It jogged a faded memory. A dildo, was it, or a vibrator – an old world device. I gulped, not knowing what to say.

"I hope I am not embarrassing you," she said flatly, tossing the sinful object into a corner. "He has to use that now. There were other things too but we had to leave them behind in New Eden."

"Why are you showing me this?"

She looked at me with tears in her eyes. I so wanted to reach out and cradle her in my arms, instead I paced her living room, grateful that the door to the bedroom was shut and that her son was at school.

"Because I am trapped. He is my husband and I cannot abandon him. I am grateful for your help. If there is any way I can repay you – let me know. That's how we settle debts where I come from – in any way we can."

I shivered and opened the file folder. For the next twenty minutes I kept my concentration on their moving arrangements and made a quick exit without broaching the subject of repayment. My heart was heavy and my appetite raw. After many months, I felt the stirrings in my loins and did not care about feeling guilty. I had once refused the unspoken tug from Kamala, how long could I go on denying nature?

During my visits since that day I have become her father confessor. She says she got used to unburdening to her priest as a Catholic girl, when her stepfather abused her. Doug gets her to perform unnatural acts of sexual gratification, sometimes while their son is in the other room – no wonder the poor lad has the volume of the Communicator up so loud. That's all Doug can do now—his mind is sexually starved. It's an artificial way to find relief. But they both find relief, and she is bonded to him in her Catholic sort of way "'til death us do part." I also suspect she enjoys her body and misses the more natural ways of sexual intercourse. But why am I talking this way?

How long has it been since Agnes and I . . . too long! Better not talk about it. It only highlights the emptiness between us. We decided to live our separate lives a long time ago—it was easier that way. So Agnes took the evening shift at the hospital and I got immersed in my civic duties. Helping others—that's how monks and celibate priests of pre-Flood times kept the cravings of their bodies at bay. Not all of them were successful; some ended up performing heinous crimes against children and young girls, which led to the bankrupting of organized religion in the Old World. Were we wrong in outlawing self-gratification this time around? Didn't it ruin an entire civilization? But now Delia makes me want to look inward again, look at all these sexually unfulfilled years . . . Is self-gratification wrong? Why did we label it a sin?

*　　*　　*

Agnes cut the roses neatly and placed them in plastic wrappers. It was the third week of June and the heat was beginning to tell. She was having difficulty breathing of late and reminded herself that she had to take it slow. Still, the flowers were her contribution to the hospital's prayer room and this was the right time to pick them, just before full bloom. She also had to remind herself to keep a few aside for Frida Parks, who'd be relieving her shift at the hospital tonight. She wiped a stray wisp of hair from her sweaty forehead and looked about the garden. Gone were the wooden timbers, wiring, construction glue and other reminders of what it had taken to rebuild this place. Instead, flowerbeds lined the rectangle that was the Arthurs's family backyard, before it fell down the cliff to the Williams's house. Begonias, violets and hydrangea—tropical flowers she had only seen in her native Queensland so long ago—could grow in the warmer climate of this region now. Roses were still her favourite. She'd had roses at her wedding—the paper variety—because flowers could not grow so soon after the Flood. She'd insisted on real roses from her garden for David and Sonya's wedding, and Samson could not understand why she beamed so much during the ceremony. She uncorked the little bottle in the tea cozy and took a quick sip. Brandy increasingly made her feel better and more lightheaded. What did Samson know!

She heard a sound behind her and was thrilled to see David parking his bicycle under the overhang. Oh, it was nice to see her David, tall like his father, but more sensitive and caring. He was her one consolation in a marriage that was slipping away from her. Maybe David could take her mind away from things at the moment. She quickly tucked the bottle under the cozy again.

"Hi Mum! How are the roses?"

"Hello, darling! It's a great day isn't it?" She looked around her. From the summit of Sunset Hill, the lake-ocean gleamed back. It was flat in the summer heat.

"Stopped by to see how you were doing. The students opted for a research hour and did not need me."

"And he comes to see his dear mother, that's sweet. I wish your father would do that. He usually finds something else to do with the unforgiving minute."

"Dad gives of himself a lot. So do you. Have you booked that vacation yet?"

"Your father and I wouldn't know what to do with so much time alone together."

"Oh, come on—there will be a lot of catching up to do."

"He spends more time over at that Stone woman's place now."

"What do you mean?" David asked.

David looked alarmed and she wished she had kept her mouth shut. But who else could she talk to? "Haven't you seen what he's been doing lately? Buying them groceries and medications. He's always 'checking in' on them."

"Dad's doing the decent thing. He's their sponsor from the Executive Committee."

"There's something weird about that family." She saw David blanch even more at that statement.

"Let's go inside." David started to pick up the plastic wrappers with the roses.   Agnes quickly grabbed the tea cozy and let him lead her indoors. Inside the kitchen, she felt hemmed in. She had spent so many years in this kitchen and now it was confining. Her breathing became more laboured. She wished she could have another drink but didn't want to upset David.

Instead, she blurted out: "For all the progress since the Flood, I don't think we've advanced at all."

"Come now, mother—what did you expect? We were coming back from ground zero." David put the kettle on. "Cup of tea?"

"Love one!" She sat down at the table. "It was a heavy price to pay. We women went back to the nineteenth century, chained to things like that old stove at the back, while our men were stolen away from us to rebuild everything we had taken for granted and lost."

"It keeps Samson alive, he says. Gives him a purpose and mission."

"Maybe, maybe. But we don't all have his zeal for rebuilding."

They drank their tea in silence.

"Ethan's coming back next week," David said after awhile. Now she knew why he had come to see her.

"It would be nice if you and your father cried once in a while."

"What—?"

"Never mind—because I cry all the time. You are worried about Ethan?"

"Dad says Ethan is going to run for election."

"And you are worried?"

"It's not 'worried.' You know what a bully he was growing up. He just doesn't play by the rules."

"You've got to stand up to him, David. Bullies get their due, eventually."

"But not until they do a lot of damage."

"I wish I were young and strong enough to yell at him like I used to when he would shoot at your birdcage in the back yard with his catapult—remember?"

They laughed at the memory. She enjoyed sitting with him and talking about those times, hard though they were.

"I am more worried about the days ahead than I was ever worried during the Flood," she said.

"Why?"

"We haven't built our New World yet, David. I wonder whether I will even see it in my life."

"The Bible promised us a thousand years of peace."

"But not until we weed out the evil that lies within us. The Flood only gave us a respite. There are still a lot of restless emotions running around in this place. I can feel it."

"Next thing, we will be crying over all this and spoiling a perfect day."

She drained her cup. "You're right. We have to put on a bold face. That's what your father said. And that's what has gotten us this far."

When David left, she returned to the tea cozy and drained the bottle. She would get another one on tonight's late shift at the hospital. Soon she felt the knots in her stomach loosening. She began to sing; she always sang when she was drunk; it was a great release. She staggered slowly into the bedroom and set her alarm for 6 p.m.—that would give her a good, two and a half hours to bask in this euphoria. It was better than having an orgasm, but then she had never had a real one or maybe she couldn't tell the difference. She had tried and at times had been close, just like the many times she had been so close to having a second child. In the end, she had lain back and "serviced her mate" as all good Tolemacian women did. It was the topic of many subdued discussions among the church ladies; they found solace in sharing. Perhaps the post-Flood lifestyle had destroyed women's ability to find pleasure. With long hours of back-breaking work in sooty kitchens, child-bearing, child-rearing, building houses for oneself and for others who were unable to do so, setting up hospitals and caring for the sick, creating schools and the services that were once provided by governments, where was the time to think of oneself? And yet, it was so . . . so unfair. But this euphoria got rid of all that. She knew she wouldn't be disturbed because Samson would not be home till well past eight o'clock. Within minutes she was snoring.

*   *   *

June 30, 2045—Ethan Williams returned to Tolemac

The who's who of Tolemac society were invited to the big party Burgess threw to honour the return of his older son. There were the Arthurs, the rest of the Executive Committee and their families and numerous visiting dignitaries from the NADF and the FHS among the two hundred and fifty guests in attendance. David went, not because he was anxious to meet his old nemesis, but out of curiosity to see how Ethan had evolved with exposure to the Capitalist world.

Burgess's house stood near the summit of Sunset Hill, a few steps below Samson's, and faced the southern end of the island. It was blazing with light as guests crested the hill. The temperature was 42 degrees Celsius and everyone was damp with perspiration after the walk. Copious quantities of grape juice cocktail were made available. Burgess made it with a slight twist; he always added a small amount of alcohol to get in under Tolemac's dry laws: "1 percent alcohol" was the tolerable limit. Everyone liked Burgess's grape-juice cocktails. Barbecue stands lined his vast garden that sprawled downhill—one could pick from the pork, chicken or beef stands or the plain vegetarian one. The barbecue was a Tolemac tradition; it was spawned when early post-Flood Tolemacians cooked out in the open before their houses were properly equipped with kitchens and plumbing. At this barbecue, the kids were running around helping themselves to morsels of food while the adults chattered in little groups on the lawn and on the patio of the Williams's two-story marble and brick home. A string quartet played under the shade of a maple tree, but no one paid much attention to the music.

David was surprised to see Ethan's slimmed down and tanned appearance. His six-foot-four-inch frame looked taller for losing its puppy fat. A pencil-thin moustache gave him a rakish appearance and his dark inscrutable eyes were even deeper set now. Gone were the pimples, replaced by sallow skin. His clothes were impeccable despite the heat—a dark suit and lightweight cape that came down to his ankles. Ethan had learned poise in his sojourn abroad, for he no longer butted in with an opinion, but leaned into a conversation casually and made his point with quiet emphasis. He also mingled with everyone in the crowd.

David was equally caught off guard to see Delia among the guests and wondered who had invited her. When Agnes saw the younger woman, she grimaced and said, "How did she get here? Must be the influence of her executive sponsor!" David resolved to have a word with Samson about Delia and her effect on his mother. He'd just have to find the right moment and make sure he was up to a face-off on that delicate subject.

Delia looked radiant in a one-piece, red, ankle-length dress. Her red, blow-dried hair matched the dress, which was low-cut with Tolemacian-style buttons in front, revealing ample cleavage. Red sandals, slightly heeled, gave her generous hips a sensuous lift. She'd been out shopping or, as Agnes said, must have a benefactor. The allowance she now received from Tolemac was serving her well. She caught sight of David and walked over. "Hello, David!"

"Hi, Delia! Nice to see you here today." His pulse began to quicken in her presence. He realized that he felt this way every time he met her.

She flicked her head back and laughed. "It was generous of your father to get Burgess to invite me. Samson says that the faster I fit into Tolemacian society the better."

"Is Doug here?" David enquired.

"No, Joshua is minding him tonight. I thought Doug was not going to let me come at first, but I convinced him it was for our benefit—we need to meet people. Besides, he'd fallen asleep before I left."

"It must be a full-time job—minding him."

"It is. I'm glad for the break today. Joshua is very understanding."

"Well, hello my dear!" Samson had sidled over. "You look more beautiful than ever tonight! David, do you mind if I kidnap your charming companion? Delia, there are some people I need to introduce you to," and with that he whisked her off into a throng of ladies from the Women's Association.

"David Arthurs! It's been a long time!" Turning around, David was face-to-face with Ethan.

"Yes, it has."

"How's everything—the family? Heard about your growing family—two kids already? How's Sonya?"

"She's well. Actually, if you check out the vegetarian grill—I see her over there right now."

"I intend to get around to everyone before the end of the evening." It was no secret that Ethan had tried to impress Sonya during their high-school days (in fact, he had tried to impress all the girls), but she had given him no encouragement and had always considered him a crass bully. Marrying her had been one of David's milder victories over Ethan.

Ethan looked towards the vegetarian stand, but made no move to walk over. Instead, he said, "Heard you are considering running for office?"

"Is that why you came back?"

"That and other things. Dad wants me to help him with the port. It's kind of rundown."

"It looks in good shape to me. In fact our port's capacity is growing year over year."

"Oh, I know—that's the incremental stuff, right? But we've got to grow exponentially, if we are to keep up with the rest of the world."

"That's the New Edener in you. Tolemacians do not want to grow exponentially, remember that?"

"I remember that. But they won't know the benefits until they taste what growth can do for them. I intend to remind them—show them what they can achieve. It's like that old "Trading Game" we used to play—the Humanitarians just muddle along while the Capitalists grow and extend the cycle of human evolution."

"Then we will be on opposite sides in this election, as usual."

Ethan laughed and his tone was taunting. "I've always enjoyed going up against you. You'll try hard, but you'll lose this one, inevitably."

"Well, let's call it then and cut out this small talk."

"Now, now—this is my dad's big party, no need to be hostile." Then he changed his tack and became more conciliatory, "Why don't you come and see me sometime after I've settled down? I can show you some of the things I've got planned for Tolemac; they are not all bad, I assure you."

"Maybe—"

Just then, a man in a bomber jacket and military-style boots, looking somewhat out of place at the gathering, tapped Ethan on the shoulder, "Hey, Ethan—excuse me—thanks for tonight. I have to go. I'll be in touch with you tomorrow."

"Why, Sean—leaving so early?" Ethan grabbed the man's hand and turned around to David. "Here, let me introduce you to an old friend of mine—David Arthurs—a true-blue Tolemacian."

David looked at the man as he shook his hand. He had long black hair almost to his shoulders and a swarthy complexion. His blue eyes were faded. Sean must have been in his mid-thirties, but looked older.

"Sean Galloway," the man said. "Nice to meet you." His smile was authentic and David felt a connection. Sean was smoking—a habit only the very old from pre-Flood days indulged in.

Ethan continued talking: "Sean and I had some business dealings back in New Eden. He is out here looking to partner with me on a new venture and settle in Tolemac."

"That might be a bit optimistic at this stage. I'm still looking," said Sean.

"Well, look no further, my friend," Ethan said spreading his arms. "Tolemac is the land of opportunity. That is why I returned."

David felt he had endured enough of Ethan and his expansionist plans for the moment, so making his excuses, he left the two men on the lawn and went indoors.

* * *

She watched him leave the party; his bomber jacket glistening under the lawn lights. He had brought novelty to the gathering, a new face among many familiar, bored ones; a voice different from the usual. She had seen his aura: troubled, lonely. She did not talk to her husband about auras anymore. David had been "sixth-sense challenged" from a very young age. In some ways it created a distance between them that made her uncomfortable.

But the stranger had looked at her when he had come over to sample the vegetarian delicacies.

"I've stopped eating meat," he had said, grabbing a plate and piling it up with food.

After he'd eaten a couple of pakoras and a vegetarian souvlaki, he slowed down and smiled at her; a disarmingly innocent smile: "Sorry, I've not eaten in almost a day; the journey over was exhausting."

"From Oceania?" she asked, curious.

"No, New Eden."

"Oh!" she gasped. One of Ethan's henchmen?

"My name is Sean." He wiped his soiled fingers furiously on a napkin and extended his hand. "Pleased to meet you."

She took it in hers; it was firm, anticipatory. "I'm Sonya. Welcome to Tolemac."

"Ethan invited me to come over. You have a very nice group here—caring, sharing and all the nice things we yearn for in my part of the world."

His eyes were searching hers. She recognized the same hunger her husband displayed following the abstinence during her periods. In Sean's case, he was fighting his urge at the same time while trying to be respectable, to be accepted. She felt comfortable and desirable under his gaze.

"This is the usual way we celebrate," she explained. "Although Ethan's party is more lavish than some. Burgess is not sparing any expenses to welcome his prodigal son." She laughed coquettishly. She was enjoying this. Never since David's wooing of her before their marriage had a man shown such interest in her. But then the males of Tolemac respected matrimony and did not dally with married women. And David had relegated her to duty and habit. This flirting was exhilarating.

He looked at the ring on her finger and his face showed disappointment. "I find all the women marry young here," he said.

"It's our custom. Besides, there is nothing else to do after we finish our education."

"It's a pity."

"Are you married?"

"No, I'm . . . single."

They talked after that, and she forgot the time. She felt relaxed talking to him about her painting, the children, life in Tolemac. He just nodded, his eager eyes alight, drinking in her every word. He didn't talk about himself.

She heard footsteps behind her—guests sauntering in for more food. Sonya felt the yoke of inspection settle on her back. She reluctantly moved away. "I have to go. There are guests to be served. It's nice to have met you. Have a nice stay in our city."

He grudgingly pulled himself away.

"What can I get you?" she prattled chirpily over her shoulder at the new visitors, her gaze still on the departing Sean.

"My, my," chimed Frida Parks with Agnes and Kamala in tow. "You are quite lively today aren't you?"

"Yes, I am," said Sonya, turning around unflustered. For once they can see it, and I don't give a hoot!

Now, as she watched him leave the party, bidding goodbye to Ethan on the lawn, she wanted to see him again. She wanted to take a risk, something she had never done in her sheltered life.

She looked across the lawn at Delia, holding a drink in her hand, tossing her hair back and laughing at a joke that Samson had just made. Delia was flaunting herself with Samson and he was letting himself be taken along. Why only them, and not me?

* * *

Entering Burgess's house, David was struck by the collection of ornaments and plaques hanging on the living-room walls. All of them had been awarded to Burgess for his many humanitarian involvements—some were from the Executive Committee, about a dozen were from the NADF. There were even a few pre-Flood RCMP plaques. Samson, on the other hand, had no plaques on the walls in his home; he did not subscribe to such blatant self-adulation, preferring to collect memorabilia on discs and other digitized storage media.

David was admiring a life-sized porcelain lion, awarded to Burgess by the South China Republic for "great education provided to our armed forces," when a voice behind him said, "Quite a collection, eh?"

He turned around and there was Burgess, leaning heavily on his cane, mopping the sweat from his brow. "Too hot outside," he said and sat down.

"Yes, quite a collection. You must be proud of your accomplishments," David said.

Burgess gestured to David to sit down with him. David had not spoken to him in a long time, ever since Burgess had stopped dropping in and out of Samson's house and the two elders' relationship had become more formal.

"Ah, it's great to be alive today! Indeed, I feel like the father in that parable of the prodigal son." His face was flushed with pride as he spoke, gazing through the open windows into the garden where Ethan was still working the crowd of guests. David settled his gaze on Burgess's other son, John, instead. John was giving donkey rides on his back to the children, replete with party hat on his head. Kids loved harmless John, who never said much, just grunted and was always ready to play. And John, in return, was more interested in children than in adults, whom he was mostly scared of. Burgess did not even look in John's direction.

"Yes, I guess Ethan can now take care of you. And John."

"Ah, John. Yes, Cynthia left me a tough legacy, raising those two kids alone, especially John."

The story they'd heard as children—when Cynthia had suddenly left the Williams's home—was that she'd had a nervous breakdown from the stress of minding two troublesome kids while her husband was out building Tolemac. Later they heard that she had been moved to a mental health facility in Oceania and that Burgess went to visit her occasionally. After a few years, his visits stopped and no one talked about Cynthia anymore. And John would be seen at the Waterside Park on occasion, looking across the water and struggling to say the word, "Mmammamma . . ."

"I hope Ethan settles down and gets married soon. Your generation needs to ensure we have progeny to inherit this New World."

"From what I can see, marriage is not something Ethan has on his mind just yet," David said and waited for a reaction.

Burgess sat silently for a while. Outside, John came crashing down with two kids on top of him. He collided with a juice stand. Everyone, including John, laughed as the pink juice soaked his clothes.

"We were too busy you know, to focus on procreation," Burgess said. "Look at us elders—Nathan, a bachelor; Kamala, a young widow and never remarried; the others, Samson, Dr. Morden, Rocky Sabbattini, Izzy Garcia, myself, all with only a smattering of children among us, not enough for even one good-sized family. No, I don't think we did enough on that front."

David gave him a counter view. "Well, Vladimir's got three kids. And Sonya is pressuring me to have another. So we haven't thrown in the towel yet."

"Good! The future lies in expanding our population. People like you and Ethan have to get us there. I would do anything to have a handful of grandchildren now. Your father's a lucky man."

"Maybe, you need to get Ethan refocused then."

"He's a stubborn kid—doesn't listen to me—never did, even when I tried to teach him hockey, and basketball and stuff, eh? I was surprised when he agreed to return home. Maybe he has to realize his ambitions first, then he might refocus."

"He wants to turn us into another New Eden."

Burgess laughed. "Ethan is a dreamer at times. But it's good to dream. Creation happens there, doesn't it? See that piece of extra land at the back of my property? I've given it to him; he can build himself a home there. A man's got to have a home first before he starts to raise a family."

"That's very generous of you."

"What can I say? He's my boy—and the only hope of continuing my work after I'm gone."

"You've drifted away from the rest of your colleagues, Burgess. If you will pardon the observation."

"You see that, eh?"

"The last couple of Committee meetings have been eye-openers."

"Well, I have been more open to outside influences through my work on the NADF than the rest of them. I see the threats of global piracy that they do not see. When the civilized world crumbled, all hell broke loose. All of man's unchecked desires and ambitions are now loose once more. Look at the tribal wars going on in Asia. That side of the world has still not learned from the Flood. And unless we have proper controls in place we will self-destruct again."

David rose. It was time go. But he felt he had to say a few more words to Burgess, irrespective of how the older man might interpret them. "Then you'd better start having this discussion with Ethan. He's been more exposed to man's unchecked desires and ambitions than any of my generation in Tolemac."

David left him staring down at his cane. When Burgess looked out through the windows again at his newly arrived son, there was the usual look of admiration and affection on his face, but it was now creased with a slight frown.

Chapter 11

July 10, 2045—Agnes left me.

THE DAY SAMSON MADE HIS LAST JOURNAL entry about Agnes, David was working late at the school preparing for the final term set to begin in August. Sonya had taken the kids to arts camp and they were busy preparing for the one-act play that would culminate the two weeks of activities. Joey was playing one of a group of orphans and Hannah was an angel coming in over the water to rescue these lost ones. Joey was particularly obstinate that he was not lost and that he knew his role in life and did not need to be rescued, especially by Hannah, and Sonya kept reminding him that this was only a play, written by a teenager in the camp.

Suddenly David's Communicator went into voice mode and he recognized Frida Parks. "David . . . is that you?"

"Yes. It's been awhile." He remembered his absent-minded wave to her on the street the day he burst in on Delia Stone's solo sex act.

"David, you must come at once. I can't find Samson. Your mother is in the hospital."

"What!"

"She's had a heart attack. Please come as soon as you can."

He rushed out, got on his bicycle and dashed off. The hospital was uphill from the school and he was winded when he arrived. There was no sign of Frida Parks, but one of the nurses on duty, Dagma, a regular attendee at the Church of the New Covenant, quickly ushered him into the intensive care unit.

When they neared the ICU, she said, "David, you will have to wait here. The doctors are still trying to stabilize your mother."

"But can I just look? See if she is all right?"

"Please sit outside here. I will page Dr. Karya for you. Can I get you anything in the meantime?"

"No, thank you. Dr. Karya is attending to Mum?"

"Yes. He also has our correspondent heart specialist Dr. Phillips in Oceania on the Communicator in the ICU."

David felt partially relieved; he'd heard good things about Dr. Karya, a product of the post-Flood like himself.

As Dagma turned to leave, she paused, "David, one other thing. There is a gentleman in the waiting room. He's the one who found your mother fallen in the park and brought her in. He carried her half a mile up Sunset, as he did not know how to get help. I believe he's a newcomer to Tolemac. He said he would stay until the patient's family arrived."

"Can I see him?" David felt a sudden gratitude towards this unknown Samaritan.

"I'll send him up. Please sit tight and try to relax. Can we contact anyone else while you are waiting?"

In his rush to get to the hospital David had left his mobile at the school. He gave her Belva and Kamala's addresses from memory. They were his mother's closest friends. He also asked Dagma to leave a message for Sonya.

"How about your father?"

He'd forgotten Samson. David listed a number of possible places his father could be at the moment: the church, the city hall, the building society, even the Stones's. Dagma left to see what she could do.

The moment he sat down, the elevator doors opened and Frida Parks came stumbling out.

"Oh, David, there you are. I've been trying to locate your father all over the place."

Then David remembered that Kamala had given Samson a gift of a mobile Communicator last Christmas. Samson was not at all interested in carrying one, but Kamala had insisted.

"Call Kamala, she may have the number of Samson's mobile, in case he is carrying it."

Frida went off to try Kamala. The ICU quieted down. A generator purred behind big metal doors where doctors and nurses were busy saving the sick or just keeping them alive. David felt exhausted by the sudden turn of events. He had never seen someone close to him die. People were living longer these days. Only the really elderly died and they usually did so in nursing homes for the aged. Hospital facilities like this had helped extend life expectancy. He looked at the clock; it was seven o'clock and beginning to get dark outside. He began pacing.

The elevator doors opened again and the man he had been introduced to as Sean Galloway at Ethan's homecoming, stepped out and looked curiously about him. Sean was now sporting a beard that made his lean features look more hawk-like. He still wore the faded bomber jacket, which in the light of the brightly lit room, looked like it had seen better years.

Relieved for the company, David said, "It's Sean, right? Was it you who found my mother, Mrs. Arthurs?"

Sean nodded, but continued to look around the ICU in wonder, before speaking, "This is a great facility. Is it true that your medical coverage is taken care of?"

"It's the benefit of contributing to the Medical Fund. What happened with my mother?"

Sean unconsciously fished out a crumpled packed of cigarettes. "Can I smoke in here? I'm dying for a cigarette."

David was getting impatient. Didn't the man know that all of indoor Tolemac was a smoke-free zone, especially hospitals? He pointed instead to the "no smoking" sign and said, "Can you please tell me what happened?"

"Darn! I guess I'll have to go outside then. Come with me and I'll tell you what happened." Sean put the pack of cigarettes back in his jacket and turned to leave.

They rode the elevator down together. At close quarters, Sean smelled of the sea, as if he'd been in the hold of one of those fishing vessels coming in from the Californias. Or maybe he was boarding in a hostel near the port, one frequented by sailors and transients.

On the porch, tension drained from Sean's face as he dragged hungrily on the cigarette, ignoring his companion's impatience. David hadn't seen too many people smoke. Nathan Goldman smoked cigars occasionally, but he did so with great poise, more for effect than need.

Sean began slowly. "I'm staying at the Waterfront Hotel and went down to the park this evening to stretch my legs. I saw your mother, about two hundred yards in front of me. It was just getting dark and the park lights hadn't come on yet. The place was deserted, except for a couple sitting on a park bench some distance away. I could make out your mother. She was walking away from me, trying to go faster and faster, as if she were running away from something—or someone. Then she clutched her side and fell."

"I wonder what she was doing there at that time? She doesn't take that route home normally."

"Don't know. I ran over to help her. She was in pain, gasping for air. I've seen heart attacks before, so I looked for help. But the couple who were sitting on the bench had suddenly left."

"What did you do?"

"All I could see was the big 'H' of the hospital sign through the trees up the hill. So I carried her and ran uphill through the park, then cut over to the road. When I hit the road, pedestrians came to my aid and helped me get her inside."

"I can't thank you enough, Sean."

"No problem, that was the least I could do. I hope she recovers soon."

For awhile they stood lost in their own thoughts. Sean continued to draw on his cigarette. David's curiosity took over. "The other night, Ethan mentioned that you were an old associate."

"Yeah. I did some work for him in New Eden."

"And you are thinking of moving here permanently?"

"I've been looking for a new place to hang my hat, so to speak. Checked out Alberta and Saska-Manitoba. Nothing interesting there. I'm here, on a temporary visitor permit."

"Anything I could do to help?"

"Well, I'd like to get some information on how to apply for permanent residence here. In case the deal with Ethan doesn't work out."

"What kind of work do you do?"

"I'm a pilot."

"A pilot!" David was intrigued, yet mildly disappointed. There was no work for pilots in Tolemac. The island had no commercial airplane service. All land was split between farming, housing, the port and the microchip factory. The

Executive Committee was opposed to funding an airstrip, due to its consumption of land and the risk of noise pollution. The closest airport was in Oceania.

"You might be out of luck here. We don't have an airport."

"Helicopters," Sean clarified.

"And what did you use them for?"

"I ferried oil workers between New Eden and the oilfields offshore. Ethan ran a courier service in New Eden. I did drops for him when he was short of pilots."

Frida, rushing out of the elevators, cut them short at that point. "Your mother is being moved into a ward right now. You can go up to her shortly," she said. "And I left a message on your father's mobile."

"Thanks!" David said.

A car screeched into the hospital driveway. It was Kamala's red Arrow. Belva, Sonya and the kids piled out.

Hannah grabbed David's hand. She still had her angel costume on. "Daddy, please let's go to Grandma. I have to talk to her."

David had trouble restraining the child's energy. "Hang on Hannah. We can't go in just now."

"But we must," Hannah insisted.

"Go with her, David," Sonya said. "She's been agitated for the last hour."

He complied. Sonya knew best in this situation.

Dagma led them to the ward. Agnes had been placed in a semi-private room, which she shared with two older women in their eighties. She was asleep, her breathing laboured. Her face was pale and drawn, as if she had been through extreme physical exertion. There were tubes sticking out all over her. Hannah broke away, ran over and grabbed her grandmother's free hand, the one without the intravenous tube in it.

"Hannah, be careful," David hissed.

Agnes opened her eyes and stared at the little angelic figure holding her hand. Her voice croaked, "Ah, it's my little angel. Have you come to take me home to God, then?"

"Hi, Mum," David offered.

But she was looking at Hannah. "Is that true, my dear?"

"Grandma. Be happy. The angels love you. They told me."

"That's good to know, darling."

"It's nice up there, trust me—I've seen."

At this point, Sonya and the others arrived in the room. The women surrounded Agnes's bed making David feel out of place. He looked at Joey, who was also trying to find something to focus on. "Come on, son—let's go outside for a while. Grandma is in good hands."

Sean was standing outside. He was permanently sewn into this picture somehow.

"I'd better be going now," he said, but did not make an effort to leave.

"Will you come and have dinner with us sometime? We must meet again," David said.

"Oh, could we have steak-burgers when he comes?" Joey suddenly came alive.

"You know that too much meat is not good for you, Joey. We've had steak burgers four times in the last two weeks already."

Sean laughed. "You have steak-burgers here? Used to eat 'em all the time in New Eden. There was a place there that made the world's biggest steak-burgers."

"Can we, Dad?"

"Perhaps, if Sean comes," David caved in. "We have a new place that's opened up on Dundas," he explained to Sean. "Owner is from Alberta. I can't keep the kids away from there."

There was a commotion by the nurse's station and Samson came barging in. "Where is Agnes?" He was out of breath and his eyes had a haunted look. David had never seen his father like this before. Samson gave Sean a cursory glance and a nod, and seeing the huddled group inside the room, rushed over.

The women parted as Samson approached Agnes's bedside. Only Hannah stayed, still holding onto her grandmother's hand.

"Agnes? Honey, say you are all right?" Samson said, soothing Agnes's damp brow.

"She is going with the angels soon, Grandpa," Hannah said, her eyes widening.

Samson was not amused and stayed focused on Agnes. He gingerly took her other hand with the tube in it. Then he began crying. David, following silently into the room, had never seen his father cry before. Samson's giant frame shook with muffled sobs.

"I told you Grandpa, you don't have to cry," Hannah insisted. "She is going to be with the angels."

Belva, started to shoo everyone out authoritatively. "I think it's time for Samson to commune with her. Let's retire to my place and pray for our dear Agnes."

"Hey, wait a minute. Who's talking about dying?" David protested. Then he saw Dr. Karya framed in the doorway.

"Mr. Arthurs, David? A word, if you will—" Pulling David aside, the doctor said, "I think you'd better leave your father with her. She's had a tough attack. She'll pull through, if she does not have a relapse. Perhaps Samson at her side will be best for her now."

Something in the doctor's tone alarmed David, so he returned to Agnes's bedside and took her cold, shrivelled hand in his. On the other side of her bed, Samson mumbled, "Agnes, you will stay and fight. We fought all this time. Please . . . stay . . . please . . ." He was willing her. "I can explain it all . . ."

Then he heard Sonya whispering in his ear, "David, let's go now." Reluctantly pulling away, he felt Agnes's faint tug on his hand; then she let go.

Everyone, including Sean, bundled into Kamala's car and drove to Belva's home halfway up Sunset Hill on Somerset Drive, a few streets away from David's home on Lilydale Crescent. David peddled after them on his bicycle. A roar broke out as he passed the hockey arena—contained excitement released by a population that now played and watched this sport year round. These were comforting sounds, but the natural sense of home was now tempered with a sense of loss as he rode through the dark and familiar streets. The streetlights were just starting to come on and people were taking their after-dinner strolls. He'd never felt lonely before. Samson had explained it to him many times—how people roamed the dirt tracks that were once the early streets of Tolemac, mourning their losses. There were two types of people he'd said—those who mourned and those who built. "Be a builder," his father had said. Samson also explained that many who held onto their grief without mourning, had passed away of various illnesses within the first five years of the Flood.

When he got to Belva's, she was serving vegetarian goulash; a potato salad was well dug into and the loaf of sourdough bread was almost gone. She then served her guests bowls of her famous vegetable stew with chunks of bean curd clogging the steaming surface. "Come along, David you must eat something. Had I known of this earlier—well, how can you ever know of these things—I would have got some meat from the market."

"No more meat for a while" David pleaded, looking at Joey.

"Belva, I'll get you some tomorrow" Sonya offered. "My kids will eat your larder dry at this rate."

During what was a sombre meal for the adults, Sean asked questions about Tolemac. The locals were glad for his presence and curiosity.

"You must spend a lot of time cooking?" he said to Belva. "Peeling those potatoes—"

"We grow the skinless type here," Belva explained.

"Our farms have genetic variations of the older forms of vegetables," David said.

"But you still have to cook them, no?" Sean shook his head.

"We still like the naturalness of cooking," Belva said. "Don't tell me you folks get away without cooking?"

"Well, we prefer our food prepared in packets. Just heat and eat."

"And lose all the nutrition?"

"No. In fact, our genetic variations are such that they taste better once pre-prepared, frozen, then heated and eaten."

"And what are you doing in Tolemac?" Sonya asked, looking directly at their guest.

Sean spooned his soup before answering. "I'm visiting."

"He's a helicopter pilot," David said. "And may apply for residence here. If he likes it."

"We are not exactly as exciting and dynamic as New Eden. And we don't have helicopters." Kamala said.

"But you have a caring community. I see it in this room."

"We look out for each other. It's our legacy."

"It should have been ours, too. But we went into reverse."

"What do you mean?" Sonya interjected.

"Competition intensified with us Capitalists. I think we got scared about scarcity and went into overdrive."

After dinner, Sean excused himself to go outside for a cigarette, while Belva arranged the prayer circle and guided the others into a meditative mode. They prayed for Agnes. During the session, David tried connecting with his mother; he thought about the little things they had done together, their conversations. But his mind was preoccupied and nothing came easily. When they were finished praying, Sean was standing in the doorway staring curiously at the little circle.

"Amazing!"

"Why? Have you never done prayer-meditation?" Kamala asked.

"No. I've never prayed in my life. Teach me."

"We pray all the time like this," Hannah piped in.

Sonya smiled and ruffled Hannah's curls gently. "Sure. We have classes for newcomers every Thursday evening down at the Veteran's Centre on Dundas. Come on over sometime."

"Sure. I'd like to try," Sean's eyes lit up at the offer.

Later, after he had thanked everyone and bade them goodnight, Sean pulled David aside at the front door.

"You have a wonderful family. Thanks for including me tonight. I hope your mother recovers quickly." Then he pulled his jacket about him and walked off into the night.

*　*　*

At about three in the morning, David heard voices in his sleep. He awoke and felt across the bed for Sonya, but she wasn't there. He was fully awake now and could tell that the voices were coming from Hannah's room. He tiptoed across the landing, past Joey's room to Hannah's where the door was ajar and a dim light shone through. By the light of the bedside table lamp, he made out Sonya kneeling by Hannah. The child was upright in bed, facing the window.

"Grandma, we will be all right," Hannah said.

Then, after a pause, she continued, "And I will look after Joey. No, I'll try not to . . . fight, or anything like that with him. Well, not all the time at least. Will you tell him, too?"

David was about to open his mouth to speak when Sonya turned around, placing a finger across her lips. Suddenly, in Hannah, David saw the young Sonya who had spoken to her "ancestors across the water" so many years ago in the Waterside Park. He did not interrupt.

"She's gone now, Mama," Hannah said turning to Sonya. "But she said she will visit me again."

"Your grandma is with the angels now, honey. It's time for you to go back to sleep." Sonya kissed Hannah, stroked her golden curls, and laid her down on the bed.

"Mama—"

"Yes, honey?"

"She looked, sort of unhappy or something. Why is that?"

"I don't know. Maybe, she will tell you more when she next visits you."

David had heard enough. He staggered into the living room and switched on the Communicator. There was a message waiting. "Call the hospital, urgently," it said.

*   *   *

When David arrived back at the hospital, Samson was sitting outside the ward, drinking a mug of coffee. His eyes were bloodshot and his beard was a mass of tangled hairs. He stared into his mug. David placed a hand on his shoulder. "Dad, you need to get some rest."

"She had another attack in the night."

"The doctor warned us about that."

"She never woke up, David. Not once, while I was by her side."

"But she was conscious at times. I felt her."

"I so wanted her to fight, for life. Like she did with me all those years we were raising you."

"Maybe there is a time to stop fighting and let God's will prevail."

"I let her down, David."

David remained silent. This was not a time to tell his father about his mother's growing bitterness. The jealousy in her final days. He had promised to talk to Samson about it, but now it was too late. Inwardly he kicked himself. He had been reluctant to seize the day, and now the day had slipped past.

Samson continued, "One day I'll have the nerve to tell you. But right now, I just need to finish this coffee and lie down for a while." He drained the rest of the mug and rose wearily. "Let's get some rest. In a few hours, we have to bury our dead again."

Chapter 12

LEO PATIMKIN TURNED HIS COMMUNICATOR OFF and looked out of the window. He was never going to get this math thing right. And the assignment was due tomorrow. Try as he might, he did not have his father's brains. There were many things worrying him today, math the least of them. When the Patimkins had returned from the synagogue, he dragged himself into his room to complete this assignment, but couldn't get past the first problem. Sally Morden was troubling him. She had invited him to her place for a twinning exercise, something Mr. Arthurs had arranged, and Leo had surreptitiously hinted at, as a solution to his math problem. The first thing he had seen was a picture of Joe Sabbattini on Sally's desk in her den. That had ruined his concentration, Sally's dark beauty and confident air notwithstanding. He didn't know Joe and Sally's relationship had progressed this far. Heck, Joe Sabbattini was still turning lots of girls' heads. Joe was not ready to settle down, even though most Tolemacians did marry in their early twenties or even late teens.

Then Leo had met Johnny Garcia at the synagogue and found out that Johnny's dad, Izzy, wasn't going to be serving on the Executive Committee anymore. He was just too ill with cancer and was refusing the new cell transplant procedure, for it was against his religious beliefs. Leo liked Izzy, who was half Jewish and half Mexican Catholic. He was a quintessential Tolemacian. He went with his family to the Church of the New Covenant on one weekend and to the synagogue on the next, a true multilateralist who embodied Humanitarian values. Johnny had promised to drop by later and help Leo with his math exercises.

Johnny had also told Leo that, at a party last night at Joe's place, a drink laced with something had been introduced, and the kids who took it had gone pretty wild.

"Was it alcohol?"

"Not sure. Must have been something stronger. Joe said he had gotten it from some 'connections.' "

"Did any of the adults notice?"

"No, we had a vacant suite at the Waterfront. You know, Joe's dad's pretty generous to us on the weekends. He thinks that we play group games and debate philosophy."

"Yeah, but if he found out?"

"Well, Joe is good at getting us to clear out before his father's curfew."

"What happened to the guys who took it?"

"One of the guys—that show-off Reggie Theophilus—said that it was better than an orgasm."

"Oh, yeah?"

"Oh, yeah! He shags daily—he should know!"

Leo winced. He shagged too, not daily though, but he was angry with himself when he succumbed. "That's pretty dangerous. He's flouting the rules."

"We all do, some more than others. The rules are wearing thin now."

"Still—"

"We are getting pretty bored, you know. And this is Joe's way of being popular. Hang out with Joe—he keeps you popping with all the stuff we hear about on the Capitalist side but can't experience."

This last statement still echoed and bothered Leo. Just like the nightly urgings of his loins. "Turbulent as the waters, you will no longer excel, for you went unto your father's bed, onto my couch and defiled it"—Jacob's condemnation of his first-born son, Reuben, for masturbating. These were the teachings that had been drilled into his head from an early age, the legacy of the Flood. Leo found strength in denying the raging beneath his navel through meditation and through intellectual discourse. The free meditation classes introduced to all ages in Tolemac were supposed to curb these unnatural desires. Yet, when he sat around Sally and smelled the freshness of her skin, he wanted to go the other way, and he sometimes did. So he prayed and meditated and masturbated and dreamed that one day he would marry Sally.

Tolemac, if one followed the rules, worked. It worked for people like Leo who did not stand out in the crowd. The rules would put people like Joe Sabbattini in their place and make Sally Morden choose wisely; make Leo match up to the Joes of this world in areas where intellect mattered more than popularity. Accordingly, Leo had embraced the Humanitarian cause and had set his sights on becoming a member of the Executive Committee one day.

But the rules were too tight and people were finding loopholes. Leo was just worried that the things he was raised to believe in were slowly eroding and that popularity could be bought by fancy drinks laced with mind-altering drugs.

*   *   *

For David, the two weeks following Agnes's death went by in a blur: the funeral proceedings, the many well-wishers who gathered to pay their respects, the constant presence of new and familiar faces. The people came in dribs and drabs, in trickles and rushes, at various times during those two weeks. Samson met everyone, embraced, talked, laughed and cried with them, as they reminisced about old times. He held a dramatic funeral service for his beloved Agnes that reduced many in the church to tears, himself included. He seemed to be able to cry freely now, since Agnes's passing. Sonya suggested that David stay with Samson and not leave him alone during the wake, and in the nights immediately following the funeral. So David temporarily moved into his old bedroom back at Samson's house, to the room that held his childhood memories. It was still intact, as if Samson and Agnes had expected him home any day—all the old books, even the computerized reading tablet he had received when he was five, they were all there, and dusted, too. But the room felt small and cramped. After taking a look around, David chose to sleep in the living room instead. He did not want to shatter the image of his somewhat cloistered but relatively happy childhood.

Despite his loss, Samson was in control during those two weeks. He rose early in the morning to putter around in the garden, and then he went into the kitchen to make breakfast. This was followed by a trip to the funeral parlour for the wake and to meet well-wishers. A quick detour to the church and to City Hall to "check on things" rounded up his day. He took special care of Agnes's roses, which were in full bloom now. This was something he had never done before, the garden being Agnes's preserve. At sunset, Samson and David would sit out on the back porch, out of the summer's heat and catch up on the day. Sometimes Samson peered through the giant telescope mounted on the porch, overlooking Tolemac. From as far back as David could remember, this had been his father's pastime, surveying the city, ensuring that everything was running smoothly. If he missed Agnes, Samson tried not to talk about it. He appeared to have compartmentalized her into one of those caskets in his mind, where the rest of his deceased family was placed.

One evening, as they were sitting on the deck looking down into Burgess's backyard, David asked his father, "How come you got the house on the hill and Burgess got the one below you?"

"We fought for it," Samson said, smiling.

"I thought Tolemacians never fought?"

"Well, not exactly 'fought.' The summit could only take one small house, although the next level could take a larger one. I was never one for large houses, but I wanted to see Tolemac take shape. The higher elevation was important for me. So Burgess and I had a wrist fight to see who would get the summit."

"And you won?"

"No, I lost." At David's look of consternation, Samson carried on, "When Burgess saw the land area he had fought over, he had second thoughts. He'd always wanted a big house and all the trimmings he'd lost in the Flood."

"So he just gave it to you?"

"When I was elected Chairman of the first Executive Committee, he shook my hand and gave me the title deed to the summit saying, 'Here, this goes with the territory.' I wish he had told me his real reason for giving me the title deed. Afterwards, he built that big monstrosity below. It took ten years to complete, with all the supply problems we had in those days."

"Yes, I remember."

On another evening, David decided to be bold. "Were you disappointed in Mum in any way?"

"No. What made you think that?" Samson replied, scowling this time.

"Well, she seemed to think so. Blamed herself for not being able to have any more children after me."

"That's nonsense. Any life after the Flood was a gift. I was so glad she bore you."

"Did you tell her that?"

Samson looked down at his feet and then out over the city lights below. He rose and walked over to the telescope and peered through it for a while. "Sometimes we say things and only we hear it. I guess Agnes either did not see or hear my gratitude, or I did not speak it in a way that she understood."

"You were busy."

"Yes, I was. And so was she. I guess we overlooked pure and simple communication."

Samson was fiddling with the sights on the telescope, as if he couldn't quite get the focus he was looking for. "Sometimes, it's easier to start from scratch than to go back and sort out old messes." Then he let the telescope fall back into its idle position.

There were no further conversations on this subject, and David returned to his home at the end of those two weeks, sure that his father was on top of his grief, but unsure that he was on top of his own. His mother's death had been inconclusive for him; she had left with many questions unanswered. He felt all bottled up. One thing was sure—he had lost a confidante. Would Sonya fill that space? There were things they discussed as husband and wife, but Sonya had not yet arrived in the space his mother had occupied. Maybe time would tell.

* * *

David ran into Sean again at the Royal City Bank on Dundas, a couple of days after he had returned home. It was a nice sunny day and he had decided to walk over to the bank to do some old-fashioned banking instead of doing it online. Sean was arguing, rather furiously, with a teller. He looked confused. Then, finishing his conversation abruptly, he walked away shaking his head.

David quickly completed transferring digital cash to his mobile Communicator at the walk-in kiosk and caught up with Sean. "Hello, there!"

"Oh, hi, David! Nice to see you again," he said, looking preoccupied.

"Having a hard time with our banking rules?"

"Yeah, I couldn't understand why my first pay stub was reduced so much?"

"You're working? Why that's great! Where?"

"I joined the port's new air transportation unit. Ethan's job finally came through. And he's got me a permanent residence visa."

David felt a lump in his throat. "That's great!"

"He's planning to introduce an aerial ferry service for the port. You know, get urgent spares and personnel across the water in emergencies. Even carry passengers, if there is demand."

"He'll never get that one past the Executive Committee."

"Why not? It has a good business case; the financials make sense even for a small place like Tolemac."

"Sean, we only use helicopters for medical emergencies, not for commercial ones. And there too—Oceania runs the air doctor service for us. We do not believe in commercial emergencies."

"Well, Ethan is going to propose it to the port's board and then to your Executive Committee. In the meantime, he's signed me up as his lead pilot and consultant on this project."

They walked up Dundas in silence. David felt like he was on the basketball court again, with Ethan edging past him. Burgess Williams owned the major share in the port of Tolemac. Nathan Goldman held a minor share. Nathan's main interests were in the microchip factory and the farmlands that he had bought and leased out to the many residents of Tolemac, including the early migrant workers. Ever since he had tried to hatch his plot to attack the port in the fictional Trading Game, David always had an uneasy feeling that Ethan was going to do exactly that in real life one day. The port was the nerve centre of Tolemac; without it, no microchips could leave the city; food exports and imports would be blocked, too. He, who controlled the port, controlled Tolemac. With Burgess entering retirement, Ethan was hungry to step into his father's shoes; that was his main reason for returning to Tolemac. Running for political office was secondary. When David had raised his suspicion with Samson on many occasions on the back porch during the last two weeks, his father had shrugged it off, saying there were too many "checks and balances" in the Humanitarian system to let that happen. According to Samson, the Executive

Committee could overrule any monopolistic moves by businesses that disadvantaged citizens of Tolemac, especially the poor.

"Why do they take so much out of our paycheques?" Sean said, interrupting David's thoughts.

"Well, you contribute to the Medical Fund and the Defence Fund automatically. And you may have signed up for the Voluntary Contribution, in lieu of taxes."

"Yeah, I did. I thought that was a good idea at first. Now I'm thinking again. The woman at the bank tried to explain that to me. You mean we have no option but to make a voluntary contribution? To whom?"

"To society, so that the underprivileged or those unable to earn their income can be cared for. You could have refused or decreased your contribution if you wished. You have that option, especially if it places a financial burden on you. But when there is no compulsion, people usually give more."

"And why is my income available for everyone to see on the public Infoway?"

"Because incomes here are transparent. We all know what each other makes."

"Don't you have any privacy in these matters?"

"We do, in things of a more personal nature, like relationships. You see, after the Flood, the survivors had to pool their resources in order to get by. Food, clothing, everything was shared. So they grew up with a culture of openness about material possessions."

"But the Williams family practically owns the port."

"Yes, ownership is okay. In fact, the maxim 'more will be expected of him to whom more was given' prevails here. That's why 'affluent' people like Burgess Williams and Nathan Goldman volunteer so much of their time on the Executive Committee and other causes."

"They do not get paid to govern this place?"

"The Executive Committee members' expenses are covered, yes, but their time and expertise is voluntary."

"I see. So everybody looks after everybody else and nobody starves here. And you have quaint institutions like banks to manage your communal money pot, while we got rid of those bureaucracies, years ago?"

"That's right. And we give them nostalgic labels from pre-Flood days—just like we name our streets, you may have noticed."

"They were right when they asked me to come here," he said, as if to himself.

"Who are 'they'?"

"The folks in New Eden."

"Why?"

Sean shrugged and did not elaborate. Instead he said, "Well, I might as well get used to living on a reduced income then. There's not much to spend it on here anyway, so I shouldn't grumble. I'm just grateful to be working again."

They had reached the corner of Dundas and Kennedy, and David had to cross the road and head back to the school.

'When are you going to come over and have dinner with us?" David asked.

"Oh, yes! And I won't forget to bring the steak burgers for Joey. Make that 'soon'—just as soon as I am settled."

"That's a deal! But don't take too long."

When Sean walked away, David realized why he was beginning to like him. Sean was different—foreign and unaccustomed to the ways of Tolemacians. Yet he was curious and leaned towards this way of life, however hard it was to comprehend at first.

Later that evening, David went over to Samson's house to retrieve some laundry he had left behind during his recent stay. Upon entering the garden, he stopped short. Delia Stone was coming out of the house. For a moment, David wondered if she was one of the stragglers, coming to pay her last respects to Agnes. Samson came out after her and he appeared to be in a lighter mood. He even laughed as he greeted David.

"Hi, son! We have a special visitor!"

Delia was dressed in a body-hugging, sleeveless T-shirt and pants, and her red hair was pulled back over her head and tied in a knot at the back. David felt the blood rush to his head again.

"I'm sorry to hear about your mother, David." Sincerity shone through her sensuality.

"Thanks for coming," David said.

"That's what good neighbours are for, isn't it? Your father has been most kind to us. Anyway, I was just leaving. I really do hope things settle down soon."

Samson gave her a small parcel he held in his hand. "You forgot this," he said. She quickly put it away in her handbag. "Thanks," she replied. There was something unsaid as their gazes locked. Then she went down the steps, waved goodbye to the two men, and walked down Sunset Hill.

"She's done marvellously since they arrived here, hasn't she?" Samson said, standing at David's shoulder, looking after Delia as her figure disappeared in the gathering dusk.

"I guess Tolemac has given the Stones a new lease on life."

"Not Doug, unfortunately. He continues to deteriorate and this puts a huge strain on Delia and Joshua. She wants to work, but can't leave Doug unattended."

"Can't she get a nurse or one of the hospital volunteers to look in on him?"

"He wouldn't let her. Kicks up an awful fuss."

"It's a shame. I think they have a strange relationship."

Samson, who had turned to go inside, paused on the stairway. "How do you mean?"

David wanted to tell him what he had seen the other day at the caretaker's cottage, but he held back. Instead he said, "It's just a hunch I have—you know my instincts and all."

"She had a hard time having Joshua the natural way. The child was artificially produced in one of those labs on the Capitalist side."

"Mum wished we had labs like that here. I could have had more brothers and sisters."

Samson looked irritated. "That kid is also very sickly. Has an attention deficit disorder and suffers from asthma. God did not ask us to procreate unnaturally."

And with that Samson went indoors. David followed. After he had retrieved the laundry, David said, "Do you know that Ethan is trying to set up a commercial helicopter service?"

"Yes, there has been talk about it."

"Aren't you concerned?"

"No, he'll not get far with that. We have principles, as you know, and this project does not meet those."

"The Committee will not approve?"

"Not unless there is a majority in favour. I don't see anyone going for it other than possibly Burgess, just to salve his son's feelings."

"But why do we have such rigid principles? Personally, I don't see anything wrong with a commercial helicopter service."

"Knowing Ethan, he's aiming to open a direct air route between Tolemac and New Eden. That's just the entry to full blown trade with the Capitalists. And that is why the Committee will oppose the helicopter deal."

"I've never quite known why we have this aggressive stance against the Capitalists. While the post- Flood 'don't trade with the capitalists' message continues to get hammered away in our schools, Oceania has cautiously open limited trade links now. Surely there must be a few common areas where we can trade while still respecting each other's differences?"

"They don't abide by our laws, and we find their rules of engagement abhorrent. We can't even get them to keep back their own refugees, let alone start opening trade links. And if we have a trade dispute, 'might' will triumph over 'right.' You would have learned that in school, surely?"

"And I continue to teach it, too. But I'm not totally convinced. I think trade is achievable, if we attempt it."

"Oceania has also encountered drugs in their city, and there was that bomb explosion recently. You open the door and all this stuff comes with it."

David changed subjects, "You are spending too much time alone these days. Come by for a visit with the kids sometime."

"I will. Give them a big hug from me. I miss my Bible debates with Joey. And Hannah can throw the odd curveball with her visions of angels and the like. But I am also busy with the mid-term elections. It keeps me from having to brood here every day."

"I forgot the elections. Have Izzy and Nathan confirmed they are dropping out?"

"Yes, finally. We old guard never stop running. We kind of fade away as our health problems get the better of us."

"And you are going to stay on?"

"I have to. But this will be the last time. I need to see you younger folk on the Committee. And what about you? I can't keep asking every time there is an election, you know?"

David remained silent for a while before speaking. "There are some days when I feel that I am not cut out to be a politician."

"Ethan is running this time."

"That was a foregone conclusion."

"Yes, and Peter Lowry, too. They are coming in as observers to our next meeting. And once they complete the observer status period, they will declare their candidacy." Then his face got serious. "David, you know that we've got to have balance on the Committee, that's why the old guard keeps running every term. But I worry about the younger crew coming in—the likes of Ethan and Peter—they do not share the same vision we had. You are by far the most balanced of the new generation—probably your mother's trait, for which again, I did not thank her. We need you on the Executive this time!"

Suddenly and involuntarily, David found himself saying, "Count me in."

Samson stopped in mid-stride. "You mean that?" There was the beginning of a smile on his face.

David hung onto his statement. "Yes."

He saw Samson's eyes light up with relief and happiness. "Aha!" Samson roared as he took David by both shoulders and shook him vigorously. "At last— and you will make a great leader of this city!" There was nothing but admiration in the older man's eyes. He hadn't been so animated since the time of Agnes's death. Allowing no room for afterthoughts, Samson performed a little skip over towards the Communicator. He quickly voiced a message to his colleagues that David Arthurs would be another candidate submitting a nomination. "There!" he said as the message transmitted. "Let's drink to it!" He poured out two little glasses of sacrificial non-alcoholic wine: "To the next generation of Arthurs!"

As he pedalled his bicycle home later that evening, David wondered what had caused him to make that commitment out of the blue. Was it having Ethan pushed in his face? Was it his awareness of the mounting disappointment of his father, who had asked him to run three times during three prior election terms? Was it to compensate Samson for his recent loss of Agnes? Or was he coming of age finally? Maybe it was all of the above. It was exhilarating to feel committed. It was also strangely frightening.

* * *

That night he broke it to Sonya, after the kids had gone to bed.

"You're running? And you did not even discuss it with me?" she said.

"I can't let Ethan run away with his madcap plans. He's going to use the Executive Committee to get his way."

"David, you sometimes imagine the worst of Ethan. He's nothing but an overgrown bully."

"Well, I know him better. He is past bullying. He is more calculating now. Still a bully, but in a more dangerous way."

"We Tolemacians are a gentle people. His message will never sell."

"Honey, we can't let reckless forces like Ethan run amok. We need balance. I feel obligated to be that balance."

"So, it's all about you and Ethan, and living up to each of your fathers' expectations. What about us?"

"What about us?"

"Are we going to end up just like Samson and Agnes? Your mother was bitterly unhappy when she passed away—you know that. They were hardly acting as husband and wife anymore."

David remained silent on this point.

"It's easy to lose oneself in the politics of this place," Sonya continued, pressing home her point.

"Honey, now you are talking as if you resent our life in Tolemac. We have to give back, you know. Samson needs me on the Executive Committee."

She walked away from the dining table and went into the bedroom. David followed her. "Will you support me, then?"

"I don't know, David. I want to. But I'm afraid of what this means. The examples I have seen aren't good ones." She started to undress for bed and he felt an overwhelming desire for her olive-skinned body. Her long black hair fell down past her shoulders as she undid her hairpins.

"Your mother did all right? She did all right on the Committee, didn't she?" he said.

"But that's all she did in the end—her job and her work on the Committee, since father died. She has no other life, except to see her grandkids occasionally."

He decided to take her in his arms and put an end to any further conversation. He wanted her to offer herself to him like she had done on many countless occasions, like all dutiful wives did in Tolemac, or in Biblical times, so he could lose himself and forget the onerous responsibility he had just accepted. But that night, for the first time, she did not comply and was far away in thought. He rolled off her eventually, unconsummated, and lay awake for a long time. The image of Delia pleasuring herself floated into his vision—wanton, extracting her pleasure at will, absentee husband notwithstanding. For a moment he wanted to be the instrument of that pleasure. He wanted to replace Delia's face with Sonya's, see his wife squealing with delight as he thrust himself harder and harder into her. But he knew that did not work in real life, not in his, anyway. It went against the rules and roles that husbands and wives had carved out for each other in post-Flood, Humanitarian society. Sex was a hunger to be satisfied periodically, and for procreation. To take it beyond that and to revel in its hidden pleasures would lead to the debauchery that preceded all cataclysms—the Flood, Sodom and Gomorrah—he had learned those lessons well. He placed a pillow over his swollen manhood, which the image of Delia had generated, and forced himself to go to sleep. But troubling images of Samson coming out of the house behind Delia, the latter writhing on crumpled sheets with a hand between her legs, bothered him through that restless night.

Chapter 13

TOLEMAC HELD ELECTIONS for its Executive Committee once every five years. There were eight members on the Committee. This five-year term's members were Samson, Burgess, Nathan, Kamala, Vladimir, Asif Murtaza, Dr. Morden and Izzy Garcia.

Izzy was the committee's conscience on matters of governance, but had been absent a great deal in recent times due to his cancer. A cocktail of drugs kept him alive— barely, and he refused riskier, modern medicines that claimed to have eradicated most strains of the disease. He was the Committee's representative of the "Dependents Program," aimed at less fortunate citizens unable to earn their income due to disability or illness. Under Humanitarian rules, if two or more members of the Executive Committee resigned, or were unable to carry out their duties during a term, by-elections were held for their replacements. This was the election they were going into because Izzy and Nathan, who had both served since the founding of Tolemac, were stepping down in the middle of their terms. Izzy due to his health and Nathan because he wanted to work on some philanthropic projects before he "got too old to do it."

Candidates volunteered for election. Political fundraising was discouraged and rarely practised, but candidates were allocated equal blocks of time over the Infoway to broadcast their manifestos and face questions from citizens at public meetings. It was a relatively simple process and politics was given a minimal role in the life of the citizens of Tolemac; a dramatic reversal from pre-Flood days when the line between politics and commerce had blurred and led to excesses.

Traditionalists claimed that it was this unholy union that had contributed to God's wrath by way of the Flood.

Those in political office were respected, and it was their personal character and record of humanitarian activities that got them elected. Orderly succession was very important to Tolemacians; therefore, new candidates were eligible to submit their nomination only after they had completed a minimum of three months as observers on the Executive Committee. A selection sub-committee declared those finally eligible to stand for election. This election's selection sub-committee, comprising of Dr. Morden, Asif Murtaza and Vladimir Patimkin, was looking for a candidate's good understanding of the current issues, character, endurance and commitment to serve for the long term. Given the volunteer nature of the role, not many came forth, and Tolemacians had, more or less, entrusted the running of their city to the Executive Committee and their groomed recruits, who had wisely steered the city since its founding thirty-three years ago.

*   *   *

When David attended his fourth meeting of the Committee on August 20, an unprecedented storm broke out. All committee members were present that day, including Izzy, now restricted to a wheelchair. Also present were Peter Lowry and Ethan Williams as observers. David liked Peter and shook his hand. He remembered Peter's pacifism during their Trading Game and felt that even if he had Capitalistic tendencies there was a sense of moderation in him. Peter had broadened physically and his five-foot-five-inch frame resembled a wrestler more than a budding politician. Ethan had placed himself behind Burgess—observers were relegated to backbencher status behind their sponsor Committee members, who were the only ones eligible to sit at the round table. By now, David had pushed himself to sit behind Samson in the Committee chamber and not up in the balcony.

Kamala presented her recommendations on the priority for mid-term funding re-allocations for projects that had been requested of her several meetings ago. She was a very methodical woman, and had taken her time on this assignment. Years of judicial practice had taught her how to place the facts in the right place and interpret them with humaneness. She presented detailed costs and benefits for each of the proposals, with a summation and recommendation at the end. In her report, funding for the sea wall and Vladimir's request for firewall-server capacity took precedence over the increased contribution to the Defence Fund. When the available funds were finally allocated, the sea wall got its full request; Vladimir got only part of his request, but it would enable him to begin the initial phase of his project; the Defence Fund request was deferred to the next budget period.

Burgess, who had been silent throughout the allocation process, rose passionately. "This is unacceptable! You are making a big mistake!"

"Kam's assessment is fair, Burgess," Samson said and looked around to the rest of the Committee. "Do you all agree?"

There were nods around the table.

"But it's very easy to allocate funds to obvious causes; it's the hidden ones that are difficult to identify," Burgess persisted.

"Can we prevent a 'hidden one' like another Flood, no matter how much funds we have in Defence?" Samson countered.

"If it happened today, at least we'd be better prepared," Burgess shot back. He was looking directly at Samson when he uttered his next words. "If we'd had our own helicopters back then, if we'd had our own blood supplies . . . damn it, Samson—you know we would have done better the last time!"

Samson did not answer but flushed red. Kamala interrupted, "The Flood was an act of God. We could not have controlled it. Acts of terrorism or territorial disputes are acts of man, and within our power to avoid, if we act sensibly. Burgess, we should try diplomatic methods first, rather than building large military machines that become powers unto themselves after awhile."

This being the divisive issue, Kamala's recommendations were put to a vote, and not surprisingly, passed six to one. Burgess was the only dissenter. Samson did not even have to cast his deciding vote.

"Before we move off this item, Mr. Chairman," Nathan cleared his throat, "What progress have you made in your attempts to open dialogue with the New Edeners on the refugee issue? We talked about this three months ago, but have not yet seen any progress."

Samson ignored the question and shuffled his papers, eager to get on to the next agenda item.

"It's important, Sam," Kamala said. "We need another round of discussions soon, particularly on this refugee issue."

"And then you could get around to discussing Defence-related stuff with them, too," Nathan said, looking at Burgess. "I think the miscreants who are causing trouble in Oceania, and giving the Defence Fund this extra work, are the dispossessed, filtering in from the Capitalist states."

"Yes, yes—I hear you," Samson said. "I'll present you a plan within the month on how we can have another go at this."

"My WorkOUT plan is almost complete," Nathan announced. "Even if it's not ready for approval in Tolemac yet, you could have a draft to engage the New Edeners in a fresh dialogue. This plan, by the way, will be my parting contribution before I step down."

Ethan leaned over and whispered to his father. Burgess nodded. Then, just as Samson was about to present the next item, Burgess piped out, "You've been slow opening this dialogue Sam. This is not your typical style. Are you protecting someone? Someone you don't want repatriated, if we strike a deal with New Eden on the refugees?"

"What do you mean?" Samson was getting red again.

"Well, you've been seen in the company of certain New Edeners recently."

"Burgess, I resent your insinuations. This very committee accepted the Stones into Tolemac three months ago. I have done my best to get them settled."

"Your attention is somewhat lopsided towards these newcomers. Have you paid the same courtesy to that new fellow—Galloway? The guy who found Agnes in the park? The man is a cancer survivor and nobody has given him any time or attention, save Ethan here."

Kamala brought relief to the table, "Gentlemen, gentlemen . . . stop! This is getting far too personal."

"Hear, hear," echoed Dr. Morden, who had been sitting impatiently through the proceedings. "Sam, could we get to the next item on the agenda. I have a surgery to attend in an hour and I can't keep my patient waiting."

Samson and Burgess settled down, the former red-faced and swallowing his comeback, the latter looking smug.

The next item on the agenda got even closer to the refugee issue. This time, Izzy was on the mat. It appeared the "Dependents Program" was over budget, again.

Izzy cleared his throat and spoke hoarsely—the cancer had extended down his larynx, despite surgery in that area six months ago. "What can I say, Mr. Chairman. We've had too many refugees in recent times, a net inflow. Also, the first generation of Tolemacians is now entering its retirement years and need more care and support. We are all draining the Fund." He paused for breath and drank some water.

Nathan spoke: "But everyone can do some sort of work based on their abilities—no? Remember our motto Izzy, 'from each according to his abilities . . .' you still serve despite your health challenges. That's the principle behind my WorkOUT plan."

"But you cannot force people. Who are we to judge their abilities, or disabilities?"

They debated for another half hour. Nathan frequently waded in with his fledgling WorkOUT plan as the panacea, in lieu of the "welfare" that Humanitarian governments provided its needy citizens. WorkOUT, according to Nathan, would match the types of available work for those who were unemployed, based on skills, abilities or handicap, and earn those in the program a living wage without arbitrarily putting them on welfare. Only residual gaps in earnings would be covered by welfare. The conclusion reached, and this was one of the Committee's customary consensus decisions, was to have Nathan present his draft WorkOUT program at an upcoming meeting, as soon as it was ready. The Committee requested that the proposal detail the types of work inductees would perform and the conditions under which the program would be administered, before they decided on it.

"This will be a big change for the people of Tolemac," Samson concluded. "If we decide to go this WorkOUT route, it will involve a lot of communication and a lot more compassion."

"But times are tough, Sam," Nathan said. "We can't sustain our present level of funding, as you know. And we cannot afford abuse of the system, especially by freeloaders."

The final item on the agenda was the proposed helicopter service. David pricked his ears up on this one. Burgess presented the proposal.

"My friends and colleagues, I may not be in a particularly winning situation today," he began, "but I want you to seriously consider this proposal to run a helicopter service from the port of Tolemac to neighbouring communities, and abroad."

"Define 'neighbouring communities,' " said Vladimir Patimkin.

"Well, certainly Oceania is foremost. But we do have a lot of exiles and people with family connections in Philadelphia, Saska-Manitoba, Alberta and New Eden—"

"New Eden!" Samson cut in. "Is this another bid to open trade with them?"

"Hush, Sam, hear the man out," said Nathan.

Burgess resumed, "The journey by boat to Oceania takes sixteen hours. We could cut this down to one and a half hours by introducing a helicopter service. We rejected proposals for an air service in the past because the proposals required land for runways. But helicopters use vertical takeoff and landing and do not incur any space, except for parking."

'What else do you plan to transport?" asked Asif Murtaza.

"Well there's all kinds of emergency needs, spare parts, computer supplies— Vladimir, you know, you've had problems of breakdown at the Communications centre, and recovery has taken many hours if not days—we could cut out all these delays."

"Have you considered financial viability?" Nathan said.

Burgess leaned behind and Ethan handed him some papers which were distributed around the table. There was meticulous detail in the plan—revenues, costs, probabilities, load factors, potential boat traffic volumes that could be siphoned off to the helicopter service, frequencies, and growth plans—Ethan had done his homework.

"As you can see, my friends," Burgess's voice had regained its confidence because he knew that he had their attention. "This plan pays for itself in eighteen months. There is a pent-up demand for this service. I am willing to test the plan with the port's own finances. At most, I will be looking for funding from the City of Tolemac only to expand the operation, if the test is successful." Then he cocked an eyebrow in Samson's direction, "and that funding need not necessarily come only from Tolemac's public purse. We could get private finding from our destination points, too—remember, the service is bi-directional."

"And that would mean that New Edeners and other Capitalists could have a say in the way we do business?" Samson concluded.

"Sam, much as I dislike the Capitalists, this helicopter plan has merit," Nathan said, pouring over the financials.

"And we cannot remain isolated forever," Vladimir said. "The Communication Centre will certainly benefit from this proposal."

Dr. Morden weighed in, "So will Tolemac General. There's some great research done in private hospitals in some of those Capitalist states that I don't mind paying for. Good research saves lives."

Kamala looked across at Samson with concern in her eyes. "Sam, I know you have your concerns on the trade side. But we need to open a new dialogue with our neighbours. When we do, this may be the start of something positive between our two realms. And we don't have to compromise our principles just because we open an air service with them."

"Capitalist information flows into Tolemac via the Infoway are controlled," Vladimir added. "If we fear contamination, we could introduce similar controls on the transport of people and emergency goods."

David saw that his father was trying hopelessly to stem a rising tide of enthusiasm for something new, for change.

"How do you know that our helicopters will be allowed to land in the Capitalist states?" Samson asked.

"We have already covered that," Ethan piped up from behind. "I've secured route licences and landing permits. The Capitalists invite everyone to trade with them. They have no hang-ups."

"They just don't play by our rules," Samson growled.

From there on, there was no stopping Burgess's plan. In typical Tolemacian fashion, however, a whole bunch of controls were built in: route plans to be approved by the Executive; initial routes to be limited to a daily service to Oceania and an 'on-demand' service to New Eden; no paying passengers to be picked up in Capitalist states (that would signal open trade); only passengers who paid for a return fare in Tolemac would be boarded at Capitalist destination points for return home; cargo from the Capitalist states to be restricted to emergency supplies and personal goods from former Tolemacians living there; quarterly audited statements of performance of the new service to be reviewed by the Executive, and so on. The deal was finally passed in a split vote, with five to two in favour of the proposal (Izzy and Asif voted against it). Samson did not have his chance to veto the vote, even though he was still opposed to the proposal.

In summing up the decision, Samson looked crestfallen. "Well, I was mistaken. You are obviously open to breaking with tradition. Today, two out of our three agenda items went to a vote. That's a first! Much as we may think this an innocuous step, this vote opens the door to full-blown trade with the Capitalists. I hope you know what you have voted for."

Chapter 14

OVER THE NEXT MONTH, David felt his relationship with Sonya cool off. It became evident in little things. Dinner was sometimes not prepared when it was her turn to do so; long silences ensued at the breakfast table, and whenever they were broken, Sonya limited her comments to Joey and Hannah. Regular sexual intercourse, that one predictable ritual between them, became infrequent, with ready excuses on her part to avoid it altogether. This was not one of those tiffs that ended within hours or even days; it had a slower burn that was moving them into greater reticence.

David continued to attend Executive Committee meetings as an observer, and the issues were becoming more and more engaging. Now he felt compelled to participate, as if this was a vocation he had been previously running away from. When he filled in the nomination form and asked Sonya for her co-signature (a candidate's spouse was supposed to endorse the nomination, to ensure domestic life was not compromised), Sonya vacillated. But he pushed the issue, and, finally, she signed, which sent her even deeper into aloofness. She began returning to her art gallery in the evenings after preparing the children's meals and helping them with their homework. Sonya had graduated in the fine arts and her paintings were well known in Oceania and other parts of the Humanitarian Federation. When David asked her why she was spending so much time at the gallery, she said that an upcoming exhibition was taking up more of her time than she had bargained on. He tried to compensate by spending additional time with the kids in the evenings. He figured that she was trying to send him a message: how she would feel when he got into political office. Teaching at the school and attending to city work would wear him down and leave him no time for his family.

One evening, when Sonya was at the gallery, he dropped the kids off at Belva's, with the excuse that he had an unexpected errand to run. Belva adored Hannah and Joey and was always willing to spend time with them, especially now that her own children and grandchildren lived in the New Settlements.

He went down to the gallery. It was about seven o'clock, and Tolemac's sky was in twilight. The streetlights were coming on along the two arterial roads running downhill to the water, and mixed with the dying colours of the sun, they provided a kaleidoscope of unity between what was man-made and what was natural. The sounds of the waterfront and port had started to die down while the crash of the surf had increased. He walked down the string of shops along Main Street. Clothing that all looked alike peeped out of shop windows; only the buttons were of different colours, shapes and sizes. There were lots of capes, which had come back in fashion about ten years ago, something to do with the fact that warmer coats could now be dispensed with. He peeped in the closed shop window of the bookstore to see if any new titles had come in; they would normally be illuminated on the big screen in the centre, but tonight the screen was switched off. All he could see was the bank of print-on-demand machines where customers could download their purchases onto their personal Communicators or print them on paper. The bookstore, especially the sections on history and literature by pre-Flood artists, was a great place to get lost in. He had spent a lot of time there waiting for Sonya to finish her work in the gallery, in the days when meeting after work to walk back home together had been so much fun. As he passed by to the next door, he saw dim lights inside the art gallery; he heard voices as he pushed through the front door with its "closed" sign.

Sonya specialized in impressionistic styles of landscapes and street scenes. Her gallery was the place to come to for a bird's-eye view of Tolemac. As she was also a distributor for the artworks of other Tolemacian painters, she graded the paintings in chronological order, some even predated the Flood. Thus, in her "historical" section, she had paintings of street scenes from the now submerged cities of Toronto and Niagara Falls. David marvelled at the depictions from that period; of old streetcars and that tall tower, whose antenna was still visible from what was now the greater Lake Ontario. The later paintings, many of them her own, depicted the lush cornfields of rural Tolemac; factory scenes in the microchip assembly line; people going to work on their bicycles; the monorail inching its way out to the New Settlements with passengers hanging on from all sides; the March of the Lamps ceremony; and her most autobiographical—a little girl talking to the spectral shape of a handsome man who hovered above the waters offshore from Tolemac's waterfront. This last painting never went on public display but remained in her private collection.

David had spent a lot of his leisure time in the gallery, watching Sonya at her work. When visually exhausted, she would become more analytical like her mother and sort through the many paintings that came in daily, judging them on their merits and deciding where each would hang. He found this strange mix of artist and accountant fascinating; it was part of his attraction to her—that unknown side that he hoped never to fully discover, but always to be in awe of, 'til death did them part. He had spent hours with her as she sat by her easel in the outdoors, whether out in the country or on Sunset Hill or down at the Waterside Park, conjuring images that were only in her head and adding extra dimensions to those everyday scenes that lay before them. Today, he felt even more intense about those moments they had shared, due to the gathering gulf between them. David paused in the doorway. He winced when he saw Sean, who was paying close attention to every word of Sonya's as they walked together around the exhibit area. The theme of the upcoming exhibition, she was saying, was to do with "dream consciousness"—images people see in dreams or meditation. There was a lot of colour in the paintings on the walls, subdued by the dim lighting in the gallery.

"There will be extra lighting on the day of the show," Sonya said, as if pre-empting David's thoughts, "and that will lend more vibrancy to these colours." She stopped upon seeing him enter. "Hello, David. Look who dropped by!" Her voice became strained upon seeing him.

A stumbling "Hi there!" was all he could manage at that moment. He felt relieved that Sean was present. From out of the blue, Agnes's words came to him, "Samson and I would not know what to say to each other if we were alone together." David's palms started to get clammy.

Sean broke the silence. "I didn't know Sonya was so talented. Tolemacian painters are brilliant!"

"Sean's taking part in our prayer-meditation classes, too. He's been over at the meditation centre all week," Sonya said.

"Oh! And how's the new job?" David enquired.

"Great. We got delivery of the first two helicopters last week. Ethan's looking to buy a couple more. He's seeing so many possibilities already."

"Four helicopters? I thought you were going to have only one!"

"Oh, no. Now that we have your Executive's clearance we are really going full bore on this."

Sonya looked irritated at the conversation slipping away from her. "Gentlemen, since you have so much to catch up on, I had better get on with my work."

"Oh, I'm sorry, Sonya—we got carried away!" Sean apologized.

"No, perhaps it's me," David said. "Sorry I butted in."

Sean bowed gallantly at Sonya. "Well, O artist of the Humanitarian world, I am indeed ready to return to this personal tour. David, let's catch up some other time, shall we? And, oh, I did capitulate to the dinner invitation, by the way. Sonya twisted my arm beyond any more hesitation."

"Yes, he's coming over next Saturday," Sonya said, taking Sean's hand graciously and moving on to the next portrait. "Now, this one illustrates the messages we get in the dream state. Notice the lighting—white with flashes of brilliant maroons and blues, reminiscent of the flashes through which we receive these messages . . ."

David decided it was time to leave; he wasn't sure why he had come in the first place or what he had achieved by doing so. He was also burning with a sense of hurt for being left out.

*　*　*

Sonya knew her mother would not approve, but she felt the only way to deal with the issue was to talk about it. She decided to visit Kamala on one of her rare days off from her various civic and volunteer duties. Within minutes, their conversation turned to the new entrants to Tolemac.

Sonya threw out a line. "I am terribly attracted to Sean. Is that bad?" She felt unburdened in saying it. Now she had passed it onto her mother, just like she had channelled many of life's difficult questions when growing up.

Kamala nodded as if expecting this comment. She moved over to a picture on the wall, one of Sonya's recent paintings of the waterfront, and pondered it.

"It's not right. That's not the way we were brought up." Kamala said after a pause. She tried to reposition the painting, for no obvious reason, and kept getting it off centre. Sonya went to the rescue.

"That's not the way we were brought up—my generation. There was far more openness in your time while growing up in the old world," Sonya said, holding the picture on one end as they finally righted it. "Your generation narrowed the world for us after the Flood."

"We are still inclusive of all people—Capitalists and clairvoyants alike," Kamala almost snapped the last few words.

"Yes, but your laws neuter us in other ways."

Kamala ignored the comment, and straightened up, looking at the painting again. "Tea?"

"No, thanks. I have to get back to take Hannah to her music lessons."

Her mother's shoulders drooped, as she made her way over to the living-room sofa and gently sank into it. "I would stay away from Sean Gallagher if I were you. It can only lead to temptation."

"Is that why you stayed away from Samson all your life?" Sonya was sorry for blurting it out, but she was irritated with her mother's casual dismissal of her feelings. Like a true *Tolemacian—bury feelings with rules.*

Kamala sucked in a deep breath. She looked indignant momentarily, then exhaled and looked out of the window, all, without saying a word. Sonya saw the light surrounding her mother go from red to blue and fluctuate in between.

"I'm sorry," Sonya said, coming over and sitting by her mother.

"You have seen that all along, haven't you?" Kamala spoke finally.

"From the time I was a child. I could see the change in your aura whenever Samson came by."

"But what would I have achieved by baring my feelings—destroyed both our families in the eyes of our fellow citizens?"

"Instead you clothed yourself in the lonely life of widowhood. You didn't even marry again."

"No one else interested me. It was easier to focus on things that made sense for the greater good."

"Did you ever tell him how you felt?"

"No!" Kamala rose and began to tidy her already neatly arranged papers, work she brought home daily after a full day at the judiciary. "But I am sure he knew. We never spoke about it."

"And now he is openly flaunting himself with a much younger woman."

Kamala turned to face her daughter. Her eyes were piercing, having regained her composure from a few moments ago. "That is his choice and yours, too. Stay away from temptation. That's all I can tell you."

* * *

On the following Saturday, David included Samson and Kamala in the dinner arrangements. It was time to get Samson out of his work and into the midst of the family again, especially with the grandchildren. Besides, Hannah loved her grandfather's tall tales of the "good old days." Joey usually listened in silence, unable to break through Hannah's total domination. And Samson loved this indulgence. Kamala's presence would add sobriety to them all.

Sonya looked radiant that night. She wore an ankle-length cotton dress that hugged her body and served to further stoke David's smouldering passion. Her black hair was pulled back and hung in a ponytail at the back. When Samson arrived, he was whisked away to the kid's room for the usual half hour of Hannah's news. Kamala came in soon after and Joey hijacked her, pleased that his sister was busy and out of the way. Kamala, in her thoughtful way, always brought gifts for the kids; this time it was crunchy chocolate marbles, all the way from Oceania, with simulated sugar modifying the chocolate to reduce the risk of tooth decay, yet retaining the sweetness that kids loved. It was at times like these that David missed his own grandparents who had passed away in the Flood, never having had the chance to indulge him.

By the time Sean showed up, the grandparents had managed to partially extricate themselves and were playing Maslow's Pyramid, a psychological board game, in the living room with their grandchildren.

Sean was better groomed than on previous occasions. Gone was the shoulder-length hair; now it was shaved into an army-style crew cut. The beard, the bomber jacket and the military boots were also gone. He was dressed in a plain blue shirt, khaki pants and shoes.

Samson remained aloof when David introduced Sean. Kamala was her warm self, but probing; she instantly got into a discussion with their visitor about how he was taking to life in Tolemac. Her eyes were piercing, studying, classifying.

Hannah volunteered to say grace and proved she had certainly moved past the "rub-a dub-rub, thank you for the grub" stage when she gave everybody a controlled and adult prayer, partially to impress her grandparents. It went something like "Lord, please bless this food, and the people who are about to receive it, as they have worked hard to earn it." David saw the gleam of pride in Samson's eyes, as this little golden-haired angel, eyes closed in fervent concentration, concluded her prayer.

Sonya had outdone herself with the dinner, which consisted of roast duck with pumpkin, beans and mashed potatoes. The gravy and stuffing were the best. But more importantly, her artistic flair in presenting the dinner was evident in the table arrangement, replete with candles, sprigs of parsley, coriander and fresh fruit interspersed between the crockery. Sean enjoyed himself, spooning several servings during the meal. And Sonya was always at hand to help him with whatever he needed. Kamala burped on more than a few occasions, mostly when her daughter hovered around their guest.

The conversation during dinner was discreet and neutral, and David hoped the rest of the evening would be much the same. Hannah announced to everyone that she was now into painting and wanted to do portraits of her family so that Sonya could display them in the gallery. That got some lively discussion going. And Joey wanted to know why they could not get the old "cowboy and crooks" movies in Tolemac. Apparently, in an edited Oceania documentary shown in school, these movies were still widely available for download via Communicator in the Capitalists states.

"Well, that period of history is no longer valid," Samson explained. "We have our own 'Wild West' today, only thirty-three years after the Flood. But we use more humanitarian methods to restore order now. Not the 'shoot 'em all up' stuff they preached in those old movies. We don't want impressionable young people getting the wrong notion."

"I wish they'd had some sort of control like that back where I used to live," Sean said. "Your grandfather is right, Joey, sometimes having everything available is not necessarily the right thing." For the first time, David saw Samson give Sean a nod of approval.

When the kids had retired to the den after dinner, the adults went out on the porch with their coffee mugs, and the conversation took a different turn.

"I didn't know you were afflicted with cancer. I'm sorry to hear that," Samson said suddenly, looking at Sean. There was a momentary silence as everyone felt uncomfortable with his directness. Embarrassed, David kept his eyes straight ahead, looking beyond the curve of Lilydale Crescent towards the lights coming up on the waterfront in the deepening twilight. Samson continued unabashedly, "I'm also sorry we have not paid you too much attention since your arrival in Tolemac."

"Oh, it's okay. You've had your own share of worries recently," Sean said.

Sonya's eyes were wide open with concern. "Sean, I didn't know . . . about your illness, that is. Is there anything we can do?"

"No, I'm all right now. I was in hospital for a spell before it went into remission."

"Was that why you came to Tolemac?" Samson asked.

"Yes, as a matter of fact. I lost my job when I went back to work. Nobody gave me an explanation but I figured it was on account of the illness. You're toast when you fall off the treadmill down in New Eden."

When David dragged his gaze back to the tableau on the porch, he saw Kamala looking at Samson, pleading with her eyes for him to change the subject. There was nothing but concern and admiration in Sonya's eyes as she looked fixedly at Sean.

"Well, in Tolemac, we don't believe in anyone becoming 'toast.' We have laws here to protect the fallen," Samson continued evenly.

"Yes, and that's why I am eternally grateful for you folks taking me in, even offering me a job and giving me resident status—all in the space of two months."

"And now you are going to be running helicopter traffic between our two states— trading with those who rejected you." Samson said.

Sean held Samson's gaze. "Samson, I know how opposed you are to this deal. I'm sorry you feel that way. But if we manage it properly—and I aim to—there are a lot of good things we can get from New Eden."

"Without giving away the shop?" David asked, hoping to help ease the tension.

"Absolutely. I have contacts. I know how to play them at their game, if necessary."

"That will be difficult," Samson shook his head. "The Capitalists look for 'net gain' not 'win-win' and more so with us because we are the smaller cousin. It even happened before the Flood when little Canada tried to trade with the once mighty United States."

David broke in, "But it's no longer about Canada and the United States. Our land masses are mixed. Our people are mixed. It's more of an ideological divide that exists now between Capitalism and Humanitarianism."

"And that's a much more serious division," Samson said.

"I don't think you're being fair to the Capitalists. We can always set some ground rules with them, and not play if they don't abide by the rules."

"But they break the rules every time," Samson countered.

"That is why we have a presence at the International Tribunal," Kamala said.

"Those tribunals take a long time to get things resolved and in the meantime we lose," Samson said.

David decided to change the subject: "Sean, how's the meditation coming along?"

"Great. I can't say that I am at the level of you locals yet but I am beginning to see glimpses of dimensions beyond me." Sean looked at Sonya and smiled, and she returned his smile. "Thanks to Sonya. The meditation is also helping me deal with my rejection."

"Rejection?"

Sean shrugged. "Oh, it's a long story. I told it in class once and reduced a few people to tears. Perhaps Sonya can tell it better than I."

"I guess being rejected by your country and employer at a time of your greatest need is enough to cause those feelings," Kamala said.

"Yes, that and other things."

Sean was not going to elaborate and David felt that his attempt to steer the conversation towards calmer waters was not meeting with a lot of success. At that point, Kamala sailed in and got the conversation going on Sonya's upcoming art exhibition; that topic took everyone into a less contentious zone for the rest of the evening. David saw Kamala casting apprehensive glances towards Sonya and Sean during the conversation, as if every new discussion point she brought up would prevent her daughter from looking adoringly at their visitor.

As he bade Sean farewell that evening, David wrestled with conflicting thoughts. Sonya was obviously smitten by Sean, and he by her. Sean was confiding in Sonya—she knew more about him than anyone and yet had not known about his illness. Were there other things he was keeping in the closet? They were also probably seeing more of each other, too, now that Sean was in the meditation class. Were they seeing more of each other beyond the class? That night he felt those pangs again, of what he had now determined was jealousy. He had never felt anything so strongly before. He'd read that jealousy was rampant in pre-Flood society, just like depression, anxiety, greed and other vices. These vulnerabilities were supposed to have been wiped out—that seemed to be the only rationale for a cataclysm on a magnitude of the Flood—but now they were back, and infiltrating the people who were creations of this new landscape, people like him. His mother had said, "There are still a lot of restless emotions running inside us."

That night he woke up from a bad dream: a flood of water had broken into the art gallery and soiled the painting of the little girl talking to the spectre across the water.

*　*　*

"Why do you distrust New Edeners so much?" David asked.

It was the following weekend and he was helping Samson repair his roof. The shingles were worn out and an entire section needed replacement. The warm sunshine had squeezed the sweat out of their bare bodies, just as David was hoping this moment of bonding would force some answers from Samson.

Samson kept hammering in the new shingles and remained silent. The shingles did not need nails anymore as they had an all-weather adhesive on them. But Samson insisted on nails since, according to him, "that's how shingles were always laid." David kept the question hanging and proceeded to place the replacements in line so that Samson could get to them with his hammer and pail of nails as they worked the bald stretch of roof.

"It's not as if I haven't tried. We've gone in delegation three times on different occasions over the last thirty years."

"Why did talks break down?"

"Because they wanted fundamental changes to our way of life that we were not willing to compromise on."

"Like?"

"The Dependents Program, for instance—they called it a subsidy. They don't believe in subsidies to organizations or to people."

"Can we not show them the success of our program?"

"But how do they measure success of a program? In the numbers of people it has given a second lease of life to, or by its financial viability? If it's the latter, then we don't have a story they'll be excited about. You heard Izzy the other day . . . the program's losing money although it's helping a lot of people."

"But you could argue that we have become New Eden's dumping ground for its fallen ones. That we are subsidizing them."

"But they don't care for the fallen. They never have. Sending the fallen to the 'colonies' is their answer to the problem. On the other hand, they argue that their system of 'winner takes all' attracts the best and the brightest."

The last shingle was in place and David was stowing the ladder and tools away in the work shed, when Samson said, "Come on, I want to show you something. Get your bicycle and follow me."

They free-rolled their bikes from the house on the top of the Hill and headed part way down Sunset before turning off towards the cemetery. The leaves were still green on the trees for this warm October day. In the bright sunlight, one could distinguish the pre- and post-Flood vegetation. The pre-Flood trees were old and gnarled with dark leaves; their post-Flood counterparts were lighter, more luminous. David wondered if that was indicative of humans, too. Were the post-Flood denizens such as he, more enlightened than the pre-Flooders? That said, the old trees nestled comfortably amidst the younger ones, while the latter did not encroach on the spaces staked out by the old veterans.

The cemetery was busier than usual, this being the weekend. Some Tolemacians even held family picnics here, as it gave the departed ones a chance to join their living kin at these gatherings, or so the popular belief held.

Samson headed towards the Arthurs family mausoleum. When they were inside, he knelt in front of Agnes's tomb for a few minutes. David knelt beside him. It was a nice feeling—for a fleeting moment they were a family again. It had been a long time since he had felt that way, not since his early years as a child.

"I miss her," Samson said. "She kept me anchored."

"We all miss her."

"Hannah told me the other day that Agnes visits her in dreams."

David started to say something about not taking Hannah seriously and decided against it. That girl was special and he had sworn to take her seriously.

Samson continued, "Your mother was unhappy and unfulfilled. Hannah told me that in her sweet little way. And I feel responsible for it. I was not around when she needed me, especially in those last days."

"There's no point in harping back to the past, Dad. Is this why we came, here?"

"No, no. I was distracted for a moment. I'm sorry." Then he crossed the cold marble floor over to another tomb. "I spent many moments in this tomb in those early days in Tolemac, reconnecting with my departed family. You weren't around when Adele passed on," he said.

"No, but you told me lots of stories about your life together as children. And about that time of her passing."

"Yes. But what I did not tell you was how she passed. She had a rare blood type and had lost a lot of blood during the exodus, due to her premature labour. Many of us refugees who were stranded up on the Hill at that time needed blood and medical supplies. And the helicopters that came around from time to time couldn't attend to everyone." He sat down on a lower step in the mausoleum, remembering. His eyes were watery.

"You told me all that." David said.

"We appealed for blood. The only place that could provide her type was a hospital in the former New York State, which had coalesced into New Eden. We sent SOS messages on Vladimir's communicator, time and time again. But they wanted payment—money talked for them, even at that time when the world was crumbling about us. We had no money to lay our hands on. Finally, she died. And the blood never came."

They sat in silence, each lost in his own thoughts. "You know, she cried when she knew she wasn't going to make it. She said she wanted a baby—that was all she was hoping to have in this life and was that too much to ask for? I promised her that I'd have one for her. Now do you know how special you are?"

David took his father's hand and gently got him to his feet. There was no need to talk anymore. They cycled back up the hill to his home and Samson was steady at the wheel, pedalling with purpose as they climbed Sunset. David understood then how his father and the entire old guard kept their minds from drifting—work, physical exertion—things that keep dark thoughts from percolating in the mind.

When they had parked the bikes, Samson thanked David for helping him out in more ways than one that day.

"I'd better keep my eyes on you from now on," David said. "Now that you are 'un-tethered,' as you say."

"I hope that does not mean spying on me?" Samson laughed.

"No, no—but you need your family around you at this time."

Samson started to go indoors, then paused. "You know, it's very hard for me to talk to the New Edeners on the refugee resettlement issue. Yet, the Executive has ordered me to do this. Will you give me a hand?"

"Why . . . sure! I'd love to!" David was elated and taken aback by the request. A plea for help from Samson? The man who was always above help, because help was something only he doled out in unlimited quantities to those around him? "I'll speak to Sean—he has contacts," David said.

"Be careful," Samson looked serious and thoughtful again. "I still do not know the extent of Sean's allegiance to Ethan."

"I think Sean can think for himself. Besides, I think he endorses the Tolemacian way of life. Nathan himself said it—we can't do this alone—we need help. Inside help."

Samson shrugged and went indoors. On the threshold, he paused, "Okay, see what you can do. Let's get together again tomorrow and discuss this. I'm too bagged today."

Later, as he cycled downhill to Lilydale, David stopped steering and let the wind course through him, not wanting to control things anymore. At last, a chance to play in the big leagues. He felt like he was on a wild ride now— definitely entering centre stage and wanting to abandon himself to wherever this entrance was going to take him.

Chapter 15

THE NEXT TWO WEEKS MOVED FAST, as David got busy for the upcoming trip to New Eden. Despite lingering pangs of jealousy, David called Sean, asking for help with contacts on the other side. Sean suggested meeting Congressman Marc Gordon. "Marc Gordon helped me out when I fell ill," Sean said.

David invited Sean to meet him in the newly-opened Coffee Boutique by the port. It was relaxing sitting in the newly opened café, with the coffee aromas mixed with cinnamon, orange and cocoa; coffee beans were now grown with these different flavours. The news of the helicopter service had added to the flurry of activity at this eastern end of the port, where older structures were being torn down, making way for trendy boutiques and shops like the one they were in. Samson on the other hand, preferred his coffee black and straight and usually went down to the older coffee bars on the western side of the waterfront, where the street markets were held and where the first boats had ferried relief into Tolemac.

Sean was dressed in a pilot's uniform and looked suave and upbeat. David realized that every new encounter with Sean showed his rapid reintegration into the world of work.

"What makes you sure Marc Gordon will help?" David asked.

"He's in New Eden's Congress, similar to your Executive Committee. Gordon's a man of considerable wealth, who lost his wife a few years ago. Since then he has refocused his life, entered politics and is giving back most of his fortune to the needy. He offered to take my case to court but I told him not to waste his money and came out here instead."

"So there are philanthropic types in the Capitalist realm, after all!"

"Yes, but they are a dying minority. I'll call him today and arrange for a conference link with you."

The following day, David met with Nathan and they reviewed his draft WorkOUT plan. The plan was still missing a few touches but its essence was clear. Nathan suggested that they could safely assume it would pass through the Executive Committee and that they should send Congressman Gordon a copy to study before their New Eden visit.

A few days later, Samson, David and Sean were on the Communicator in Samson's study to Congressman Gordon who had received the advance copy of the WorkOUT plan, plus a copy of the near-bankrupt Dependents Program for comparison. Samson paced up and down before the call came through.

"I can't remember this Gordon fellow. Wasn't around during my dealings with them," Samson said.

"He's new. He entered politics four years ago and has made quite a name for himself," said Sean. "He doesn't follow the herd."

"And Nathan's WorkOUT plan—it's not even ratified in Tolemac yet." Samson was still pacing.

"But it's just what we need to show them that our plans do expect human effort in return for charity." David said.

The Communicator light went on and a raspy voice said, "Gordon."

"Hi, Congressman, sir! It's Sean Galloway."

"Galloway! Nice to hear from you again. So you made it?" The voice was kindly and measured. Samson flicked the two-way video switch and a grey-haired man with aristocratic features came into view. Samson also stopped pacing so the congressman could see him and the others in the study.

"Yes, and thanks to you. Mr. Gordon, sir. I have Sam and David Arthurs from the City of Tolemac with me. As I mentioned in my earlier note to you . . ." and Sean went on with introductions. Gordon smiled as he spoke. He did not look like one of the dreaded Capitalist power types, but rather like the fine-boned, well educated and refined old type one met at university. This became more evident as his picture got clearer—the reception was not always the greatest between the Humanitarians and the Capitalists—there had been no real investment in Infoway infrastructure between them, unlike within their respective realms. Even Samson's skeptical eyebrow began to smoothen out as Sean concluded the introductions.

Gordon got right to the point despite his collegial air: "Gentlemen, I've read your plans—the Dependents one will not fly here—it has no return. But the WorkOUT one might have a better chance."

"Thank you!" David piped in, fearing Samson would say something controversial.

Surprisingly, Samson followed with, "Mr. Gordon, we really do appreciate you trying to support us on this. Believe me, I have tried many times in the past."

"We do have an emerging group of influential people in this state who are interested in your ideals. Some of these people are even in Congress now. I've arranged for a cross section of them to meet you when you get here. I hope you can respond to all their questions appropriately. I caution you, they do not stand any weakness."

Samson smiled. "Arguments we can always provide. It's intransigence we've had to deal with so far."

"Well, I'll see about opening doors on this side. When are you coming?"

"A week Thursday."

"Good. We'll be ready. Here's some homework I want you to do before that."

Gordon went on to point out some areas in the WorkOUT plan that looked weak, and David promised to work on them with Nathan. For the next ten minutes of discussion, David began to get a warm feeling about Congressman Gordon—his kind exterior was tinged with toughness. He was also a sharp businessman, keenly aware of, and expecting good returns on investment.

"I think you've sold him!" Sean said, after they terminated the call.

Even Samson was beginning to look optimistic. "This is the best luck I've had so far."

David smiled. "I guess we needed some inside help after all."

*　*　*

Leo Patimkin took deep breaths trying to quell his panic attack. He was getting them more frequently of late. He blamed it on the exams. He was definitely going to flunk math. Why the heck did his father not see that and play to his strengths? They'd had another row this morning, when Leo had asked Vladimir about letting him apprentice at the Communications Centre after high school, in lieu of attending university. Didn't his father know that he was a practical type of a guy, who learned by doing?

But he knew it was the other thing that was bothering him more. Yesterday, he had caught Joe and Sally having sex in her den. Having sex! Just like that. He had called over for his twinning session, half an hour earlier than expected, and seen Joe's car parked outside. He should have turned back, gone away and come back at the right time. But, no, his curiosity got the better of him. He'd gone around the side of the Morden house and peeped in through the window. The rest of the house was in darkness. Joe was straddling Sally on her desk. The look of utter pleasure on her face made him gasp—she was enjoying herself! Joe climaxed with a roar and they rolled off the desk onto the cushions below and Leo heard her say, "Oh Joe, that was great—I wanna do it again and again and again . . ." Damn fools, they were breaking the law—again and again and again! Premarital sex was illegal in Tolemac—didn't they know that? He slunk away from the window, completely dejected and lost.

Then yesterday, to add to his misery, Johnny Garcia had come by and said that he had got his hands on a sample of that stuff they'd had at the party a few months ago.

"How did you manage that?"

"It's easy. You can buy the stuff out by the docklands now. Joe has connections."

"Did you try it?"

"Well, I was kind of forced to. We were at this party last week, see."

"At the Waterfront Hotel?"

"Yeah. Everyone was taking a hit, as they called it. Came around to my turn, how could I refuse?"

"You . . . bastard!"

"Cool it now! What could I do?"

"You could have refused!"

"And be the odd one out? I don't know about you but I have difficulty with that. I was sick afterwards though. Try anything once I said."

"And you had your simulated orgasm?"

"Joe gave us some pictures—dirty ones from New Eden—said he got them off one of the boats. After we took the stuff, some of the guys did it with the girls who were there. Right there on the floor. It was kind of creepy to see people I knew so well act like that. I was too scared of that. So I shagged instead. I must have done it about six times!"

"Six times!"

"Yeah. Do you want to try it? I pinched a couple of 'hits' from the party. Try it—you feel kind of shitty afterwards, but it's great while it lasts."

Now he was sitting in his bedroom staring at the two yellow capsules that Johnny had left behind. Artificial stimulation would give him the orgasm he knew he could never enjoy with Sally Morden. He was too frightened to take them in the house, though, not knowing how he would behave, and his kid sisters, Olga and Larissa, were always snooping in on him. "Try anything once." He swore if he took them, it would only be to check them out; he was never going to get hooked. But he could not stifle the waves of panic that surged through him.

He slipped the capsules into his pocket and left the house through the side door. It was just after nine o'clock, and the rest of the family was watching an old movie on the Communicator. "Be back soon," he said to his mother who looked up anxiously as the side door creaked open. His father did not even look up; he was still simmering from their argument earlier in the day.

Leo headed for the Waterside Park. There, amidst the shade trees and hidden from everyone, he could try this stuff and get it over with. Very few people were out at this time of the night; just a few dog walkers and some young married couples stargazing. He took the capsules out and stared at them. "Try anything once." "And lose everything you've stood for," another voice said. "I'm only trying it so I know the pitfalls my generation is getting into." "Yeah, yeah—you know that already—why do you have to take the wretched stuff? You just want to shag yourself silly and blame it on these drugs. Leo is a coward; he can't get Sally Morden!" The voice kept taunting him. His heart was racing and suddenly he had burst out of the shelter and was running full tilt for the sea wall. En route, he nearly knocked down an old lady and her two dogs. The animals started yapping behind him and the old lady was panic stricken to see this wild youth running as if he was about to jump into the sea and drown. As he hit the railing, Leo flung his arm in an arc and the capsules sailed out and were lost in the waters below. He hung there, half over the railing, panting; he was drained and relieved at the same time.

"Are you all right, dear?" It was the old lady, whom Leo recognized as Frida Parks, the city's favourite spinster. Her dogs were nipping at his ankles.

"Yes, I'm all right. I just had to get rid of something." He was still panting. Then the regret of blowing his chance to experiment took over, and he lost it. "How did you manage to live without having sex all your life?"

"Well, I'll be . . ." Frida jumped back, swelling with a mixture of anger and embarrassment, flummoxed by the question coming from this strange youth, who looked vaguely familiar in the deepening dusk. "How dare you!"

Immediately, he felt sorry for what he had said. She pulled her dogs back and strode away, remarking, "I just don't know what this younger generation is coming to!"

"No, no," he called after her. "I didn't mean it. I need your advice . . ." But Frida Parks and her dogs had already been swallowed up by the night.

*　　*　　*

A day before their departure to New Eden, David sat in his school office staring out the window, wondering if he had everything ready for the trip. He had spent a lot of time fine-tuning the WorkOUT plan based on Congressman Gordon's feedback. He hoped that he, Nathan and Samson had covered all the angles. Somehow he needed to link WorkOUT with historical examples of where similar programmes of mixed Capitalist-Socialist principles had worked before the Flood, but the data eluded him.

His mind was a maze of thoughts. He had never been to any part of the Capitalist realm before. He had only been out of Tolemac twice—to Oceania on both occasions—in 2035 and last year. Both times, he had accompanied Samson, who was attending the annual conference of the Federation of Humanitarian

States. The trips had been by boat; David remembered being met by a large number of dignitaries at the other end and being treated with great respect during the visits.

Oceania was about three times larger than Tolemac and benefited from large tracts of agricultural land. Given the larger population base, it also had a strong industrial core and was the leader among the Humanitarian states. David was surprised to see familiar faces during their visits—many Tolemacians had been lured to the larger state for the opportunities it presented them. While Samson attended the first conference, David had explored Oceania and found it flatter than Tolemac. The monorail system was well developed, with routes extending everywhere from the core. Purchasing a day pass, he travelled to most parts of the state. Towns dotted the island and Oceania had successfully devolved its administration throughout most population hubs. He also spent a considerable amount of time at the University of Oceania, wandering through the old halls of that venerable institution which predated the Flood and had withstood the earthquakes. He read many pre-Flood manuscripts, some still water-soiled. As someone who had never attended a bricks and mortar university, U of O had been the highlight of his first visit. Not having the population base to sustain a traditional university, most Tolemacians, including David, attained their tertiary education degrees and diplomas through distance learning by dialling into research libraries around the world via the Infoway.

Samson's comment on that first visit ten years ago was, "There is a lot we can learn from Oceania, and they are keen to share, without pressuring us to follow. The beauty of the Humanitarian Federation is that it respects the freedom of the individual member states, yet is willing to lend a hand when necessary, without interfering in our internal affairs." Upon their return, Samson proposed the monorail system for Tolemac. Following two years of deliberation and evaluation, it was built, and subsequently spurred the birth and growth of the New Settlements.

On his second visit to Oceania last year, David noticed more progress. Most visible were the huge digitized billboards advertising consumer products, some that he had never seen before. Samson was worried during that last visit. "They have loosened trading ties with the Capitalists due to the pressure to remain competitive. If they don't keep a lid on things, this could spell trouble in the long run." News of drugs, and of arson in a factory that had led to a huge explosion in one of Oceania's industrial parks, was heard soon after their return from this second trip.

Now, in the solitude of his office, on an impulse, he dialled up the political history section of the U of O library and scanned the last hundred years preceding the Flood. A lot had happened: the fall of imperialism, the rise (and fall) of Communism and Fascism, two global wars, terrorism, the rise of Capitalism again under quaint terms called Reaganomics and Thatcherism and the fall of the world financial system in the giant stock market slide of 2008, culminating in the Flood that had finally bankrupted the countries of the Old World. But somewhere after the second of those global wars, between 1955 and 1980, there had been a period of peace and flourishing in Western Europe, North America and Australasia where economic growth and care for the individual had moved in lockstep, bringing waves of immigrants to the nations in those prospering regions. A Middle Way had flourished! That was his proof. He copied those sections and added them to the appendices of the WorkOUT presentation.

"But they never lasted," he said, rubbing his eyes and switching his attention to look outside the window. He was pleasantly surprised to see Sally Morden and Leo Patimkin in animated conversation under the giant ghost maple tree, now ash-grey in the early autumn.

Sally was a natural, an A-student, bright and attractive. Leo, on the other hand, was at the bottom end of the class due to his math problems and was now approaching the pinnacle of his inability in that subject. Unfortunately David was not qualified to teach math to the senior classes, so was unable to help Leo anymore. If parents are supposed to endow their children with hereditary genes, this was one instance where that had not happened. The only common denominator between Vladimir and Leo was their mutual attraction to Communicators—Vladimir, to build their systems and infrastructure, and Leo to use them. Leo was the Academy's resident expert on chat lines and information databases and was well versed in the political and economic trends of the day. In this regard, he was a throw-back to his father in those early days of "news central" down at the Patimkin tent.

Still, David was glad to have twinned them, in the hope that Sally's mathematical talent would rub off on Leo. He had also hoped that the hormonal imbalances at this time of youth would not get in the way of their concentration—Leo's mainly.

But all did not seem well out there under the ghost maple tree today. Leo was gesticulating animatedly at Sally, who was trying to quiet him, it appeared. Suddenly, Leo dashed his soda bottle onto the ground, splattering its contents on both of them and strode away angrily. Oh, oh—seems this twinning thing wasn't going so well, after all! But with his impending trip to New Eden, the exams to deal with, an upcoming election and an unsettled wife at home, David was not in a frame of mind to step into another of life's conflicts at that time. His wristwatch pulsed six o'clock as he wearily shoved the printouts into a file and saved the soft copy to his mobile. Time to look over these documents one more time after dinner, he mused, making his way to the exit.

Chapter 16

SHE LAY AWAKE, WATCHING HIM dress in the semidarkness. Normally, he would have approached her for sex last night. But she knew her iciness of the last few days had kept him from reaching out for her, as was his customary habit. She had slept turned away from him, a pillow tightly clenched between her legs.

She felt she was losing him. Not that she knew much about him. Even though they had been married all these years, he still felt like a stranger to her. Was it the yoke of custom that kept them from melding hearts as much as they melded bodies?

On the surface, he was a dutiful husband, a good father, an upstanding member of the community; and now soon to be an elected leader of the city. Any Tolemacian woman would have told her that she had chosen well and made a marriage that she should be happy and grateful to God for. And yet . . .

Was it this apparent loss of David that was driving her towards the foreigner with the lost eyes and open feelings? She felt that Sean Gallagher would hold her in his arms, caress her face, kiss her, enter her body with a passion that matched hers. All the things a dutiful Tolemacian husband could not do. She could see it in the restrained desire Sean had revealed to her at Ethan's party and later in his openness, the night he had come to their home for dinner. But they had not crossed the line yet, even when Sean had held her hand tenderly while on the gallery tour. It had sent a tingling down her spine. They had been so close that night in the gallery and she would have succumbed had David not shown up.

And now, as she watched her husband zip his bag and look anxiously in her direction, she saw him slipping out of her hands in his quest for self actualization in the political arena. She suddenly wanted to cross that line with Sean, if only to hold onto something she never thought attainable in her entire life.

* * *

Kamala drove David and Samson down to the port. Two helicopters sat on the helipad; the other two, were probably in the air somewhere, already at work. They were met by Sean and escorted on board one of the helicopters. The craft held eight seats, including the pilot's, and had a rear area for light cargo. Sean invited David to sit next to him in front. Willy Lo was also on board; he promptly announced that he was going to arrange university entrance for his son Manny. "Gotta get a good education for my Manny, you know—the best kind. New Eden State University is the best," Willy said, buckling up next to Samson. Two engineers from the microchip factory, attending a conference in New Eden, made up the rest of the passengers.

As Sean made final preparations with the ground crew, David's thoughts drifted back to leaving home that morning. While packing his bag in the semidarkness of the bedroom, he realized that Sonya was awake and watching him.

"I'm off!" he'd said, trying to sound cheerful, "I'll bring souvenirs when I return!"

"There are only a few things I look forward to in this marriage. And what I need, I can't get," she'd blurted out. Then she just kept staring at him, making him uneasy. Did she mean sex, or his time? She was definitely confusing him. He shook himself. It must be his time he concluded; sex had been an unarticulated problem between them for a very long time, even before his entering politics.

"Listen honey—this is good for us. If we get this deal clinched, our refugee problem will go away, for good!"

"But after the refugee problem there will be another problem and another. You know that. All you've done this week is prepare for this meeting and work at the school. Once you're on the Executive, we will rarely see you at home."

He grabbed at straws. "Honey, we'll work it out. We'll agree on a plan for balancing my time between commitments. And if the Executive becomes too much, I'll drop the volunteer math classes for the lower grades."

"Just when Joey is going to need your help?"

Realizing his faux pas, he parried. "No, I could take care of Joey at home."

"When, David? When will you have the time for that?"

"Honey, we'll work it out." But he knew he hadn't convinced her. When kissing goodbye, her lips were wooden, dry, but her eyes were alight with suppressed anger. The one redeeming feature was that they had exchanged more words then than in the other half dozen conversations over the past month.

A shuddering broke his reverie. He couldn't hear a word Sean was speaking into the microphone in his helmet. Then they were lifting off and David grabbed his seat feeling he was going to fall off, despite being strapped in. The white rooftops of Tolemac lay symmetrically grid-shaped near the port beneath them as the helicopter spun over the mainland for a few moments before striking out across the water. For first-timers, it was a glorious sight. The roar subsided after initial lift off, but they still had to shout across the cabin to be heard.

The water was muddy brown clearing the shore. "Flood debris still hugs the shoreline in this area. It's the same over in New Eden, only dirtier," Sean explained. As if to confirm this, he swooped down lower and David could see objects under the water: remnants of rotting vehicles, asphalt, concrete, even whole portions of buildings now calmly reposing beneath the risen waters. On David's two previous voyages these objects hadn't been as visible due to the churn created by the boats he'd travelled in. But from up here, all was revealed, the vanished cities that had once been the north-eastern corner of North America. "But it gets clearer when you go further out," Sean assured his passengers.

A craggy rotting platform, sporting flags of both the Humanitarian and Capitalist realms went by below them.

"Brady's Island Bar," Samson spat from the side of his mouth, loud enough for all to hear. "The original one. Now's he's opened another one further up ahead."

There were boats moored alongside the island bar, and many others were coming and going. Brady was running a thriving business.

"And you still haven't shut him down, eh?" Willie Lo said.

"Sometimes our Humanitarian laws are too kind. And I'm not the only one making them. He just manages to stay out of our reach."

"See that mast sticking out of the water?" Sean pointed to a needle-like column rising out of the water. "That's all that lies above water of the old CN Tower. It's a landmark for boats. Might not last too long as there is erosion at its base."

Samson leaned over and waved at it, his displeasure over Brady easing. "I climbed that tower as a boy. It was the world's tallest freestanding structure at the time. Remember, Willy?"

"Sure. We don't build that tall anymore," said Willy, giving it his builder's eye.

As they headed further into the lake-turned-ocean, the water began to turn into a beautiful turquoise and the roar of the helicopter became monotonous. The scenery settled into endless, gentle rolling waves upon clear water. Small boats, bobbing up and down, came into view.

"Passenger boats?" David enquired.

"Fishing boats," Sean replied. "The ones carrying passengers hug the coastline. These ones come right out into the middle of the ocean to escape the polluted coastal waters. I still think the fish here are suspect, although they put them through irradiation processes back on shore. People who eat this fish live out in the 'colonies.' It's poor man's protein."

Another dual flag-waving platform came into view, much larger than the previous one. It had a larger vessel that looked like a passenger liner moored alongside.

"Brady's sure hit the big time with this one!" Sean said. Samson remained frowning in the back seat. The newer island bar had a sign on its rooftop, pointing skywards and was clearly visible to those in the helicopter. "I guess he's out to attract air traffic too, now that we have a helicopter service."

"And don't you dare take him up on his offer!" Samson growled.

"Will we pass any of the colonies?" David asked.

"Sure, I'll swing by one. Some are not too far offshore from mainland New Eden."

One of the colonies came into view about twenty minutes later. At first it appeared to be a little island, demure and innocent in the middle of the water, surrounded by oil platforms. But as they neared, the ground was black, with sparse vegetation. Small, dirty houses dotted the island in no particular order; they seemed to have sprouted up wherever there was a bit of available land.

Large industrial plants resembling oil refineries passed below. Oil drills swung to and fro like giant birds pecking to rhythm in their quest for food—up and down and around and all over again. People were busy at manual outdoor work. A few peered at the sky and stared at the helicopter as it passed by. Some stopped working altogether. Sean swung the helicopter in close to see the blank stares on the faces of those on land. It struck David as odd that most vehicles like helicopters and cars now ran on liquid hydrogen or on alcohol-derived fuels, while fossil fuels were still used extensively in manufacturing. It was almost as if the Flood had set the world back technologically in some industrial sectors, while in other sectors, like the computing industry and the genetics industry, it had caused the opposite effect.

"Jersey," Sean explained, looking down at the blackened land mass. "They produce half of New Eden's oil."

"The people down there obviously don't share in the wealth. And they don't have any entertainment down there either, the way they are looking at this helicopter," Samson said.

"Yeah, the wealthy ones, the ones who own the oil fields, are back in mainland New Eden. In the gleaming towers—you'll see," Sean said.

"I have seen," said Samson "You'd better show David."

"How come the people in Jersey have no say or share in the oil wealth?" David asked.

"They are just the workers on fixed wages," Sean explained. "They come here from New Eden. None are forced. Personal economic conditions, caused by bankruptcy, health or marital breakdown, bring them."

"Why?"

"It's cheap to live in the colonies. No minimum wage, no maximum either. One wage will feed a family of four. There's nothing much to buy and no standards to maintain—skid row. Life expectancy is also low. It's the end of the road for someone who can't find a job on the mainland—the bottom of the barrel in our population—the fallen ones."

"Delia and her family would have ended up here if we hadn't taken them in," Samson said.

"Me, too" said Sean.

"You?" David said.

"Yes, after I fell ill and lost my job."

"Must study," Willie broke in, "be best at what you do, then you don't have to worry about colonies."

"If education will ensure good health—sure," said Sean, and swung the controls pushing the helicopter back over the water again and towards another distant shoreline that they were soon to discover was New Eden.

This land mass was much bigger. Its coastline was crowded with boats, many big ones that looked like ocean liners or freighters. For the first time, they saw other helicopters moving around in their airspace. Larger aircraft that looked like airplanes were ascending and descending over a point somewhere inland—New Eden International Airport. What caught David's eye were the glimmering towers along the shoreline: tall buildings, encased in glass or gold, that caught the sunlight and threw it back.

They landed amidst the towers in the city centre. Sean explained that it was a downtown helipad for business travelers, and that it saved the commute to and from the airport, which was about forty-five minutes away. The whole street was in a shadow thrown by the towers, which made everything look cold and damp. "New Eden does not have a problem with flooding. These buildings had foundations reaching deep underground," Sean explained.

All foreign visitors had to line up in front of a bank of Communicator kiosks and complete a landing script. A plastic digitized card automatically popped out as a receipt. Burly NADF guards, armed with rifles, peered closely, ensuring that each visitor scanned his new smart card at a security gate reader that subsequently opened, allowing exit from the helipad. When David enquired about this, Sean laughed. "That card is part visit visa and part marketing device. It has a radio frequency and makes a record of all the places you visit while in New Eden. This helps people like the police keep track of you. It also helps the establishments you visit, especially the shops and entertainment venues. They'll send you marketing information after you depart. It's a real pain. I suggest you leave this card behind at Congressman Gordon's and use it only when exiting New Eden."

The speed at which everything moved was pronounced. Cabs lined up to collect passengers: yellow cars that all looked the same and that zipped in and out of traffic to get passengers to their appointments on time. Willie was whisked off in one of them.

Sean hailed a cab, too. People walked fast on the sidewalks and did not seem to know each other. If they did, they did not slow down to say 'hi,' as they did in Tolemac. And there were no cyclists, although rollerbladers were everywhere and some even had skates with motorized blades that gave out a hissing sound as they whipped in and out of traffic.

David could see why everyone in Tolemac was crazy about the material goods of New Eden: gigantic stores lined whole streets and "for sale" signs were everywhere. Giant digitized screens, about ten stories high, stood at every street corner running glittering commercial advertisements. The images were jarring, and convincing. Passing the Fruitalicious drink advertisement, David suddenly felt thirsty! Very soon his temples began to throb. In timely fashion, Sean remarked from beside the cab driver, "Do you feel the buzz? New Eden does this to me. It takes getting used to. We call it the frenetic energy of Capitalism."

"It sure is. But who are those people on the sidewalks sitting with what looks like all their earthly possessions?"

"They are the 'fallen ones' as we call them, looking for their next opportunity. Some are newcomers to New Eden; they usually walk around in a daze for a while, gaping at everything before finding work."

"And do they find work?"

"Oh, sure— the resilient find something. And if one is unsuccessful, at the other end of the opportunity spectrum, there's always the colonies."

"I must get some gifts for the kids," David remembered.

"There's a department store a block ahead on the Avenue of the Classic Americas. We'll pull over and circle while you duck in and out. Don't be long, for we could get ticketed," Sean gave instructions to the cab driver. The man appeared reluctant at first. Then Sean slipped him a bill and the driver nodded, picking up the pace, and cutting in and out of the slow-moving traffic in the city core.

Sean carried on his commentary, "Most of the buildings are less than ten years old. They knocked down all the old ones after the Flood, as they were unsafe. Fierce competition for real estate makes landlords build more facilities into their buildings all the time, so obsolescence is very high. So are the rents."

The cab let him off at the corner of the Avenue of the Classic Americas, a straight broad street with tall buildings on either side. Samson decided to stay in the cab with Sean. Morby's, the department store, was at the intersection of the

Avenue and Madison Street. It was a huge building, eight floors—all of it a department store. And yet it looked dwarfed by encircling larger office buildings. David pushed through the imposing brass doors, where two armed security guards in full combat gear stood in attendance. Entering, he was transported into another world. Not having seen a department store before—Tolemac only had general stores and strip malls—he was ready to be educated.

First, there was the piped music playing softly in the background and following him down soft, carpeted aisles—gentle and relaxing sounds that shut off the blaring traffic outside. The vapours in the air changed and took the theme of the various departments within the store. Beautiful women hovered around— shop attendants, he soon discovered, who made it a point to accost each customer, trying to sell them something. They all appeared to be in their early twenties. They all had the same hair and eye colour and he wondered which factory had cloned them. As he was looking for books, they shooed him into the library department where the air smelled of ink and classical music played. They even knew him by name and all he had done was flash his smart card at the store entrance where a greeter stood with a device in hand and a wide smile on her face. As he turned the corner into the children's section, carnival music took over and the classical strains faded. Sean had mentioned building upgrades, and the acoustics in here were cleverly designed to transmit the customer from one world to the next in a matter of steps. A beautiful, blond salesgirl, whose name badge read Mandy, plied him with books on children's adventure—there were titles and authors he had never even heard of—where had all these writers been? And he thought he was a reading aficionado! Declining the salesgirl politely, David moved on to the section on painting and crafts to look for a book for Hannah. The choice was daunting, so, closing his eyes, he grabbed the first one. Then he went back to the adventure section and picked up an old "cowboys and crooks" book for Joey, even though Samson would not approve of his choice. Heck, he even felt like reading all this stuff, lost from his own youth! Moving onto the confectionary section, the air first smelled of chocolate, then liquorice, then candy apple. The selection was enormous and he felt the beginnings of a headache. Mandy had handed him over to Sandy, the confectionary expert. People around him were stuffing their shopping carts as he walked around scared to choose anything, just marvelling at the variety. Sandy soon lost interest in him, and with a "If you need me, just call…" moved onto another customer who was pushing a bulging shopping cart.

David was agape in the food section. There was no smell of raw fish and no jumble of fresh produce as in Tolemac. Everything was in packets, precooked, and looked very sanitized. No wonder this section could be adjacent to men's clothing!

He ambled over into the men's clothing and accessories department and was just beginning to wonder why men in New Eden needed so many support mechanisms to maintain their physical appearance, when he spotted the thief. The man didn't look out of place, and was elegantly dressed like most of the customers; however, when David observed him closely, his suit looked like a prop; it did not become him. The man's swarthy features, rough manner and darting looks were unlike those of the mainly urbane people in the store. Curly locks of black hair fell on his collar obscuring it. He had a device in his hand, which he held momentarily over selected pieces of merchandise. After zapping an item—a watch, a shaver, a pocket communicator—he would quickly pick it up and deposit it into a bag he was carrying, which did not sport Morby's logo. He moved swiftly, dodging the prowling salesgirls. David followed him instinctively, mesmerized by this man who was deliberately going about his thieving business in broad daylight. One part of David wanted to shout out and warn employees in the store; the other part was struck dumb with fascination. Just then two big security guards, clad in combat gear and carrying guns, descended the escalator. One pointed in the direction of the man and they both jumped the last few steps and ran toward him.

The thief took off, pushing and shoving people out of his way, heading in David's direction. David remained frozen. Then an inner voice, nurtured on Tolemac's persistent teaching of social justice, screamed inside, "Don't let him get away!" As the thief grazed past, David mechanically stuck out his leg, tripping the man and sending him headlong into a clothes rack that collapsed, bringing down all the clothes on top of him. The thief gave a David a deadly look and violently struggled to escape, but the guards were on him by then. One guard placed his gun at the man's head and shot a bolt of electricity that made the thief convulse violently and flop back into the pile of fallen clothes. The second guard grinned, saying, "Better play it safe," and shot a second bolt of lightning from his gun into the fallen man whose torso jerked and smoked on the floor. The guards grabbed the man like a piece of discarded merchandise and hauled him out of sight of the staring customers and staff.

The break in the normal flow of store activity was over quickly; shoppers and salesgirls looked curiously at the limp thief being carted away, and resumed their shopping and selling.

David shivered as he made his exit from the scene. In the brief instant that their eyes had met, David had seen flashes of the thief's character—the humiliation and anger at being caught, and the defiance to continue doing what he did if another chance presented itself.

*   *   *

"They sell those 'zappers' in some of the underground stores here," Sean explained later, in the cab. "It neutralizes security tags on the merchandise, so the thief can pass through checkouts undetected."

"But that makes the sale of these zappers illegal?"

"It's not a case of legal or illegal. Everything is on sale here. The bad guys have equal chance of success as the good guys. The good guys just have to be smarter and on the side of the law or we will sink into anarchy. Those security guards must have used some pretty sophisticated equipment to track the man in the act—not forgetting the help they received from a vigilante like you!"

"Why did they shoot a helpless man?"

"Oh, they taser them all right. Given the double-dose he got, that guy is probably only good for the colonies now."

"Welcome to New Eden, son," Samson intoned from the back seat and gazed out of the window.

The cab drove through the city and into its outskirts and the high-rises began to thin out. Soon the road led onto a ramp and David got a shock as they merged into a giant multi-lane highway with about ten lanes of traffic going in both directions. There were vehicles whizzing around at very high speeds.

Sean chuckled, "Hold on to your seats folks—this is the expressway taking us into the suburbs of New Eden—we are heading into Palm Hills, an exclusive hideaway for the rich and famous—Congressman Gordon's stomping ground."

After about twenty minutes, they took an exit ramp and the geography changed. They were into rolling green hills, a landscape dotted with large houses spread far apart from each other with high walls and cameras mounted on them. Most had armed guards patrolling their perimeters.

"The rich need protection," Sean said.

"From the fallen ones?" smirked Samson.

The cab drove past a grove of trees and turned into a lane. The drive down this palm-tree-lined lane was soothing and the shade welcoming. They pulled up at a large gate. There was no guard, but Sean announced their names into a microphone at the gate and it opened automatically, shutting behind the moment the cab pulled inside. The driveway led to a large brown three-story house with bay windows and gables. It was an architectural relic of pre-Flood days, but because of the wooden trim around the roof and doorway, it looked very recently built.

"I guess, this is where I leave you," Sean said, helping with the bags. "I've got some business in town. David, if you feel like sightseeing, here's my number downtown. I could pick you up around seven this evening. And remember our flight leaves at ten o'clock tomorrow morning, on the dot."

David immediately recognized Congressman Gordon who met them at the large oaken front door. He was tall, dressed in a blue blazer and tie with navy pants and black shoes that gave him a pre-Flood, retired naval commander look.

"So glad you could come!" Their host ushered them into a spacious foyer. A staircase led off from the main lobby into the rooms upstairs. They passed a living room full of ceiling-height bookcases, sturdy reading tables and lounge chairs, and went out into a large back garden, which even for November was leafy and full of flowers. High walls ran around the entire property shutting it off from the outside world. This was very different from Tolemac, where low fences separated properties, if at all. At a table in the middle of the garden, a group of men and women, dressed in conservative dark suits, were engaged in animated conversation but stopped the moment the newcomers stepped through the living-room doors.

Congressman Gordon introduced his guests to the dozen or so members of what he called the Knights of Eden, a group dedicated to the restoration of human rights to all citizens of New Eden. Although there were many people there that day, David only remembered the most important names in the ensuing conversation—Luke, Matt, Jean and Marc, which was Congressman Gordon's first name. He figured he'd call them the "four apostles" as a memory jogger.

The two attendants serving tea were an interesting twist on the notion of wait staff. They were mechanized robots, almost human in appearance down to their liveried uniforms, answering to voice commands delivered by Congressman Gordon. David had a hard time taking his eyes off them. He had never seen such creations in the Humanitarian realm—except perhaps for those fictional robots in the old sci-fi movies from Samson's collection.

When everyone had settled down and been served tea by the "attendants," Marc Gordon rose. "My dear friends, thank you all for coming today." Turning to Samson, he remarked, "We have studied your proposal for stemming the outflow of refugees and restoring dignity to our fallen ones—the WorkOUT plan, not the other one. It has great promise. But we have many questions, naturally, and I hope you will indulge us for the next few minutes . . ."

With that, they spent the next hour grilling Samson on the various aspects of the plan, his modus operandi to sell it to Tolemac's Executive, the funding formula, the payback, the results, the expected uptake on it and so on.

Samson got increasingly energized as the questioning deepened. For the first time in all his efforts with the New Edeners, he was in front of an audience that was interested and engaged. They were very intelligent, too, most of them being retired business people who certainly knew their ROIs and demand-supply theories.

"Have you tested WorkOUT?" Luke asked.

"No," Samson replied openly and David came to the rescue saying, "We hope to implement it based on our principle of 'to each according to his need and from each according to his ability.' Tolemacians were raised on this principle and could relate to it easily—we expect this to be more of a communication challenge rather than a selling one."

"Who funds the shortfall on your Dependents Program today?" asked Jean, a hawkish-looking woman who was inspecting the charts in fine detail.

"Well, that is a burden of our greater society and every Tolemacian needs to bear it, even if it means higher contributions to our governance budget. We need to give according to the needs of our fellow brethren," Samson said.

"So you would expect the citizens of Tolemac to subsidize WorkOUT, too, if it does not meet expectations?"

"Yes. In the end, someone pays; we like to spread the burden."

"Yeah, I can relate to that," said Matt. "Otherwise you pay for it some other way—increased security for the rich, or the poor guys come and steal all our stuff anyway. That's what I have been trying to get our folks in Congress to see all these years."

As the conversation progressed, it became clear to David that this group was a strong lobby in their Congress. The Knights of Eden were trying hard for reforms to their existing system. And they were trying to strengthen this bid by building similar coalitions in other Capitalist states.

"But let me remind all of you, dear colleagues," said Congressman Gordon, "ours is still a fledgling movement and we cannot push too fast too soon."

The meeting broke up with a firm commitment by the Knights of Eden to twin with the Executive Committee of Tolemac and to work together and keep each other informed on progress of the WorkOUT bill's passage through the Executive.

The meeting was followed by a sumptuous lunch. Alcohol was served and the conversation became garrulous at times. But no one was rude or irreverent. The robot attendants answered commands speedily and methodically as Marc Gordon spoke directly to them, issuing new orders. They stopped whenever he spoke, listened, and resumed working.

"Don't worry," Jean, sitting next to David, said. "The attendant will bring you your soda. He's had so many requests, it's sitting in his queue somewhere. But he will get to it in order of priority."

She'd no sooner finished speaking when the soda arrived at his side. David turned instinctively to say "thank you," but the robot had moved on to attend to his next task.

"A small step forward," Samson said later, as they made their way to the guest rooms where they would spend the night. "But further than we've ever come in all these years. Thanks for introducing me to Marc Gordon."

"It's a pity you two did not meet earlier. I guess he was busy building his business empire, while you were building Tolemac."

Then Samson chuckled, "I was going to say something about those robots, but thought better of it. They could have eliminated machines and provided employment to about four 'fallen ones' instead."

"That would have been pushing it," David agreed. "But you know, I couldn't help but think the Capitalists are the real creators in this world! Just the stuff I've seen today—mood-altering interiors, wide highways, glittering buildings, mechanized manpower and all that stuff. They are stretching our imagination to the endless possibilities that still exist on this planet. We Humanitarians, on the other hand, apply technology in our farms and microchip factories. But we do not create anything—well maybe buttons instead of zippers. These guys are the real architects while we are the construction workers."

"Now, now—no sense in knocking what you have—'the grass is always greener,' they say. Remember, we had all those things before the Flood and it did not help us."

"I get the feeling these Knights of Eden are trying to do what neither the Humanitarians nor the Capitalists have done—fuse the best of both our worlds. And they could be onto something." David saw Samson pause at his words, before going into his room. As David let himself into his own room, which adjoined Samson's, the "Middle Way" idea began to percolate in his mind again.

*   *   *

That evening, Congressman Gordon took them on a tour of his estate in a jeep, one of four vehicles in his garage. His property was double the size of the Waterside Park and horses grazed in the tall grass.

"We don't have a lot of farmland, just grazing fields for cattle and horses. Our food is imported from Alberta and Mexico," Gordon explained. He went on to tell them that he was childless and that after his wife had passed away five years ago, he had retreated to this ranch to raise horses and work for causes such as the Knights of Eden.

Samson tried to look interested in the ranch and its environs, but because material wealth and possessions didn't catch his fancy, it was hard for him. He kept flicking at the black flies buzzing constantly in and out of the uncovered jeep.

"You must have worked really hard to buy this spread," David said.

"The building industry was very busy in the post-Flood stage. That was my line of work. I guess I was lucky," Congressman Gordon replied.

"And you got to keep all your money?" David asked. Having explained Tolemac's voluntary contribution system to the Knights of Eden during lunch and getting some raised eyebrows, he was keen to know how the other side treated the accumulation of wealth.

"Well, it's an 'each man for himself' system here. I get to keep all my earnings, but I also get to pay for my own security and for Medicare. Some of us pooled our monies for economies of scale and for bulk buying of some of these services, but it's pretty scattered. But then with our system, there's always someone willing to offer you a deal."

"I prefer our system," Samson said smugly.

"Yeah, yours has merit. But our challenge is going to be to get everyone contributing to a WorkOUT program over here. No one sees the problem until they are in it themselves, and by then it's too late to start anything."

Sitting out on the open prairie in the cool evening breeze, David found it difficult to believe that this was also part of the big, bad and bold New Eden that Humanitarians often spoke of in awe and fear back home. If not for the broader panorama and bigger buildings, they could have been back in Tolemac. The only reminder that even people like Congressman Gordon were never really secure from the threat of being robbed or harmed by the less fortunate, was his portable Communicator always at his side. It tracked the movements of potential thieves around his property to a master console under surveillance by his security guards back at the house.

Congressman Gordon pointed to a black patch on the wall of his barn as they passed. "We had a security breach a couple of months ago. Someone broke into my property and started a fire to stampede the horses and ride them away in the confusion. We lost a couple of animals, but, more importantly, my bodyguards shot all the thieves."

"Shot them? Isn't that taking the law into your own hands?" David said.

"We do have the power and freedom of self-defence, and the right to bear arms to do that. Without that ability, we would be overrun by the 'fallen ones.'

Do I like it? No. But what alternative do we have, unless we neutralize miscreants with your type of programs?"

"I am glad we met," said Samson. "I've been looking for someone like you in New Eden for a long time."

"Oh, we've been around. We've just been smothered in New Eden's drive to find its balance. The 'nice to do' things got left aside. But it is now time to remind ourselves of what it means to be human again. It's just such a long road back." Marc Gordon was suddenly looking rather tired.

When they arrived back at the house, a man toting a rifle, who looked familiar, met them at the garage.

"Nice day out there, Billy," their host said.

"Billy!" Samson exploded and leapt out of the jeep. "Billy White Dove—well I'll be darned!" He embraced the small, armed man and hugged him tight.

"Nice to see you, Mr. Samson!" Billy said. It seemed to David that Billy had gained weight and lost most of his hair since he'd last seen him.

"You know each other?" Congressman Gordon asked. "Billy is one of my longest-standing bodyguards."

"He is also one of our lost sheep. Why did you take off just like that, Billy? My God, we have such a lot to catch up on." Samson was still pumping Billy's hand, grinning from ear to ear.

"Oh, it's a long story, Mr. Samson—maybe I'll tell you one day," Billy said, looking around furtively.

Just then a short, squat woman of about thirty-five came round the corner of the garage, carrying a baby, with another toddler in tow. Billy looked awkwardly at her and said. "Mr. Samson, this here is my wife Rosa and two of my 'Capitalist children,' Pedro and Felicia."

The woman smiled shyly, showing gaps in her teeth. She wore faded, but clean clothes.

"You have a wife—another one?" Samson's face started to cloud over and Billy shifted his feet. Sensing the tension, Congressman Gordon said, "Billy, can you put the jeep away? My guests need to rest. Perhaps we can all catch up a bit later, yes?"

Samson nodded stiffly at Rosa and mumbled, "I'll see you later," to Billy and let himself be steered back to the house with David following closely on his heels.

"Well—I'll be! He was a drunkard once. Now he is a bigamist too!"

"Not anymore," Congressman Gordon said. "Billy went on the wagon ten years ago when he left that Brady outfit and came to work for me. Got married again—said something about an annulled marriage before that—"

"Which is a lie—he still has a wife back in Tolemac who waits for his return every day. His Tolemacian children can hardly remember him; we literally raised them, after Billy ran away."

"I see. Well, we can't prosecute him in New Eden. We do not recognize your laws, yet. Maybe we will one day. Billy is a good and trusted worker though, and a kind and loving family man. Come, a nice cup of coffee would be just the right thing now."

"I guess so," Samson agreed. "Things were going so good, until I saw Billy."

Chapter 17

DAVID TOOK UP SEAN'S OFFER to spend the evening in town with him. Congressman Gordon and Samson got engrossed in a game of video chess all through the late afternoon and into the evening; heated discussions on the pros and cons of their respective political systems occurred periodically. Billy White Dove did not make another appearance.

Sean was at the front gate of the Gordon estate at seven o'clock in the same yellow cab. As they sped off along the expressway in the gathering twilight, the golden towers in the distance transformed into glittering columns of light. Nearing the city, David felt his pulse heighten again; there was a stepped up vibration here, he realized, that could be addictive to someone who lived for long periods in the city core. His heart was racing by the time they slithered into the slow-moving downtown traffic. With nightfall, the giant neon signs had amplified their presence and throbbed to cacophonous music as the cab rolled down Jefferson Avenue, the city's main drag.

"Electric, isn't it?" Sean shouted over the blaring sounds. "Always gave me a buzz when I used to live here."

"You must find Tolemac boring."

"No. Not now. I think I am slowing down. New Eden's good for the occasional visit—not to live in permanently. Besides, this buzz is not good for my health anymore."

The cab let them out on a side street leading off Jefferson, in front of a mammoth neon sign that read 'The Pink Gypsy.'

"This was my favourite nightclub, once. Not too mean. Nice music. Watch out for the girls—they can be predatory."

"And this is good for your health?" David said, his excitement mounting. Tolemac did not have nightclubs or bars. He felt a sense of abandon, like an errant seventeen-year-old; perhaps he'd be more understanding of his students when he returned.

At the entrance, a woman in her late thirties, with wild blond hair and a heavily made-up face, broke away from a group of men and headed over. The men were dressed in sleek bomber jackets similar to what Sean had been wearing when he first came to Tolemac. They stared curiously in David's direction.

"Well, well, if it ain't our good old Sean the Brawn himself?" The woman gave Sean a big hug and smacked him a kiss full on the lips. "Where have you been hiding out, honey?"

"It's been awhile. David—this is Sugar—a friend from the old firm."

The woman threw David a purring, inviting look that gave him goosebumps. She perused the newcomer from head to toe, and tried to hide her disappointment. She turned back to Sean, "Where have you been—it must be two years? You kind of dropped out of the scene."

"It's a long story. Let's say I emigrated."

"You didn't go to one of those colonies?"

"Oh, no. Better. I live in a very civilized place now. Tolemac."

"Ah, you've gone over to them socialists then, have you?"

"Yes. But be kind—my friend is a socialist. They call themselves 'Humanitarians.'"

The woman smiled teasingly at David. "Didn't mean to be rude, honey. But you are welcome. C'mon in."

She stepped between the two men, slung her bare arms around their shoulders and herded them inside. David could smell the combination of perspiration and strong deodorant on her, and it was exciting. Other than Sonya, he'd never been so close to a woman that he could actually smell her!

The room, the size of a huge hall, was vibrating with music, and psychedelic colours changed on the walls continuously. There was a raised stage in the centre. A bar ran right around, stacked with bottles of varying colours. The walls seemed to dissolve and return, as colours wove around them in the pulsating light. Tall attractive women in slinky outfits emphasizing large breasts were busy serving patrons who thronged around the bar. A bikini-clad waitress led them to a table close to the stage—Sugar had connections. The stage was by far the most riveting part of the room and David sucked in his breath when the next act came on. Three men and three women stepped into the footlights wearing overcoats. After an introductory dance number that was quite sensual, they doffed the heavy coats, revealing stark nakedness underneath and paired off into various acts of copulation—two men, two women and a man and a woman. David's eyes were glued to the stage and his pulse quickened with each parry and thrust of their bodies. He was also embarrassed to note that an erection had taken hold and was getting harder by the minute. He dropped a napkin over his crotch and hoped no one would notice.

"Exciting huh," Sean shouted over the din. "Don't worry; they are actors, teasing everyone into the mood. They don't actually fornicate in public. The real pros are working the floor as you can see. There are private rooms for rent upstairs, if anyone is so inclined, after the show."

Looking around the room, David saw other women now, not as thinly dressed, but appearing quite businesslike, walking from table to table, chatting up the men. There were elegantly dressed male types too, doing the same at other tables where women were seated. "There is prostitution here?"

"No, this is sex among consenting adults, for a fee or for mutual gratification. Man meets woman at the bar. The music, drinks, and show put them in the right mood; they retire upstairs and fuck their brains out. It's a complete package. Welcome to my beautiful city!"

Sugar giggled and pulled out what looked like a long black cigar from her handbag.

"Weed, honey?" she asked Sean.

"No, thanks. Went off that stuff long ago."

"Oh, what's up? You are too clean! What happened to that mean streak I loved?" She dragged on the cigar and her eyes glazed over. She slid her hand down onto his crotch and started nibbling his ear. Sean laughed but didn't restrain her.

"I met Ethan in one of these places," he said.

"That explains how he keeps his sexual appetites at bay." David said.

"He is a wild one. Still flies out here, although he's more secretive now. After all, he's got a reputation to maintain back in Tolemac."

The waitress returned and plunked three different-coloured drinks on the table. Sean inserted a bill into her panties; it seemed the place to deposit payments because many bills hung from that rather fragile piece of clothing, which barely covered her well-shaved pubic area. "Try the cocktails—the red one is the strongest—gin/poppy margarita." David sipped it tentatively. The alcohol, which he had never tasted in his life, burned all the way down his throat, and he started coughing. Within seconds, he started to go numb, a sense of euphoria taking over. Poppy—so there must be opium in it, as well—he was really graduating with honours tonight! The apprehension that had surrounded him since leaving the security of Congressman Gordon's house started to lift. He took a few more sips. A sense of relaxation, almost bravado, was taking hold. This was getting to be fun! Sean finished his drink and signalled to the waitress again. Sugar lost interest in Sean, got on the floor and began dancing by herself. David noticed others doing the same thing from time to time; then they would either retire to the bar, or sit down, or disappear somewhere. Frankly, he didn't care anymore. He downed his glass so as not to be left out. He suddenly wanted to be a part of this scene.

"You know, you are a lucky man, David," Sean was saying.

"Hah? Yeah, this is great! Glad I came."

"No, not because of this. Because you have Sonya."

"What!"

"And Joey and Hannah."

"What the heck are you talking about?" David was coming down to earth with a bang and needed the second drink that had magically appeared in front of him in the last few seconds.

"All this big-city stuff wears out after awhile," Sean said.

"It beats dull old Tolemac any day," David replied, suddenly feeling obstinate. He gulped down the new drink and wanted more. He was spinning out of control, but liking it.

"I was married once," David heard Sean say through a myriad of flashing lights. He pulled himself up only to see that the lights were those reflecting off the walls. The moment he relaxed again, the lights dissolved and Sean's voice seemed to be coming from afar. Like the voice of conscience.

"Yeah? So what happened?" Silly bugger, what's he telling me all this shit for now? Yeah, talking like that—tough, like Bogart in Samson's old movies, sure sounds good. This glass gets more interesting by the minute. Sip, gurgle, course, absorb, relax. This was a great routine. Let the voice go on, let the colours blur all around, let the music make crescendos, like waves from the ocean around him. Sip, gurgle, course, absorb, relax! And do it all over again. Hey, waitress—another please!

"David—better go slow—this stuff hits you harder—later. They mix drugs in them too, sometimes."

"What happened? Go on tell me. What the hell have I got to be so proud of?" He must have been shouting, for even Sugar floated into view from somewhere and said "Everything okay, honey? Come and dance with me."

"No, take David here. He needs some exercise."

Suddenly he was up on the floor and it was great to have a woman's body, Sugar's he guessed, pressed up against him. He sucked in her perfume. He liked her smell. His erection was firm against her and he let her swaying hips cradle and coddle it for a while. God, he needed coddling at that moment.

"I haven't had sex for a month," he said into her ear. "The wife and I—not getting on."

"Oh, you poor darling."

"Yeah, and he says I am lucky!"

"Sean?"

"Yeah. How about you? Do you have sex?" He had become very courageous. This was something he could do now—no restrictions, no Tolemac, no Samson, no Mum, no Sonya and no bloody moral code—hooray for freedom! But he noticed that he was having difficulty staying up on his feet. His knees were buckling and Sugar kept propping him up.

"I have sex all the time honey, simple as eating and sleeping. But you are in no shape for it today. Why don't we sit down now, huh?"

The next thing he knew, he was sprawled on a chair and voices were saying, "Let him sleep it off. Come on honey bunch, we need to catch up on old times in more ways than one. Be wicked to me once again."

"Now, now—don't expect much. I am a reformed man."

"Oh, you are a tease. C'mon let's go upstairs!"

"Come to think of it, it has been a long time!"

Hey, what about me—don't leave me out of the action! But David's knees were paralyzed and his body stuck like a dead weight to the chair. Then Sean and Sugar were gone and he was left with swirling colours, pulsating music and the ebb and flow of people in the hall, like ghosts hovering about the threshold of his consciousness. Before he passed out, it flashed across his mind that this is how it must have been for many people before the Flood, when alcohol and drugs flowed freely—garbled thoughts, paralyzed actions—as they staggered in delusion towards the abyss.

*   *   *

"Slow down" David had his head out of the window and the rushing breeze was blowing the dizziness away. He felt like retching for the umpteenth time and tried to hold it in. "Can't you stop?"

"We can't now, we are on the expressway," Sean said, as the cab raced back to Palm Hills. "Hang in, it shouldn't be much longer."

David had woken from his stupor at the Pink Gypsy, sick and surrounded by his own vomit. Sean helped him clean up in the toilet and gave him a pill for the hangover. David never saw Sugar again.

"I am never, ever going to drink that stuff again," David said, as the waves of nausea shifted around him, thinning out slowly.

"Good! I wanted to give you a once and final dose of it. You Tolemacians live in a dream world."

"I've got such a headache." David leant back in the seat and closed his eyes. Recollection was flooding back. "You said something to me in there, before the lights went out . . . What was it? You were married. Was it?"

"No sense going over that old story again. I'm in no mood for it now."

"No, finish it. Tell me what happened."

"She dumped me. That's all that happened."

"Why?"

"A cancer victim is not a provider anymore."

"But aren't spouses supposed to stick together, especially in the tough times?"

"That's according to your philosophy, especially when you are sober. I'm betting there were times last night, when you felt like calling it quits to wife and family, right?"

David fell silent. Alcohol and drugs loosened and rewrote the rules, however hard coded they were within.

"Who's Sugar?"

"A girl at the helicopter operation where I used to work back here. Knew her before I got married. She somehow came back on the scene after my divorce. She's easy, no long-term commitment—just good 'sex to go.' "

"'Sex to go'?"

"David—get this into your head—in Capitalist society, nothing is for keeps. Everything changes and evolves with time—relationships, health, money, family—everything is 'to go.' "

"Then you folks must be forever in flux."

"My parents divorced when I was ten. They had maxed out their relationship by then they said. We kids just had to cope. They have each remarried three times since then, with respective children from all three marriages. It's normal and expected. Nothing is forever."

"But there are exceptions . . . Congressman Gordon, for instance."

"A few . . . only a few."

Dawn was creeping through on the horizon when they turned off the expressway into the soft, semidarkness of Palm Hills.

"Thanks for the outing," David said. He wished he could sleep another twenty-four hours. He felt warmth towards Sean, something he'd felt right in the beginning when they first met, but had since got muddied over Sonya. "It was certainly an education."

"An education, huh? What happened to the tough talk from last night?"

David blushed and looked out the window.

Chapter 18

SAMSON WAS QUIET ON THE WAY to the helipad. David was sure his father had observed him slinking into Congressman Gordon's house at dawn. The light in the older man's room on the second floor was on at the time. Samson never enquired about the previous evening, nor did David volunteer information about it, although his puffy face and bloodshot eyes said it all.

There were five passengers travelling back with them. A Tolemacian family had attended a relative's wedding in New Eden. While going through departure formalities in the terminal, David saw Sean on the tarmac, looking at his watch. Just a few minutes before they boarded, a man in uniform got out of a car painted in the same livery, and headed over to Sean. They spoke for a while and the man handed Sean a parcel, which he signed for and tucked under his arm. As the two men parted, David recognized the uniformed man.

"That was Jermaine! One of the Brady twins," he said to Sean later, as they boarded.

"Yeah." Sean said. "He runs a courier company here that carries regular parcels for Tolemacians back home. Uses us for express deliveries."

"I went to school with the Bradys, not my greatest friends. Jermaine moved down here after high school. His twin, Jeremy runs a warehouse at the Port of Tolemac."

"They're bad news!" Samson interjected from behind. "Just like that drunkard father of theirs. I'd be careful of what you carry for him."

"Well, mine is not to reason why," Sean said. "I reckon it's pretty innocent stuff anyway. Letters and gifts for the relatives back home and that kind of thing. At least, that's what the customs declaration says."

"Why don't you open it and check?" Samson said.

"And risk getting fired by Ethan? No thanks! I need this job. What can be so dangerous anyway, if it's headed for Tolemac?" Sean tossed the parcel into the baggage compartment, made sure all his passengers were buckled up, slid into the pilot's seat and began preparing for takeoff.

The ride back was uneventful. The Tolemacian family was full of stories of their "shopping expeditions" in New Eden. They were in awe of the place and were planning a follow-up visit soon, much to Samson's chagrin. David gave up his seat in front to one of the family. Forced to sit next to his father in the second row, he was keen to keep the conversation from getting to the events at the Pink Gypsy.

"Did you get a chance to meet Billy?" David asked cautiously.

Samson continued to look out of the window for a while. "He came by the house after you were gone. We chatted."

"Did he tell you anything more?"

"Said he was happy now. That woman is not his wife, she just lives with him and has given him two of the five children he has in New Eden. The other three came from another relationship."

"I heard about these transitory relationships in New Eden."

"Still, Billy says he is able to provide for all five of them and his new mistress. He thanks New Eden for giving him the chance to get over his affliction with alcohol."

"How so?"

"Brady hired him to manage the supply chain from New Eden over to his island bars. Billy is a binge drinker, imbibing when he is depressed. He was constantly surrounded with the stuff working for Brady. He had so much alcohol he developed an aversion to it. He claims to have gotten up one day from his usual hangover and walked away from his habit—just like that."

"I don't believe it! Alcohol is addictive. I'm sure he must have had terrible withdrawal symptoms."

"That's just it. He says once the mind has moved past the addiction, one is cured. He moved past his addiction that day and hasn't looked back since. Like the cripple who picked up his bed and walked in the Gospels."

"So the cure then is to have an excess of the problem till one gets fed up with it and moves beyond it?"

"Seems like it, at least according to Billy. What we practise in Tolemac is keeping temptation at bay, instead of indulging it. Prohibiting it with our laws. There are times I wonder if that has been too restrictive?" There was a frown on Samson's brow.

As the helicopter circled the helipad on the Tolemac end, Delia Stone was standing by the landing area. The wind from the helicopter swirled her flaming red hair. She clasped her hands tightly around her upper body, forcing herself against the blast. As soon as the craft landed, she hurried over.

"Samson, he's taken ill. I think he is going, this time."

"I'll come at once," Samson said. "David, take care of the border formalities, will you?" And with that, taking her hand, he strode away. Tolemac's customs and immigration formalities for returning residents were quite simple. While foreign visitors had a separate line-up and were grilled to ensure that no bogus refugees were making an entry, Tolemacians just had to fill out a form and hand it to a bored-looking border guard in the customs shed at the end of the helipad.

Waiting for the taxi—which took about twenty minutes to arrive—David tried to figure out how to account for his hung-over appearance. Sonya would be at the gallery at this time, so he had till late afternoon to recover and look decent. But what was happening to Doug Stone? And he was uneasy of the role Samson was playing here. Was Samson doing so wilfully, or was he allowing himself to be dragged into it by Delia's vulnerability?

As the taxi rolled up Dundas, he was startled to see posters on the street wall. "When it's time to vote—make sure it is for Ethan Williams—the man with the future vision for Tolemac." How the heck was Ethan out breaking the rules and campaigning, when nominations were only closing next week and campaigning couldn't officially start until then? He directed the taxi to turn around and head to the Executive Committee office. He ran inside, and Mrs. Appegio, Garry's mother, who was the administrative assistant of the office, looked up nervously.

"Well . . . hello there, David," she tittered.

"How come Ethan's declaring his hand so early?" he bellowed.

"Please sit down." The woman shifted, looking over her shoulder.

He stood. "Come on Mrs. Appegio—what's going on?"

"Well, David, Nathan is here—dropping off some papers. Perhaps you would like to speak to him?"

Without waiting for a reply, she rose and scurried into a back office. Nathan came out smiling, hand outstretched.

"David! Back from big, bad New Eden already? My, you look kind of worse for wear?"

"Why is the campaign off so quickly?"

"Oh, that—"

"Yes, that indeed!"

"Well, calm down. Sit down." When Nathan saw that David was doing neither, he continued. "It's like this you see, and I'm reporting this second hand, so don't quote me. I'm not on the selection committee. That's Vladimir, Asif and Morden's job. They received three eligible nominations for the two open positions by the end of last week: Peter Lowry's, Ethan's and yours. Since you were the only candidates who had passed the three-month period as observers, the selection committee decided that nominations were as good as closed. So, a notification went out from the committee yesterday opening the campaign, a week ahead of schedule. You should have the note in your mailbox when you get home. I know it's a bit unusual, but that's what the selection committee decided this time around."

"But it's not fair! I was away."

"Yes, but it usually takes a couple of weeks before the campaign kicks into full gear anyway. No one expected Ethan to spring into action so soon. Would you have been ready, had you not been in New Eden?"

"No, I guess not. Ethan must have been planning this for a while and moved as soon as my back was turned."

Nathan sat down. He took out one of his classic cigars, then remembering that he was indoors, refrained from lighting it, letting it remain in his mouth, like a pacifier in an infant.

"You know, David, that's what I fear some days. Ethan's got the tenacity the pre-Flood generation had in their 'dog-eat-dog' world. I remember that from my Wall Street days, and I still try to keep it alive in business dealings without harming anyone. In Ethan's case, it's a genetic trait and his sojourn in New Eden has sharpened it. It's an edge your generation has lost."

"Is it that vital for survival?"

"I believe so. We Humanitarians have started to 'hunker in the bunker' too much. But enough of this. Tell me that you have some good news from New Eden."

David gave him the brief upshot on their trip—just the parts about the meetings with the Knights of Eden.

"That's great! WorkOUT will spread outside of our borders. It might even be the start to integration with the Capitalists."

"You really think that integration is possible, even necessary?"

"Of course, but your father and the others on the Committee will never hear of it in their lifetimes. We are all one, David—or at least were before the Flood. But we were a sinful bunch then—united in our sinfulness. Now we think that sin is on the other side and we are truly the saved ones. I'm not so sure anymore."

"That's the second person on Committee expressing doubt about the last thirty three years, in one morning."

"Samson too, eh? Wisdom comes from doing, then reflecting. I guess some of us on the Executive are entering that reflective phase."

David left Nathan chewing on his cigar and returned to the taxi that had run a big tab by now, simply idling.

Dropping his things off at home and taking a shower to cool off, he hoped his agitation would ease. It didn't. He was still mad as hell. As the kids were still in school and Sonya was away at the gallery, he decided to pay Ethan a visit at the port.

The administrative offices were about half a mile from the helipad, and right off the main entrance of the port, in the heart of the emerging trendy area. The receptionist looked tentative when he asked for Ethan. "Do you have an appointment?" she asked.

"Yes," he lied, and did not catch himself for a change. He was too agitated to worry about conventions and truth-telling at the moment, precepts he had been raised to believe in. The receptionist made a call. Then she hung up and said that he would have to go over to the adjacent building in the rear. She had him escorted to this building, which had a great big sign above it saying "Williams Enterprises." David had never seen a business advertised so boldly in Tolemac before, especially one tucked away among other port facilities and warehouses. The garish lettering resembled the Pink Gypsy's. Another receptionist greeted him—a man with swarthy features and slicked back hair. He had an air of indifference and spoke with a throaty accent; he wasn't a local. "Mr. Williams's office has no record of your appointment."

"Tell Mr. Williams that we made the appointment on his father's lawn four months ago. I am here to see him, and will not be leaving until I do."

The man made another call. He was transferred a couple of times and each time his indifference softened a bit. Finally, in a voice as soft as jelly, he said, "Yes, Mr. Williams, I'll show him right up."

The man, who then introduced himself as Ogaki, led David through a series of offices up several floors. On each floor, he spoke to the receptionist on duty. All of the offices had interesting names on the walls: Williams Trading, Williams Air Charters, Williams Port Services and finally, the holding company, Williams Enterprises. It was like penetrating an onion to get to its core and Ogaki seemed to have special dispensation. David was surprised to see a security guard with a rifle standing outside the great oak-panelled doors that looked like the end of their quest. To his added consternation and surprise, the guard, a hulk of a man with a broken nose and cropped blond hair, frisked him before letting him in the door.

"What's this for?" David protested.

"Formality sir, for unexpected visitors," the guard muttered and carried on, squeezing every nook and cranny of David's body with a smile of delight that got wider as he progressed. He even squeezed David's crotch.

Finally, he was inside Ethan's office, and the oak doors closed behind him. The room was cavernous. Large windows on either side overlooked the water. The room had a lush, carpeted floor and a huge screen behind a desk that sprawled the entire length of one wall. Ethan, dressed in his signature dark suit, rose from behind the desk and came towards him.

"David—finally, you pay me a visit!"

"What's with the rough-handling guard outside?" David said. His crotch still hurt. Everything hurt, after last night.

"Oh, I'm sorry. I did not have time to instruct Hal that you were an old friend. He's trained for surprises. I brought him along from New Eden when I moved. He's good."

"But you don't need bodyguards here? This is Tolemac, for God's sake?"

"Oh, it's a work habit that I got accustomed to. Besides, Hal runs personal errands for me as well. He's a minder of sorts, and I'm lost without him. Can I get you a drink?"

Without waiting for David's reply, Ethan moved to a panel on the side and slid it open revealing a large refrigerator, full of refreshments of all kinds.

"Water will do," David said.

Getting a bottle of mineral water and a can of grape juice for himself, Ethan gestured to a couple of lounge chairs by the windows. "Make yourself comfortable. Now, what can I do for you?"

David got to the point. "You've launched the campaign already."

"Oh that!" Ethan smiled and sipped his juice. "I was trained not to waste time in business, so I got on with it. What about you?"

"I'll be starting—soon."

"Good! David, I hope you didn't come here just to beat me up on politics. There are a couple of things I want to show you."

Again, brooking no protest, Ethan rose, went over to his desk and picked up a device. He clicked a couple of buttons and the shades came down on the windows and the lights dimmed. The screen behind his desk came into perspective and turned into a giant map of the post-Flood world, with arrows radiating from New Eden in the centre to all ends of the screen.

"While I was apprenticing in New Eden, I worked for a trading company, and we were looking to expand into markets beyond our borders. The Humanitarians didn't want to trade with us. So we looked at Indo-China, which was locked in a civil war under a totalitarian regime at the time. Communication with the outside world was censored and their citizens were thirsting for information and new ideas. Our trading company was also a broker for an information syndicate in New Eden, and we started supplying information and exporting recycled Communicators into Indo-China. We started giving away the hardware, literally for free at first, and had to use black-market channels to do that. It didn't cost us much because the merchandise was destined for the scrap heap anyway. We quickly established a market and swelled the ranks of revolu-tionaries in their villages and towns. When our information started piping through, it constantly reminded them of what they were missing in life— what other 'free' states had in relative abundance. The dictatorship soon fell and once the republic was established, we jacked up prices for our information services; we even established a more realistic price for our hardware, with profit margins built in. Indo-China paid, as this was now considered an essential service. It still is a very lucrative market for my former employer, and we really fulfilled a need for those people. I used that philosophy when I started my own company."

"Are you trying to do the same thing in Tolemac with your helicopters?"

Ethan smiled in the semidarkness, his voice gently mocking. "You catch on fast, David." Then he flipped another button and the map changed to a view of Tolemac in the centre with arrows pointing out from it.

"This is a 'work in progress' map. It's my vision for Tolemac, when I am elected. We could be the trading entrepôt for the whole of our New World, if we desired. And we don't need to produce everything ourselves—just be the transhipment and repackaging centre."

"And we would sacrifice the lifestyle that we have known so far?"

"Change is good, David. Sometimes you have to give people a dose of what's good for them—even shock them into seeing the possibilities. I am asking you to join me in this quest."

"You are welcome to your vision, Ethan. Only, I prefer not to push people but lead them gently towards the changes we know we must make. At least, let's be clear that we will be on opposite sides of this issue, during the campaign."

"So you came here to throw down the gauntlet?" Ethan flipped another switch, his voice going icy.

A different set of images lit up the screen: whirling psychedelic lights, a drunken couple hungrily grinding their pelvises into each other on a dance floor populated by other couples in similar states of arousal. The camera zoomed. David made out Sugar's buxom body, wildly splayed blonde hair and makeup mixed with sweat dripping down her face. He recognized himself, even more pathetic, groping, eyes glazed and trying to focus: he was not shaking to the music, he was trying to keep his feet under him.

"You bastard!"

"Interesting couple, eh, David," Ethan chuckled. "You should get out more often. Take Sonya with you."

David sat back in his chair. He gulped down his water, hoping to loosen the knot around his heart.

"Don't worry, David. I won't be using this clip in our campaign. This was just for my amusement. The look on your face is priceless."

David struggled to rise. "I was drugged, unbeknownst to me."

"Oh, yeah? Rumour has it that you were diving into those margaritas pretty quick."

On the screen, David was staggering now and falling flat on the floor. Other than for Sugar, looking helplessly down at him, none of the other dancers paid any attention.

" Drugged, eh?" Ethan noted, studying the screen. "I guess so – you passed out before you could really indulge. Reminds me of that old politician who is recorded in the history books that he 'smoked but did not inhale.' "

David rose. "I came to tell you that I did not appreciate you jump-starting this campaign for one thing. And that I am going to do my darndest to see that Tolemac's growth is ordered and balanced. And that we do not lose the values of generosity and kindness we have striven so hard to salvage from the ravages of the Flood."

Ethan walked back to his desk. "Goodbye then, David. See you at the debate. And say hello to the wife and kids for me. Hal will show you out."

Chapter 19

DAVID WENT HOME AFTER LEAVING **W**ILLIAM'S **E**NTERPRISES. There was still no one around the house and he paced the den. Why was he so upset? Because Ethan had stolen one on him? It was an election, for God's sake! What did you expect an opponent to do? Still, he preferred playing by the rules, the way things had been done in the past, when all candidates launched their campaigns simultaneously, and platform policies drove votes, not extended campaigning, squeezed in with pre-emptive strikes. Were those times on their way out? And would Ethan keep his word about that damning video clip and not risk exposing his own forays into the seamy world of New Eden?

All David could do now was get a move on and launch his own campaign and not let these fears bog him down. He sat down at his Communicator and scribbled notes, then deleted them. He was feeling very tired and the headache had not left. He needed to speak to Samson. He needed his advice. So, he picked up Samson's suitcase that was still lying in the hall with the other luggage and set off for his father's house. When he got there, he realized that Samson was probably at the Stone's or the hospital or wherever, attending to that family's latest crisis.

About to turn and leave, he decided to drop the suitcase off anyway, so he let himself in through the side door with the spare key Samson always left with him. There were voices coming from the bedroom. By reflex, he started to go over to the door; then stopped short. The last time he'd spied on people in the privacy of their bedroom, he had received a rude shock. But something propelled him forward. After all, this was his father's house, the home he was raised in. He had a right to walk in whenever and wherever he wanted. However, the voice that mesmerized and drew him, was a woman's, coming from the room. Dreading the worst, yet wanting his suspicions nullified, David paused just outside the bedroom door, reluctant to go any further. The voices were clearer now.

"It will be a relief in a way." Delia's voice was distinct.

"You've had your hell on earth. Paid the price in full," Samson said.

"I worry about Joshua. He needs a father."

"He never had one. He will now."

"Oh, Samson! I wish I had your strength." The springs on the bed creaked and David had heard enough.

He tiptoed across the hall and exited via the side door. Reaching the street, he realized he was still holding Samson's bag. Just as well, too, leaving it behind would lead to more questions now. He walked back home, thoroughly deflated. Everyone was beginning to betray him, just as he had betrayed himself last night in New Eden.

He found himself heading towards Tolemac General. He also felt he was stumbling from one calamity to the other, unanchored, looking for explanations and just plain out of control, since landing in Tolemac less than four hours ago. He wanted to bury himself in Sonya, but even she had spun out of his orbit, and the last thing he wanted with her right now was another argument.

At the hospital, Dagma was on duty and seeing David's agitated state, she took him straight up to Doug Stone's ward. David approached the sick man's bed and they were suddenly alone in the three-bedded room. The profusion of wires sticking out of Doug only made his appearance ghastlier. The dying man's eyes were puffy, the blond hair on his head had grown long and straggly and hung to one side of his red face. A streak of spittle ran down his mouth and disappeared somewhere into the bed sheets. Doug opened his eyes after David had been standing silently by his side for awhile.

"Josh? That you boy?" The voice was raspy. More spittle oozed out as he spoke.

"No, it's David Arthurs."

Silence.

"Need to talk to my boy."

"Where is he?"

Another silence.

"Came with me to the hospital." Long pause. "Went to find his mother."

Then, as if in response to the question, the hapless Joshua was in the room beside him.

"Dad, I can't find Mom. She's not at home. She said she was going to get some help."

"Let her be. You come over here, boy!" The scrawny hand, tethered with wires and tubes, extended and took hold of the boy and clutched him to the bed. David wanted to leave them to their privacy, but the boy looked at him, pleading silently not to be left alone.

"Your Dad is going to be all right," David said.

The boy shook his head. Doug's voice increased a notch. The pitch was nasal and strained and kept fading. "Josh—remember . . . it's all about you, boy. Don't leave it to anyone. Don't trust them. Especially when they come with their sweet smiles. The women . . . they are the worst. Remember . . ." The voice was fading fast and the grip weakening. David stepped over to Joshua and put his arm around him. The boy was trembling.

"It's okay, Joshua" David whispered. "I am with you."

"Remember," the voice squeaked on, "don't trust—"

Then two nurses came in and asked them to leave. David led the boy out of the room. There were a couple of chairs in the corridor, and they sat down. Joshua was looking down at his feet, sucking in his breath, trying to hold everything in. David fished in his jacket pocket and found the two chocolate bars he had bought in New Eden. Well, Hannah and Joey were going to have to be contented with sharing a bar between them!

"Chocolate? Got this one from your hometown. Downey's Milk and Nut."

Joshua's eyes lit up when he looked at the bar, but he made no move to take it. Then he looked toward his father's room anxiously, as one of the nurses rushed out. "Come on, let's go for a walk," David said, and thrust the bar of chocolate into the boy's hand. For the next ten minutes they walked the corridors and Joshua busied himself with the confectionery.

"How's school?" David asked. "I heard you are in Joey's class."

"Yes. Joey is smart."

"Well, all you kids are smart. At least, when compared to my generation."

"I'm not."

"Who says so?"

"Everybody in the class. Well, they don't say it, but I know that's what they are thinking."

"Well, you've probably learned things differently when you were in New Eden, right?"

"I didn't go to school there 'til I was eight."

"And why was that?"

"Because my Dad and Mum couldn't afford to send me. Dad was ill most of the time. I tried reading on the Communicator, but the math was difficult."

"Next year, you will be in my volunteer math class, I can help you with extra lessons." What was he saying? Wasn't this was the piece of workload he was trying to give up in order to balance his life!

"Will you, sir?" Joshua looked interested for once.

"Sure," David said and looked away from the small face that for a moment had lit up with hope.

Returning to the ward, they found two visitors: Delia and Samson. Delia's hair was scraped back in a bun and she smelled of fresh apricots, just as his mother had. Perhaps she had been daubing herself with Agnes's perfumes while in Samson's bedroom! She looked relaxed but resigned. Samson too was relaxed. Seeing them together, a nerve started to pulse in David's temple.

"Mom," Joshua pulled away and rushed towards his mother. She embraced him and kissed him and David could see that the emotion between them was genuine. David did not look at Samson; he was worried his mounting temper would get the better of him. Samson and Delia went into Doug's room but David hung outside.

"David!" a voice from behind made him jump. It was Frida Parks, in her primly starched pink volunteer's uniform. "A word with you my dear, if you will."

"Let's take a walk," he said taking her hand and walking down the corridor. Right now, Frida Parks was just the distraction he needed.

"You look rather worse for wear," she said. "Are you well?"

"Oh, I'm all right, just a bit worn out from travelling. We returned from New

Eden today on Executive Committee business. What is it you want to talk about?"

"It's about Doug Stone, you see—"

"He seems pretty low right now."

"I was looking through his medical records—"

"Are you are allowed to do that?"

"Dr. Karya trusts me after all these years of volunteering."

"And—?"

"Well, it's odd. Maybe, it's just me, but I think . . ."

"Come on Frida, I've had a long day."

"All right. Well, let me tell you this straight then. I think Doug Stone is suffering from an overdose, wittingly or unwittingly!"

"What!" He must have raised his voice, for a couple of nurses looked back at him in surprise as they passed in the corridor.

"Hush, keep it down, David. Well, you see. I looked at his chart. He is on a very powerful new drug called Cancerl, to keep his blood levels balanced. He is supposed to take it once a day, usually at night. I was the first at his bedside when he was brought in. When I asked him when he had last had his dosage, he mentioned after lunch. Then when I was leaving, he mumbled whether he would be all right to take his second dose at night, like he normally did. At first, I thought he was disoriented about the time. But now I think not."

"What do you mean?"

"Well, if he is on a regular double dose, the medication can have the opposite effect and drive his blood levels so high that he could die of internal haemorrhaging."

"Why haven't you told Dr. Karya?"

"Well, I am so worried. You see Delia is the one administering his medicine. Knowing her—er—closeness to your family, I wanted to be certain first, before I said anything to anyone. I owe Samson and Agnes so much. Agnes was the only one I could call a true friend."

"Well, thanks for sharing this information, Frida. Don't say anything until I check with Delia and Samson. There is probably a very logical explanation for all of this." He tried to keep a straight face as he bade her goodbye.

"You will let me know, won't you? I can't keep this secret to myself forever. It's making me very anxious!" she said, as they parted.

When David returned to the ward, Doug's room was closed off and Delia, Samson and Joshua were seated outside. Delia was sobbing this time, deep sobs that shook her. Her hair had come undone and was a splash of red across her shoulders. Samson had his arm around her and she was leaning into him. Joshua was staring at the empty Downey's chocolate bar wrapper, as if hoping the chocolate would be restored. David fished out the second bar and tossed it over to the boy.

"He's gone," Samson sighed.

"Can I have a word with you?" David said.

"Not right now."

"Yes. Right now!"

A shadow crossed Samson's face at the deliberateness in David's tone. Excusing himself, Samson followed David down the corridor. They had barely stepped out onto the hospital patio when David erupted. The tension that was bottled up inside him came out, surprising even him, for he had never spoken to Samson like that in his entire life.

"The man was dying and you were making out with his wife!"

Samson flushed a deep red. "I wasn't 'making out.' We were sitting on the bed, talking. Why do you suspect the worst in things you do not see?" Samson started pacing and his voice lost its edge. "I am deeply attracted to her and care about her well-being. She needs comforting."

"Like hell, she does! So did Mum, but you were never around!"

Samson maintained composure "Your mother and I, God bless her soul, we drifted apart. It's a terrible thing to drift apart."

David started pacing as well. They paced in opposite directions to each other, stopping at times to hurl an accusation or a reply. David knew with each outburst he was hurting his father but he couldn't stop. Maybe, he was finally coming to terms with his own mother's death, and the buried anger was finding an outlet.

Samson came to a standstill and looked out at the parked ambulances. "Spousal abuse is a terrible thing."

"So is neglect."

"Delia did not neglect him. But he treated her terribly. And Joshua, too. She was married to him and in an abusive relationship for fifteen years—a long sentence for someone in the prime of her life."

"I wasn't meaning Delia's neglect of her husband. I was thinking closer to home!"

Samson's face turned red again but he did not respond. David wished he had. A good punch up would have been preferred—something David had never done in his life. But he knew that Samson would not descend to that level.

Then, as suddenly as it had gushed out of him, David found his anger ebbing. He decided not to push any more of the older man's buttons. The question on the Cancerl drug would have to wait for another time. Samson was looking his full sixty years now, even older.

"I think I'm going home now," David said.

As he was about to exit the patio, he heard Samson say, "Son, I did not neglect your mother. We were both in a time and place I hope you will never have to face. We were the builders. When you build, you expect everyone to do his or her bit, side by side. There is no time to nurture. That's the word—nurture, not neglect. When Agnes died, I knew that I had lost the chance to nurture her forever. You can't blame a man for trying a second time, can you?"

*　*　*

Sonya laid the mats in a circle on the floor. She had come out early today, hoping to avoid meeting David on his return. She did not want him to distract her from what she had in mind. After the class tonight, Sean would stay behind; she knew it. She would ask him to stay if she had to. And she would discover him, intimately.

She marvelled at her determination to go ahead with this dalliance, for dalliance it must be, at least in Tolemacian eyes. For a moment she hesitated. Samson had warned her about the evils of the Capitalists. Was Sean representative of this malevolence? Was the insidious creep of Capitalism's sensory temptations manifesting itself in this secret desire for extramarital sex? She shook her head and continued to straighten the mats on the floor. Samson had also said "it was easier to do than think" and second-guessing was not a facet of Tolemacian life, even if the "doing" was sometimes misguided. And Samson himself was being sucked into the vortex of Capitalist pleasures. For a moment, panic hit her and she wondered if there was a way she could shake off this strong desire that had gripped her.

A knock sounded on the door. She looked at the clock; there was still half an hour before the students came in. As she opened the door, she wondered who it could be at this time. It was Sean. He was standing on the doorstep, his head askance, looking longingly at her. His face was drawn, and his hair, which he had been allowing to grow back over the collar, was tousled and unruly.

She wanted to grab him, pull him in, have her way with him before all the doubts running through her had won over. Instead, in habitual tongue-tied reticence she said, "You're early."

"You do look lovely," Sean replied, staying in the doorway, reluctant to come in.

"Are you attending the class today?" she asked, impatient.

He nodded and stepped in gingerly, swiping back his hair, the new surroundings making him conscious of his bedraggled nature.

"Then you'd better come in. Can I get you a cup of ginchenachea tea?" She did not know what more to say or do. She had to keep busy. She went back into the room and put the brew pot to boil. She realized that she was not good at seduction.

As she focused on making the tea, she felt his eyes following her every move. He had paused in the middle of the room just a few steps in from the doorway.

"Sonya, I'm not worthy of you."

She did not want to look up. The tea spilled, scalding her hand. She took a damp cloth from the sink and held it to the burn, wincing.

"Did you hurt yourself?" The concern in his voice was sharp. He quickly stepped over and massaged her reddening hand. His touch was tender.

"There's butter in the refrigerator," she said. Her legs felt like rubber in his proximity.

Then he was applying the butter on her, slowly, deliberately.

"What did you say just now?" she asked.

"I am not worthy of you."

"Why do you say that?"

"I just think that."

She reached out her good hand and felt the roughness of his cheeks. His face was a puckered line of hills and dales, bones sticking out proudly amidst cavernous and sunken cheeks. A day's stubble added roughness and masculinity to strong jaw lines that melted into blotchy flesh at his neck. Her hands were moving all over him now, excitement mixed with disappointment as the image of the idealized male was juxtaposed with the tired creature under her touch. Then his hands took hers and pushed firmly outward.

"Stop! Enough! I came early to tell you that we have to stop this charade," Sean said, moving completely away from her.

She felt slighted, hurt. "Is this your style? Lead a woman on a dance and then walk away?"

Tears were in his eyes and the anguish on his face was overpowering. She immediately felt bad for lashing out.

"Sonya, what we are doing is wrong. I wouldn't have thought twice about our actions if this was New Eden. But here—somehow—it doesn't feel right. It feels unclean. I want this to stop before it goes too far. I will never come back here again if this makes it easier for you, for us."

They remained silent for awhile. He coughed involuntarily. She poured the tea and left the cup on the table for him to get if he chose. He spat phlegm into a tissue.

Catching his breath, Sean said, "You do have a good family—I found that out on my trip to New Eden this time."

"You say that every time we meet, yet you know that I am extremely unhappy."

"It's not David's fault, not everything is. We live in imperfect worlds. It's unfair to take out all our frustrations on the ones closest to us."

She felt close to tears herself. His words hit like nails. She felt dirty, unworthy; all thought of carnal pleasure had vanished. "I don't think I can conduct today's class. I am not in any state to do it now."

"I am sorry to have burdened you with this today."

She was grabbing at straws now. "Will you stay for the class? It will be better. I can't have you leave now. It . . . it would destroy me completely."

"I'll stay, if that helps. It's easier for me to idolize you from afar. I have delved too much into the seamy side of sex and women."

"Drink your tea." She straightened, catching herself. *Silly fool, what had I been thinking?* And yet, Sean's vulnerability triggered her. *If only David would just reveal that occasionally.*

There was a knocking at the front door again. The first of the students had arrived.

*   *   *

When David got home, Hannah and Joey were waiting anxiously for him and for the gifts they were expecting from New Eden.

"I'm sorry kids, but I only got you these books. Didn't have a lot of time to shop around." David fished around in his bag, which still lay where he had dropped it.

"Wow! The Adventures of Roy Rogers," exclaimed Joey, picking up the book and racing to his room to let all his friends know via Communicator chat line. Roy Rogers was only available in Tolemac on an infrequent show over the Communicator, a severely edited Alberta-based production, beamed from Oceania. Hannah took the book on the Art of Visual Imaging with a satisfied look on her face.

"Where's Mum?" David asked.

Hannah was already into her book. She tossed her curls from behind the pages and said, "She said she was leading a late class at the centre. Oh, and Sean called too, to find out if the class was still on."

David felt a knot tighten around his stomach. He had to get to the meditation centre as quickly as possible.

A dim light emanated from the main hall when he arrived at the centre. A low chant greeted him. A group of men and women, dressed in tights and T-shirts, sat in a circle. They were in lotus positions holding each other's hands in a linked chain. Candles in the centre of the circle provided light, while incense burned in the background. Through the fragrant haze, he recognized Sonya in the centre, leading the meditation. Sean was seated next to her, holding her hand. David held back just outside the door. Being an ardent practitioner and teacher of the art, he was respectful of the meditative state, even though he was in anything but that condition right now.

Sean looked at peace. It was hard to believe that just last night he was wading quite comfortably in a den of alcohol, drugs and sex, dragging David with him. Yet, Sean was bored then. Today, he looked rejuvenated. David remembered his words: "You are a lucky man." He also recalled how Sean had laughed and followed Sugar up to one of the back rooms. And now he was holding Sonya's hand.

After what seemed like an eternity, really only fifteen minutes by the clock, the meditation ended. David barged in, even while members in the circle were stretching themselves and rising indolently from their relaxed state. His agitated aura must have grated on them immediately, for they stared at him making his way over to Sonya and Sean, who were still holding hands, enjoying the fading fragments of the session.

"David!" Sonya said, disengaging quickly from Sean. She was genuinely pleased to see her husband. It occurred to David, that other than during his three trips abroad, they had never spent a night away from each other in their entire married life, and despite their recent estrangement, her face was inviting. He took her in his arms roughly and kissed her in front of everyone.

"David!" she blushed, looking around sheepishly at her students. "That was nice. Welcome home!" She was smiling and looking at him askance.

"You are a lucky man indeed," Sean said from somewhere in the back, but David's eyes were solely on Sonya. She looked beautiful.

"I came to take you home," he said.

Her reserve resurfaced. "But I have to close the centre. It will take a few minutes."

"I'll wait," he insisted.

"I can give you both a ride back," Sean said.

"That won't be necessary," David said abruptly. "I want to be alone—with my wife." The rest of the group had started to depart. Looking around him, Sean shrugged. "Well, I'd better be heading off too, then. Sonya, thank you again. I'm glad I made it tonight. It was especially uplifting. Goodnight!"

The moment the last straggler had left, David followed Sonya upstairs to the office. She was bending over some files when he swept up behind her.

"David! What's got into you?"

"Shh!!" he moved her onto the couch and kissed her deeply on the mouth once more. He felt her small firm breasts under him. He squeezed them and heard her gasp. Not in pain, but in delight at his deliberateness. It had been so long. After her initial surprise, she yielded to him, aggressively. They ate hungrily of each other, unashamedly, noisily, like animals. Her passion surprised him, but he didn't care anymore. Screw ritual. The face of Delia swam in front of him momentarily. Then the face disappeared and it was Sonya that he was with and he was getting lost in her, letting go and she was taking him with her to that moment of release. She was taking control of her pleasure and he was letting it happen. Too much had happened today; he couldn't control things anymore, so he let someone else be in charge. They climaxed together and rolled off the couch, laughing, hugging, and crying.

They lay on the floor, perspiration streaming off their bodies, bewildered by the fire that had engulfed them.

"I didn't know that one could enjoy this so much!" Sonya said, running her fingers up and down his chest. "What got into us there?"

"I think we went past ritual today. I missed you honey."

"Me, too. Ever since we were married, come to think of it. What happened just now?"

"We were wanton."

She shook her head. "That must have been the big O. The one we Tolemacian women rarely discover."

He did not want anything to spoil the moment. It was as if he were opening that door in the dream, the one that had been out of bounds all this time. He placed his hand gently over her mouth and mounted her again, slowly this time. And her body melted around him, drawing him in. This, too, a second time in one night, was a first in their relationship. But her hunger, radiating from every thrust and pull of her body, egged him on. This was so much better than all the times before.

He never had that recurring dream after that day. And all he'd done was let go.

*　*　*

She stretched out on the floor of the tiny office, her body a bath of sweat, the sweet, sticky kind covered in an aroma of intense heat that she had never experienced before. It was frightening. So this was what it was to experience Orgasm—and she had thought it could have only come with the outsider Sean, not her tried and true spouse. Over to her side, David groaned and turned over, satiated. All these years she had slept beside him, opened her body to him, but they had never experienced the union of two bodies like they had just done.

She smiled—satisfied that this experience was hers to have again—legally. Yet the other side of her reflected on the loss of so many years gone by.

Chapter 20

Doug Stone was entombed two days later. Considering that he was a newcomer to Tolemac, quite a number of people gathered to pay their respects. There was the Executive Committee, who having authorized the Stones to remain in Tolemac, was still their custodian. Familiar faces from the hospital also showed up: Dr. Karya, Dagma and Frida Parks, whom David tried to avoid eye contact with. Bringing up the remainder of the gathering, along with the Stones' neighbours, was the Arthurs family. Joshua Stone struck up a conversation with Joey, trying to keep his mind from the proceedings. Joey was co-operative. Hannah stuck her hand into Joshua's a couple of times, especially during the sadder parts of the ceremony.

A car pulled up, and Ethan Williams got out, wearing a well-tailored suit with his hair slicked back and moustache groomed for the occasion. David figured that from now until Election Day, Ethan would be at all the baptisms, weddings and funerals,

Doug was interred in the public area of the cemetery. It was a rundown part of the property that flooded often during the rainy season. On that day, the ground was muddy and sludge oozed over shoes and boots, as attendees trod around the nondescript tomb. Samson delivered the funeral service in traditional Christian fashion—"Dust to dust, ashes to ashes."

Delia was dressed in black slacks and a body-hugging white blouse, with her shock of red hair hidden under a black scarf. A scarlet, sleeveless vest protected her from the coolness of that early November day. After the coffin was moved into the tomb, she thanked everyone for their hospitality and caring: "Joshua and I are indebted to the kindness you have all showered on us, since our arrival. We will be eternally grateful to the people of Tolemac for adopting us as your own, something we never experienced in our native land. I hope we can repay you in some way." It was an eloquent message, delivered in a soft but measured tone that surely earned her many sympathizers.

As the gathering started to disperse, a frail hand gripped David from behind. "A word, my dear—"

It was Frida Parks. David stumbled with an apology. "Sorry, Frida. I didn't get back to you since we last spoke."

"No, no, it's okay. You've got lots on your mind with the election and all." She was dressed in a navy blue suit and hat to match.

"I didn't get a chance to discuss that issue with Samson."

"It's okay. You see, on the day Doug Stone died, Dr. Karya was about to order an inquest. But Samson talked him out of it."

"Samson did?"

"Well, there is no reason to suspect anything, now is there? I must have been paranoid. The man was going downhill fast and his death was a mercy in itself. Besides, there is no reason to torment that family anymore. At least, that is how Samson explained it to Dr. Karya."

"How do you know all this?"

"Well, I was in the room cleaning up. I overheard them talking."

"Thanks for telling me. I guess that puts an end to that."

"Yes, I'm so relieved. If Dr. Karya is okay with it, then it should be okay. Now we can all move on, right?"

"Well, well, if it's not our dear Frida!" The voice came from behind, before David could answer. Ethan had sauntered over and was bowing graciously to the elderly spinster. During the funeral service, Ethan had made it a point to whisper greetings to each of the Executive Committee members. He had condoled grandiosely with Delia and Joshua, and now it was Frida Parks's turn to receive his charm.

"Why, hello Ethan!" she replied smiling at him demurely. Ethan nodded at David and made as if he would like to speak privately with Frida. David held his ground.

"You have some very interesting posters," said Frida. "That's the first time we have seen such a thing—very creative!"

"Well, thank you! I thought we should spice up the elections this time. It's gotten too boring over the years. Won't you say, David?"

David remained noncommittal, but Ethan didn't lose his ebullience.

"David, let's catch up on the election some other time shall we? Right now I just wanted to say hello to Frida here!"

"Why that's so kind of you, Ethan," said Frida, beaming.

Realizing that he was the one intruding now, David said. "Goodbye, Frida. See you at the debate, Ethan."

As David stepped away and hurried after his family, he heard Ethan say, "Can I give you a ride home, Frida?"

"Why, I'd love that. You have such a nice car" she said, giggling nervously.

*　*　*

November 7, 2045

She looked lovely at the funeral today, dignified in her loss. And she is free, like I am. And what I just committed with her will be debated in this community for years to come when these memoirs are finally revealed.

I went to her home after the ceremony. I knew that Joshua would be with Joey and Hanna, a generous offer by Sonya to have the boy in happier surroundings at this sad time. Delia opened the door as if expecting my knock. She had taken off her scarf and her lush red hair cascaded over her shoulders. The white blouse had the two top buttons open, inviting me into her comforting and enchanting bosom.

"Thank you for coming," was all she managed to say before I took her in my arms for the first time, despite all the many other times I had withheld myself. We ate hungrily of each other, staggering across the tiny living room. We never made it to the bedroom, our passion was so intense. There on the floor outside the bedroom door, I entered her and gasped as if I were entering a promised land that had been denied me for aeons.

Later we rolled in each other's arms, delivered, happy, liberated and not giving a damn about who was going to judge us anymore. I held her tight as we lolled in the afterglow of our lovemaking, knowing and trying to shut out the doubts and second guessing that was bound to intrude in all subsequent acts such as this that our bodies and souls had finally committed.

*   *   *

The next two weeks passed by in a blur for David. The exams were held, and students and teachers worked hard. Leo Patimkin had a tough time. While on invigilator duty, David saw the boy struggle. Leo was stoic in his efforts however, never complaining but tackling the papers on his Communicator with all the concentration he could muster. The strain showed by the end of exam week and Leo wasn't among the throng of liberated teenagers partying and whooping it up at the Waterside Park after the last paper. In fact, one of those celebrations got so wild that one of Joe Sabbattini's clique, who had recently moved out to the New Settlements, drove his father's car into the lake with three of his buddies inside. No one was hurt, but the car was a write-off. This was a first in Tolemac. There was talk that some of the kids had been "under the influence." That rumour was quickly quelled by Rocky Sabbattini, who had sponsored the party for the teens.

Ethan Williams's (and now Peter Lowry's) poster campaign became more pronounced around Tolemac with each passing day. Word circulated that Ethan had recruited the Academy of Learning's most popular student, Joe Sabbattini, and friends, to help with his campaign.

There was disturbing news coming out of Oceania. The rise in drug use among teenagers had increased, and a few teen crimes were now being reported. There was an unconfirmed report of a smuggling ring feeding in from the Capitalist states. The people of the Humanitarian realm, being conservative in their outlook, had been hitherto smug about recreational drugs ever taking root in their midst. But that was changing. Samson was chagrined over the developments in Oceania. "We are going backwards again," he said, during his Sunday sermon. "We must be vigilant never to regress. The Flood wiped out all those retrograde ways. This was our fresh start. We must never give into temptation!" His face was charged with more emotion than usual when delivering those lines. He was also spending more time with Delia now, and they were seen together at civic functions, where she arrived as his guest. Joey even mentioned that he had seen Grandpa down at the Waterside Park one day, having a picnic lunch with Mrs. Stone. And that Frida Parks, who had been walking her dogs nearby, had crossed the road in a hurry.

The ecstasy that David and Sonya had experienced at the meditation centre never resurfaced, as David started to focus on the election ahead. Even though Sonya was more accommodating, he believed she still secretly resented his involvement in politics.

The election came to the forefront of David's life when, a couple of days after the exams, Leo Patimkin showed up on the Arthurs family doorstep one evening with a bright red poster that read: "Vote for David Arthurs—our kind and beloved leader." David was taken aback. Before he could say anything, Leo blurted out, "Mr. Arthurs, sir—we've designed this poster for you. And we plan to support you throughout this campaign by running flyer drops at homes."

"Leo, I'm flattered! But don't you have other things to do on your holidays?"

"Well, we . . . I, figured you needed some help, given the huge campaign running for the other guys. Besides school's out for the next month anyway."

"Why, thank you Leo! That is most encouraging. But we don't run big political campaigns in Tolemac."

"But that's changed already. Ethan Williams saw to that."

"I'd rather spend the time and effort figuring out how to present my platform to the electorate."

"Well, you are taking too long, if I may say so, Mr. Arthurs. I could rally the troops and hold a think-tank session, to get things moving, if you'd like."

"And who are the 'troops'?"

"You'll see. Meet us tonight at the youth centre. I'll arrange it, no problem. There is no more time to waste."

David hesitatingly agreed. Leo was right; time was marching on, and he had been standing still on the election.

It turned out that Leo's troops were comprised of Izzy's son Johnny Garcia, Natalie's niece Rita Sacic and Sammy White Dove's cousins Billy Junior and Gary.

Until Leo had prompted him, David had made no concrete plans to fight this campaign that was running away from him. Samson had gently nudged him, but given their frostiness over "the Delia factor," his father had not pushed him. All David had as a plan of attack was a series of visits to the worker centres—the port, the microchip factory and over to the New Settlements—to listen to the diverse views of these key voting groups and pitch his platform. After that, there would only be time to prepare for the public debate, the night before the election. The debate usually drove the majority of votes, particularly among the undecided.

What was going to be his platform? The idea of a "Middle Way," which had sparked off again at Congressman Gordon's house, had germinated in his mind since his return from New Eden. If he could campaign for retaining the community values of Tolemac, while being open to new ideas from the outside, and towards implementing change (as long as it was congruent with Humanitarian beliefs and principles), he was sure that was the answer the Executive Committee of Tolemac and the Knights of Eden were both seeking from each end of their respective political spectra. The more he thought about it, the more the Middle Way seemed like a good platform to him. That night, he proposed it to the "troops" when they met down at the youth centre.

"Too bland, Mr. Arthurs," said Johnny, after everyone had digested the argument.

"It's neither here nor there," mused Rita.

"Hang on, guys" Leo disagreed, "Mr. Arthurs's Middle Way is just what Tolemacians will vote for. They want change, yet they are cozy with the life they have. Ethan's too far out in right field for them. He can paint all the bright pictures he wants, but will Tolemacians go for it?"

They went back and forth on the issue and David enjoyed their youthful passion and sincerity. Finally, it seemed that giving the Middle Way a shot was realistic, given that Ethan was indeed an extreme right winger and Peter only a couple of steps behind. The White Dove boys went along with everything Leo said. For a kid struggling with math and skirting depression, Leo came alive when it came to politics.

"You've also gotta have something for the youth, Mr. Arthurs," Johnny said.

"Yes, especially since those aged sixteen to twenty-five now comprise about twenty-five percent of the voting public," Rita concurred.

"Our generation is very politically savvy. And with all this stuff about the drugs in Oceania and all," Johnny gave his team members a veiled look, "I think we have to take a stand on drugs."

"Johnny's right, Mr. Arthurs," Leo said. "I'll draft messaging on youth issues into your speeches."

David was intrigued. "You think we have a drug problem here?" Sometimes he wished he could get more into their world, which he saw only in the controlled environment of the classroom.

"Oh, we have issues Mr. Arthurs." Billy Junior spoke up for the first time, winking at Leo.

"Like?"

"Don't worry Mr. Arthurs," Leo interjected, "I'll give you some points to talk about."

David persisted. "But I thought the generation gap was beginning to dissipate in the post-Flood era!"

"It may have been in your day, Mr. Arthurs, when you were building side-by-side with your parents. But now that things are more settled, we are drifting apart again."

"It's the story of life on this planet. We'll always have a generation gap. We'd be lost without it," Rita mused, fluttering her eyes at Johnny.

David decided to drop the argument and fall in with their greater wisdom; a generation gap did exist and youth issues needed to be addressed.

"And we must launch the poster campaign and organize lots of rallies," Johnny said.

"Yeah, we must. We've gotta give Ethan and Peter Lowry a run for their money," echoed the White Doves.

"It's a given," said Rita.

Looking at Leo's triumphant grin, David reluctantly caved into this suggestion, too.

With the strategy thus settled, the students divided the tactical issues among them. Johnny was responsible for the staging and video facilities at David's public meetings; Rita was the art director of posters and other image-related things, including David's dress on the night of the public debate. The White Doves were in charge of distribution and Leo would become press secretary. And they would co-opt other helpers from their class to assist as required. Everyone was pumped up by the time they officially kicked off the campaign with a prayer that night.

His students' views apart, David needed to hear from the real power base—the electorate at large. Therefore, the first stop of his campaign was at the microchip factory located on North Dundas. The factory had a strange history associated with it, now the stuff of local lore, which explained how Tolemac got its reputation for microchips. It was said that as things were settling after the Flood and the earthquakes, a group of computer programmers from a nearby software manufacturer were among those marooned on Sunset Hill. Defaulting to their specialty, these intrepid pioneers started off by building spare parts for the Communicators that began sprouting all around Tolemac, often pulled out of personal belongings hurriedly packed during the exodus. Vladimir Patimkin worked as an apprentice in the first microchip factory these programmers subsequently built. He later led a team that invented the "city firewall" concept. Nathan Goldman, seeing an opportunity, funded the factory from his stashed earnings, which subsequently made him a rich man, although now he gave most of his wealth away to the less privileged. Thus Tolemacians were generally known as the microchip manufacturing experts in the Humanitarian realm and had built market leadership around it. When David visited the factory, however, a different side of this legendary success story emerged.

The first annoyance was to see Ethan Williams's posters, with customized slogans for the factory population, dotting the well-manicured lawn outside: "Partner with the best, Compete with the rest. Let's show them that Tolemac can take on the microchip world!" Peter Lowry also had his, less ambitious, signs that proclaimed, "The age of liberalism is here. Let's burst beyond our frontiers." The White Dove boys promptly went about setting up David's red campaign posters alongside the black ones of Ethan and the orange banners of Peter's.

Now in his late fifties, Sandeep Patil, the factory head, greeted them and escorted them around the facility. He was one of the original programmers stuck on the Hill during the Flood. David got a fleeting opportunity to meet and shake hands with the workers, most of who were hurrying about the place in starched white overcoats. They walked down long hallways that had several air-sealed doors leading off into work areas, which Sandeep explained, were contamination free for production work. There was a different buzz here, unlike in the laid-back streets of Tolemac. Many of the workers knew Samson, and therefore extended their respect towards David. Sandeep had organized a town-hall session in the cafeteria and the audience was starting to swell as David made his way to the podium in the centre. Many arrived for the special event, for this was the first election where a political rally was actually taking place inside the workplace, even though David's erstwhile competitors had already come and gone, leaving their calling cards behind on the lawn.

Being in the front line of voters was a far cry from being with a bunch of rambunctious teenagers in a classroom, and David was nervous. As the town-hall session went from speeches to "open-forum" period, the questions and statements took on a direct and pointed tone. The session started to blur and Leo helped by slipping David notes with some of the answers scripted ahead of time. David paused to drink copious amounts of water in between the difficult questions. The ones he remembered the most during that hour-long session and which they taped for follow-up review, ran something like this:

(Question from audience) "When will you open up for exports with Alberta and New Eden?"

(David's response) "We will review the need for this before proceeding. Capitalists play by their own rules as we know and we have been spared the fallout by not playing with them so far. But times are changing and I agree that we need to be open. I am building a case for this. Please send me your reasons why such a move is necessary and I will be happy to convene public discussions before we move forward with a proposal to the Executive Committee."

(Statement from audience followed by a snicker) "We badly need the latest equipment, and the best ones are in New Eden. That should be reason enough!"

(Another statement from the audience) "Alberta has also gotten into the microchip game, after New Eden did last year. And they are looking at European markets, while we are stuck trading with just the Humanitarian states on our side of the Atlantic."

(An authoritative voice from the audience) "We need to broaden and expand our customer base in order to lower unit costs."

That was when Leo had slipped him the note with a smiley face that said "Smart Ass!"

(Another statement that raised cheers from the audience) "Ethan Williams says he will introduce trade with the Capitalists within six months of being elected."

(A more doubtful voice from the audience) "That's rhetoric. How could he do that on his own? The Executive Committee makes collective decisions and Ethan's only one member." But an influential one at that, David thought. He decided not to respond to Ethan's boast as this opposing viewpoint from the audience had covered it.

(Another question) "What are you going to do to keep the drugs off our streets?"

(Another note slipped by Leo, thank God!) David glanced down at it and read, "Our border security is tight and we haven't compromised this to date, nor will we in the future." His eyebrows rose at Leo's next lines, but he continued reading, "And we will organize focus groups among the youth to discuss the issues they face and get them out in the open. Often, rejection and isolation drive individuals to artificial forms of release or expression. Our inclusive society is a counter to that; we must maintain that value at all cost." He got applause with those statements and David nodded his gratitude to Leo.

(Another voice) "But the drugs are getting through."

"We don't have any conclusive evidence of that," David said.

(Guffaws from the audience.)

In closing, David summed up the issue that was most troubling to everyone: the threat of losing their livelihoods to external, mainly Capitalist competition. He promised to work for more openness in terms of trade with the Capitalist states and to consider the audience's requests, yet tactfully promised to implement none of these requests until after a full review. As David bid goodbye, Sandeep said, "David, thank you for coming out today. I'm sorry for putting you in the line of fire but our sales have been slowing down in the last couple of years and we are facing intense competition. The workers are beginning to feel it now. They are even crabbier after we were forced to shut down our 'quiet rooms' due to cost-cutting measures. I think they are looking for change."

David and his followers all returned to the youth centre, which had by now become their de-facto campaign office. David got feedback from his team:

"You were too wooden, Mr. Arthurs," Rita said.

"Yeah, you've gotta come across as more natural, sincere like, you know—" Johnny said.

"Make decisions, even if they are premature," Billy Junior said.

"Hey, like that one about free trade with the Capitalists within six months," Gary said. "Ethan must be dreaming!"

"But it registered with the voters," Leo said.

A couple of days later, they held their next rally at the Waterside Park, where the crowd was more garrulous. Key constituents were port employees, downtown business people and residents. While the downtowners were mostly conservative, the Port employees and boaters were not, and David was mindful of this polarity. The "red team," as he had dubbed Leo and his helpers now, had to mount a cleanup first, for Ethan and his gang had held a big party the night before and the park was strewn with posters, flyers and litter from the free barbecue stands that had kept the audience fed during the proceedings. After two hours of backbreaking work, the red posters were flying all around the park and it finally started looking like the David Arthurs rally.

The recent decision by the Executive to invest in bolstering the sea wall bode well for David and the audience spared him when the topic came up, given his family connection to Samson, who had been most in favour of funding this project. David took a more strident stance and focused his speech on the need to be centred, in a time when change was being forced on Tolemac from all sides. "We are being pressured to follow the Capitalists, but is everything the Capitalists do good? Is the closing down of quiet rooms in our factories a good thing? How do stressed out workers unwind? How are the marginalized treated? If one of you were to have an accident while at work—and we have seen many take place in this very port—do you want to end up in the colonies or would you want to benefit from work-persons compensation and rehabilitation that we have always enjoyed in Tolemac?" A few nods and few guffaws in the audience. "Balance and openness is what we need," he concluded and the red team, arraigned behind him on the stage, waved their posters in response, and a few people in the audience applauded. Then one man, who seemed a bit drunk (David wondered how he managed that—maybe he'd come off a boat that stopped off at Brady's Island Bar!), rose and said in a loud voice, "Why the devil did you allow the helicopters to run here? You are ruining the passenger traffic on our boats!"

"Well, there was a demand for the helicopters. I doubt the Executive will ever expand this service into any form of larger fixed wing traffic," David explained.

The next day he felt like an idiot, when Ethan was reported quoting the following statement during his rally in the New Settlements: "Given there is still so much land in the New Settlements, all this growing suburb needs is an airport to connect residents with the outside world. The rising traffic figures of our helicopter service—that is now up to four helicopters and will be soon going up to six—could very shortly support a daily twenty-four-seater plane ride between Tolemac and Oceania." This statement apparently got a lot of support from the people in the New Settlements. And David got a message on his Communicator from someone down at the port that simply said, "Liar!"

David's last call was on the New Settlements, which was about a forty-five minute drive over Sunset Hill and at the northernmost point of Tolemac. Given the paucity of cars and motor transport (other than the monorail service that plied between the New Settlements and downtown Tolemac), only the most mobile or self-dependent came to live here. Garry Appegio had moved his family over to the New Settlements a few years ago and he was their main contact who helped set up the afternoon's rally. The red team arrived in the morning, erected banners and made all the logistical arrangements. David took the monorail from downtown at midday. As the crowded train, packed with people visiting relatives in the New Settlements, inched its way through lush green fields of rural Tolemac, David glanced out of the window at the produce conveyor at work again, hauling the year's second harvest of fruit and vegetables up and over Sunset Hill and down its other end to the port. Despite the crowded monorail train, the parallel two-lane paved road running adjacent had only the occasional car driving past, a sharp contrast to the buzzing expressway he had traversed in New Eden. Testament to where Tolemac had chosen to focus its investments— it certainly hadn't been on roads! The New Settlements were strings of houses of the mainly urban young who were starting to move out of the core of Tolemac into bigger homes on larger plots of land. Strict zoning was still in effect, as arable farmland surrounding the Settlements was protected from encroachment. Given the increasing population in Tolemac over the next ten years, housing would become expensive and people like Garry were sowing the seeds of their future wealth by coming out early. David had once been tempted to move here, but his involvement in the school and Sonya's in her gallery had made them give up on the idea. Besides, he did not own a car.

Arriving in the main square of the New Settlements, where the rally was being held, he felt like a pop star from the pre-Flood days. This election was beginning to hark back to that time, and it was unsettling. Samson wouldn't be enamoured with the show biz factor. About five hundred people were gathered; David Arthurs was the weekend entertainment for this suburban community. There were lots of young families and children running around, plenty of distraction for a political meeting.

David launched in to his well-practised, slick pitch on the Middle Way and immediately, one of the young men in front raised his hand. "David, with respect, you are talking to the risk takers of Tolemac, not the old gentry who live out faded dreams in the downtown core. We are the pioneers of our generation and we want to see some change around here. What new changes do you propose?"

"Well, openness to dialogue with the Capitalists, for one," David replied. "As you know the Executive has been reluctant or unsuccessful in going that far. I will work to make that happen."

"What else?" another shouted from the back.

"WorkOUT—I believe in it. I believe we have a good working model now and I'll work to see it implemented."

"Well done!" said a man in the middle somewhere. He looked older than the rest and vaguely familiar. "It's about time people realized there is no free lunch."

"Do you support the airport proposal?" the man in the back shouted again.

"No," David said and realized that he was going to pay the price for his honesty with this largely, pro-airport group. He saw Leo's face go pale.

"Oh, hear that? He does not support the airport!" The heckler carried on.

"Well, we don't all support the airport," another voice chimed in. "Especially, if there are no proper noise regulations."

David pounced on this sign of dissension. "We need evaluation of all changes. Change for the sake of change is not good. I've been over to New Eden recently, and the roads are not all paved with gold."

"Hear, hear!" It was the man in the middle again. Then David recognized him as Juan Gomez, the former migrant worker whom Samson had talked about so much. It was nice to see that he had become a settler here.

"We need increased monorail service to the New Settlements," another male voice shouted out from the back. "The population has increased five-fold in the last three years and we still have the same frequency of service as we did five years ago."

"That's what public services do for you," the heckler came back in. "And look at Ethan William's privately owned helicopter service—gone from one to four helicopters in a few months and more are on the way." He got some cheers for this comment.

"And there is no harm in having a few more consumer choices in this place, especially if we have the means of obtaining it," another person said, and got many grunts of approval.

David promised to look into the monorail issue. Remembering the blinding array of choice he'd had in Morby's department store, he did not comment on the consumer choice issue—that would open a whole can of worms around trading with the Capitalists and he did not want to go there.

When he wrapped up the session, David felt he had made some allies, alienated a few others and not really made an impact on many of the pro-change New Settlers. It was a bittersweet end to the campaign. There had been no major breakthroughs in swinging voters. And his father's track record had not done much here, either. Now all he could do was get ready for the debate.

*   *   *

When he returned home that evening, David was surprised to see Samson watching "Camelot" with the children. Joey was sucking on a candy bar at Samson's feet, while Hannah was cradled in her grandfather's lap. For a ten-year-old, Joey still exhibited many childish traits; he was indulged in a way that David had not been. At times like this David wondered if parents of his generation were overprotecting their kids.

"You don't get tired of this movie, do you?" David said, bringing a soda into the living room and falling down on the couch as Part One of the movie wound down. He closed his eyes and knew what would follow: King Arthur proudly inviting his men to the round table while Guinevere frolicked with her ladies and attendant knights in the forest, during the 'lusty month of May." Samson always stopped the movie at this part, at least for the sake of the children. It was a happy part of that ancient story, the culmination of the founding of Camelot among the ignorant people of ancient "Merrie England."

"It's fun, Daddy," Hannah said. Her tone implied that he should shut up and watch the movie.

When Part One ended and the kids had ambled off to their respective rooms, Samson said to David, "I want to talk to you about the election. I'm worried."

"Why?"

"Support for Ethan and Peter is growing. You are trailing."

"I've had no support from anyone but my students."

"Each candidate is supposed to stand on his own merits; those are the rules of the game."

"Those were the rules. Rules without teeth of enforcement. Ethan's using his personal funds to get elected. Free barbecue lunches at rallies don't come cheap. Next he'll be getting corporate sponsors to help him."

"That will not be allowed; he would be disqualified."

"He's too smart for that. He will push us to the brink of tolerance and then ease back. But he will get his way in the end."

Samson looked resigned. "We never had competitiveness like this run amok before. When we ran for office, we trusted each other."

"But you also became a band of cronies. The voters I've met on my campaign want change. So we have to change."

Samson abruptly switched subjects. "How are things at home?"

"They are okay."

"I mean, really. Between you and Sonya. This election has put a lot of strain on you. I should know, I've been there."

"We've worked things out."

Samson remained unconvinced. "If I can give you some advice on what to avoid, keep her involved in this job. Public office is a vocation, not a hobby. And it's got to be hers, too. And the children's."

"How's Delia?" David asked, wanting to get off the subject.

"She's well. I told her that you knew—about us, I mean"

"And?"

"She felt relieved. She wants to belong. She feels that Tolemacians regard her with suspicion for all the kindness they've shown her family."

"People are beginning to talk about you two."

"I don't care anymore. I've given enough for the cause."

"You won't do anything impulsive, will you?"

"I'm too old for that." He rose to leave. "Well, apart from the movie and visiting with the kids, I came by to tell you to put on a good show at the debate. No matter what Ethan drums up with the rallies and posters, it's the debate that's going to be the clincher. Good luck, son!"

Chapter 21

DEBATE NIGHT. David had prepared for all eventualities. The format would be a three-way discussion between the candidates in front of the cameras. David had been worrying incessantly that Ethan would reveal his sole night of philandering in the Pink Gypsy. But there was nothing he could about it; Ethan had the power to destroy him if he chose to. All he could do was be alert and be prepared to drag Ethan down with him if the subject ever arose. Still, he could not contemplate the disastrous damage to his reputation and to his family afterwards.

David practised for several hours in front of the mirror; he had not received any formal media training so he studied his moves as best he could. He asked Hannah and Joey to critique him. He had the red team critique him. He even asked Sonya to critique him.

"You're too serious, Dad," Joey said.

"Loosen up, Mr. Arthurs," Johnny Garcia said.

Sonya's contribution was, "David, you've got to entertain them. Make it light. The world is not going to fall down on us again."

It was hard keeping all this feedback in mind. There were times when he wanted to pack it in. Why had he embarked on this foolish quest? There were too many conflicting voter needs to be met. But whenever he saw Samson in those days leading up to the debate, David knew he had to carry through and do it better than his father had. After all, if the current generation did not outperform the previous one, how would the species evolve?

"How can I please them all?" he asked Samson one evening.

"You can't. You have to pick the most practical course of action and stick to it. People will show resentment initially, even ingratitude, if things don't start out well. And they never do. But if you stay the course, you'll get there in the end. And the electorate will be grateful to you, for making tough calls on their behalf."

"Meaning they blindly follow? Praising their leaders when things go well and dumping on them if their lifestyle is compromised?"

"It's been that way throughout history. It changed for a while during the early post-Flood years, when people banded together and shared and didn't criticize. But when stability returns, people go back to their old ways. Leading the herd is a lonely job."

David studied clips of past debates. The candidates were sober individuals, articulating the wisdom and experience they were bringing to office. They got elected that way—for honesty, integrity, courage and intelligence. Not for showmanship and illusive dream weaving. He watched Samson's performances. His father was eloquent yet passionate when cornered on issues, especially Humanitarian ones. Samson did not compromise or flinch when making a point.

The evening before the debate, David went down to the youth centre to get some notes from the campaign office. It was deserted, except for a basketball game going on in the adjacent court. He hadn't been sleeping well the last couple of nights. The dull thump- thump of the ball on the boards next door kept pace with his heartbeat. After a while, he could not tell which beat was louder. The red team would be decorating the inside of the Communicator studio at this time and David didn't expect to see anyone in the tiny recreation room turned campaign office. Therefore, he was surprised to see Leo in the room, furiously writing and muttering to himself. The boy was scribbling on pieces of paper, with a number of past attempts lying in balls on the floor. David held back at the door momentarily, only to see Leo push back the desk angrily, and pace up and down.

"Leo, what's up?"

Leo spun around, with anguish on his face. "You've gotta win this debate, Mr. Arthurs! Or we're done for. I've been writing speeches for you, but I can't seem to get them right."

"Okay, slow down. It's only a debate. It's not the end of the world. And I've got all the speeches I need. I just have to get them straight in my head."

"You don't understand. We can't let Ethan win."

"This is a democracy Leo. The people will vote for who they think is best. All we can do is do our best. Your team has done an excellent job and I wouldn't have made it this far without you. But we cannot let this get to our heads."

"But you're our hope for the next generation, Mr. Arthurs. Don't you see that?"

"Not all of your generation may support the Middle Way."

"It's the only way—we'd be stupid to polarize to the left or right."

"But it's not proven. Past civilizations have tried it, but they came unglued in the end, too."

"I've been reading up on it. The ancient Incas did it for several centuries in the former South America, until the Spaniards invaded."

"Yes, and there was always Camelot. I even found a more recent example after the last World War. But greed undid those attempts in the end. That's what we must be vigilant against—greed!"

Leo paced up and down lost in thought and David tried to cheer him up. "Don't worry, we'll win. I wish everyone were as smart as you; that would make our job easier. The problem is they aren't. Samson calls them 'the herd.' " David busied himself with his papers, trying to memorize all the possible cues and responses. He felt a mild headache coming on.

All the while, Leo paced about the room silently. Suddenly, he said, "Joe Sabbattini was down here earlier and said they were getting ready for a party to celebrate Ethan whipping you in the debate tomorrow. They think it's a done deal already. Something's up in their camp, but Joe's not letting on."

"He's learning Ethan's intimidation tactics. Ethan used to pull those stunts on me. I wouldn't get sidetracked if I were you."

"Sally Morden was with Joe. She supports Capitalism, too."

David was beginning to get a bit irritated. And the headache wasn't helping. "So this is about Sally then, is it?"

Leo had the look of a hurt animal at David's comment. "Mr. Arthurs, I can't be a loser anymore. Do you understand? Not again. You better win tomorrow." And then he fled the room, slamming the door behind him.

* * *

The studio lights were smack on his face when David took the middle podium with his name on it. He barely saw Ethan come in from the right and Peter to the left. After he had blinked a dozen times and adjusted to the lights, David made out the portly form of Heather Bradley, Tolemac's Communications anchor and moderator of the debate, dressed in her usual brown suit that matched her brown hair. She was standing directly opposite him. Then he realized that with the light in his face, and with Peter and Ethan spared that discomfort, whoever had arranged the podia hadn't done him a favour. But they were "live" now, and to complain would make him the spoilsport in front of all Tolemac. Again, the feeling that this was all a big promotional stunt, rather than a serious debate about Tolemac's future, gnawed at him.

Ethan wore a black cape that gave his tall frame a dashing cut. His pencil-thin moustache looked glued to his face in a rakish angle that accentuated the cape. Peter, on the other hand, was dressed in a bright orange suit with a zippered front. Well, guess where he's been shopping lately! The red team had settled on a white shirt and white pants for David, with a red blazer to match his campaign colour.

Opening speeches gave the candidates an opportunity to unwind. David was nervous and glad for the blazer that hid telltale signs of perspiration. Ethan was eloquent, projecting a sincerity that was difficult to associate with him; smiling often, he looked directly into the cameras all the time. Peter was his measured self, intellectualizing on his points and making them in a forceful manner. It was hard to imagine that most, if not all, homes in Tolemac would be glued to their Communicators that night watching this hot little studio with its bright lights and three sparring wannabe politicians.

After they had all described their platforms—David's Middle Way; Ethan's right-wing stance; and Peter's, which had shades of both but was more right leaning than David's—Heather pulled out the questions that the citizens of Tolemac had submitted.

"David—this one is for you—and other candidates, you are free to express your view or challenge the respondent—tell us how WorkOUT will help us in the future?"

David took his time and picked up his notes, reminding himself to look into the camera before speaking: "WorkOUT is not a punishment. That's important to understand. It's our way of giving those marginalized the chance at earning back their self respect by doing meaningful work for a living wage."

"But it will take away individual choice," Peter said.

David shot back: "These people do not have a lot of choice anyway. They sit at home today and wait for Welfare cheques, which do not really help their self esteem."

"WorkOUT is also a way of undercutting the laws of supply and demand for labour," Ethan said, smiling. "The WorkOUT salaries do not reflect economic value and are therefore a subsidy. It's like getting prisoners to work for whatever you can afford to pay them." David decided to let the people decide that one. Ethan was not going to draw him out into dangerous territory.

Instead, David continued, "The Middle Way is exactly that—balancing economic and social needs with compassion as the yardstick." Something told him that the people of Tolemac would register that one.

Heather said, "Peter, this one is for you. You have preached 'liberalization' yet you have held back from complete liberalization. Are you an advocate of David's Middle Way, or are you really trying to step out of the box? The questioner here says it's hard to get a fix on your position. What are you really advocating?"

Peter smiled and pulled himself up. He took a sip of water and looked deliberately down at his notes for a while. Then he spoke out, stridently. "No, I am not for the Middle Way or whatever you call it. That's neither here nor there. We need to pick a few things and do them really well—like developing world-class capabilities for our microchip facility and port—that would mean bringing in the best experts and technology, be they Humanitarians or Capitalists, and investing a disproportionately higher sum of our annual budget to strengthen these facilities."

"So, you are advocating 'focus,' but in a few areas?" Heather summed him up.

"Yes."

"That does not go far enough," Ethan said.

"And why do you say that?" Heather turned to him.

"We are a small population—no matter what we do locally, it will never be enough. We need to join forces with Capitalist states that have the money. In that way, we will not be competing all the time, but aligning with them where it benefits us."

"Would you compromise our Humanitarian principles in those types of partnerships?" David said.

"Be careful there, David," Ethan said looking into the camera again between words. "We can be self-righteous by hanging onto our principles. We Humanitarians think that everything in the Capitalist states is bad."

"Would you be comfortable having the Capitalists telling you how to run your business by surrendering too much economic control?"

"I wouldn't give up that much control. You have to maintain the balance of power. Have you not yourself gone in delegation and met similar-minded folks in New Eden, looking to forge partnerships?"

"Yes. But these are partnerships aimed at advancing our Humanitarian ideals."

"I think we can do the same in business deals," Ethan said. He smiled into the cameras at the end of that exchange, knowing full well that he had scored.

"A question for you now, Ethan," Heather said, after the candidates had sufficient time to regroup. "You have been hailed as the great modernizer, but are you not concerned with how the changes you propose will affect the lives of our citizens?"

"I am not ramming home these changes. The people are asking for it. There is a new generation of citizens in Tolemac today. People my age or younger dominate the population of our state now. We want more out of our lives and for our children. And if my generation is expected to govern in the future, well then, we need to have our hands unfettered to do that."

"Ethan, your changes do not take into consideration our fragile environment, let alone the people," Peter interjected. "Your airport proposal is not acceptable to everyone—have you considered the environmental impact on the New Settlements?"

"There will be a proper study done before anything is attempted. I will bow to the recommendations coming from such a study. But let me ask you, Peter, have you not yourself asked for expansion of the sea wall as part of your port development plan? Have you considered the environmental impact there? I am only suggesting an alternative that would take some of the pressure off these existing facilities. An airport would do just that."

"Give us your views on the moral repercussions that might be felt as a result of our being open to all these new influences, Capitalist ones especially," Heather said.

Ethan pulled himself up to his full height. He swung his cloak behind him with a subtle flourish and delivered lines that must have been rehearsed in anticipation of this cue. "Heather, we are in a moral vacuum now. Yes, you may look at me in shock. But Humanitarian youth are falling prey to external influences because of their sheltered existence. Take the drugs in Oceania. Our neighbours there cannot discern between good and bad, because everything to date has been only good in their lives, after the Flood faded from memory. There is no problem in New Eden, where drugs have been legal since that state was founded. They exposed themselves to the danger and dealt with it."

A look of anger creased Heather's brow, although she tried to remain neutral. "But surely, Ethan you are not talking of turning our beautiful little state into a seedy little whorehouse with all of the vices of the Capitalist states?"

Ethan was unfazed. "Take Alberta. They were facing the same problem Oceania has today, until they legalized drugs five years ago. Now they don't have a problem."

David jumped in, "But they have more addiction centres per capita than any other state in the Capitalist realm. Is that a fair trade-off?"

Ethan smiled and said: "Addiction centres are now closing down in New Eden due to the declining number of patients. There are always short-term adverse effects because of change, but they level out. We cannot hide ourselves under a bushel forever. We certainly need to educate our youth to the dangers out there. They need to see and know what's going on and make intelligent decisions for themselves. I'm not saying that we will not have casualties, but that, overall, you will have a stronger generation going forward."

David felt his blood rise. "I teach young kids and have a young family. Do you think putting them in harm's way is going to make them strong?"

"Yes, I do. And that's the fault of our founding fathers—'cocoon the young' they said, as they braved the elements to build a post-Flood society. Now we have a whole generation of kids with unformed wings. I don't think the older generation did us a favour. We can't compete with the big boys because we don't know how to."

"Maybe we just don't want to," David said and thought, if I can just keep him talking like this, very soon he's going to alienate himself with the good people of Tolemac. He decided to press on, braving Heather's frown that indicated she would like to change the subject. "You say the older generation led us astray?"

"No." Ethan replied. "They did a great job in imparting us with strong values. But they need to let go now."

As if on cue, Peter interrupted. "Ethan, are you casting aspersions on the very team you are aspiring to govern this state with?"

"Peter, as much as I respect my esteemed colleagues on the Executive Committee, I am not afraid to admit that some of them have impaired judgment now. And we need to change the 'old guard.' "

Peter was on the attack now, "That 'old guard' is still the majority on our Executive. And you say that this majority have impaired judgment?"

David sat back and let them knock each other out. All he had to do was remain silent and watch.

Ethan continued without faltering, "I am not here to cast aspersions on those members in whose company I will endeavour to govern Tolemac in the future. But if you ask me to speak my conscience, then I will say—yes!"

"Gentlemen!" Heather interrupted. "May I remind you that this is a debate on political issues not a personal attack against anyone."

Peter said, "But Ethan has started something. Let him finish."

"Yes," David agreed, trying to keep a straight face.

There was a moment of silence before Heather said, "Okay, Ethan you have one more comment before we exit this question."

"Well, I have reasonable evidence to suggest that some of our esteemed colleagues on the Executive lead double lives. I intend, if elected, to force an inquiry into personal conduct and have those responsible step down from the Committee." He was looking directly at David now. "For example, standing up in a pulpit and preaching morality to churchgoers on a Sunday and then living in sin with a neighbour's wife, with the neighbour himself dying under suspicious circumstances, is to my mind not the right moral fibre for our society. That behaviour is more insidious than drugs or other Capitalist vices we are so paranoid about. So let's clean up our own house, before we go looking at flaws in the Capitalist camp."

"I resent that insinuation!" David pounded the table in front of him, nearly losing control. "How dare you!"

Ethan was calm and even-tempered in his response. "I intend to expose these transgressions when I am in office. You may resent it now, but the good citizens of Tolemac deserve to know the truth. This is not idle chatter on my part, I have proof of serious breaches of conduct by these individuals and I will furnish it when I am authorized to do so."

There was hushed silence in the studio and Heather sucked in her breath. The clock ticked on the wall and the sound was like nails pounding into David's skull. Rivulets of sweat ran down his sides and soon he felt them run down his face and into his mouth. Peter and Ethan had orchestrated this one well—and just when he thought he'd had his old foe on the ropes!

"Well, thank you Ethan for that," Heather's irony was stinging after what must have been an eternity of silence. "I hope you can sincerely back up that statement. These are pretty damaging indictments on the present state of our nation. But we have to move on . . ."

The rest of the debate passed in a blur and David was totally distracted. He knew that Ethan had hit the jackpot. He was not sure how the people of Tolemac were going to react but public questions on Samson's activities were now on centre stage—and David had not a shred of evidence to refute it. And all along he had been worrying about the Pink Gypsy! What a great deflection Ethan!

David imagined that his pale face on camera for the rest of the debate must have looked like further evidence of Ethan's damning indictment on Samson.

When the debate concluded, David left the studio immediately, not waiting for the ensuing chitchat and refreshments. Ethan would pump many hands tonight. Members of the red team were not in sight and David did not want to face them at this moment. They must have slunk away, defeated. He did not know where he was going but returning home to the family right now, was something he did not want to do. When he finally broke out of his preoccupied thoughts, he discovered that he had made his way towards the church and to the caretaker's cottage at the rear.

He walked up the stairs and pounded on the Stone's front door. There were sounds inside as if a great many things were being moved. Joshua finally came to the door and Delia shouted from inside. "Joshua, we are not at home. Tell them to go away."

"It's Mr. Arthurs—David," the boy said, reluctant to shut the door. Delia appeared and dragged both of them inside.

"Sit down, David, thank God you have come! I couldn't leave without talking to at least one of your family. Josh, go into the room and get the rest of your stuff into the small suitcase."

As Joshua meekly complied, David looked at her. Delia's hair was loose in a shock of rumpled red, and her eyes looked teary. She was dressed for travelling—black pants and leather jacket zipped up, her sexuality hidden today. Her face was pale and drawn.

"Where are you going?" David said.

"You think we can live here now? I watched the debate."

"Did you kill him?"

"He's best off where he is now. Where he cannot hurt anyone anymore. Why are they raking up all this stuff?"

"You cannot play God, you know."

"Do you know what misery he put me through? For fifteen years. And the last four, when he became impotent from the medication, they were the worst!" She clenched her hands and the edges of her eyes brimmed with tears.

"Still, mercy killing is a criminal offence here."

"What else would you have done?" she said, as tears welled over and rolled down her cheeks. David pulled a tissue from his pocket and handed it to her. For a brief moment, their hands touched. There was a vibration there—a desire to live, to survive, masked behind the veil of widowhood she had recently embraced. He had received that same vibration in the look from the thief in Morby's department store, before the man was tasered by the security guards. It struck David that his mother had never shown this latent fire; all Agnes had salvaged in the end was bitterness.

"Did Samson know?" he said.

"No. And he must never be mixed up with this. Joey and I are leaving on an overnight boat. Belva has offered help. Her friend runs the boat. I will write to Samson and explain everything when we are on safe ground again."

He was still not convinced. "Frida Parks saw Samson talk Dr. Karya out of performing an autopsy on Doug. That smacks of collusion. I bet you that old woman has not kept a word unsaid in blabbing to Ethan."

"If Samson talked to Dr. Karya, it was in kindness. Samson is not involved in this. I take full responsibility. Maybe, one day I'll get to tell them my version."

"Where will you go?"

"Back to New Eden, for now. It's easy to get lost there. And without Doug to hinder me, I can get work again, honest work."

"You will break Samson's heart. He was just beginning to live, after all his nation building. And he wouldn't understand flight. He is a stand-and-fight guy."

She rose and walked towards the window. "Not all people are made like Samson. David, please try and understand. He is a wonderful, sensitive and caring man, a fix-it man. For once in my life he made me feel like a woman. Desired and lovable. But every time he looks at me now, Doug's death will stand between us. Doubt kills, doesn't it?"

Then she came over to him and held his hand again. This time the touch was motherly and he hadn't felt this in a long time. He looked into her bloodshot eyes, the high cheekbones that gave her an aristocratic bearing and the hair that made her so feminine. "You are so much like your father, in a way. I am sorry to have hurt your chances of winning this election. Please understand. No matter where I go, I will always live with that."

"Goodbye, Joshua!" He said to the boy who had come out of the room and was watching sadly. These endings must have played out too many times in his young life. David took out his notebook and scribbled on it. "Joshua, here is my Communicator mail address. Write to me when you get to New Eden. We must keep in touch okay?"

"You mean that, Mr. Arthurs?" He looked unconvinced.

"Yes, I do."

"It may not be wise for you to be associated with us," Delia said from behind.

"We are kind of 'family' now Delia. And one thing Samson taught me was that family stick together."

"Goodbye then," she said and kissed him lightly on the cheek. And for the first time in his handful of encounters with her, this being the closest, David did not get breathless.

He walked home through the dark. It was finally beginning to get cold for early December. Soon Tolemac would celebrate Christmas. He wanted to go and see Samson but felt he would be a failure in his father's eyes. He turned in to the Waterside Park instead and sat on a bench. He did not know how long he sat there. The cold was becoming intense but he continued to sit. He wanted to feel numb. He wanted to feel pain. He was in pain—and shock—from the evening's events. The lights were on in the park and the wind was drifting in from the water. There was no one around, or if there were, maybe no one wanted to associate with a loser. After an eternity, he rose and walked uphill to Lilydale Crescent, shivering in the red jacket he was desperate to get out of.

*　*　*

She had sent the kids to bed before David arrived home. He was stooped and looked like he'd aged ten years. That had been evident on the Communicator during the debate. Each blow that Ethan had struck after Samson's secrets were revealed had caused David to slump deeper and deeper behind his stand on the studio floor.

She had prepared a steaming pot of hot chocolate. Ginchenechea was good to calm a person down, but with his spirits as low as they were David, needed a boost.

He flung the red jacket on the floor, threw himself on the chair opposite her and stared at the blank wall.

"I'm sorry about what happened. I didn't know it would get so ugly," she said after awhile.

"Me neither. Our politics have gone back to pre-Flood days. I rehearsed for all possibilities, except the personal attacks. Samson said it was not part of our culture anymore. He was wrong."

"That's why I was worried about your involvement."

"I should have paid more heed to your sixth sense."

"There's always tomorrow."

"They vote tomorrow."

"And we can all get on with our lives after that."

"I know our relationship has taken a beating since I got involved in the

242

political affairs of Tolemac. But can you see yourself living under the leadership of the likes of Ethan? I am more determined than ever to fight his right-wing threat to our way of life. We owe it to our children, honey!"

She put down her cup and went over to him. She reached out her hand and drew him to her. Her nightgown opened and she was not wearing anything underneath. He sucked in his breath looking at her body, her small, firm breasts with erect nipples. She knew it and felt beautiful in his sight. "Come, honey—make love to me tonight. Like that last time. It seems so long ago now. And there is so much catching up to do."

She was convinced, even before he took her, that this was going to be a special night again. She had felt life leap in her womb after that night at the meditation centre. And there should be many more moments like those to come, now that the politicking was over and done with, at least temporarily.

"And we'll fight those bullies tomorrow—together!" she said, before crushing her mouth on his.

Chapter 22

The next morning dawned no different from any other. It was a clear day with no bad weather in the forecast and a full moon was expected that night. Mrs. Wang's ballroom class was running in Martyrs Square as usual, the dancers dressed in sweaters due to the cooler weather. There was no activity on the street to signify anything special. Yet it was Election Day and voting was taking place in the privacy of people's homes. There would be no more campaigning; it was too late for that now. All one could do was vote and wait for the news when the computer-tabulated results were announced at seven that evening.

Waking up from a night of languid and frequent lovemaking, David switched on the Communicator and placed a check mark beside "David Arthurs" on the personalized ballot delivered to his email box the day before. "May he rule forever," David laughed ruefully. Then he jumped back into bed and buried himself between Sonya's breasts.

"Well, at least we discovered something new through all of this," she whispered stroking his head. "These are not flashes in the pan. And they are real." He lay in bed, agreeing with her and drifting back to sleep. When he woke again, she was in the kitchen and the smell of grilled bacon was strong, making him realize how hungry he was.

After a hearty breakfast, he spent the first half of the morning with his red team down at campaign headquarters, bolstering their flagging spirits. "Anything could happen now. All is not lost—not everyone is in favour of Ethan's madcap plans for modernization." His team appeared to be holding up well. But they were not saying much, nodding their heads for the most part, averting eyes. And he did not like the vacant look on Leo Patimkin's face. Something was ebbing from the young man.

In the afternoon, David went over to the hospital. "Is there evidence of foul play in the Stone case?" he asked Dr. Karya.

Dr. Karya was noncommittal. "I cannot rule out anything until we have a formal inquest. If Ethan carries out his threat, he will first have to file a formal criminal complaint with the hospital or the NADF. It's only then that we can subpoena records and reopen this case."

"With his father being our head of law enforcement, you can expect Ethan to do that."

"The signs of death may have indicated an inaccurate dose. However, the drug Cancerl decomposes in the body within a very short time. It's almost a month since Doug Stone's death. It will be hard to prove that overdosing did take place."

David's heart leaped at that bit of news. He knew that it was wrong to feel that way; wrong to look for technicalities over justice. What had happened to that idealistic young man who stepped up to the plate to run for public office just a few months ago? Since then, he had been exposed to illicit sex, drugs, jealousy, envy, suspicion, anger and now cover-ups—all those pre-Flood emotions, acts and vices that had accompanied the fall of that early civilization. Was the clock turning backwards? But then, he had also discovered how to express his feelings and love his wife.

*   *   *

When David got to Samson's house, the sun was setting on what had been a sunny cold day. The days were short now and sunset came at about five o'clock. David had put off this visit until now, but needed to confront Samson sooner or later. His father was in the living room, in his pyjamas, and it looked like he hadn't gotten out of them all day. The neat, spare house looked rumpled, and papers lay on the floor and on Samson's armchair. The Communicator was on and David saw the familiar figures from Camelot on the screen. The control panel said "rerun # 3." There was one difference this time. The faces of Guinevere and Lancelot were contorted in anguish as they held each other in a deserted garden, singing parts of a song that he had never heard before. Then David realized—Samson was viewing Part Two of his favourite movie—the forbidden one that David had never seen as a child.

The older Arthurs did not speak as David sat down on the couch beside him and watched the movie through to its conclusion. It looked like Camelot was unravelling. The knights were fighting amongst themselves. King Arthur's illegitimate son, Mordred, was loose, sowing seeds of dissent and scandal among those entrusted with noblesse oblige. David watched silently until the movie ran through to the final battle scene between a jaded and tired Arthur and his once-loyal knight, Lancelot. Arthur tells his trusted old assistant, Sir Pellinore, "Pelly, greed undid us and now they want revenge. All our plans to build a noble kingdom have come undone. We were ahead of our time." Then he turns to a boy who had followed him to the final battle scene. Arthur knights the boy and shoos him away from the battlefield, shouting, "Run, my boy, run and live and tell them that there once was a spot for 'happ'ly ever aftering' called Camelot." The movie ended with the haunting theme song.

Samson let the final credits run and his eyes were blurry. "I'm sorry about how the debate turned out. I let you down."

"It's all right. I'm glad it's over."

"We are still no different from the denizens of Camelot, David. We still want to vanquish the opponent at all costs, by any means. As a civilization we aren't out of the woods yet."

"Is that why you never wanted us to see this movie?"

"Well, I thought that our chance had come this time around, with Tolemac. Delia's left, you know."

"I know."

"You do?"

"Yes. I went to see her last night on the way home from the debate. I was surprised that the two of you were not watching it together."

"I wanted to be alone last night. The debate was my world—the world we built here in Tolemac. When I saw you on stage, I saw myself those many years ago and I was proud and happy for you. When I went to see her later, she was gone. She'd left a note."

"What did it say?"

"She thanked me for one bright shining moment in her life. She said I had made that difference for her. In a strange way, she did the same for me."

"I'm sorry, Dad!"

"Did you know about this suspicious death business?"

"Frida Parks hinted about it. Did you?" said David, looking directly at his father.

Samson was reflective in his response, "Delia asked if I could help. She said Doug had destroyed his monthly prescription in one of his mad rages. She was worried he'd worsen without the medication until he was due for his next re-fill. So I got her an extra dose—"off prescription"—so that the hospital wouldn't ask too many questions the next time she went for Doug's monthly supply. I was just trying to help."

"How did you get the extra dose?"

"I know the pharmacist at the hospital very well. I helped build his house after the Flood. He used to get your mother her supply of 'devil's brew,' without a prescription."

"The pharmacist knows! Oh, God, now you're really in trouble!" The image of Samson handing Delia a parcel outside this same house a couple of months ago, flashed in David's memory.

"I guess I will have to face the consequences. I can't run away from it."

"Given your position, she shouldn't have asked that kind of favour from you."

"I can't question her motives nor judge her. And we don't know beyond a doubt if she is responsible. Conjecture only plays havoc. All I know is we were very happy together."

Then David asked the question that had been foremost on his mind. "Did you break the moral code?"

"Adultery?"

"Yes."

"No."

"How about 'Chastity Before Marriage'?"

Samson continued in even keel. "I guess I will have to make a public admission of this sometime. You can judge me then. You wouldn't believe me if I told you now."

"Delia said the same thing to me."

"Events like this destroy trust. That's what I am most sorry about."

The clock struck seven. David jumped up. He had forgotten the election results. He quickly dialled the local news channel. Heather Bradley came on-screen in her brown suit and matching brown earrings.

They sighed, mostly out of relief, when the results were announced. A total of 35,500 people (ages sixteen and above only) were eligible to vote and the final standings were:

Ethan Williams: 14,150

Peter Lowry: 11,250

David Arthurs: 10,150

Heather announced: "In light of the results, Ethan and Peter will be invited to join the Executive Committee next week. We wish them the very best in their political careers! And we wish to thank David Arthurs for his spirited campaign."

David raised a mock glass in tribute. "And thus ends the short-lived political career of David Arthurs!"

"Oh, you'll run again. Here's to the next time!"

"There may not be a next time."

In the interview that followed the announcement of the results, Peter gushed with his plans to propose the expansion of the microchip facility and the port. He was all numbers and figures. Ethan was interviewed in his home and he had his father's ebony lion as a backdrop. With his cloak draped over the animal, Ethan cut a dramatic figure: "We will be bold, venture into the unknown, tame it and clean up our house—once and for all—the future is now!"

"They still want to win at all costs," said Samson, rising from the depths of his chair. "They have not learned in over a thousand years. You'd better get home. I'm going to turn in."

*　*　*

Samson watched his son depart, and then scooped the papers strewn on the floor. He did not want to look beaten to his next visitor who would be arriving any minute now. He wished he had spent more time consoling David, but that would have to wait.

He changed into casual clothes—jeans, T-shirt and sandals—and he slicked his hair and beard into a presentable shape. He placed Delia's letter into his journal. It was all he had left of her now. It had been brief but so rejuvenating. She had taught him the art of lovemaking. Of not only taking but giving, giving until it hurt. But, in a different sense, hadn't he done that all his life, for his fellow Tolemacians? Worked, built, organized and planned so that people could have a second chance. And the moment he had started to relax, they'd got him; and his son, too. He was glad he made the call today. The doorbell sounded.

The man standing at the door stepped in quickly from the porch light. He looked different from when Samson had first seen him. Gone was the lean and hungry look. His stride was purposeful, yet he looked about with caution.

"Sorry about the election. Hope David's all right?"

"I left myself open. I should have listened to Congressman Gordon earlier. These guys play by a different set of rules."

"We are glad to have you on board finally."

"I have no choice now."

"You are the only one who can help us. We've done all the digging on the outside. Here's something to keep you going. It's as far as we've got." The visitor pulled out a sheaf of papers and handed it to Samson.

"I'll do what I can," Samson said as he glanced through the papers and raised his eyebrows.

His visitor began to cough. "Do you have some water?"

"That's a bad cough," Samson said, handing him a glass of water from the portable drinks trolley.

The man drank his water and the cough eased. "Here are the instructions for the hook up." He handed Samson another sheet of paper. "Do you think you can get it set up?"

"I have contacts, although recently, they have gotten me into hot water more than anything else." Samson chuckled.

"When can I expect to go 'live'?"

"Give me a couple of weeks. I'm going to move fast, before I lose my Executive privileges. I sense Ethan's going to have me suspended. And he has grounds."

"He'd be hard pressed to pin foul play on you."

"Oh, but he will create so much noise I'll have to resign anyway."

"You expect too much from yourselves. With your laws."

"Sometimes we try to escape our mousetraps by building others."

"I have to go. We'll be in touch." The man drained his glass and rose.

As the visitor slipped quietly away, all Samson could see of his departing figure was the moonlight glinting off a bomber jacket.

Chapter 23

WHEN DAVID GOT HOME, the family was unusually quiet. They had dinner together, making small talk. During a lull in the sober dinner conversation, Joey proclaimed that David's loss at the election was no big deal. David in turn promised that he could help his son with math in the new school term. Joey said that wasn't a big deal either, if David did not have the time for tutoring. And David insisted that he would find the time. Hannah then came around and sat on her father's lap and said that she had a dream that he would lead Tolemac one day. After the children had gone to bed, Sonya and David sat out on the back porch. It was cold, but they hunkered down in blankets, warming up with mugs of hot chocolate.

"Sean said I was a lucky man. Now I know why."

"You'll run again."

"And you'll be at my side?"

"You were destined to run, honey. It was foolish of me to think that I could stop you. Just include us in the good times, as well as the bad." Then she turned her dark eyes on him. "And don't ever stop making love to me like you did last night."

"That's what Samson told me. About having you involved in the good times and the bad."

The Communicator's emergency voice-channel light started flashing. David had switched off the ring alert because he did not want to disturb the children. Who could it be at this time of the night? He did not want to answer right then, being snug in the blanket on the porch with Sonya, yet he couldn't take his eyes off the hypnotically beckoning red light.

Finally, when Sonya said, "You'd better get that. Something tells me it's not good," he moved.

It was Vladimir Patimkin. He sounded distraught. "David, sorry about the election, but please come down here quick! We are outside the Waterfront Hotel. Leo's gone crazy."

"What!"

"He's got a gun from somewhere and shot Rocky's kid. He's holed up in one of the rooms of the hotel."

David was reeling. "Vladimir, what are you saying? This is Tolemac for goodness sake!"

"I know. But David I can't describe this any better. He's also holding Sally Morden hostage. We don't know what to do."

David was seized by Vladimir's seriousness. "I'm on my way!" he said, switching off the Communicator and grabbing Sonya who was coming in through the screen door.

"Come with me. I'll explain later."

"I can't. What about the children?"

But he was insistent. "This is big, honey. I'm sure they will be alright. We can call Belva enroute and ask her to look in."

He threw her a coat, grabbed one for himself, filling her in on the sketchy details while herding her out the front door. His heart thumped as they freewheeled their bicycles downhill to the waterfront.

The hotel was bathed in light from temporarily erected flood lamps. Burgess and his troops were lined up around the hotel. Blue and black uniforms and helmets announcing "NADF—Tolemac Division," gave the policemen a scary appearance in the night. David had never seen so many law enforcement personnel concentrated in such a small area before. A flood lamp was focused on the windows of a room on the second floor. There was a group of partially dressed people draped in blankets, standing in the chilly air behind the police cordon. These were the hotel's guests, hurriedly evacuated during the emergency.

Burgess quickly gave David the story. Joe Sabbattini and his helpers had been at the hotel, gearing up for Ethan's campaign celebration and awaiting their leader. Sally was with Joe at the time. Leo had turned up, and without uttering a word, walked up to Joe, pulled a gun out of his school bag and shot him in the chest. Then Leo grabbed Sally and locked her with him in a second-floor room of the hotel, threatening to shoot her if Ethan and Peter would not resign and call for a new election under the old format, in Leo's words, "sans the character bashing that went on in the debate." Joe was rushed to the hospital where Rocky was with him now.

"How'd Leo get a gun?"

"I don't know. Maybe he got it from one of the sailors in an illicit deal. My men do random searches for guns and drugs on the boats coming in via the Capitalist states, but that does not go far enough."

"I'm not impressed."

"Let's not argue, David. You know I've raised the issue of providing adequate funding for Defence many times at the Committee, yet no one listens."

Vladimir, looking dishevelled and confused, came over with his wife Tanya in hand. David could see their preteen twin daughters, Olga and Larissa, huddled in the NADF car behind the police cordon.

"Please save my boy, David." Tanya, in contrast to her erudite husband, was short and matronly. She grabbed David's hand: "Please ask them not to shoot him." She was dressed in a housecoat with an overcoat draped on top. "He respects you. He will listen to you. He does not listen to us anymore."

"David, whatever you plan to do, you'd better make this quick," Burgess interrupted. "We plan to rush the building soon. We've got to get him while he's still unsure of his movements."

"You will do nothing of the kind!" Sonya said. "Until David has a chance to talk to him."

Burgess shrugged. "Okay. I'll hold my men off for as long as I can. Remember, there is an innocent young woman being held hostage in there."

David was undecided. Suddenly, people were relying on him. He looked at Sonya. "Go to him David," she said, her eyes steady. "He needs you now, more than ever."

Nodding, David stepped out into the spotlight and made his way towards the hotel. Leaving the safety of the police cordon, the distance to the entrance doors appeared to be a long walk. He saw movement behind the curtains in the room on the second floor.

"Leo!" he shouted, "I'm coming over, Leo." He didn't think anyone heard him. His throat felt constricted.

The lobby was deserted, except for two armed policemen wearing gas masks and combat uniforms, standing at either end of the stairway.

"We'll give you cover, David," one of them said, and his voice sounded familiar.

"No, thanks," David replied hastily. "I'll be all right. You can come up once I manage to get the girl out of the way." But he felt he was making a big mistake by not taking them along with him. Yet something kept propelling him forward. He looked at the policeman again. "How do you know my name?"

The policeman removed his mask. "I'm Paul Samuel. Remember me from school?"

Paul Samuel, who had gone on to join the NADF in Oceania after graduation! "Paul! Why, I thought you were in Oceania?"

"I'm on loan here temporarily. I'm with the NADF's drug squad in Oceania. They sent me down to investigate a drug connection in Tolemac."

"Drugs? Here?"

"We think Tolemac is being used as a trans-shipment point to get drugs into the larger Humanitarian states, like Oceania. But there is usually leakage locally when that happens."

"I can't believe we'd succumb to this."

"That's what we are here to find out. I'm not sure Tolemac can be kept totally out of bounds of the drug trade anymore."

"What's Leo and Sally got to do with drugs?"

"I was following an anonymous tip we received tonight that some 'retailing' was going on around the waterfront and it led me here. Why don't you go upstairs and find out for yourself?"

"What room are they in?"

"Two zero eight. On your left."

The single flight of stairs took forever to climb. David's coat was damp by now and he had sweated right through his shirt. All his life's work as a teacher, building up the next generation was about to fall apart in Room 208 and he could not let that happen without at least a damned good fight. He was finally outside and tapped on the door. "Leo, it's David Arthurs. And I'm alone."

"Come in Mr. Arthurs." Leo's voice was faint from inside. "I unlocked the door for you. Bring no one else. Please!"

David pushed the door open and stepped in, shutting it behind him. The scene that met his eyes completely obliterated the tense police scene that he had just come through.

Sally was seated on the floor with her schoolbooks spread out around her. Leo sat across from her. Apart from the tension in their faces, they could have been studying together, as David had once urged them to do. Then he saw the gun reposing on Leo's lap. The boy had a faraway look of accomplishment in his eyes.

"It's time to go home now, Leo."

"Not yet, Mr. Arthurs. Not yet. Sit down." Leo's fingers tightened around the gun momentarily and his voice took on a strange high note. The boy fished out a little pouch from his jacket. "Want some of this Mr. Arthurs—it's giddy stuff. Makes you do anything you want to do."

"No, thanks. Where did you get that from?"

"My secret." He grinned gleefully and popped what looked like a pill into his mouth. "We can't let them win, Mr. Arthurs."

"It's not about winning and losing, Leo. It's about treating one's neighbour as one would want to be treated." David saw Sally's fearful expression increase a notch.

"They're gonna get you in the end Mr. Arthurs. After they've done with your dad. But don't you worry, I'm gonna stop them. And Sally is going to help me. Aren't you Sally, darling?" His eyes were glazing over and beads of sweat covered his brow. "This stuff really motivates."

The recollection of similar behaviour struck David. He was back in that loud bar in New Eden, rubbing his crotch against Sugar and feeling he could do anything he wanted. Leo had gotten himself a handful of the same drugs.

"And you wrote my speeches on how to combat drugs."

"Sometimes you have to join the Devil and play him at his game, Mr. Arthurs."

How far gone was Leo? David decided to chance it, hoping he sounded convincing. "Okay, Leo, you win. Let's have some of that stuff and tell me how you are going to beat our competition."

Leo tossed him the pouch. There were three tiny capsules in it. How many does one need to pass out? He'd had three in New Eden before he collapsed.

Maybe if he hit one and Leo hit the other two? What if these are double or even triple strength? What if he passed out before Leo did? How many has the kid taken already? Sally was looking at David quizzically, wondering whose side he was on.

David popped a capsule into his mouth and tossed the pouch back. He tried keeping the pill under his tongue, hoping it would not dissolve.

Leo was laughing, "Joe, he wasn't a bright kid after all. Took one look at me, and fell down like a poleaxed bear. Hah, ha!"

"Guns are great equalizers, for cowards!" Sally burst out, then checked herself and began to sob. With a sinking feeling, David felt the covering of the capsule begin to melt and immediately the sweet taste of its contents hit his palate.

"Yeah. This gun is great. Has that punk Ethan resigned yet, Mr. Arthurs?"

"No. And it's not going to happen, Leo."

"Might as well get comfortable then, 'til he does. It's going to be a long night." Leo rose and went over to the Communicator in the room and switched on the audio channel. His step was unsteady. "Sally, let's dance." He yanked her up and put his arms around her with the gun hanging from one hand. They stumbled across the room in an awkward two-step. "See, I can get any girl I want if I play their game, Mr. Arthurs. You gotta do it, too. Or else they'll destroy you."

David's mind was racing. Should he jump the boy now? But the gun flapping in Leo's hand was scary; it was right up against Sally's back and the room was too small to have bullets go off inside. Besides, David's eyes were glazing over and he was beginning to feel light-headed, too. Sucking in his breath he tried suppressing the feeling, but the euphoria was too good to resist. After all, he had just suffered a humiliating defeat in an election. Wasn't he entitled to a bit of relief? Who cared if there was a drama going all around him? Life was a drama!

The audio was interrupted and Vladimir's voice came in over the line. They had intercepted Leo's Communicator channel. Vladimir's voice sounded strained and high-pitched and the reception was crackly. "Leo . . .Leo. Please put down your gun and come outside. Please son, we implore you!"

Leo stopped dancing. He stumbled over to the Communicator and wrenched the tuner off and the line went dead. "He's another coward! Always did it the 'right way.' That isn't the right way. You've gotta play them at their game and beat 'em!"

Sally had fallen back on her knees. And Leo was stumbling about the room. David crawled over to her. The drug-induced side of him wanted to have sex with this poor innocent ebony babe, the other side of him was furiously trying to stay afloat. "It'll be over soon," he whispered in her ear. He was pretty sure that was the higher side of him speaking.

"Hey, Leo!" David said, staggering to his feet. "This stuff is awesome. Let's have some more."

When Leo handed him the pouch again, David took out another capsule. "One for you, and the last one for me."

"Mr. Arthurs, don't——", he heard Sally pleading in the background, but he put a capsule in Leo's hand. "Let's hit this nice and high, Leo."

"You bet, Mr. Arthurs. You're my man!"

In moments, the room was spinning. "Show me your homework," David said trying to retain the last hold on his higher self.

"Nah . . . Don't need this stuff now. Sally, come here. I need to have sex with you, baby. You don't mind, eh, Mr. Arthurs! I feel good and hot right now. Yeah baby!" Leo was spinning in circles, groping for Sally who had crawled over to the door.

"No, don't!" The look of horror on Sally's face temporarily dampened David's own drug-induced designs on her.

"Sally is going to do it with me!" Leo was salivating now as he ambled towards her. "Thought Leo couldn't get his girl, did you?"

David lunged across and grabbed Leo's leg and they both came crashing down on the floor. The gun fell out of Leo's hand and went spinning somewhere out of sight. "Sally, get out of here!" David gasped.

He heard the door slam, and then it was just Leo and him entangled in each other. David's vision was narrowing and all he could see was Leo's struggling face.

"She's getting away, Mr. Arthurs. She's our trump . . . card. Can't let her get away. . ."

"Let her go, Leo!"

Leo was thumping him, and crying at the same time. "But you're always like that . . . Mr. Arthurs! You're too good! Letting the chances . . . slip. Where's my gun?"

David held on to him, determined not to let go. There was a crash by the doorway and Paul Samuel and his companion found David and Leo pawing around each other and flailing helplessly for a gun, which lay innocently at the opposite end of the room.

All David heard Leo say as they hauled him out was, "You let me down, Mr. Arthurs! You betrayed me! Hey guys, has that punk Ethan resigned yet?"

*   *   *

The next day, David woke up with the biggest hangover to find Sonya hovering around him with a hot cup of ginchanecea tea. Hannah was lying patiently on the bed beside him, hands cupping her chin. "Daddy, you're a hero! They are talking about you on the news!"

"Now, Hannah let your Daddy rest. He's had a rough night."

"I'm going to tell all my friends in school!" she said, and went off somewhere.

David closed his eyes again. The same dryness of throat and throbbing of the temples from the morning after in New Eden was back. Then Sonya's lips were on his cheek and they seemed to suck the dryness and pain away.

"Oh, stay there. Don't go away," he croaked.

"Now, now. We can't be at this all day," she said, drawing away and straightening the blanket around him.

"What happened . . . afterwards?"

"When they took Leo away?"

"Yes."

"Ethan showed up on the waterfront after you went inside the hotel and made out that he was prepared to resign if that would get the boy out."

"A great chance to make a grand performance!"

"Precisely. I told him not to bother, as you had the situation under control. When they brought Leo out however, he was the first to demand the boy be arrested and charged with shooting a teen and putting another's life in danger."

"Where is Leo now?"

"Mother had arrived by then and put a jinx on Ethan's plans. She told him

260

that as Leo was below eighteen, he became a ward of the state and would be given treatment and rehabilitation instead of a trial. Mother was in good form. She said that if ever justice were to be served it would be on those who had got guns and drugs into the hands of teenagers. Leo was taken to Tolemac General. He was diagnosed as having suffered a complete nervous breakdown."

"Poor kid. And what about Joe and Sally?"

"Joe's out of critical condition. The bullet grazed a rib and exited from the other side without much damage. And Sally is with her parents—she's shaken, but she'll mend. She's a strong girl."

"I can't remember anything after they took Leo away."

"We brought you home in the police car. You were pawing and trying to crawl all over me. And we were all having quite a laugh. 'Grown man takes bad drugs to overpower kid and attacks wife in the process.' A great headline for a news story. I'm relieved Heather Bradley was not around to see you in action!"

He was blushing. "I did all that? Can't remember a thing!"

"I was surprised at you. If the NADF guards were not around in the car I might have actually liked what you were doing, apart from the mumbling and fumbling."

He knew she was kidding him and gratefully took her hand. He set the cup of tea aside and was fast asleep within minutes. Nodding off, he smiled, realizing he had just lost an election, yet saved young lives—all in the same day!

His feeling of victory was short-lived. The next day, Ethan announced a "Get the Facts on Drugs" campaign, an education program on the pros and cons of imbibing mind-altering drugs. Another grandstanding opportunity.

Two weeks later, soon after Ethan and Peter were formally inaugurated into the Executive, Ethan introduced his first action to the Committee: a formal complaint to suspend Samson Arthurs for aiding and abetting the suspected murder of Doug Stone and for breaking the moral code of Tolemac.

Part 3

Retribution

"Consequently, just as the result of one trespass was condemnation for all, so also the one act of righteousness was justification that brings life for all."

—Romans 5:18

Chapter 24

December 21, 2045

I̶T̶ ̶I̶S̶ ̶A̶ ̶L̶O̶N̶G̶ ̶T̶I̶M̶E̶ *since I have written anything in this journal. It was my companion during tough times. In good times, I neglected it; like a spouse, or a loved one we take for granted. Today, the prodigal, I drag myself back to its faded pages.*

Father, forgive me! I sinned. I broke the commandment, sought a moment of peace and comfort, became selfish for a brief moment in my life and paid heavily for it. In this lifetime, I was intended to be a producer, not a consumer; a giver, not a taker. I should have seen that the day You spared my life during the Flood. When all those people were falling behind, I wondered why I wasn't one of them. That's because I was intended to go on to build the next chapter of our human story. That was Your plan.

But what of that plan now—our beloved Tolemac riddled with drugs, plagued by consumerism, surrounded by alcoholic sirens in our waters, our founders trespassing the laws that were set up to protect us and keep us whole, my beloved Executive Committee torn asunder with the new blood we infused into it. New blood I should have seen was evil the day I plucked it out of the womb of its helpless mother and gave it life.

And my beloved Agnes, why did you leave me so soon? If I'd had the chance to talk to you on your deathbed and tell you what you had imagined that day was not what it was. Oh, that we had not drifted into our silences over the years. And, oh, Agnes that you could believe that I would have a second chance of finding love, the love I know you so wanted to give me but which our customs and laws prevented us from sharing in equal measure.

As for Delia, who finally released me from those shackles. The events of the past few days have tarnished what we had, but I would like to treasure those times before all this unravels, before the accusations, the innuendo and the charges in court.

Regarding my dear son David, sad is the day when the sins of the father visit the son. I preached this so much in church. How stupid and unassuming was I to not realize that our lapses come back to haunt us? How will I motivate him to go on when his first attempt to serve publicly has ended in humiliation, far worse than mere defeat?

I talk of lapses here, of errors in moral judgment. But are they the doors to human experience we are all preordained to live through, that we stifled with laws and traditions, which were the product of our own post-Flood demons? Why did we legislate pleasure as a bad thing? What was so wrong in looking at Delia enjoying herself in my arms? Of that pure glow of ecstasy in her that raised my own spirit and made it soar? Something I never experienced with Agnes, who yet showered on me a different kind of love.

Father, you used to inspire me during those early days on Sunset Hill, never to give up. That's all that's keeping me from calling it quits—never giving up. Yes, one has to go on, I know. If we don't do that, what are we? But this time we have to recalibrate our rules of engagement. We went too far left. David talks of the Middle Way, but it is too soon for that now. Swinging a ship that has keeled over too far left requires a sharper swing to the right first. Let me do that then. Once we have righted the balance, David can travel the Middle Way. I think his generation will be able to do that quite successfully. But we, the old guard, who caused the keeling, have to right the balance first.

And that will take pain and conflict, which still lies ahead. But therein lies the challenge. To stride the land like an avenging angel and rid this place of malcontents that preyed on our weaknesses and brought us to our knees. There can be no holding back now, no compromise. Already the evidence with which to strike back is beginning to gather, thanks to those relentless Knights of Eden, from whom we can learn valuable lessons. And we need to rewrite our laws. We cannot legislate emotions—that was the mistake. What a fatal mistake!

I feel better already, this journal has been a great help—a well in which to bury my troubles and be cleansed for the journey ahead.

It is late, as this year comes to a close. Father give me the courage to go through the humiliation that lies ahead and let me not veer from the path I have now chosen. Amen.

*　　*　　*

That is the last entry in Samson's journal. It's as if he never intended to record anything more. It had sounded like a prayer.

It is late indeed. It is well past three in the morning and I have spent these last few hours reading about events in Samson's life, making them trigger memories of my own life and trying to understand the genesis of what transpired in the last four months of his.

I close the journal and am about to head for the bedroom when I realize that I promised to help Hannah fix her password. Switching on the Communicator, I navigate down to the master password index that Sonya and I control, and reset Hannah's. Then to make sure she will not have trouble with it in the morning, I test it by opening her mailbox. Sure enough, it works. As I am about to shut the machine off I see a folder in her mail file called "Joshua Stone." Joshua? Corresponding with Hannah? It's a big folder judging from its size, and it is active, as there are unread messages in it. I guess I have been prying into people's lives so much in search of answers that I reflexively open the folder, promising myself not to snoop too much. But Joshua intrigues me; I did not know that Hannah and he had so much in common. The correspondence is a text thread. I go back to the beginning and scroll down.

December 18, 2045. Hi Josh! Why do you not write? You said to send notes, not voice. And I have done that ever since you left. I have missed you so much since you went away. I've no one to fly my kite with. Joey says it's only for young kids—but you're not young, yet you played with me. When are you coming back?—Hannah

December 25, 2045. Happy Christmas! Josh if you don't write, I promise I will never write to you again!—Hannah

December 26, 2045. Hannah! How are you? We just got a place in New Eden and I wanted to write straight away. How are you and your family keeping? Sorry I did not reply earlier, my mum and I were searching for a place. And then when we found one, we had to wait to get an Infoway connection. Sorry we don't have voice, only text.—Josh

December 26, 2045. Oh Josh, thank God you replied. I was so upset with you! What do you mean you have no Infoway connection—every house, every person has one. And why can't you get a voice connection? My dad is feeling very down after he lost the election. I don't know how to console him. Maybe I can write him a letter or something just like I have been writing to you. Writing cheers doesn't it? Write soon!—Luv Hannah

December 30, 2045. Hannah, you may have free Infoway connections in Tolemac, but we have to pay for it here and my mum had to get a job before we could do that. Can't afford voice, only text. I am also working in Mr. Kim's grocery store after school. I hope to buy his store when I am bigger (it's very small and does not make a lot of money, so I think it will be cheap to buy). Maybe I can turn it into a bigger store like Morby's where they sell the best chocolate. Too bad about your dad. My mum is also very hurt about having to leave Tolemac —we both miss our time in Tolemac—we were happy there. At least, you were my friend. Mum does not talk much about it but when she comes home at night she sits down at the Communicator to write something, a letter I think, but then she deletes it and goes to bed sobbing.—Luv 2 U 2, Josh

December 30, 2045. Oh, you poor thing. What do you mean you have no friends? I have tons of them here. The problem with you is you never wanted to go out with them much—always in your house, until I would come and get you. Why don't you come back to Tolemac? I miss you.—I like 'Luv 2 U 2'—clever. Grandpa says they used to write that way when they were kids when the Infoway was called the Internet.—Hannah

I find it hard to stop reading this string that does not seem to end, between two children on either side of the socio-political divide of our present world. I quickly scan down to the bottom. Their innocent chatter also holds some of the answers to our adult world and it is refreshing, for once, to get down into a child's orbit again, where the problems we think we have, don't exist. But I have snooped enough tonight, and my eyes are blurry. I shut off the Communicator and head to bed.

The streetlight that comes in through the window of our bedroom shines on Sonya, who is lying on her back, one arm thrown over her head. She sleeps like that now due to her expanding belly; our third child, conceived that night at the meditation centre, is to be born in a few months. The blanket has slipped down to her waist and the strap of her nightdress has fallen off her shoulder. I see the rhythmic rise and fall of her breasts, the sprawl of her dark hair against the white pillows. A wave of desire sweeps through me. I want to make love to her right now. Not the way I pawed her in the police car that day under the influence of drugs, but in the way we have made love in these last few months since that pivotal night in the meditation centre. I lay down beside her. Instinctively, she snuggles up and leans her side against me. I take her breast gently in my hand and she murmurs in her sleep. But I cannot follow through. There is still too much on my mind. I need to put all the events of the recent past behind me before normalcy can return. I take my hand away from her and lay it at her side. I stare up at the ceiling. So let's get on with the "inquisition" then and have done with these sleepless nights.

*　*　*

The New Year had just dawned when the Executive Committee convened its inquiry into the allegations brought against Samson. Kamala kept away from our house during the two weeks leading up to the hearing, as she was the presiding judge and had to remain neutral. I know it must have been very hard on her, for she missed the kids over the Christmas season. She, unlike most other people, still maintained the tradition of exchanging gifts and even had a little tree decorated in her home every year, which Hannah and Joey thought was cute. Not many people celebrated that festival anymore.

I went to see Paul Samuel down at the local NADF office a few days before the hearing and caught him just as he was leaving. He had a suit bag in hand.

"Hope I haven't come at a wrong time?" I said.

"No, but we can talk in the police car taking me down to the heliport. I'm heading back to Oceania today. My work here is done for now."

In the car, he told me how far his investigation had led.

"One of our 'retail' suspects is a guy called Nick Sagar. Nick runs a passenger and cargo boat out of Tolemac to the Humanitarian states. Have you seen him before?" Paul showed me a picture. I recognized the man at the Waterfront Park on the day of my election rally, the one who had claimed that the new helicopter service was depressing boat traffic.

"Why don't you arrest him?" I said.

"Not yet. We need the big fish."

"What about the drug users? Can they be forced to give you leads?"

"We don't know who the users are until they display signs of distress—when the drugs become addictive or when an overdose is taken, such as happened with Leo. By then, they are incoherent and unreliable. The problem is that these are ordinary people. If I could categorize them, I'd say that a majority of them tend to be either stressed, emotionally needy or plain bored."

"Which could be a lot of us."

"Precisely. But, we know how the system works. Nick is the retailer. He's got a wholesaler somewhere in Tolemac, who's also focused on larger markets like Oceania. Tolemac is a good sideline, gravy. Retailers are recruited from among the disadvantaged. We've got enough evidence on Nick and can take him out of the game anytime. But getting Nick wouldn't solve our problems; we've got to hit the mother lode and there are many layers between the likes of Nick and the ringleaders."

"Is there anything I can do to help?"

Paul fished out his card. "Here's how to reach me if you come across anything. We've tailed Nick quite a bit. One of his frequent haunts warrants checking out further. It's a warehouse on Water Street, down by the port. Run by a guy called Jeremy Brady, remember him?"

"Of course! We went to school with him. His twin runs a courier business in New Eden."

"Yes, that's why we think there might be a connection. We've got our folks keeping tabs on Jermaine Brady in New Eden, too. Jermaine also owns an aviation maintenance company—he's quite the success story over there. We are not sure if all that money has been legitimately earned. Keep your eyes peeled. Let me know if you stumble on anything. Unfortunately, the distribution web is getting more complex in Oceania. Hence my superiors need reinforcements down there and have recalled me. We had to temporarily pull our surveillance off Brady's warehouse, too."

We had arrived at the heliport by then and I was surprised and pleased to see Sean readying the helicopter taking Paul back to Oceania. I hadn't seen Sean since the election campaign, although Sonya had mentioned that he was still visiting the meditation classes, albeit with less regularity now.

I had a chance to talk to Sean when he came by the tiny passenger lounge. He waved to me to come outside, as he was smoking. He looked pale and tired. He lit another cigarette from the dying embers of the one he had just finished.

"It's been awhile, Sean!"

"Yes, I've been busy. We are preparing for the arrival of two new helicopters. Had to recruit additional crew and see about setting up our own maintenance facility now that we will be up to six choppers." He looked distracted and coughed as he exhaled.

"That's stuff's not good for you." I said.

"Can't help it. Pressure of work, I guess." Then, as if remembering, he said, "Give my regards to Sonya. Tell her that I'll try to get out to a class soon."

He bade me a hasty farewell, stubbed out his cigarette and headed off to board his helicopter. I wished Paul goodbye and watched the big bird fly out across the water.

*   *   *

Sonya was strained in those days leading up to the hearing. The exuberance of being pregnant was not enough to ward off the tension. We made small talk most of the time during the day, and at night tried to forget the pending inquiry with lovemaking that had taken on a kind of desperate escapism. Now I understood why Delia had sought the pleasure of her own body to avoid the harsh world around her. One morning at breakfast, I mentioned that I had seen Sean at the heliport and that he had promised to attend a future meditation session.

She brightened at the mention of Sean. "He keeps so much inside—he needs to get out to our classes more often," she said.

"Is that why you find him attractive?" I ventured, smiling.

"Yes, in a tragic sort of a way. He has none of the things we all take for granted." Then she smiled. "Are you jealous?"

I blushed. But I was not feeling threatened anymore. I think we had crossed a milestone in our relationship that was making me very secure. I was so grateful for having her around at this time.

And what of Samson? He was spending more time on the boat that he had bought a few years ago and used sparingly during the summers. He was overhauling the engine and giving the boat a coat of fresh paint. Whenever I went by the waterfront, he'd be hard at work, not bothering with his customary chatting to passersby. Once, I went right down to the quay and he was on the landing dock with a device in his hands. He hit various buttons on it and the boat reversed, spun a full circle and fell back into its moorings. For someone who was not fond of technology, he was applying himself to this tool with zest. I had been standing there about fifteen minutes before he noticed me.

"You look like you are on a mission. New toy?" I said.

As he turned around, I caught a glimpse of his maniacal determination, but it disappeared as he brushed the hair across his sweaty forehead. His countenance relaxed, changing into a wide grin. "David! Yes, you could say I'm on a mission. Getting this boat fixed up. This is a portable navigator to help me steer the vessel remotely from the dinghy when I'm out snorkelling."

"Are you going to take that overdue vacation after the inquiry is behind us?"

"Perhaps. At least, I'm thinking of taking a long journey."

"Is there anything I could do to help with the hearing?"

He put the portable navigator away and wiped his hands with a cloth. Then he reached into a cooler and pulled out two bottles of iced ginchanecea tea and tossed one to me. He opened his bottle, took a gulp and sat on the railing looking out to sea.

"There is nothing you can do for me now, son. Except tell the family that I'm okay. How are Sonya and the baby coming along?" This deflecting small talk was beginning to bother me.

"Fine. Sonya's a bit sick in the mornings, that's all. Could you not get Delia to testify? Clear up this whole thing?"

"Leave her out of this. I've got to face the music."

"You still haven't told me what happened between the two of you."

"Come to the hearing and find out. And be patient till then." His jaw was set and I knew that we were not going to get much further on this subject.

"What's with the spare fuel tank?" I said, changing subjects. There was an unfamiliar portable fuel tank on the deck and judging by the way it sat solidly on the gently swaying boat, it was full.

"I told you. I will be taking a long trip one of these days, and I need all the fuel I can get." He winked at me, drained the bottle of iced tea and dropped it back into the cooler. I capped my bottle and slipped it into my carry bag to have for later—one good Tolemacian trait—'waste not, want not.' Taking my leave of him, I paused at the dock entrance and looked back. Samson had returned to his work, whistling, and there was that same deliberateness of movement again, as if he were in a hurry to get somewhere.

*   *   *

I didn't forget Leo. I went by the psychiatric ward a couple of times. The first time, the nurses told me that he was still violent and had to be sedated; visitors were out of bounds. The next time, the day before the hearing, he was able to see visitors.

Waiting to see Leo, I got my first opportunity to watch the inmates in the public area. Most were middle-aged or older, many having suffered the trauma of the Flood and never recovered. Some muttered to themselves, others wrung their hands and got exasperated, while others just sat in silence. The more expressive ones tried taking their clothes off or bothering their calmer brethren—at which point an attendant would appear and take them out of sight. One particular act was most interesting. At different intervals, a few of the old-timers would start making waves and flapping their hands like giant birds. Another group would cower down beneath them and close their ears as the wave makers got louder and louder. Then with a shriek the wave makers would race over the cowering ones and run to the end of the room reducing their noise and flapping as they passed. Both groups laughed hysterically and the act would be repeated with the cowerers reversing roles with the wave makers. The attendant escorting me explained that the inmates were re-enacting the Flood. It was the last event they remembered before going off their heads.

Leo was among the scattered inmates, sitting in a corner with a younger woman who looked sedated. But as soon as he saw me, he got agitated and shouted "turncoat— traitor . . ." and a few other choice words. The attendant had to re-escort me to the front desk. Leo's antics aggravated the rest of the inmates in the hall, for everyone started chattering and wave making and cowering and taking their clothes off and all the other things I had witnessed, with a higher level of intensity. A flock of attendants descended to calm everyone. After that day, I decided to give Leo a rest for a while, but I resolved to return and try and to get through to him again.

Chapter 25

ON THE MORNING OF THE HEARING we gathered in the Executive Committee's public chamber. When Sonya and I arrived, Samson was seated at the centre table, facing the judge's bench. From our seats I could see him in profile. Members of the Executive Committee were on the left side of the room. The witness stand was on the right. The upstairs gallery, normally empty, was full of spectators. Muted voices tittered in packed rows of wooden pews on both levels, until Kamala entered from a side door and took the bench. She was impeccably dressed, in her judicial red suit and black gown, and her manner was businesslike. The tittering stopped. I looked around at the faces in the chamber. I had known many since childhood. Most were in the over-fifty group who attended our church services regularly; there was a mixture of curiosity and uncertainty amongst them.

"Good citizens of Tolemac," Kamala began, "we are gathered today on a matter of utmost gravity. A member of our Executive Committee stands accused of complicity in the death of a refugee living in the community. It is charged that the death of Douglas Stone occurred because of a wilful overdose of a drug called Cancerl, supposedly administered by the deceased's wife, Delia Stone, who has since departed Tolemac for parts unknown. Samson Arthurs is accused of providing Mrs. Stone with excessive and unauthorized quantities of this drug. You will hear the testimony of witnesses today. The Executive Committee will act as jury in this preliminary hearing, and you may wonder, why? Why not a properly constituted jury from the general population? Let me explain. Our laws demand integrity and selflessness from those who serve publicly. It is a tradition that defines who we are in the Humanitarian States—and especially in our beloved state of Tolemac. We need to deal with our own problems expeditiously, and the Executive will stand in the public eye during this forum today, addressing its internal issues of alleged misconduct, if indeed there has been misconduct. If proof of guilt is established, criminal charges will be laid and a formal trial will be set for a later date.

"Those of you presenting evidence, please do so in good faith, you will be under oath. Those in the public area, please reserve your judgment, comments and applause. We are dealing with a grave situation today, one unprecedented in our short history as a post-Flood society."

Taking a deep breath and bringing down her gavel, she said, "Let us begin . . ."

The parade of witnesses began, questioned in turn by respective members of the Executive, who had been delegated certain areas of inquiry relevant to the case. I sucked in my breath when the first witness was called: the pharmacist at the hospital, who confirmed issuing a prescription of Cancerl to Samson Arthurs on August 10, 2045. The hospital logs confirmed his testimony. The pharmacist went on to say that he had done "favours" in the past for Mr. Arthurs and other respectable people of the community, but due to the potentially lethal aspects of Cancerl, had decided to log the prescription this time. The man kept his face averted from Samson all the time and had a hangdog expression. He seemed to be wrestling with himself and at times his speech was indecipherable. Samson looked on the witness with pity and a hint of scorn.

After the pharmacist stepped down, a nervous Frida Parks took the stand. She was dressed in a sunny yellow print dress on this cold winter's day. She glanced anxiously about the room.

Frida testified to Doug Stone taking twice-daily doses of Cancerl instead of the recommended once-daily dose. To the question posed by Asif Murtaza as to why she had not disclosed her information earlier, Frida blushed a beet red I never thought possible for such an elderly and frail woman. "I was convinced that Sam—Mr. Arthurs, was right in his judgment. But the longer I thought about it over the following few weeks, the more uncomfortable I felt. I finally couldn't keep it inside me anymore and decided to report the matter."

"Why did you bring this matter to the attention of Executive Committee member Ethan Williams and not to the hospital authorities or the NADF?" Asif asked.

Again, she looked nervously around the room and up into the gallery: "Well, you see, I was not sure how to proceed. Then I had a conversation with Ethan, who convinced me to make a full disclosure."

"But you left it up to him to report the matter," Asif concluded with a scowl and sat down. That must have been a lucrative car ride Ethan had with Frida, following Doug Stone's funeral!

The next person to take the stand was Samson himself. He was low voiced and restrained. His shirt was well-pressed and his flaming red hair was slicked back, the curls falling down on his collar. Burgess rose to ask the questions this time.

"Sam, were you aware of the properties of this drug?"

"No. I took Delia's—Mrs. Stone's—word on it. She was quite proficient in treating her husband."

"That's a lot of trust, Sam!"

"She showed me a copy of a prescription from Tolemac General. She told me that Doug had smashed the current prescription to pieces in one of his fits of rage. Having witnessed him in those rages, I believed her. She didn't want to attract attention to her domestic discord at the hospital and asked if I could help get her a replacement, discreetly."

"Couldn't she just tell the hospital that she had dropped the prescription and spilled its contents?"

"She had done that just the month before, when Doug destroyed the prescription on that occasion, too. You could check that with the hospital logs. She was running short of excuses for Doug's behaviour."

"We will check those logs. But could she have been lying about the second occasion? Or even, about the first?"

Kamala interrupted, "Burgess, we don't need Samson's speculations. Please stick to the facts."

Unfazed, Burgess continued. "I'd like to introduce some evidence, your Honour." With that he introduced to the court subpoenaed subscriptions that Delia had with an online medical journal. Her click-throughs on the Communicator had been focused on a section that provided research on dosage levels for Cancerl.

"Would you say, Sam, that she was an expert on Cancerl and its properties?" Burgess said, looking triumphant after his painstaking detailing of the records. "That she had enough information to know a double dose would kill him?"

"Or that a half-dose taken twice a day would also sustain him!" Samson shot back. Burgess lost his cool.

"And how the hell could you have known that?"

"Because that's what she told me! Since when do we have to doubt everything people say? Have we not progressed since the Flood?"

"Burgess!" Kamala sailed in firmly. "Let me remind you to stick to the facts and not to upbraid the witness. We will have medical testimony from Dr. Karya later. You can ask these questions of him. Now proceed, if you have any further questions."

Burgess took a deep breath and lost himself in his notes for a while until he calmed down. He took a sip of water. "Did you ever question Mrs. Stone's care giving towards her husband?"

"No. I think she was a wonderful caregiver. More than we were to our own spouses, Burgess." The titters returned to the room and I saw Burgess frown. Samson continued, "It's ironic that she had to pay such a heavy price just to provide that care. Doug Stone was a leech that sucked and sucked and—"

"I am not interested in the character of Mr. Stone. What was your involvement with Mrs. Stone? Your relationship?"

"I—" Samson paused and wrestled with his thoughts; then he carried on, "I spent a lot of time with her. Eventually, I fell in love with her." The tittering was getting really loud now, and Kamala came down hard on the gavel. When the pin-drop silence returned, Samson continued, "And I had every intention of asking her to marry me, if she hadn't left Tolemac." And then he turned around and looked at me. It was as if he was giving me the answer I had long been waiting for.

Burgess carried on. "And this relationship—did it exist even when your wife was alive?"

"Let's say it blossomed soon *after* Agnes died. I was lonely, and Delia knows how to care for a man."

"Did you two ever commit adultery?"

Kamala intervened. "Samson, let me remind you that your privacy, by virtue of our laws, entitles you not to answer this question. Breaking the moral code is a punishable offence only if a citizen voluntarily confesses to it or is found guilty by three separate witnesses. It cannot be extracted on a witness stand under oath. I am merely reminding you of your rights, at this stage."

"I appreciate it, your honour. But I'd like to answer that question. After all, we made those laws. Now we must taste their judgment."

The silence in the room was getting very loud, as everyone braced themselves for what Samson would say next. I could feel the thundering in my temples. Then someone coughed, a suppressed cough, and the tension immediately released, like the air going out of a balloon. Samson took a sip of water from the glass beside him. He appeared to be waiting for the air to leave the balloon. Then he said, "If you define adultery as having sexual relations with someone else while one's spouse is alive, then the answer is no!"

"But you were in a sexual relationship with her at the time of her husband's death?"

"No. We became lovers after Doug's death," Samson said, putting his glass down firmly on the table.

The room was breathing normally now—its inmates getting accustomed to the ebb and flow of point, counterpoint; to the bait and switch of these two elders.

"So, you had sexual relations with her after Doug Stone's death, but before you two could be formally married." Burgess said aloud, looking towards the audience. Kamala released a slow breath.

"Yes." Samson turned to me again. He was not asking for forgiveness in that look, but laying himself before me. In the instant our eyes met, I read that he was more interested in my verdict on him than the rest of Tolemac's. I gave him a thumbs-up sign and he smiled. Sonya squeezed my other hand, concurring with my support.

Burgess continued, puffing himself up, "How do you reconcile that behaviour with your paradigm, preached most Sundays from the pulpit, of chastity prior to marriage, which is a fundamental part of part of our moral code?"

Then Samson said something that made me very proud of him. "Burgess, I've learned something over the last couple of months that I've also preached many times from the pulpit but only understood in biblical theory, and that is to 'live in the moment.' Delia and I are adults, who lived unhappy married lives before we met. This was our chance to reverse that situation and grab at a fleeting chance of happiness. At least, that is how I saw it. I admit that it was an error of moral judgment on my part and makes me a charlatan of the pulpit, but I am very glad that I seized the moment."

"And broke the laws that we enshrined to protect and help us lead a righteous life."

"My dear Burgess, how dare we moralize that the only ones traumatized by the Flood were those who took their lives or languish in psychiatric wards. We were all traumatized. So, we insulated ourselves from further shock by invoking tight laws that denied our humanity. We felt smug about it, but can you really legislate human emotions? We went too far."

"I have no more questions, Sam." Burgess said and sat down.

When he stepped down from the stand, Samson walked back to his seat with a firmer step.

The final witness was Dr. Karya, who had the results of the exhumation. He referred to a large file during his question period with Dr. Morden, who represented the Executive. Dr, Karya's responses were matter-of-fact and confident. "As we had expected, there were no significant traces of Cancerl in the remains of Doug Stone. Note that this exhumation and autopsy was done almost three months after Mr. Stone's death. Cancerl breaks down in the body very quickly and is almost untraceable after about fourteen days. So we are unable to prove beyond a doubt, any theory of an overdose."

"What about the possibility of two half-doses a day, as Mr. Arthurs has suggested?"

"That's possible. Dosage tolerance is related to the physical condition of the patient, his or her disposition towards the medication and the progression of the disease. We are still trying to establish optimal dosage levels with this new generation of drugs. Besides, Cancerl is not an easy drug to take. There are many side affects—pain and muscle stiffness being foremost. It's very possible that Delia Stone gave her husband half-doses to keep these side effects under control and that she believed she was administering the appropriate dosage all the time."

"Dr. Karya, let me repeat my question. Can you prove that Doug Stone succumbed to an overdose?"

"No, I cannot conclude that." Dr. Karya closed his file.

"Thank you, Dr. Karya!" said Kamala as Dr. Morden signalled that he had no further questions, "You may step down now."

The hospital logs were brought back for scrutiny and it was confirmed that Delia Stone had been issued with a duplicate prescription of Cancerl on July 10, 2045 (a month before she received the second duplicate from Samson) under a statement given by her that said "The prescription accidentally dropped and its contents were destroyed while being administered to the patient." The Executive then retired to deliberate on the verdict. They were cloistered for about an hour.

When the members of the Executive returned, the verdict was more or less as I deduced. Samson was exonerated from any complicity in murder or attempted murder. So was Delia Stone. He was held responsible, however, for a serious error in judgment: in influencing and obtaining, through unauthorized means, a potentially lethal drug. With regard to breaking the moral code, which Samson had self-confessed to, Kamala sentenced him to three months of community service without pay. After the verdict was delivered, my father tended his resignation from the Executive Committee. Ethan looked satisfied with the verdict.

In her summation, Kamala addressed Samson and the room at large. "We have passed a watershed today—a tenuous one. It is reassuring to know that everyone in this room sought the truth, and the resolution of this case leaves the integrity of the Executive Committee, our justice and governance structures intact. As we move on from this chapter, I want to thank the Executive for its honest deliberations, the witnesses for their co-operation, Mr. Arthurs for his honesty and openness and to you dear citizens for sharing in this rather painful, but necessary hearing." Kamala's voice was strained while she made her closing comments and she paused twice, once to drink from a glass of water, the second time to reflect on what she was about to say.

Just then Nathan Goldman, recently retired from the Executive Committee and sitting in the front row of the public area, rose: "Madam Justice, may I say a word in the presence of the good people of Tolemac?"

Kamala looked surprised and had her gavel poised to dismiss the session. Instead, she lowered it and said, "Yes, Nathan, if you will keep it short."

Nathan cleared his throat and turned toward us. He looked more erect than usual. "My good citizens of Tolemac, as a former member of the Executive

Committee, it would be remiss of me to leave this room and not recognize the contributions of the man upon whom we all sat in judgment today. Shakespeare, if any of us still care to read him, once said, 'The evil that men do lives after them; the good is oft interred with their bones.' But we need to talk about the 'good,' too, or else we learn nothing from our experience.

"I am deeply honoured and privileged to have been associated with Samson Arthurs over the last thirty-odd years. Many of you thank me for my philanthropic contributions to Tolemac, but, I ask you, what good is money if it cannot be put to good use? And my dear friend Sam here showed me, showed all of us, just how to do that—not just with money, but also with time and effort. He was the capital E in the word 'effort.' A man of meagre means, who scorned amassing personal wealth, Sam has done more for this community than I have ever done or can aspire to do with all the money I've made. During the early days of the Flood and ever since, he has worked tirelessly, never took a vacation or a break. And his effort was mainly directed at others and for others, not for himself. When we faltered, he pulled us up with his rallying cry, 'keep going—we have to keep going.'

"Over the last thirty years, he steered the Executive Committee through choppy waters to give us the stable society we have today. He showed me the value of pursuing wealth and then redistributing it, of staying in Tolemac rather than fleeing to the Capitalist states, where I would have made more money but ended up a less fulfilled man. I want to thank him for that. I also want to thank him for his courage, not only for rebuilding our beloved state, but also for rebuilding his life when he lost his dear Agnes. Many of us are afraid to love—I am—and, as a result, I have been single all my life. Many of us are afraid to love because we lost all our loved ones in the Flood and some of us, including me, have lived in morbid fear of ever losing again. And so we have bound ourselves in laws that, today, look rather outdated. Maybe it was a geological seismic shift after all that caused the Flood. Maybe we were simply due for such a shift, like the dinosaurs were for theirs. Maybe it wasn't God punishing us after all, and we read too much into it. Maybe we punish ourselves with our own foibles and fears.

"As for my friend Samson, he's had the courage to love and to lose, to love again and lose it all again. And knowing him, he will keep going. So, as much as we bid farewell to you from the Executive today, Sam, I want to thank you for being our hope and beacon of light. We saw you stumble today as you admitted to an error of judgment. But didn't someone say that 'to err is human'? And by God, I am glad that you did, because for that we love you even more. Sam, my dear old friend, I wish you and your growing family, all the very best in the days ahead. Your Honour, thank you for letting me speak."

It was a speech, delivered with equanimity and poise. Kamala finally brought down her gavel, dismissing the session. Yet no one moved as she made her way slowly from the bench, as if dragged by a heavy weight. She stumbled on the threshold, heaving a sigh before exiting the side door. Then people started rushing out of their seats to press Samson's hand, to thank him and to wish him well in the next chapter of his life. Looking at the faces, I saw hints of shame, for snooping into the life of one of their own, especially someone acknowledged as their undisputed leader. The herd had returned ashamedly back to the shepherd, albeit too late.

Vladimir passed by and he looked harried. He still took the time to pause. "Thank you for looking in on Leo," he said.

"I did my best for him. I'll go and see him again, as soon as he is a bit better," I said shaking his hand.

"I tried to do the best for your father, too. We wrestled with the decision behind closed doors." Vladimir looked apologetic. "But he broke our laws. That was hard to bypass."

"No, you did your best to uphold the laws of our state. Thank you."

He shook my hand again and departed. There was an unspoken look in his eyes, as if he were telling me he'd like to help, in anyway, as long as it did not get him into conflict with those 'laws.' For he was, after all, a law-abiding citizen; we all were. Suddenly, that seemed like a problem!

With Sonya in tow, I helped steer Samson through the throng of well-wishers. On the steps of city hall, Burgess was leaning on his cane, smoking a cigar, lost in thought. I couldn't resist a jibe and pulled away from Sonya and Samson, momentarily.

"I hope you are satisfied with your day's work, Burgess?"

He stared into the distance. Then he turned towards me with hooded eyes. His normally impassive countenance was showing the strain. "It was Ethan's decision," he said.

"You mean, you couldn't decide for yourself?"

"It was Ethan's decision to prosecute," he repeated and leaned heavily on his cane as he made his way down the steps to his car. "I was only supporting my son. Besides, it is imperative, above all, that the Executive be free of scandal. Society crumbles when its leaders are corrupt."

In a flash of anger I looked around hoping to catch sight of Ethan, wanting to vent my steam on him, but he was nowhere to be seen. He was never around when he could be at the receiving end.

*   *   *

I accompanied Samson to his home, leaving Sonya to shepherd her distraught mother. We trailed our bicycles up Sunset Hill. It could have been just another blustery winter's day, except that the sky looked dark on the horizon, not the dull familiar grey of winter. We got bad rainstorms at this time of the year and they would come down suddenly.

I made two mugs of hot cocoa in his kitchen and Samson and I sat outside on the porch steps, looking down at the city below, while the sky darkened overhead. The telescope hung limply on its stand, a lone sentinel.

"What now?" I said, nursing my mug.

He remained silent and inscrutable.

After awhile, I tried to make conversation again. "Why don't you write that book on the history of Tolemac now? My students have been waiting anxiously for it."

"My work is at an end here," he said finally.

My false enthusiasm evaporated into the air like the steam from the mugs. "What do you mean?"

"I've put a lot into Tolemac. It's my only legacy."

"This is your home!"

"Yes, but the status quo is never an option. You will have to work hard to keep Ethan Williams in check. And to get our antiquated laws modified."

"Not all our laws are bad." Had he forgotten the transparency laws and the social safety net they had provided, not forgetting the impending WorkOUT bill?

"No. Not all of them were bad. We just got carried away in places."

"You want me to make changes. And I'm not even in office!"

"But you will be, if you work at it! I'm going to turn in. It's been a long year." He made to rise but I held him back.

"Dad—"

"Yes?"

"I'm glad you clarified that thing about Mum and Delia in court today. It sits better with me now."

He ignored my compliment, or didn't hear it, for he slumped back on the porch steps, lost in thought. "You asked me what we were doing in my bedroom the day Doug died and I told you that Delia and I were talking and you didn't believe me. Do you still not believe me?"

"I believe you."

"That was the day I swore never to let her come so close to me and yet keep my distance. When I went to see her the following day, we became lovers."

"I know the feeling. Sonya and I have discovered it, recently."

"Only recently?"

"We were being a dutiful Tolemacian couple before that."

"Your mother and I were dutiful all our lives. What a waste, it now seems."

"So what will you do now?"

"You know, there is a sense of restlessness that comes when you get too comfortable. Then, change for the sake of change becomes desirable, even if it's the wrong kind. I feel that way now. Ethan recognized that complacency in our present generation of Tolemacians and tapped into it, while I missed the cue." He was being philosophical again and evading my question.

He rose and went indoors, and I sat outside for a long time, looking down at the city we were both falling out of step with.

Chapter 26

For the next three months our family hunkered together, nursing wounds and giving each other sustenance. The children were constantly into new things, and I wished that I could follow their example. Joey started a hockey card collection and Hannah began to play the piano in earnest, giving her painting a rest. Their actions suggested that I too should bury the past and move on. The new baby was making itself more visible every day. I enjoyed the mornings I spent cuddling with Sonya, and because our level of intimacy had improved, this baby's arrival was going to be different than Joey's and Hannah's. When they were born, we'd been Tolemacian stereotypes of husband and wife; now we were enjoying our joint creation in a spirit of love and giving. I made breakfast for Sonya most mornings and ensured that the food types that made her sick were off the tray, something I'd never done on the two previous occasions. Agnes and Kamala had been around then, counselling Sonya, sparing me that responsibility.

Kamala came down with pneumonia soon after the trial, and was laid up in bed for two weeks. Sonya and I took turns visiting her, bringing her food and medications. On the first few visits, Kamala was mostly in bed, reading legal briefs and coughing incessantly. She told us not to worry and to leave the goods we had brought her; she would sort it out later. Sonya often complained about her mother's obsession with work and came home in tears one day, saying they'd had "heated words" over this issue. Sonya was worried such tension and disagreement might aggravate her mother's illness. Given Sonya's pregnant condition, and her tendency to get more than usually emotional at this time, I asked her to take a break from her mother, and went to visit Kamala myself the following day.

I was surprised to see my mother-in-law out of bed and in her study. She was fully dressed and elegantly groomed, although still somewhat pale in complexion and unsteady when she moved about. She had brewed tea in anticipation of my arrival and was reading a novel. There was sitar music playing in the background, remixed with nature sounds that created a calm ambience in the room.

"Come in, David. How's Sonya?"

"She's well."

"I'm sorry I upset her yesterday. Tea?" She paused to catch her breath then poured with great dexterity. Her fingers lightly glided across the cup as she handed it to me.

"I brought you some herb and garlic mushrooms. It's a new genetic mix in the store," I said, placing the parcel I had brought on the side table.

"Thank you. You children are so thoughtful. I won't starve, you know. In fact I am feeling a lot better. Sonya's home truths did me a world of good."

"I'll let her know. She was beginning to feel you were unreachable."

Kamala looked thoughtful as she sipped her tea. "I probably have been, all these years. Samson's testimony in court changed that."

"How so?" I said, keeping my eyes on the cup.

She continued sipping her tea. "Well, when you discover that you have been upholding laws that deny people their humanity, it starts to make your life seem rather . . . unlived. That's probably why I fell ill."

"It was overwork, more likely. You need to take a break sometime, you know."

"Overwork I can handle. Denial is something I can't. I was a young widow, too, once. When I decided to embrace widowhood and work for the good of our fledgling state instead of looking after my own interests and desires, I denied myself. Samson forced me to face that in court the other day. It was a . . . rude shock."

"I don't think he intended it that way."

"No, certainly not. But it was a wake-up call to re-examine the things we have done. Take our blinders off and look at the next phase of our evolution—a kinder, more understanding phase, perhaps?"

"You look better today."

"Yes, after my blow-up with Sonya yesterday, I put away those legal papers. This morning has been pleasantly reflective." She smiled.

She was back to work the next week and came to visit with gifts for the kids and a bouquet of roses for Sonya.

*   *   *

The Executive Committee passed the WorkOUT bill at the end of January. Many people signed up, but it would be months before we could tell the outcome. The school term began, and I was getting to know my new batch of students. I also set up an hour, twice a week, to take Joey through his math. My duties at the Executive had ended upon losing the election, and I did not have to understudy proceedings anymore.

The Executive, however, was embroiled in another pivotal issue. We heard that New Eden was demanding reciprocal landing rights for two of its private helicopter services, and if not granted, were threatening to cancel our service into their state. Ethan came on the evening news urging Tolemacians to support a reciprocal deal because our growing helicopter service was now deemed essential. Public debate on the issue had begun.

Sally Morden went to university in Oceania, Manny Lo in New Eden. Leo Patimkin was still in the psychiatric ward of Tolemac General, but according to Vladimir and Tania was doing well and responding to treatment. Joe Sabbattini got out of hospital and began working for his father at the Waterfront Hotel. He also enrolled in our distance-education program on Hotel and Property Management. There were no more reported incidences of drug problems in Tolemac, although the problem appeared to be worsening in Oceania and had now started up in the Humanitarian state of Saska-Manitoba as well. Public debates were running in Oceania, on the question of whether they should follow Alberta's example of five years ago and legalize recreational drug use, within certain limits.

We attended a couple of local weddings, very traditionally done. They helped remind us that Tolemac was still a good place. Belva's daughter Rose finally tied the knot with Juan Gomez's son Julio. Rose was in her thirties and had promised to remain single as she believed that men always leave their wives after awhile, her father being a great example. Finally, the handsome Julio who had been raised in the migrant labour camps and had gone on to own and run a very successful construction company in the New Settlements, convinced her otherwise. It was a traditional wedding, replete with Christian vows. It was held in the rented hockey stadium and the customary barbecue (indoors this time, due to the weather) followed. Belva was excited and even more radiant than the bride. This was her second accomplishment of the week. Two days earlier, Samson had resigned as pastor of the Church of the New Covenant. "Charlatans should not be in the pulpit," was his reason and Belva was appointed interim minister, until a formal selection for a new incumbent took place.

Johnny Garcia and Rita Sacic also got married. They had exhibited a strong attraction to each other while on my red team and I knew it was only a matter of time before they followed Tolemacian custom and married young. Johnny was taking over his father's hardware store, now that Izzy had settled into retirement to focus on fighting the dreaded cancer that forever nipped at him. Johnny and Rita's wedding ceremony, performed in the synagogue, was symbolic and reverent. Sitting there in the pews, I closed my eyes and wondered if it had been wrong for the Executive to pass all those laws. In the end, we had become a stable society because of them. It was finding the balance that was important—the Middle Way. It was indeed a shame that people had not seen the value of the Middle Way and had been blinded by Ethan's promises of growth.

Samson signed up as a WorkOUT candidate and opted to clean out the sewers in the port. It was back-breaking work. I visited him one day and he was covered in grime but smiling as he installed pipes down the sewer shaft with a gang of other WorkOUT workers. I recognized the workers as people who had always lived in the subsidized housing section of the city. Their children had passed through the Academy, some with a great desire to succeed, others with the same apathetic air as their parents. When I visited however, everyone was upbeat, their filthy conditions notwithstanding, and Samson seemed to be the catalyst for their mood. He was cracking a joke about the "magician and the drunk," one I had heard before as a child, and many of the workers in the vicinity had stopped to listen and shook their heads with furtive smiles when he delivered the punch line.

"And there's my son, in whom I am well pleased," he raised his voice to everyone upon seeing me. I blushed. "What brings you, David?"

"You are in a great mood considering these working conditions!"

"Never been better! I am with the salt of the earth, eh, guys?" There were nods and guffaws as the workers went back to their tasks.

"I came to see how you were doing. Can I get you anything?"

"Muscles are a bit stiff. But otherwise, I'm okay. How is the baby coming along?"

"Well. I hope you'll be out of here by the time it arrives."

"Oh, I'll be done by then—three months, that's the sentence. Although I have never felt better. This takes me back to the time we were rebuilding after the Flood. It was just the dirt and the grime and the sweat and working side-by-side with people who didn't give a dime about rank, position, wealth, any of that stuff."

"You never could get used to the easy life. You are a born socialist."

"Humanitarian, my boy. I've also got some information that I will be able to share with you shortly. Things are moving along well—you'll be on the Executive shortly."

"Now that is the biggest joke! Have you shared that information with your buddies here, too?"

"No need to be sarcastic. You will be, mark my words. Now, I've got to get back to work. Drop by the house sometime, I usually get back around seven o'clock."

"That's a long shift!"

"That's what I signed up for. It cleans the soul, though it hurts and soils the body. See you later!" With a wave of his hand, he hobbled back into the mine shaft.

* * *

The early breezes of spring were starting to gust a week later when I received a call from Vladimir Patimkin. He said that Leo was due for release from the hospital shortly, having made a speedy recovery. But now, with his release nearing, the boy was getting agitated again. Vladimir wanted to know if I could help. Remembering Leo's reactions to my earlier visits, I wanted to be sure that I did not make matters worse. So I decided to meet with Vladimir first and assess the situation.

I went to see the elder Patimkin down at the Communications Centre. It was a concrete, dome-like structure, midway up Sunset Hill on North Ontario Street. I had visited the older centre, on a school excursion about twenty years ago, when it was located down on the waterfront in a hastily constructed wooden building. A string of computers were lined against a wall in a ventilated room, I recalled. The new building was more cavernous and enclosed. I had to go through a retina scan and a corresponding computer check on my identity at the Humanitarian States central ID office in Oceania before the security guards let me in. Mercifully, all of that took only five minutes. Doors opened and shut, as an attendant escorted me into the command centre.

My breath clouded as I progressed deeper into the building. Vladimir's working area resembled a giant hockey arena. Like his son, Vladimir was tall and gangly with that defining protruding forehead. However, the older Patimkin was calmer and more poised—age and the Flood had bestowed a wisdom in him that Leo had yet to acquire. Today, however, Vladimir's calm was overlaid with strain, a strain that I had begun to notice since the night of Leo's misadventure. He straightened from a terminal and picking up a coat, similar to the one he was wearing, came over and shook my hand. Since I had last seen him at the hearing, he had also developed a nervous twitch above his left eye.

"David, it's good of you to come. Here, put this on. We keep it cold in here. The computers heat up, you know."

We were on a raised platform on the periphery of a room that overlooked a hollowed-out central area below containing three concentric circles of computers.

"This place has grown from the old shed I last visited," I remarked.

"Let me give you the quick tour," Vladimir said. He seemed relieved to be talking about his world, rather than the murkier one of his troubled son.

"Those circles of computers below are our three lines of firewall defence from the outside world," he said. "In the old days, one line was sufficient. Not anymore. Software piracy is getting smarter every day. I call a code red any time the second firewall is compromised."

"Has that happened?"

"At least four times last year and once already this year, despite the reinforced logic patches we installed recently."

"How come we never hear of any of these attacks?"

"And panic the good citizens of Tolemac? No, these battles are best fought alone by specialists." I looked down at the three innocent-looking rings of computers. I made out people walking among them, checking consoles and making notes on hand-held devices.

"It looks like we are still at war."

"We are, in a way. Fortunately, it does not take human lives like traditional battles did. But if vital systems fail—such as those at the hospital—we will have fatalities. That's why continuous funding is so critical. Your father understood this. He is a regular visitor here, checking to see how well our defences are holding up."

"Where do these attacks come from?"

"All over the world, but mostly from the rebellious, rogue states of Asia. But recently I've gotten a few well-funded ones from some of the Capitalist ones in North America as well."

"Have any attacks been launched internally? I mean, from within Tolemac?"

"Oh sure. That's why I have been so keen to acquire new funding for the Centre. So far our defences have focused on external threats, but internal threats are growing. With the funding approved last August—you were at that meeting—we've built a sniffer prototype that can get into private networks, especially companies and small businesses in Tolemac, through their public firewall connection, and check those organizations for viruses or illicit activity."

"Sounds great! When do you release it?"

"Not for awhile. First, we need more funding to make it robust enough for public use; it's only a prototype at this stage. Next, we need Executive Committee approval; there is a privacy issue here. Business users have to give us consent to use this sniffer on their internal networks and you know how paranoid everyone is about their privacy, thanks to the transparency laws. No, we are still some ways off from implementing this solution. It's a pity we lost Samson on the Executive. He was a strong proponent of this project."

"Why don't you use this technology to fight the drug smugglers?"

Vladimir had an awkward look on his face and chose his words carefully. "Again, our privacy laws prohibit us from spying without evidence of criminal activity."

"For heaven's sake, Vladimir, isn't Leo proof enough?"

His expression turned to pain. I immediately apologized for my impetuousness, "I'm sorry. It's just so frustrating when we have to follow the law and the miscreants don't."

"That's the same thing Samson said. But I have the onerous duty of upholding the privacy law in the operation of this centre." The tick over his left eye had increased in frequency. Then, as if to end the discussion, he moved quickly to two computers hooked up in parallel on the platform we were on, with a giant monitor between them. "Come on over here. Let me show you one of our experiments."

A music program was running on the screen. "This is how we breed viruses to kill other viruses that invade us. The first computer is running one of our home-grown applications—a musical broadcast. Now I am going to infect it with a virus we captured from the outside recently and stored on this second computer." He hit a button and the screen started to crumble with jarring sounds. "Now I'm going to send in the antidote we developed, which is stored on the first computer." He hit another button and the image began to correct itself and the jarring gave way to the original music, albeit shakily.

"Now let's have a bit of fun. I am going to get both virus and antidote programs to run against each other with our artificial-intelligence application acting as referee. Each program will try to outsmart the other and get stronger and fiercer as a result. When one program runs out of options to improvise, it dies. We save the survivor to act as protection in case we get attacked again. Our research findings are discreetly exported to other communications centres in the Humanitarian realm."

He typed in some commands, and the images started to ebb and flow before me— first the music, then the jarring sounds, then the music again followed by louder jarring sounds, then silence, then the music again and the image became clearer. "Let them fight while we talk," Vladimir said, taking my hand and leading me towards a bench.

"How is Leo?" I asked.

"He has responded well to the medication. He is now out of sedation and has been moved into a private room, although he is still hyper at times."

"But can you reach him? Talk to him, I mean? He kept referring to the generation gap during the election campaign."

"I'm not sure. This is my world you see around you. I am preoccupied with survival. To provide my family a good and safe life, and spare them the ravages I went through as a teenager. I've kept them insulated from this world, and perhaps that was a mistake. Leo does not see things the way I do. He does not see the dangers we are exposed to each day down at this centre. He takes my insularity for a sign of weakness."

"But he does advocate the Middle Way."

The program behind us had lapsed into steady music now. Vladimir looked over his shoulder and his eyes gleamed with satisfaction. "It looks like we just killed another threat to our way of life." He rose quickly and went over to the two computers, saved the programs and shut the machines down. "David, I'm not against the Middle Way. We have to be open to the outside world. The competition makes us stronger, just as these viruses do. But we can get hurt, too."

"You know Vladimir, I don't quite see it that way. In many ways you two are alike. Leo believes you need to adopt the enemies' tactics in order to be good. And you breed viruses to combat others. You are both variations on the same theme."

He looked down at his feet for a while. "Maybe we are. I hadn't quite looked at it that way."

"Why don't you get him to work alongside you here?"

Vladimir frowned. "Here?"

"Why not?"

"Leo did talk about serving a formal apprenticeship at the centre once . . ."

"It'll do him good to work alongside you. He really likes working with computers. Perhaps, you will begin to understand each other. I'll go now and talk to him. I hope he is still not sore with me for getting him apprehended that night?"

"He would have faced kidnapping and manslaughter charges if you hadn't."

"There's something I want you to promise me," I said.

"What's that?"

"You'll back off pushing him to go to university when he gets out of hospital. He does not have your mathematical talent, even though he resembles you in spirit. You've got to let him find his game."

Vladimir wrestled with this one. Finally he said, "All right. I'll play along. I guess I haven't much choice now."

"And listen to him—however hare-brained his ideas may be. I wish I had, during my election campaign."

"I'll try."

"My last batch of students—Leo included—are great kids. But they've grown up in a different environment, not in a room like this."

I left him in his cold chamber, amidst the banks of battling computers and went in search of fresh air and daylight. Vladimir was the prototypical Tolemacian old guard—a stolid, law-abiding technocrat, even if the boundaries he placed around himself and his family hurt him personally. But I had made a dent in his armour. Or had the events of the recent past already caused that dent, just like they had in Samson, Nathan and Kamala?

*   *   *

Leo was now in a private room on the second floor of the psychiatric ward. The private area ringed the central public core where new arrivals and long-term incurables were housed. As I crossed the ground floor, the regulars were at their usual antics. The wave makers and the cowerers were arm wrestling with each other and a few interns were trying to calm them down. I was relieved to take the stairs and enter the private area.

Leo was striding up and down his room when I entered. "Hi, Mr. Arthurs!" He said out of the side of his face, and continued pacing. His hair was combed and the regulation orange uniform was cleaner than on my last visit. He certainly looked healthier, though not quite there yet.

"Good to see you, Leo, you've made great progress." He didn't reply but kept pacing. I tried again, "Soon you'll be coming out. And spring is here. We can rope you into the Spring Charity Drive. Kamala is looking for volunteers."

"I'm not going out, Mr. Arthurs. Gonna stay here a bit longer."

"Now, now—come on Leo! It's nicer outside—trees, waterfront, people."

"I saw what 'people' did to your father." He motioned over to the Communicator in his room. "They are out there. I don't wanna come out, Mr. Arthurs. Until they are gone!" His voice increased a few notches in that exchange, so I decided to take a different tack.

I tried his favourite topic—politics. "Do you know that our WorkOUT plan is making inroads among the Capitalist states? Our policies are becoming the envy of others."

"Yeah, saw that on the news, too. But they also said that Congressman Gordon's bill was defeated by a vote of sixteen to twelve in New Eden. They still want their fallen ones sent to the colonies."

"Sixteen to twelve! That is very good news, Leo. Sixteen to twelve is extremely good news! A year ago they weren't even thinking of this stuff. A year from now, WorkOUT will be in everyone's bloodstream!"

"Not as long as they are there."

"Would you please stop pacing and tell me who they are?"

He ignored me and continued his gait. He switched on the room's Communicator and flipped channels and I let him be for a while. Then he switched off the machine and resumed his step.

"They are too powerful, Mr. Arthurs. You've gotta destroy them. You say there isn't a drug problem in Tolemac—hah! I was the silly bugger who got caught. Most of the kids are into it now. You'll see!"

His words chilled me. "Most of the kids . . .? What do you mean? Come on, quit walking around for God's sake, and answer me!"

He stopped abruptly and faced me. "That day at the Waterfront Joe and his buddies, they were all into the drugs. I grabbed that pouch from Joe before taking Sally upstairs. It was his!"

"Next you're going to tell me that Sally was on drugs, too?"

"She would have been, eventually, if Joe had his way with her. Oh yeah, and you know what, they were into sex big time. I've even seen them. Yeah, they get away scot-free while people like your dad get put down for milder indiscretions. See, I was trying to protect Sally and got snookered on the drug."

"It got me, too. Don't blame yourself. I was naïve to think this stuff wasn't going on. Sex and drugs! You kids paint a different picture back at the Academy."

"I came to tell you once, Mr. Arthurs, during the campaign? But you didn't want to listen to me. I guess I've blown it with Sally for good now?"

"I'm sorry, Leo."

Then he walked up to me, grabbed my shoulders and propelled me towards the window overlooking the central core. The nervous energy in him infected me. "You think there are only old people in here, eh? Those poor Flood survivors, right? Well, look closer. That man in the wheelchair, over on the right. He's thirty-five years old and works at the microchip factory on the night shift, a high-stress job. They brought him in three weeks ago. And a couple of days later, they brought in that young woman over on his right; she graduated from the Academy three years ago and then her husband moved to Oceania to work, leaving her with a young baby to care for. They've both been diagnosed with clinical schizophrenia brought about by abusing powerful drugs! The casualties are starting to mount, Mr. Arthurs, and nobody wants to make it public!"

I stared through the window, and what I had originally pegged as a bunch of loony old people, now revealed some differences in age. The two younger people in question were over at the far corner sitting across from each other. They looked sedated. I remembered the woman as the one sitting next to Leo when I had visited him previously.

"How do you know all this, Leo?"

"I mingle in the wards, Mr. Arthurs. The nurses let me, now that I am close to discharge."

"You still haven't told me who 'they' are."

"Ethan Williams and his bunch of Capitalists. Who else? They are creating captive drug markets all over the place and using Tolemac as their base."

Hadn't I heard this all before, from Paul Samuel? For a kid suffering a nervous breakdown Leo was clued in. "And this is your theory? Do you have any proof?"

"No, I don't. But don't you get it?"

"Leo, my father recently gave me some advice that I've started to follow. He said 'don't suspect the worst of the things you cannot see.' As much as I detest Ethan, for his madcap plans and for what he did to my father, I cannot hold this drug thing against him, without proof."

"There you go again—too trusting! You are making a big mistake, Mr. Arthurs."

"And you are mistrusting, Leo! It's not good for your health. Anyway, I didn't come here to talk about Ethan and his gang. I went to see your father today. It was on his urging that I came here." I quickly told him about my tour of the Communications centre and the gist of my conversation with Vladimir.

He seemed to calm down. "My father is involved in all that stuff? Why did he never tell us at home? He never took us to the Communications centre either, after they moved to the new location."

"He's a silent warrior, Leo. Just like my Dad. They bear their crosses in silence. They learned that in the Flood."

"Jeez!" he expelled. His pacing slowed down and he became more reflective.

"He talked about arranging to have you spend some time in the Communications centre once you are out of here. He might even arrange for a formal apprenticeship. He's also given up on the idea of pushing you into university, unless you want to go."

The tension seemed to drain from Leo's face.

"Seriously? A formal apprenticeship!"

"Seriously. And if you decide you don't want to continue your formal education, you don't have to."

"You're sure? No strings attached?"

"Ah-huh."

Then he started pacing again. But now he was thinking. I knew that I had planted the seed.

I rose to go, "I'd better be off, Leo! All the best with your recovery! And I'll see you on the outside soon."

This time he turned around to look at me squarely and there was a glimmer of gratitude in his eyes. "Goodbye, Mr. Arthurs. And thanks for coming and . . . for everything."

Chapter 27

FOLLOWING THAT VISIT to the psychiatric ward, I decided to reactivate the red team, but with a different mission in mind. Its former members, with the exception of Leo, had flexible hours as they were now studying via distance education, having graduated from high school. They readily bought into my plan; Leo's misadventure was motivation enough. They also rounded up additional volunteers from the remaining class of '45 who shared similar concerns. I borrowed Samson's telescope, telling him I needed it for a short-term project, and situated it in the church belfry that rose over the rooftops of the downtown area. There was space for two people up in the tower, which looked down on Water Street at the point where it intersected Main and headed toward the water. The telescope, once installed in its new location, gave us a bird's eye view of Brady's Warehouse.

Thus, the extended red team began voluntary surveillance shifts on Jeremy Brady's operation, hoping to come up with a lead on the drug problem. I had finally decided to listen to Leo. I also resolved not to panic anyone in my circle of friends or family, until we came up with proof. The only person I shared my plan with was Sonya, lest she worry about my nocturnal wanderings. Our new minister, Belva, was also in the know and heartily supported the cause, partly because of Billy's prior experiences with substance abuse. The team arranged its shifts in units of two at night from six o'clock to midnight, with Johnny and Rita one night, me on the next, the White Dove boys on the next and so on. It was nice taking affirmative action for a change.

Water Street is the underbelly of Tolemac. I'd seen New Eden's version at the Pink Gypsy. Water Street was milder by comparison, with rows of warehouses, hardware stores and shipbuilding outfitters. It was a narrow walking street, shrouded in shadows from the overhanging buildings. Being close to the water and at sea level, it was constantly wet and strewn with garbage bags and old equipment parts that would float about and redeposit themselves with the ebbs and flows of floodwater, whenever the seawall breached. This was one place our city's garbage collectors did not pay much attention to, as no one came down here for an evening stroll. Brady's Warehouse stood on a raised platform midway down the street and had a cavernous entrance. Inside, was stacked cargo that came off the boats. Jeremy Brady had an open office and sat behind a desk with a Communicator, processing orders, chatting with clients, hunting deliveries in a forklift while punching in location details into a wireless Communicator on the vehicle. Jeremy, like his sibling across the water, had put on weight over the years and always dressed in a sleeveless, black undershirt and shorts that showed off his hairy torso. He chewed tobacco incessantly and spat it onto the street. A couple of assistants worked odd shifts, but Jeremy was always on duty. Occasionally, he would take a client into the back office, out of sight of our telescope.

Our first week of surveillance revealed nothing, and I was beginning to wonder whether this was all a mistake, and how long it would be before we all lost interest. I'd also stored a couple of disposable video cameras in the belfry, in case we needed to take incriminating pictures. There was the usual line of suspects calling over at Brady's. Nick Sagar dropped in one evening, raising my optimism momentarily. But for a short conversation with Jeremy, he did not pick up or drop off anything. Old man Brady was a frequent visitor and was always invited into the back office. I sent Paul Samuel a note about our little venture and he was most complimentary and wished us luck. And so we waited this game out, wondering who or what would break first.

One side of me wanted to barge in on Ethan again and have it out with him. Extract the truth. But I wasn't that naïve anymore. Having learned from my previous encounters, I was sure his cocoon would be more impregnable now. "Do you have an appointment?" "Mr. Williams is in a meeting and cannot be disturbed." Ethan had built a great infrastructure that made him accessible to the world only when he needed to be.

The Executive voted to allow reciprocal landing rights to New Eden-based helicopters, as long as their frequencies and load factors matched ours. The New Edeners rebutted, claiming that reciprocal rights were not enough, and wanted two extra flights per week, or else. The Executive played for time, saying they needed at least another three months to assess if the extended service would be viable. "Trade between the Humanitarians and Capitalists had begun in Tolemac" ran the sensationalist headlines on the Communicator, while Ethan came out later the same day in an interview and said, "This is a great day for Tolemac, our possibilities for growth are endless."

I went down to the port that evening around seven, to meet Samson and get his view on things. Gearing up for the new school term, getting my surveillance operation underway and caring for a pregnant wife and two young children had given me little time to spend with him of late. I was surprised when they told me that he had pulled a muscle a few days ago and been granted sick time. In my entire life, I had never seen Samson sick in bed. I hurriedly turned my bicycle around and rode back up Sunset Hill.

As I neared the summit and strained on the pedals for the last few yards up to the house, I saw a figure step out of Samson's front gate and head downhill on the other side. It was difficult to distinguish features, as it was that moment of twilight when dusk was increasing and the streetlights had not been turned on yet.

I found Samson sitting in shadow on the back steps. The telescope was missing and the smell of liniment was heavy in the air. He was gently massaging his right leg.

"Is it bad?" I said.

"The leg? Oh, no—it'll heal. I wish I were ten years younger though. Underestimated the load I was carrying out of the pit. My leg went numb all of a sudden and I fell down. It still goes numb now and again."

"You'd better ask for lighter duties."

"I've less than two weeks left on the job—then I'll have paid my dues in full."

I asked him about the Executive's decision.

"My colleagues opened the flood gates with the helicopter service, now they are boxed into a corner. Those Capitalists play "winner takes all." They are going to get their extra frequencies. Then they'll push for more."

"What do we do?"

"We stay alert. And we have to hold back something they want. That's all we can do. How's your secret project coming along?"

"Oh, that. It's still to show results. Hope you are not in a hurry to get back the telescope."

"Take your time. I only hope you can catch the real culprits."

"What do you know about my project?" I was taken aback that he'd blown my covert operation so casually.

He laughed. "What's that old saying, "you can take the minister out of the church, but not the church out of the minister?" I go to church on my way home most days now. These are my days of reflection and prayer. Your young assistants make too much noise in the belfry."

My face felt hot and I was glad for the darkness.

He laughed again. "Don't worry, your secret's safe with me. Besides, I have decided to leave Tolemac."

"What!"

"Yes. I know you will be all over me on this. But I have decided. I am washed up here—the charlatan of the pulpit. I am going to New Eden."

"Now I've heard it all!"

"David—this is serious. I am going to New Eden—the lion's den, if you will. I am going to work with Congressman Gordon and the Knights. They not only seek to curb greedy materialism in the Capitalist states but they also wage a secret war against the forces of evil—the drug lords and other scoundrels who operate outside the orbit of the NADF."

"You can't be serious. Your whole life is here. Your family—"

"Yes, and I got lazy and complacent, and that did not help. Here, I promised to show you something the last time we met." He rose painfully and limped indoors. He returned with a file of papers and switched on the back-porch light.

That was when I had one of those "mirror moments", a moment when, after living life at an unflagging pace, you pause to take stock of yourself in the mirror and notice you've aged—hair growing out of new places or thinning in others, pouches under the eyes—signs of time taking its toll on you. Only the mirror moment this time was of Samson; in the dim porch light, the stooped form of my limping father erased the former image of the once energetic and passionate leader I had known. I shrugged the visual off and focused on the file of papers he had just handed me.

"It looks like a pile of receipts for helicopter maintenance work," I said after looking through the file.

"Yes, for services that were never rendered to Williams Helicopters. It's drug money."

"How did you get them?"

"My secret for the moment. We are getting close to catching the big kahuna. But it's risky work. That's why your young friends in the belfry should be more careful."

"And Ethan's the big kahuna?"

"We'll find out shortly."

"But then, you are leaving?"

"Yes. As soon as we get a break on this drug problem."

"Will that be before Ethan's big party to celebrate Burgess's seventieth next month? Looks like he's invited the whole of Tolemac, including the one's he's stepped on."

"It'll break when it breaks. I received an invitation too, but I'm not going."

"Me neither. Is there nothing I can do to change your mind? About leaving Tolemac, I mean. Perhaps, the baby's arrival—"

"David, we all have to follow our own paths. I have to follow mine. You have to follow yours, which ultimately will lead you to govern this place. You may not feel that now, but you will one day."

"Thanks for the vote of confidence. But that seems a long way off."

"Not as long as you think."

In retrospect, I know I should have put up a stronger argument to get him to stay, but Samson was always resolute whenever he had made up his mind on something.

*　　*　　*

A week later, Dr. Morden came on the evening news to announce that sufficient cases of drug abuse were now in evidence to warrant opening a special wing in Tolemac General Hospital to treat these patients. Ethan followed up on the next evening's news to say that more drug education classes should be held, and that he would be appealing to the Executive to release funds towards this program.

Four weeks into our surveillance mission (now toned down to tiptoeing around the belfry, thanks to my father's feedback), I heard that Samson had come over to the house to visit with the kids, but neither Sonya nor I had been at home at the time. He had gifted Joey his telescope (when I was finished with it) and given his music collection to Hannah. A fortnight later, I saw him down at the waterfront on Market Day, just as I was about to go on my evening shift in the belfry. He was shaking hands with the vendors, occasionally pausing to laugh at a comment someone made, as he worked his way across the stalls. This was the old Samson, the optimist, and even though he limped, his step was firm and sprightly. His eyes lit up on seeing me, and excusing himself, pulled me into a café by the waterfront.

The place was one of his regular haunts. The walls were covered with pre-Flood memorabilia—baseball players, old movies from the sunken city of Hollywood and a car race they called the Molson Indie. The air was tinged with cigarette smoke filtering in from the smoking section at the rear.

The only blot inside was old Brady, looking unsteady on his feet and standing by the bar, holding a huge mug of coffee. Seeing us enter he shouted across the room.

"Hey, Arthurs—how's shovelling shit working for you these days, eh? Heh, heh!"

"I've served my sentence Brady—was the best thing for me." Samson countered back cheerfully. The regulars in the café, mostly the over-fifty group, looked about unsteadily, unaccustomed to such loud and vulgar repartee.

"Now you know what it's like to get your pecker out of control, eh?"

"Served me right!"

Brady was getting more uptight with Samson's equanimity. He hobbled across the room and stood over our table. "Your regime is over, Arthurs. You guys lorded it over us for too long. Before you know it, I'll be opening up on shore."

"Over my dead body, Brady—and yours." Samson's words, cutting through the air with such sharpness, startled me. Gone was the calm; it was replaced by an edge I had seen in those old videotapes of him at the public debates.

"Heh, heh! We shall see Arthurs. We shall see." Brady threw his mug down on our table, splashing the contents on Samson's shirt sleeve and hobbled out. "Like hell, we shall see!"

Samson wiped his sleeve. "We shall see, indeed," he whispered, almost to himself. His fist encircled Brady's metal mug and squeezed it.

"He's a bastard," I said.

Samson ordered coffee for us—the black thick stuff that he enjoyed and which I had difficulty with. Over the steaming mugs he told me that Delia had sent him an online letter. Brady may not have even existed a moment ago, except for his mug that had lost its shape in Samson's grip and lay mangled on the table. Samson was totally absorbed in talking about Delia. He went on to say that she was now settled in Alberta, working as a front-office manager of a hotel and that Joshua was re-enrolled in school. She could now afford her son's tuition, as she didn't have Doug or his medical bills to deal with.

"Will you meet up with her again? It would be good for both of you," I said.

"No. That's a chapter I'd like to close. Besides, I was too old for her."

"She didn't think so."

"It was beautiful while it lasted. And I can't meet her needs from here, nor with the work I'm going to do in New Eden. Let's leave it that way. Delia is a post-Flood woman ahead of her time, at least, ahead of us Tolemacians."

"Or perhaps she has reclaimed what her post-Flood sisterhood lost?" I decided to probe further. "Did she mention anything about Doug's death?"

Samson's hand circled Brady's mutilated mug and squeezed it again. "I don't wish to talk about it. She did what she had to do." He pitched the mug into a garbage container across the room. "In a way, I'm glad it's over. Now I can move on."

We were silent. I put down my coffee after a couple of sips; the stuff was too strong for me.

"How's your crackdown on the drugs? Mine is beginning to flag over in the belfry. I'm not sure how long we can keep it up."

"Yes, I'm expecting the breakthrough anytime soon. I'll keep you informed."

"You seem keen to leave. Don't you care that people will miss you?"

"David, I have to do this, believe me! Or else all we have done will be meaningless. Your mother was like that too in the end—needy. Ask yourself, am I being selfish or are you, by clinging to me?"

I guess he had me on that point. I continued to sit there, forcing myself to drink that awful coffee, if only to prolong the last few hours I had to spend with him.

*   *   *

There is another side to the Samson/Delia story that Samson never told me, but which I unearthed moments ago while reading the correspondence between Joshua and Hannah in her mailbox.

January 10, 2046. Hannah, my mom says that she is going to be moving again. The man in her office is making "demands" on her. Don't know what she means. She is talking about going to Alberta. I'm fed up with moving again. All I can remember is packing and leaving. How can I make friends like you do when I am moving all the time? Will you promise not to stop writing to me and not to stop being my friend?

January 30, 2046. Joshua, there you go again. You are not writing to me again—have you forgotten me or are you still moving?

February 15, 2046. Oh, Hannah, are you still there? I wrote as soon as I could. We are in Alberta now—lots of flat land and cold weather here. Believe it or not, people still wear cowboy hats. Sorry I did not write, but you know that same old thing, had to pay for an Infoway connection. But guess what? I paid for it with my savings from Mr. Kim's store—didn't want to wait for Mom to get a job again.

February 16, 2046. Joshua, you are going further and further away from us. I looked up Alberta on the map today and it's surrounded by water on all sides. Did you take a boat to get there?

February 26, 2046. No, my mom's cousin lives here and he has this very big ranch—dude ranch, he calls it, where people come and stay for long periods and pay him for staying. He sent us a ticket to go by airplane—jeez, you should have seen that plane—it was huge about six hundred people in it and it got us there in two hours. They had all kinds of movies and entertainment on it—live theatre and all. My mom's cousin has given her a job in the reception area so we now live on the ranch. It's huge and I'm going to see if I can get a job tending the barns after school. It's a bit smelly down there but it's great with the horses and stuff. It's a pity I could not stay long enough to buy Mr. Kim's store, but now maybe I'll buy a ranch!

March 1, 2046. Joshua, why are you always trying to buy something? Is it that important? The people who have lots of things in Tolemac give them away to people who do not have much. What are you going to do with all that money and land? That dude ranch must be fun, though.

March 7, 2046. Hannah, now don't you go lecturing me! If you don't have money and land in this place you are dirt poor and I'm tired of being dirt poor and going from place to place. I want my own place like you have. You know my mum's rich cousin is lucky—all he had was an old horse ranch, but then they made a discovery about ten years ago in one of those salt flats on his property. It seems that there is a lot of prehistoric dinosaur bones buried there and people are coming from all over to visit. The last time they had anything in these parts was in a place called Drumheller. It's some ways from here but it got all covered up in the Flood.

March 10, 2046. Josh, now you don't have to get so touchy about my question. If you lived here, you wouldn't have to worry about those things. Dinosaur bones? That must be interesting. So, are you definitely happy there and never going to come back and visit us?

March 25, 2046. Hannah, I'm sorry I was short with you and that I haven't written. I've been working in the barns for a week now—first thing in the morning before I go to school and then in the evenings when I return. It's not too bad because we have a couple of robots, yes robots, that do all the grunge work. I just have to work their controls. But it's still awful in the mornings when you have to clear out the shit—manure, as they call it. Smells ripe and turns my stomach, but I'm getting used to it now. But in the evenings I get tips from the tourists when I take their horses away for grooming. They get a huge kick out of riding horses, which are not available in our cities. There is no animal life in the cities at all, not even cats and dogs, which we have plenty of on the farm. At this rate, I figure I could save enough money to buy voice service by next month and then to send you an airplane ticket by next summer, so you can see what I see. Will you come? Will your dad and mum give you permission?

March 26, 2046. Oh, Josh! That would be great! Joey would be green with envy—no, I mustn't say that—it's wrong according to Grandpa's sermons. He is leaving the church, you know, Grandpa, something about having broken one of the laws. When I asked him whether it's easy to break that law he said it does not apply to me—yet. I hope it never does. Imagine having laws that are easy to break? Anyway, I'm so excited, about the plane trip, although I am sad for Grandpa—that was a big part of his life—the church.

April 5, 2046. Hannah, I spoke to Mum and she says that you can come and stay with us. We have a little cabin on the ranch. Mum is working so well there now she is being made the manageress of the front office, the place where they make all those bookings for the tourists. She went out on a date two weeks ago and ever since that day has been seeing this man. He is the marketing manager I think, and he is about her age. She says they have a lot in common. She has never looked happier, although some days she gets very moody. I don't know what happened yesterday, she started crying after she agreed that you could come. It's not about you. I think it was when I mentioned that your Grandpa was leaving the church. She sat down and wrote that letter she has been trying to write these many months. Sat for hours in front of the Communicator and finally even bid it "farewell" when she hit "send." When I asked her if she were in pain, she said the truth hurt. But then she also said that I should always speak the truth, even if it hurt.

I had stopped reading their message string at that point but it told me enough. That last message was received the day before I met Samson on Market Day.

Chapter 28

OUR SURVEILLANCE MISSION WAS FLAGGING IN ITS FIFTH WEEK. Nothing had come to light. If drugs were being dealt out of Brady's warehouse, then the operators were pretty slick about hiding the fact. Our volunteers began to drop out and we were soon reduced to the core red team again. I sent Paul Samuel a message advising him that if nothing broke in the next week, we would shut down the operation.

My watch was on the evening before the storm hit, and I was alone in the belfry. Tolemac was in twilight and I was bored and absently trailed the telescope away from Brady's warehouse and along the shoreline. The fishing boats were coming in for the day—a familiar sight for a lad who had grown up here. A chop-chop sound overhead heralded the returning helicopters from their daily runs abroad. Very soon, there would be more winged craft and fewer boats, as the additional services from New Eden kicked in. Change was coming our way for sure. And yet, as I shifted my sights onto Main Street and saw the leisurely pace of evening strollers—young couples with children, older folk chatting to passers-by—I felt the world I had grown up in was still a good place. There were still more bicycles than cars. The larger structures of the port and the shops on Main gave way to ordered white houses that rose all the way up Sunset to the last house on the hill, my father's, now standing like a benign guardian surveying its handiwork below. The sight before me strengthened my resolve that Tolemac was worth defending. Samson and his old guard had built this New World; it was our duty to defend it and make it better. Samson was right; constant vigilance was necessary because complacency kills.

My telescope circled back to Brady's, and I tensed when a familiar figure got out of a car that pulled up outside the warehouse. In the streetlight, I made out Ogaki, the man who had shepherded me though Ethan's organization. Dressed in a dark overcoat, he swept inside and signalled to Jeremy Brady; then, without pausing, he went into the office at the back. When Ogaki emerged about fifteen minutes later, Jeremy was following on his heels like a cowed dog. Ogaki paused and said something harshly, then turned on his heels and got into his car. He took off, knocking around the rubbish strewn along Water Street. I managed to get one of the video cameras into position and record Ogaki's exit. Was this the connection to Ethan, or was Ogaki just an unhappy customer with delayed or missing cargo that Brady had failed to deliver?

After I shut down the operation that night, I decided to visit Samson and share this information with him. I found him pacing his study in his night clothes.

"I've got some information that might help," I said.

"Well, it had better." His agitation was palpable.

"What's happened?"

He pointed to his desk. On it was a parcel covered with delivery labels. One transhipment address label said "Williams Trading"; another indicated a final destination address in Oceania. It reminded me of the type of package I had seen Sean toss into his cargo bay the time we returned from New Eden. Its top was ripped open and smaller plastic bags containing pills of some sort spilled onto the table.

"It's a powerful hallucinatory and illegal drug called LXD."

"The stuff that Leo and I took!"

"Sean Galloway brought it to me today."

"Sean?"

"He's a covert operative for the Knights. He's building a case to get an official investigation underway on Williams Enterprises. He was getting impatient and took a risk last night; he slipped into Williams Helicopters' cargo warehouse and smuggled out this package that had been sent from New Eden earlier in the day. Trans-shipment of this consignment to Oceania was being coordinated by Brady's Warehouse."

"Good lord! That's why Ogaki paid Brady a visit today." I quickly told him what had happened and showed him the video clip. "I would never have guessed Sean was involved in this."

"Sean's been getting restless and agitated of late. I set him up with a secret sniffer program from the Communications Centre to get into Williams Enterprises and spy on their day-to-day mail traffic. He's caught a few juicy bits from some of the lower-level operatives like Ogaki, but has not been able to pin anything on Ethan so far. I think Sean threw caution to the winds in ferreting out this parcel. It was probably missed when Brady collected the goods today and must have alerted Ogaki. I think Sean's blown his cover."

"The sniffer. Vladimir?"

"Yes." Samson did not elaborate but continued, "Although we would have all liked to have caught the kingpin, between the false maintenance records, your video, the intercepted mail traffic and this LXD sample, I think we have enough to persuade the NADF to launch a formal investigation into Williams Enterprises. If we wait, the villains might fly the coup or shut down operations for awhile."

"How do we go about it?"

"I'm going to Burgess tomorrow with this evidence."

"Burgess—!"

"Yes. After all, he is still our head of security. Let him deal with this. He vowed to clean this place of corruption. He even got me. Well, this is his chance to prove to Tolemac that his sense of justice and honour transcends family connections."

"You think he will play fair?"

"My sense is he will. He is still one of us—the old guard. At any rate, I will make a duplicate set of all this evidence for you tomorrow. Send it to Paul Samuel, if Burgess does not respond."

"What if he is in league with his son?"

"I doubt it. For all his competitiveness, he is 'old guard.' Our convictions run deep—that much I'll grant him."

"And tomorrow's his big birthday bash—what a present!"

Just then Samson leaned against his desk, winced as if in pain, and sat down heavily on a nearby chair.

I leaped up. "Are you all right?"

His face was mottled, and sweat had broken out on his brow. But he smiled. "It's that darn muscle again. It hits me at the craziest of times. I'll be okay. I'll just sit here till it gets moving again."

It took a good ten minutes before he was able to walk again. I helped him apply ointment on the affected area; then we stashed away the evidence for the night.

"I could never have connected all this with Sean," I said.

Samson paused and looked directly at me. "Fighting this cause has given young Galloway a renewed purpose in life—just like it has given me. I just hope for his sake he is able to complete this job."

That strange, maniacal look flashed across Samson's face again; it was quite unsettling. It made me feel that Samson was about to do something unheard of.

*   *   *

The following day dawned cloudy and damp. The April storms (not the showers of gentler pre-Flood times!) were due anytime. These disturbances blew out mostly to sea, but sometimes they swung inland. That morning the wind was light, but the drizzle quickly became a steady rain and the skies went dark with clouds that did not look likely to move away soon. I was uneasy about what the day would bring. Samson's meeting with Burgess and my concern for Sean's well being, among other things, were playing on my mind.

We closed the school early on account of the deteriorating weather. At about four o'clock in the afternoon, after settling Hannah and Joey with some indoor tasks (Sonya was still over at the gallery), I went in search of Samson to find out what had transpired with Burgess. Samson wasn't at home, so I headed for the dock, thinking he might be insulating his boat from the coming gale. My rain poncho was dripping water down over my boots by the time I got there. His boat was not in dock. I asked the nearby sailboat owners, who were battening their boats down for the storm, if they had seen Samson. One of them, who had brought his boat into dock about an hour ago, had seen Samson taking his boat out at that time. The man remembered because he had remarked to Samson, as they had passed each other, that he probably should be heading the other way, and Samson had laughed and said, "No, this is not that bad—the met office says it's blowing over." But who ever believed a meteorological office? Had we believed their predictions, perhaps the Flood may have caused less damage. My anxiety level increased a notch.

As I pedalled my bike along the wharf and headed home, I saw old Brady tying the battered blue launch that ferried him back and forth and between his Island Bars. The boat even sported Brady's Island Bar livery on its fading façade. I couldn't resist throwing him a jibe, just to relieve my stress: "Weather's not good for business today eh, Brady?"

Brady looked up at the sky and shot back, "The Man up there always screws around with me. It's us hardworking folk who get it all the time." If he was looking for sympathy for having to shut his bars down for the evening, he wasn't getting any from me. I cycled away.

When I got home, Joey informed me that Sonya had called. Due to the bad weather, she was getting a car ride from the gallery to her class at the meditation centre and then back home. With everything going on, I had forgotten her class was tonight. What diehards to attend a class in weather like this! But it was reassuring that she was not going to be out in this weather on her bicycle, especially in her pregnant condition.

After taking a hot shower and grabbing an early dinner with the kids, I fired up the Communicator in my study and went through the daily news. Not good stuff—a Tolemacian student had been hospitalized earlier in the day on a confirmed drug overdose. A picture of the kid, Reggie Theophilus, who had driven his father's car into the water after last year's term-end school party, flashed on the screen. I remembered him; he was one of Joe Sabbattini's inner circle.

I checked my mail. The marketing messages from Morby's, which had been filling my mailbox daily since returning from New Eden, were finally abating—only three offers today. I must have been classified as a "very low probability repeat customer" in their database by now. Good!

After deleting Morby's messages, all that remained was a solitary message sent at six o'clock this evening, half an hour ago. My eyes were riveted on it and my heart started to pound. I was afraid to open it, yet knew that I must. I dragged my finger over it and hit the "open" key.

"Dear David, I decided to leave Tolemac today. Quick departures are easy—no farewell parties, no celebrations and especially no afterthoughts. My work here is done. I would like to have stayed to see Ethan's empire come crumbling down, but I will leave that to his father, an onerous burden indeed for my old partner and rival, Burgess. And I would like to have stayed and greeted my newest grandchild, but that too would have only deflected me from my purpose.

"There will be another election soon, if Burgess carries out the duty I have thrust upon him. Remember, if two or more elected members are unable to serve, the bylaws call for an election to replace them. Sometimes I think that some of our laws were not altogether bad! First me and now very soon Ethan will have to stand down, so I want you to promise me that you will not be discouraged by your first defeat and will run again. With me no longer an embarrassment to you, the field is open once again. The Middle Way is a good thing for Tolemac now.

"There is another thing I want you to promise me. After my fateful talk with Burgess today, and it was an extremely difficult one for my esteemed colleague to pore over all the evidence I presented him, I received an urgent call from Sean Galloway. After the parcel went missing, Ethan ordered a crackdown in his camp. All helicopter flights were suspended—the public reason being the bad weather. But Sean says the witch hunt has begun. That is why I feel it's the right time to get this investigation made official. I want you to contact Sean and put him at ease, for he is still under the protective custody of the Humanitarian realm and cannot be persecuted or sent back to New Eden. But he was very agitated when he called me, and unfortunately I could not meet with him in person before I left.

"Making the decision to leave has been difficult but also liberating. For once in my life, I feel untethered and free. Regrets, yes I have a few. And one I will take to the grave with me is the look on your mother's face the night of her fatal heart attack when she stumbled on Delia and me in the park. Agnes died without giving me a chance to explain. Doug had verbally abused Delia earlier that day and she desperately needed to talk to someone. Sean was walking in the park that evening and later recognized me when he came to your house for dinner. That's what we both have in common—the mark of those dealt an irreversible twist of fate.

"I will be in touch as soon as I am settled in New Eden. Until then,

Congressman Gordon's address is my forwarding address. Give my love to Joey and Hannah and Sonya and Kamala and all the people who are near and dear to me. And to the new life that is still to be born in your lovely family. And do send me pictures of the baby.

"I have left the duplicate package of evidence in my safe. You have the combination. Use it wisely and effectively.

"I have to go now for there is one more job I have to do before I reach New Eden and today is the best day to carry it out. Don't worry about me in the storm. I've dodged many before; besides, I've plotted my route to head around it. Watch out for the fires of retribution—they will burn brightly—soon!

"Goodbye and Godspeed, my son. And all the best in the new elections— they too will come, trust me! Best!—Samson.

"P.S. Along with my journal, which is near and dear to me, I have left you the Camelot tapes, which you'll find among my collection of old movies. Play Part One of that movie when you are feeling down—it tells of a better time. Play Part Two when you are at the top of your game—it will remind you of the consequences of complacency."

I must have sat there for a long time. Only the clock striking the hour disturbed me from my reverie. I had lost my father. And I had not protected him from the overwhelming forces arraigned against him. Despite his many hints and allusions, I had never fully believed he would go this far and leave Tolemac. And I found it odd that he never referred to returning or visiting or even inviting us to visit him in New Eden. It was as if he was going somewhere far way, forever.

I went outside, and the wind gusted in my face. I tied up the bicycles and put the garbage pail inside the garden shed; the gusts were picking up any loose objects now. Taking a boat, in this weather? Asinine! As if in agreement with this sentiment, lightning streaked across the sky, followed by the reluctant growl of thunder. This storm was not blowing out to sea; it was heading our way. But, then, when had Samson stopped what he was planning to do because of inclement weather? I looked over the Hill and towards the Williams's house glittering in the dark. Soon the guests would be arriving there—those that were still determined to venture out on a night like this. Some might even arrive early just to beat the storm, which, if it hit land, could very quickly flood the streets of lower Tolemac.

I went back into the house and stared at my Communicator. Absentmindedly, I typed a message to Paul Samuel: "The game is afoot. I've got plenty of evidence to show you. Get over here quick." I hit "send." It was time to bring in the troops.

I felt a presence behind me and Joey was standing there, a look of concern on his face.

"Something wrong, Dad?"

Looking at his tousled hair, dark brown eyes and the intelligent features of his young face, I wondered whether I would ever leave my son, the way Samson had left me. I wanted to grab Joey and hug him and never let him go. Instead, I said, "No, Joey, in fact the streets will be safer for you soon."

He frowned, not understanding, then said, "Mum's on the other line in my room, she says it urgent. She's been trying to get through to you but you've been busy on your Communicator."

I rushed with him into his room where his Communicator was activated. Sonya's voice came on immediately: "David, please get down to the heliport as soon as you can." She sounded a bit out of breath. Hardly the mood for someone practising deep meditation!

"Honey, what's up? Calm down!"

"Sean came in tonight, just as we were counting down, which was unusual, for he knows the rules of interruption. He insisted on speaking to me in private. I excused myself and took him up to the office, where he told me he was leaving Tolemac for good. Tonight."

"Oh, no," I said. "Too many people are leaving Tolemac for good, tonight!"

"What's that?"

"Never mind—go on."

"He looked awful—either he was very sick or drunk or something. He kept repeating that if he'd only had one break. He was so sad."

"How do you know he's down at the heliport?"

"He said something about taking off in one of the helicopters."

"At this time of the night? In this weather! Okay, honey, listen, you calm down, okay? I'll head down to the helipad right now. And don't worry. Maybe you need to get home early, too, before the weather gets really bad."

"I'll be all right. I feel safer with the class and I've arranged a ride home."

"Okay, but take care, honey. I love you!"

I turned around and now both Joey and Hannah were staring at me.

"Is Mum in some kind of trouble?" Hannah said pouting.

"No, honey." I embraced her trembling body. "But I've got to go out and help a friend. Joey, you are in charge here. I'm going to try and get back before the storm breaks. If it does, don't worry, Mum and I will be safe. Just get into your rooms and keep the Communicator on in case we need to get in touch with you."

They nodded, and when I left, were forcing themselves to concentrate on a game of Abracadabra. I free-wheeled my bicycle downhill to the waterfront. As I passed the dock, I noticed that most of the boats were in and moored for the night and that the place was deserted. Sheets of rain rocked the vessels in their moorings, their blue and red sail covers rolling helpless and dull in the moonless night. I parked my bike, chained it and ran the remaining hundred yards to the helipad. There were six helicopters now—a rapid expansion in less than a year. They stood in their white-circled landing pads, propellers swinging freely in the wind, proud sentinels to a changing society. As expected, the gates to the helipad were locked, but the NADF sentry who was supposed to be on duty was nowhere to be seen. Perhaps he was having a coffee and glad to be out of the wet weather. I scaled the thin wire fence and bruised my shins in the process.

The administrative building that housed the ticket office and customs shed was locked and dark. There was a smaller building next door, which I had taken to be a pilot's mess, as I had seen Sean go in and out of it when we took our trip to New Eden. A light burned inside.

I made my way over to this building and peered in through a window. It was a mess hall of sorts—charts and maps on walls, bomber jackets over chairs, pictures of flyers and their machines from pre- and post-Flood days. All of this was visible in the dim light of a desk lamp. Over the desk flopped a hunched figure, swaying slightly as if half asleep, or drunk. The shot glass and half-empty bottle indicated the latter. Rain poured down the windowpanes making the figure fade in and out before me.

"It's been a while, Sean," I said, and walked into the room through the unlocked door, dusting the rain off my poncho.

"David," he looked up, his face tired and thin. Then he returned to his glass.

"Want a drink? Picked this up in New Eden yesterday." He downed the contents of the shot glass and gritted his features. His clothes were wet and he was shivering.

"No, thanks! Can't add illegal drinking to breaking and entering," I said.

He poured himself another drink and stared out through the window at the swaying propellers of the helicopters. Then he said, "You won't find anything here. Ethan is too smart."

"Not smart enough. There's plenty on him to start an investigation now. Samson gave me the details."

"Ethan's goons, led by that pervert Hal, raided my room at the Waterfront today—turned everything upside down."

"Surely they can't pin anything on you?"

"My Communicator was running the sniffer at the time. They left the machine in pieces. Lucky I was out. I've been dodging them all day."

"It's not your fault, Sean. Don't take this personally."

"Do you seriously think they'll pin anything on Ethan? His father will get him out. Besides, that voice log from the sniffer program I gave your father is inadmissible in court. It was procured illegally without a search warrant. Your privacy laws are pretty cut and dried; they protect the crooked more than the innocent."

"Maybe those technicalities play out bigger in New Eden, but over here our jury might be more sympathetic to the essence of the evidence, not the means by which it was procured."

"I don't think so. I've tried to penetrate his organization for a long time but he has good cover. There are no written records anywhere that connect him. Tolemac with its funny legal system was the perfect base for him. He's a sharp bastard—the type that can only be destroyed, not defeated."

I was reminded of the layers of offices navigated that day I visited Ethan at Williams Enterprises. For a moment I felt panic. What if Sean was right, what if, after all this, Ethan got away from us on some judicial technicality?

Sean was continuing to talk, mumbling to himself: "When Congressman Gordon enrolled me in the Knights, it was my last chance to pull myself from the dung trail that was heading straight for the colonies. Then I came to Tolemac, started the meditation classes, got this job—I was on my way—finally. Flying, being in harmony with my inner self and fighting a noble cause to clean the world of all the vices that had sickened us. It was more than I could ask for. Coming up short like this is a big letdown."

"And now you pacify yourself by drinking? Would you rather run away from the problem?"

"No. I took drastic measures by stealing that contraband. And I'm celebrating what's left of my pitiful life."

"This is a pathetic way to do that, Sean." But his next words made me regret what I said.

"Pathetic. It's symbolic of my life, David. I'm dying. The cancer is back. In a big way this time. That's why I want to get this job over and done with." Then, for the first time that evening, he started coughing. Loud, wracking coughs.

I grabbed for words, for some hope to offer him. "But there are cures now, Sean."

"What if I don't want to be cured? What if it's my soul that is in need of healing?"

I rambled on, "Sonya missed you at the classes. She wondered if you had fallen ill or something. She asked me to come out here tonight and talk to you. Samson, too."

"Your dad is a good man. A fallen one, like me; we are both victims of our respective systems. That's why he took up with the Knights, in the end. Yes, you are a lucky man. You have a wonderful family. For a while back there, I imagined I could have the same, but that was wishful thinking." He downed his shot glass and wrinkled his features. "I wished Ethan had kept Tolemac out of bounds."

"It's not too late to right what you have done. Work with me and we'll ensure justice is done."

"Oh, you are so idealistic. You always believe in justice, don't you?"

"There can only be chaos without it."

Sean rose from the table and struggled into his bomber jacket.

"Don't give up, Sean!"

"Must go now. And give my regards to your kids—and your beautiful wife. By the way, there wasn't anything physical between us, although at times I wished there had been. It's a pity about my classes. It's a pity for all the things I desire but cannot have."

I reached out to grab him—to shake some sense into him, but he spun around at that moment and I saw the gun in his hand.

"I brought this along to help take care of the guards. Don't make me use it on you, David. I am leaving now." He paused to cough. "And don't try to follow me. That bastard Ethan thought that suspending my license would stop me flying. He doesn't know that my skills are up here," he said, tapping his head. With that, he went outside, coughing some more.

I wanted to follow him but held myself back. I didn't like that gun in his hand. After a few moments, I heard one of the helicopters start up and I rushed outside, unable to stop myself. Sean was behind the controls, concentrating, as the big bird lifted from the ground and hovered above the helipad. I saw the NADF guard running towards me. He had probably left his coffee unfinished in his shock and surprise at this unscheduled departure so late in the evening. The man was speaking furiously into his mobile Communicator as he hurried over.

For a few moments, the bird hovered overhead, swaying in the steadily increasing wind and creating gusts of its own. Then, with a tilt of its nose, it glided off over the water. I continued to gaze in its wake, at the disappearing blips of blue and red light, trailed by the chop-chop sound of its blades. The lights came to a stop over the water, as the bird appeared to survey Tolemac from its temporary vantage point.

"What are you doing here, sir?" The guard was beside me. Another of his associates had also appeared from somewhere and was checking the parked helicopters.

"I dropped by to see an old friend," I said, ignoring him and continuing to look skyward at the helicopter. Lightning streaked across the sky just then and illuminated the craft suspended in the air, like a predator marking its prey. I followed the line the helicopter was pointing towards. A convoy of cars was turning into the Williams's driveway, lit like an ocean liner atop Sunset Hill. Dedicated guests and Ethan loyalists who had dared to brave the storm were arriving for the party.

"You'll have to leave, sir," the guard was saying.

"No, Sean, no!" I shouted, but the words stuck to my throat.

The helicopter leaped forward with a jerk and headed straight towards the bright lights on the hill. In my mind's eye, I saw Ethan with a glass of grape juice in his hand, looking at the advancing line of cars, pleased that the inclement weather had not kept his guests from attending. His mute brother would be down in the driveway, waving the arriving cars into the parking lot, ably helped by minder Hal, who would take sadistic pleasure in intrusively frisking the guests before letting them indoors. All this flashed through me as the helicopter plunged into the house with a thundering explosion, engulfing the building in flames that were reportedly seen as far as Oceania.

Chapter 29

ABANDONING MY BICYCLE HALFWAY on the Hill, I struggled up to the crash site. Most of Tolemac had gathered by then, in the pouring rain, oblivious to the thunder and lightning. The smell of oil and burning rubber was heavy in the air and the NADF had thrown a cordon around the blaze to keep onlookers at bay. There was another smell, which I later recognized, the smell of death. A silent crowd had gathered to view the tragedy.

The fire department's three engines pumped away in an attempt to contain the blaze and I heard someone say that the two remaining vehicles, stationed in the New Settlements, were en route to lend support. The rain also helped.

"Where have you been?" Sonya caught my sleeve as I pushed through the front line of onlookers. She was hot and sweaty despite the downpour sliding off her raincoat. I began to feel the heat from the blaze at that point.

I stopped, catching my breath. "How'd you get here?"

"I'd just got home from the class when I saw the explosion. I came rushing over."

"Where are the kids?"

"I asked Belva to look in on them. Don't go in there. They pulled out the bodies a little while ago."

"Bodies . . . who?"

"Ethan and Sean. There's nothing much left of them." She looked away from me. But the tears were glinting on her cheeks in the light of the fire.

I reached for her, "I'm sorry, honey, about Sean."

She kept on talking. "And he didn't come to the classes. If he'd only come to the classes . . ."

"I'm sorry." I held her tightly and felt her trembling.

"They said it was due to a mechanical failure. Something about the storm affecting the helicopter's navigation. Could . . . could that be right?"

"It could have been," I said. There was no point in saying anymore now.

"If he had only come to the last class," her voice trailed off. At that point, I didn't want to know what had gone on between the two of them. After all, a husband and wife must have their secret places. All I knew was that I had Sonya in my arms now and that I wanted to keep her and our unborn baby safe. It made me feel strong amidst the fear, shock and death swirling around us.

From the corner of my eye, I saw John Williams walking around the blaze, pointing it out to those still rushing uphill, his eyes wide in wonder. He didn't appear to know what had happened and looked like he was participating in yet another child's game. Many of the onlookers looked just as stunned. This kind of fire and brimstone had not occurred since the Flood.

"Have you seen Burgess?" I asked, suddenly remembering.

"No. I haven't," Sonya said.

"That's odd. He should be here. He's usually marshalling troops around trouble spots."

"Maybe he hadn't arrived for Ethan's party, yet."

"But he should be here by now. Stay here, honey. I'm going to have a look."

Leaving Sonya huddled in her raincoat, I circled the wrecked building, staying on its periphery. I was soaked by now and the heat from the fire was almost a relief. Two helicopters bearing NADF insignia hovered in the air, straining to keep steady in the wind. Paul Samuel disengaged from a couple of firefighters and headed over, shielding himself from the rain.

"Paul—glad you are here!" I said, in relief.

"I came as soon as I got your message. We saw the crash as we were coming in to land."

"Have you seen Burgess?"

"No," he said. Then he looked at me and got my meaning. We both looked up towards Burgess's house, five hundred yards uphill. Like Samson's house further above, it was shrouded in darkness. "I'll call for reinforcements," Paul said pulling out his mobile as we rushed up to the elder Williams's residence.

Breaking through the front door, we made a grisly discovery. Burgess, still in his dressing gown, was slumped in a chair by the tall windows overlooking Ethan's house. He was dead. In the presence of this sudden overdose of death, I felt nauseous and had to sit down, while Paul called the medics.

When I collected my wits again, Paul was examining the contents on Burgess's desk. A printout of a mail message, queued to be transmitted at midnight from his Communicator to NADF headquarters in Oceania, lay in the centre of his desk. Strewn beside it were a number of items: the courier package from Jeremy Brady's warehouse, several fake helicopter-maintenance receipts, my disposable video disc and another disc, which I took to be the result of Sean's sniffer handiwork. My reeling brain gathered fragments of Burgess's note as Paul read the printout aloud, whistling in between sentences:

" . . . I did not realize these things were happening under my very nose . . . greed attracts powerful forces and we must stamp it out . . . As Chairman of Williams Enterprises and all its affiliate companies, I authorize a full independent audit of our books and its personnel . . . I deeply apologize to the people of Tolemac for falling asleep on my watch . . ."

"If only Sean had waited another day," I said. I was starting to shiver now.

"What?" Paul said.

I ignored his question. "I think I'll go home now. I've had enough of this. I'll catch up with you in the morning."

* * *

"Where's Samson? I didn't see him in the crowd," Sonya asked as we hugged each other and walked the ten minutes downhill to our home. The thunder and lightning was receding now, but there was still a heavy downpour. I was glad for her warmth, as the heat from the crash site faded behind us.

"He's left town," I said. Seeing my abandoned bicycle by the side of the road, I picked it up and rolled it with my free hand.

"Left town? In this weather! David, what is going on?" She'd stopped walking and looked at me for an explanation. I told her about his last mail message.

"My God, what is happening to us?" She could bear it no longer and started crying on my shoulder. I held her to me while the rain beat down on us. With the overpowering smell of destruction and death, the smoke in our eyes, and the chatter of people surrounding the crash echoing in our ears, Tolemac had become an inhospitable place. And looking over her shoulder, I could see another fire out at sea, far out on the shrouded horizon, rising like a pillar of light. I was so accustomed to fire now, I ignored it. I'd had enough with fires for one day. I just wanted to get indoors.

But sleep was impossible for me that night. Sonya fell into an exhausted slumber as soon as we had put the kids to bed, but I tossed and turned, rose and went into my study and looked out the north window that afforded a clear view up Sunset. The fire from Ethan Williams's house was still flaring in places. I walked over to the other window that looked out to sea. The pillar of light I'd seen earlier had been joined by another one further out. If I had taken a giant ruler and placed it between Samson's house and New Eden, the three fires would have been in direct line. "Watch out for the fires of retribution—they will burn brightly—soon!" Samson had said in his last note. They were indeed burning brightly tonight. But my brain was too numb to figure all this out at that time of the night. I fell asleep in my armchair eventually, but was awakened by the fire trucks barrelling past, which in turn woke the neighbour's dog and sent him barking. Sleep was out of the question after that.

*   *   *

The morning following the storm brought more developments. The air was warm and humid, and as expected, the downtown area was flooded. The fire trucks had swapped duty from the crash site and were down on Main Street pumping the floodwater back into their reservoirs. That went on for most of the day, as shops and street-level businesses were evacuated.

More intriguing news came out later that afternoon. On the midday broadcast, Heather Bradley announced that both of Brady's Island Bars had been destroyed the night before. The older bar was a smouldering skeleton of its former self, while the new one had exploded, its superstructure sinking into the waters below. It was reported that Brady's onsite still, located on the premises of the new bar, was the cause of the explosion. The explosion explained the columns of fire I had seen the night before. Freak lightning from the storm was purportedly the cause of fire. To me, that sounded too coincidental, although to Flood veterans it was a plausible answer. God had punished old Brady, finally. And just to prove the point, the old CN tower had finally broken off its rotting base and sunk into the waters too, taking the last trace of the old world with it.

A series of arrests were made that day: Nick Sagar and Jeremy Brady were brought in for questioning. We heard that over in New Eden, Jermaine Brady was also in custody, and his maintenance company to whom "payments" had been made by Williams Helicopters was sealed for investigation. Spoilt, young Reggie Theophilus, now in a hospital room, had openly confessed the night before and identified Nick Sagar as his supplier. Nick caved in soon after he was rounded up, pulling Jeremy Brady down with him. All records belonging to Williams Enterprises were subpoenaed and an investigation was kicked off immediately. An employee in Williams Trading, Ogaki, and another in Williams Enterprises, Hal Uberoth, were arrested, when clear links between them and the smuggling operation were established. A Tolemacian customs officer who was always on duty whenever shipments had come in for Brady's Warehouse by helicopter was also arrested.

All this was new evidence that came to light during the official investigation. The evidence from Sean's activities with the sniffer program was never admitted in court, and Kamala later told me that it was procured in contravention of our privacy laws and before the official investigation was launched, and hence was inadmissible. Sean had been right. Ironically, nothing was found to directly implicate the late Ethan Williams in the drug smuggling operation. Sean had been right again!

A hastily organized inquiry ruled that a combination of mechanical failure and bad weather had resulted in the helicopter crash. No evidence on the physical or medical conditions of the victims was released. There were not much left of their bodies to investigate anyway.

Tolemac mourned and buried its victims. Burgess, pronounced dead through a massive heart attack, was given a hero's burial in recognition of his pioneering work as a member of one of the founding fathers of Tolemac. Ethan and Sean's burials were more subdued—the latter was interred in the public lot, next to Doug Stone. Sonya, Kamala and I attended Sean's funeral. We were the only "family" he had left behind. Samson had been right about Burgess; his desire for public service had overridden his personal feelings, even though the consequences of that decision had been too much for him. The people of Tolemac were shocked and outraged about the exposure to drugs in their community and many public meetings were held to discuss this issue. Although I did not participate in the meetings, I heard that there was mounting support for the Middle Way now.

* * *

Leo came to see me the morning after the crash and he looked cheerful.

"We got them in the end, Mr. Arthurs!" he said.

I smiled. He looked like the Leo I had tutored several years ago in Grades 6 and 7, before the loneliness and pressures of adolescence had taken their toll.

"I told you, Mr. Arthurs—sometimes you have to play them at their game— especially when they least expect it!"

"Leo, I'm sure the NADF will be happy to have you on board with them one day. Are you reconciled with your father now?"

Leo smiled, "Let's say the generation gap between us has shrunk—although he still does not approve of my career choices. But I really enjoy working at the Communications Centre. It's like my dad has opened a whole new world for me!"

Leo was beaming with pride for a change.

* * *

Asif Murtaza tapped on our door just before we retired to bed that evening, and confirmed my anxieties that had worsened throughout the day.

"David, I've got some bad news," he began, glancing about awkwardly on the doorstep. "We've found your father's boat. It had drifted towards Jersey. There was no one on board."

I pulled him into the house with a sinking heart. Sonya came rushing out of the bedroom, pulling on a robe.

Averting his eyes respectfully from the half-dressed Sonya, Asif said, "They haven't found any . . . bodies. My men and the NADF are combing the area now."

When I looked at Sonya, I saw the same expression of helplessness she had that night at the crash scene.

Asif continued, "My crew is towing the boat back to dock. We've arranged for divers."

*   *   *

"What do you want us to do?" Nathan asked me when we regrouped later, after a fruitless night of searching the spot where the boat was found. The area was deep and thick with Flood debris making progress difficult. "Should we presume Samson missing at sea? Or leave it for now? We need to make a statement of some sort; there had been a huge public outpouring of sympathy ever since Heather Bradley released word of his disappearance on the late-night news."

"Let's leave it for now. I'm not convinced he'd go like that. He is too big for life to go out with a whimper." After all, I was going to take a leaf from Samson's book and "not believe the worst of things I couldn't see." I was also in a state of denial.

"Stranger things have happened, David. When you get to my age, you'll know. We had many plans before the Flood, but God had other designs." Nathan put his arm around me. He deferred to my judgment, however, by not making any hasty pronouncements.

And his words were only too true. Strange things did start to happen. Once Samson's disappearance was announced, people began showing up from everywhere. Flowers descended upon his home and ours, and vigils were held all over Tolemac—in the Waterside Park, at the church, over in the dockyard, even at the Executive Committee meetings. There were wreaths, flowers, poems and songs lying all around Samson's walkway leading to his front door. Finally, I had to shut his property to protect our privacy. Even then, I would go every morning and collect a new pile of flowers and sonnets that had been respectfully placed outside the wrought-iron gates of 1 Sunset Hill the night before.

Three weeks later the search thinned and was ultimately given up. Divers had combed the depths below where the boat had been found, but nothing had turned up. All that Flood debris underwater did not help.

And what did I do during those three weeks? Did I do enough? I sent out messages to everyone I knew in the Humanitarian realm and to Congressman Gordon and his team, enquiring if there was any sight or trace of Samson. I went on Heather Bradley's news show and talked about his disappearance. When asked why he was out at that time of the night in a storm, I let the world know that Samson had finally decided to take a vacation. But I covered my embarrassment while saying it. After all, wasn't the man entitled to a break after such a long run of loyal and uninterrupted social service to Humanitarianism, even though his timing could have been better? Heather picked up the story and ran a nightly section on Samson. Sightings poured in from Alberta, Mexico, New Eden, even from as far away as New Zealand, but they all turned out to be hoaxes.

Many replies came in response to my broadcast mail. The added volume of mail, combined with Morby's steady but declining marketing messages, gave me "Mailbox Full" signals every morning. Congressman Gordon's office was one of the first to reply. Marc Gordon was away on a trip in Asia and his office assistant—one John Baptist—whom I couldn't recall meeting in New Eden, wrote a condoling note that ended with the following words: "his disappearance is a great loss to our mutual cause. We trust, however, that you will not dwell on this personal loss, irreplaceable though it may be, but focus on our collective efforts at advancing balanced human ideals. Congressman Gordon will reply when he returns, but until then, please keep the faith and keep up the battle—sincerely! J.B."

I received another surprise note, from young Joshua Stone, which greatly touched me: "Dear Mr. Arthurs, I am sorry to hear about your dad's disappearance. I know it's hard to lose a dad, however good or bad they are. Mom says that she will write to you when she has the strength. Your dad was really kind to my mom and me. Mom has missed him since we left Tolemac and is quite upset about his disappearance. Other than that, we are both okay. I am in school and math is tough but I am trying. I hope you find your dad soon. Give my regards to Joey and Hannah. Bye!—Josh"

I sent him a reply, saying that I had started a tutoring class for Joey and his classmates and that he was welcome to join in via Communicator. I got an instant response, "Gee—thanks! I sure will!"

The note that surprised me the most was from Billy White Dove. It was from his New Eden address.

"Dear Mister David, how are you? I saw you on the news. I still watch the news from Tolemac every day. We get news from everywhere over here—no controls. I am very sorry to hear about Mister Samson. Even though he does not approve of my Rosa, he is a good man—a saint! I will pray for him and for you. He leaves a big shadow—like my Belva. That is why I leave Tolemac, so I can see my own shadow. I am happy now with my own people. New Eden is not bad—some good people are here, like Congressman Gordon. Maybe, good will come from Mr. Samson's disappearance. Maybe, you too will see your shadow now. You are a good man. So is Mister Samson. I pray for you both.—Billy."

Burgess had left a new will, written on the day he died, leaving the proceeds of his estate to the State of Tolemac, except for a small trust fund set up to meet the care of his handicapped son, John. In the ensuing days, the port was parcelled off to a newly established Port Commission of Tolemac, comprised of a consortium of citizens, so that no one would have a monopoly on this key asset of Tolemac anymore. Nathan Goldman made an offer to purchase the helicopter service from Burgess's estate. "Don't worry, David," he told me, "there won't be any airport development in the New Settlements. Why can't they just do with helicopters like us city dwellers, eh?" His offer was accepted.

The Executive Committee declared that owing to the extraordinary circumstances around the sudden demise of so many of its members, a new election for the three replacements would be called within the next two months. This time the election would revert to the old format and excessive campaigning would be restricted. Kamala was appointed the new Chairperson of the Executive Committee. Within days of her appointment, she championed a review of our morality laws—into their effects and effectiveness. The review got support throughout the Humanitarian realm and we look forward to the reforms that will surely follow in the years ahead. Nathan, elder statesman, said that I would be a shoo-in, should I decide to run again in the new by-election, due to the Middle Way's renewed popularity and because I now had everyone's sympathy vote.

"If I do, it will be with some caveats—time off to tutor my son and spend with my newborn," was my resolute answer to Nathan.

"I'm sure they'll settle for that," he grinned. "Work-life balance epitomizes the Middle Way!"

Old Brady suffered a nervous breakdown from which he never recovered after his sons were arrested and his two sources of wealth destroyed (he had no insurance on the bars). Stubbornly independent even in his madness, he refused free treatment, which was his right as a Tolemacian, and wandered the streets talking to no one in particular about his magnificent Island Bars, occasionally stopping pedestrians and asking them to buy him a drink.

The drug-related stories from Oceania began to abate. We had broken the back of the distribution chain. But this was only a reprieve, Paul Samuel told us; soon another pipeline would open, if we were not vigilant. I spent my time at Samson's house and down at his boat, trying to understand what had driven him out into the storm, trying to fend off the images running through my mind of his final hours. I went through all his old pre-Flood movie classics—Camelot, The Ten Commandments, How the West Was Won and Exodus—signs that said my father was a survivor and a builder who had run out of things to build in Tolemac and fallen out of step with its changing times. Every night I looked anxiously for the red light to flash on our Communicator indicating a message from him, but none came.

Could God have taken him just like that? Can a random event such as a storm at sea, change a life, especially one that had endured so many larger storms? But there had been other chance occurrences too: like an innocent walk in the park for Samson and Delia, John Williams putting that lethal construction glue in his mouth, my eagerness to drop off a suitcase at Samson's house, an "off-counter" prescription; random events that had changed lives, forever. So why not a storm at sea taking Samson away? Heroes do not always die heroic deaths—just ask Burgess, if he could only talk now!

I tried concocting alternative scenarios to the one that was taking greater shape in my mind with every passing day. One scenario I particularly liked and often daydreamed about was that Samson had faked his death and gone off to work undercover for Congressman Gordon, to advance Humanitarian principles within the Capitalist realm. John Baptist, personal assistant—yeah, right! How original was that disguise? And yet, I was scared to take a trip to New Eden and find out for myself.

Sonya painted a picture during that period. It was of an angel with thunderbolts coming out of his wings, charging the Williams's house on the hill. It remains in her private collection and I have never seen it on display at any of her exhibitions.

"Sean was special," I said. "The tormented angel."

"The most authentic kind," she said, gently applying the finishing touches to the portrait.

One night she awoke from a nightmare, streaming with perspiration.

"Honey, are you okay?" I was still shaking off the cobwebs of sleep, trying to get fully awake.

"There was a boat," she said. "And a fire . . ."

"What else! What did you see?"

She shook her head. "That's the problem with dreams—they fade as soon as you wake up." She lay back and stared at the ceiling. Soon she was asleep again.

But in her sleep I heard her mumbling. "Samson . . . oh, Samson . . ."

A month into Samson's disappearance, I received a sobering message from Congressman Gordon himself:

"Dear David, I am so sorry to hear about your father's disappearance. Sorry I was unable to respond, for I was travelling in some very backward parts of Asia, with no proper communications facilities, trying to summon support for the best in our Capitalist and Humanitarian ideologies. And, believe me, even in these developing and somewhat barbaric societies, there is a glimmer of hope and a strong desire for collaboration over competition. Once upon a time we were all one. Then humankind drifted apart. But there is something in our genetic code that is drawing us together again and I see it wherever I go. But we have lots more work to do before we reach our goal.

"I have lost a loyal supporter in your father. He was the man who kindled my passion for this mission and has now left me to soldier on alone. But we are not discouraged. His message will live on and we will persevere. In fact, your father's death, if he is indeed dead, will increase his stature and make him an icon. If there is anything we can do for you or your family, please let me know. In the meantime, I trust you too will carry the torch your father carried and continue his unfinished work. Sincerely, Marc Gordon.

"P.S. You will be interested to know that I have since decommissioned my two robot servants and replaced them with a working family destined for the colonies. An excellent suggestion of your father's! At least, there is some company about the house now."

That afternoon, I went down to Samson's boat, now innocently docked at the pier, its contents undisturbed since the night of his disappearance. I had spent many hours in this boat, replaying in my mind his final scene, trying to think of a different one that would prove me wrong and indicate he was still alive, but always coming back to the most likely scenario. Whenever I looked at the evidence about me—the spare fuel container, empty but carefully stored despite the main tank holding sufficient fuel to get him to New Eden (and back!); the missing portable navigator that Samson had recently purchased; the missing mooring rope; his bag of clothes undisturbed; the fully operational ship-to-shore radio that was never used during his emergency—I knew the answer. I was just hiding from the truth. That evening, I left the boat for the last time. It was time to get on with things.

When I got home, I deleted Samson's final letter—the only piece of incriminating evidence. His secret was safe with me. So was Delia's.

"It's time," I said to Sonya after dinner.

"I'm glad," she replied gently.

"You knew?"

"I see ghosts too, remember?"

Yes, I remembered. The little girl with a water lily in her hand, communing with our ancestors.

She came and sat by my side and there was no need for words this time. She knew that I was finally ready to accept Samson's passing. I also made another resolution that night, which I shared with her. I would run in the next by-election under my own terms—work-life balance being one of them. And this time I was going to win. I was not going to be half-assed about it anymore. This was Samson's legacy to me. Sonya squeezed my hand gently in encouragement.

*　*　*

He circled the boat towards the second island bar and locked the steering. He didn't moor the craft to the platform in case he needed to make a swift exit. He transferred the code of the boat's coordinates into his portable navigator and dropped the device into the pocket of his raincoat—his insurance, in case the vessel drifted in the choppy water or the rope steps to the bar became inaccessible. Out on deck, he looked back at the flames shooting into the sky from the first fire—that had been easy, the old place was a tinderbox and went up with a single match. And the fuel used for dousing the place had helped; it was the new alcohol-based boat fuel. After a fire, no one could distinguish it from the stuff people imbibed, and there was plenty of the Devil's brew around in Brady's Island Bars! He had picked a good night too, when the bars were closed, for his issue was with the bars and their owner, not with their misguided customers, and he did not want anyone hurt.

Besides, his hunch about the weather had proven right. The storm had blown inland and all he had to contend with on the open water was light rain and tough seas. A good night for a bonfire, with plenty of wind to fan the flames! He'd seen the other fire too, the one on land, just as he was reaching the first island bar; the on-board Communicator had given him the news. Poor Burgess! But he was too far progressed in his mission to worry about things like that. "Keep going and don't stop to think," was his motto. God indeed is at work tonight!

He picked up the spare, half-empty fuel container, swung the mooring rope over his shoulder (the rope would come in handy if he needed to lower himself into the boat from another location on the platform) and jumped the three feet to the steps of the platform. The first time had been harder when the container was full. But when he landed this time he felt the familiar numbness in his leg muscle. He had to sit down for a minute until the feeling in his limb returned. Then he slowly ascended the shaking steps to the bar. The jimmy in his pocket helped him break the lock to the main lounge. His flashlight illuminated gaudy paintings—topless women, sports stars from a bygone era. Brady had no taste. But a man who lived in no man's land and was touched by no man's law was still answerable to God.

He took off his raincoat, threw it over a chair and went to work. He splashed the contents of the fuel tank liberally over the bar, the pictures, the tables, even over the new gambling section with its green baize counters. There was a door leading off the bar and he opened it. Steps descended to a galley downstairs. Shining his flashlight, he descended. Three silver metal tanks, with tubes leading from them, lined the walls. A bottling machine was situated nearby with rows of bottles stationary on a conveyor belt. Crates propped the far wall with what looked like vials of whiskey in them. Brady has got himself a veritable alcohol factory in here, he mused. He emptied the rest of the fuel container over the crates.

Back upstairs he surveyed his handiwork. Good. "Now let it work—villainy thou art afoot!" Mark Anthony, he remembered—Shakespeare. He struck a match and tossed it behind the bar. The fire swooshed up instantaneously and it was time to get out. He grabbed the mooring rope and the empty fuel container and descended the steps rapidly. He was pleasantly surprised that the boat had not drifted. He had no problem getting back on the vessel, throwing the rope down on the deck and stashing away the empty fuel container. He went into the main cabin and tried restarting the engines. Heck! The control had been transferred to the portable navigator, which was still in his raincoat pocket draped over a chair in Brady's bar!

He went back out, quickly this time. Flames were ripping apart the bar overhead, very soon the stairway would be on fire. He had to go back up; there was no option. He grabbed the mooring rope again and hauled himself up the stairs, two at a time and stumbled back into the lounge. He held his breath, for the smoke was intense, feeling his way over to the chair. He retrieved the raincoat and retreated. Just then, there was a bang from below decks and he was thrown against the door. His leg muscle gave way again and this time he could not move. He tried dragging himself outside. Now he was outside and he sucked in gulps of air. The boat was right below him. Could he jump? Too far! Another explosion went off below decks and the whole structure began to heave and tilt. It was too late—there was no way he was going to get out. And with the next explosion, the last cylinder, this hellhole was going to sink in the ocean like a stone, no doubt about it. There was only one thing he could do, and that was not to let this thing get back to disgrace his beloved son again. No trace of Samson Arthurs must ever be found in this inferno. He pulled out the portable navigator from his jacket pocket and in the staccato light, reset the controls of the boat and started the engines. Turning off the brake remotely, he sent the vessel off into the night.

Then he dragged himself back into the lounge, unslung the mooring rope from his shoulder and lashed himself to the central column that was holding the whole structure together and was dangerously tilted on its side. He started to black out and his lungs were bursting from the smoke. He managed a smile, when the third explosion brought the last of Brady's Island Bars crumpling down and sank it into the waters. Waters that he had escaped so many years earlier and that now eagerly reached out to claim his body. As he descended into the depths, to be buried under piles of debris dating back to the Flood, the waterlogged control panel in his raincoat pocket gave out, disengaging the boat and setting it adrift in the ocean.

*   *   *

So there it is. The end of Samson's story—at least, the way we arrange things to make them fit our logical maps and save us from insanity. And based on Samson's journal, which I have read tonight, this re-creation is the only one I can live with, and I will write this part to complete his chronicle. If Sonya ever reconstructs her nightmare, I think the pieces will fit my depiction.

Daylight is filtering in through the bedroom curtains. I go into the kitchen and pour myself a mug of coffee. I look out the window. Tolemac is mostly intact, now that the crash debris has been cleared and the floodwaters drained away. One thing is for sure—cataclysms like the Flood do not wipe out sins. They give us a fresh slate to repeat our foibles. A thousand years of peace is what the Bible had forecast after the Flood. There is no such thing. All this stuff has happened before. It happened at Camelot, happened right through the last century and is happening again: iterations of mankind's quest to find himself by screwing things up—hopefully, a little less each time. We just have to keep refining each iteration, and hopefully, those one thousand years of peace—our nirvana—will come one day. Hannah hit it on the head when she said, "I don't understand why they make silly laws that are easy to break."

And to convince myself that the world is still largely intact, I rise and go into each of my children's rooms to hug and kiss my children. They are blissfully asleep—Hannah even manages a sleepy giggle; my hug must have coincided with one of her "dreams." As I tiptoe out of her room, she wakes and whispers, "Dad, is that you?"

"Yes, honey. Go back to sleep. It's early."

"Dad, I had a dream."

Oh, Oh!

"I dreamed of Grandpa. He finally came to me. He was with Grandma and they both looked happy."

"What did he say?" I said half turning, a chill running down my spine.

"He said that Grandma now understands why he was taking a walk in the park that day. What did he mean?"

I smile. Now I can let *both* my parents go. "Go back to sleep, honey. And dream a bit more."

"Did you fix my password?"

"Sure did, honey."

I go into our bedroom and kneel down by my wife and kiss her on the forehead. She murmurs in her sleep and turns toward me. She is beautiful, in her slumber, even with that bit of drool sticking out of the edge of her mouth. I kiss her swelling belly where the baby is already up and kicking. And I kick myself silently for doubting her fidelity.

Then I quietly exit the house and head down for my appointment with Peter Lowry. Mrs. Wang is getting her music ready on Martyrs Square and soon the dancers will be out in their sleeveless vests, now that the weather is warming up. Old Brady is up early, too, and wandering around, looking for someone to buy him a drink. Perhaps the Medical Fund will find him a home at the psychiatric ward soon, where he can join the wave makers and the cowerers in their mindless antics. Brady, the villain, finally returned to innocence—now, that was a good outcome! The Tai Chi practitioners will also be heading down to the Waterside Park, before the sun gets too hot, Nathan among them. Yes, Sean was right. I am indeed a lucky man, and I don't have to turn around to see my long shadow in the early morning sun!

Epilogue

JULY 15, 2046. JOSH, GUESS WHAT? My baby brother was born on July 1, on Tolemac's thirty-third anniversary. Sorry I couldn't write earlier, everything's been crazy since he was born. The house is a mess with everyone rushing around, including Grandma Kamala, Aunt Belva and the church ladies; everyone's trying to help Mum with the baby. I am dashing off this note as we are leaving for the Baptism ceremony. The baby is to be named Samson Nathaniel Arthurs, and Uncle Nathan is so happy there is someone to carry his name. He promises to leave baby Sam a rich inheritance. I'm glad too, because Sam is carrying my Grandpa's name. Grandpa is at peace with Grandma—they are both very happy now. I see them often in my dreams. They hold hands and walk in a place just like our Waterside Park where we used to fly our kites, remember?

But here's the best news: Dad and Mum have agreed to send me to Alberta for the school holidays! In a plane! Dad will drop me off at the airport in Oceania—and don't worry, you can save your money. He will pay for my ticket. After Dad won the election last month, he has been very busy with a new project—multilateral trade relations—something to do with regulating those helicopter flights and working with the Capitalists on things that are important to both sides. Maybe you could ask him about it during your weekly math class. He says we need to "reach out" to the other side. If he means to people like you who live far away, I could have told him that a long time ago. Sometimes adults don't get it, do they? Will you meet me at the airport? Call me later—I'm so glad you're getting "voice" soon—writing these notes is so boring. Bye!—Hannah.

Afterword

The Evolution of Tolemac

Curious readers have asked me to describe Tolemac and its environs in detail. I refrained from elaborate descriptions in the first edition of the novel because my editors had cautioned me to avoid too much "telling." I therefore deleted swaths of physical description of Tolemac in later drafts of the novel, which are now lost forever.

That said, in acquiescence to my readers, let me try and re-create a picture of this city-state and its genesis.

When the world fragmented and drowned in the cataclysm of 2012, land masses floated around and re-aggregated under different physical compositions: where there was once land, there was now water and vice versa. National boundaries became ungovernable as they were underwater. National governments, already under pressure from the global financial meltdown of 2008, quickly declared bankruptcy and sold off their assets to private enterprise. A specially prized asset was the huge military infrastructure of the former US and Canada, which was grabbed by a group called the North American Defence Fund, who then, for a profit, provided anyone subscribing to it with security and protection.

Without the interference of big government, humans became more self-reliant, and the more ambitious ones preferred a laissez faire approach, while others who had huddled together for survival chose the collective path. This polarization led to the development of two strong ideologies along which the survivors governed themselves: the Capitalists under the motto of "Winner takes all" and the Humanitarians under the creed of "From each according to his ability, to each according to his need." Given that people were free to embrace whichever ideology suited them, the like-minded formed city-states that ran under their citizens' beliefs. This led to absolute cohesion within but polarization outside the boundaries of these agglomerations. Other than for minimal exchanges—and a steady inflow into the Capitalist realm which remained open to newcomers who could bring along competitive advantage with them (students, healthy workers, intellectual and financial capital)—the borders between the Capitalists and the Humanitarians were closed off from each other. Eventually, city-states, be they Capitalists or Humanitarians, scattered about the area that was once North America, grouped together into loose federations to trade, exchange and develop economically, giving birth to the League of Capitalist Nations (LCN) and the Federation of Humanitarian States (FHS).

This polarization was as if the Flood had also split the duality of Man into his altruistic and egotistic parts and placed them in opposite corners, each incomplete on its own, each yearning for re-unification with its other half— hence the quest for the Middle Way by David, a next-generation Tolemacian looking to rediscover his roots.

Communication largely fell back upon the Internet which was found to be working despite the Flood, as it had been originally designed to find alternate pathways to transmit its content should sudden barriers arise along its normal route; and the availability of satellites enabled the Internet to surmount the destruction on land following the Flood. Thus everything from healthcare to education to commerce was conducted via the Infoway, as it was renamed, after more investment was poured into developing the Internet's backbone. Media channels converged, as we see them coalescing today and all forms were merged into a device called a Communicator (The IPad and PlayBook weren't invented at the time I began writing this novel in 2002, but I had an inkling that these devices were on their way). I even had a strong feeling that books would go electronic at the time; hence the instant book printing machines in Tolemac's bookstore.

Infoway communication within the FHS was tightly controlled due to a fear of contamination by ideas from the more liberal LCN. Heavy firewalls were erected to prevent spyware and other malicious viruses from infiltrating. As a consequence, anti-virus software became one of Tolemac's core competencies and exports.

Face-to-face communication in the FHS states was reduced to exchanges within each state itself, and very few, like Oceania, developed their roads and highways. Tolemac's road network was largely undeveloped other than in the main downtown area. Travel between FHS states was conducted largely by boat and undertaken only in unavoidable situations. The LCN states on the other hand, like New Eden, believed in a better infrastructure that included air, sea and ground transportation links, as these were seen as enablers of trade and expansion.

In the realm of creativity and invention, the LCN states again outstripped their FHS counterparts by developing sectors like robotics and genetics, while the FHSs, rooted in a throw-back Biblical philosophy, eschewed these practices and remained economically stagnant, though morally superior. Consequently, the LCN fostered drug and alcohol addiction, high mortality rates, promiscuity, conspicuous consumption, marketing entrapment, high divorce rates and rapid human resource obsolescence, while the more vulnerable citizens of the FHS suppressed their material and sexual desires, and dreamed of the grass being greener on the other side.

As the Humanitarians bonded together, and because of their conviction that the Flood was God's punishment to a sinful Man, they began to construct strict laws governing human conduct that would never again permit pre-Flood transgressions. But laws only beget more laws and the Humanitarians soon went on a law-making spree to cover for everything. There were morality laws and income declaration laws, anti-drinking, anti-drug, and anti-theft laws. Like in any fundamentalist society, excessive laws eventually become straightjackets that protect as well as inhibit behaviour that would normally lead its citizens to discovering their true selves. Privacy became a key consideration as personal space was still a human right, and in a world in which everything had been lost, preserving one's space had become even more important. Tolemac's founding fathers erroneously believed that their strict lawmaking in other areas was counterbalanced by their equally rigid privacy laws.

By the year 2046, Tolemac was being governed by a selfless group of elders who had been in office for several years and had become stale on the job. And yet, because they had brought stability to their city–state, and because of the general antipathy towards change in Tolemac's citizens, new blood was not being generated into the Executive Committee, until David was pleaded with and cajoled to join, and then too, only when the elders saw a potential threat in Ethan Williams seeking office purely for selfish reasons.

Tolemac's secret yearning for progress is seen in its younger population's drift towards the New Settlements, in their hunger for better transportation and material goods, and in Ethan's expansion of helicopter services. Conversely, the Capitalists' desire for balance is reflected in the Knights of Eden wanting to introduce the Humanitarian WorkOUT plan in their own realm—signs of the two halves reaching out to coalesce, as do young Joshua and Hannah, the third post-Flood generation, who may actually achieve this unity.

I received criticism that this New World was not "science fiction" enough. I mean, where are the space ships and the super heroes and the androids and the intergalactic warfare? The critics are right in that respect: the world after the Flood looks eerily reminiscent of our dull existing one, and the characters could be people living in our neighbourhood today. But it is our existing world that I wanted to portray, albeit scarred, broken, and patched together after a cataclysm on a scale far greater than all of history's wars, floods and earthquakes combined. Some infrastructure that was salvaged has been redeveloped, like the Internet; others have been left to languish, like the roads of Tolemac, and by 2046, the year in which the main part of the story takes place—34 years after the Flood—mankind has just caught up, barely. As Samson says, "There is so much to do, so much infrastructure—physical, moral and societal—to build, now that we have regressed so many years. I wonder if there will be enough time in my life to even catch up to what we had."

I set out to physically describe Tolemac to you but may have drifted into explaining my rationale for painting this world the way I did. And thereby, I may have fallen into the trap of "telling," something writers are not encouraged to do anymore. Unfortunately, for writers, there does not appear to be a clear Middle Way between showing and telling, and if indeed there is one, it is a path we toil all our lives to try and discover.

I often return to Tolemac in my dreams, a world in which I spent many years during the writing of this novel, and one I wish will only remain in fiction. During my visits to this dystopia, I wonder whether one can ever judge the behaviour of those who have lost everything, and with such suddenness. If abused children later abuse, if the progeny of alcoholics end up drunks, who are we to sit in judgement on the denizens of Tolemac or New Eden for the way in which they turned out, and for the way in which they messed up their world again? Are we better served to get off our moral high-horses and emulate David in his never-ending quest to find and reconcile those two halves of himself and steer his beloved city-state back to normalcy via the Middle Way? Dear Reader, this is a question I would like to leave with you.

Shane Joseph - 2010

Acknowledgements

I wish to thank my publisher Richard M. Grove (Tai) for continuing to have faith in me. And to Kim Grove for her spirited debates on the characters within the pages of this novel.

To my editors: Alethea Spiridon who evaluated the initial draft of the manuscript, Susan Folkins who completed the copy editing, and Jake Hogeterp who was determined to give it a "once over."

To my fellow writers of the Pollard Group in Northumberland County, for their valuable observations on what detail of this brave new world and its denizens to include and what to remove.

To the readers of the Humber School for Writers for their incisive feedback on the drafts I submitted.

To Lorna Tucker and Gael Moore who gave me a reader's perspective on the final manuscript.

To my dear wife Sarah, for reading the manuscript over and over during its emergent stages and who had faith in the story to have me pull it out of my "abandoned projects" file for one final shot that saw it through to publication.

And to our children who will inherit the world of *After the Flood* — they made the writing of this novel purposeful. Let us hope that the Flood remains in fiction.

Shane Joseph

Biographical Sketch of Author

Shane Joseph began writing as a teenager living in Sri Lanka and has never stopped. From an early surge of short stories and radio play scripts, to humorous corporate skits, travelogues, case studies and technical papers, then novels, more short stories and essays, he continues to pursue the three pages-a-day maxim and keeps writer's block at bay.

His career stints include: stage and radio actor, pop musician, encyclopaedia salesman, lathe machine operator, airline executive, travel agency manager, vice president of a global financial services company, software services salesperson, and management consultant.

Self-taught, with four degrees under his belt obtained through distance education, Shane is an avid traveller and has visited one country for every year of his life. He fondly recalls incidents during his travels as real lessons he could never have learned in school: husky driving in Finland with no training, trekking the Inca Trail in Peru through an unending rainstorm, hitch-hiking in Australia without a map, escaping a wild elephant in Zambia, and being stranded without money in Denmark, are some of his memories.

Shane is a graduate of the Humber School for Writers in Toronto and studied under the mentorship of Giller Prize and Canadian Governor General's Award winning author David Adams Richards. *Redemption in Paradise*, his first novel, was published in 2004. *Fringe Dwellers*, his first collection of short stories, was released in 2008, and is now in its second edition. Shane's third work of fiction, *After the Flood*, a dystopian novel of hope, was originally released in 2009 and won the Best Novel award in the Futuristic/Fantasy category at the Canadian Christian Writing Awards in 2010. His short fiction has appeared in several literary journals and anthologies in Canada, the USA, UK, India and Sri Lanka. His blog at www.shanejoseph.com/blog is widely syndicated.

After immigrating (twice), raising a family, building a career, and experiencing life's many highs and lows, Shane has carved out a niche in Cobourg, Ontario with his wife, Sarah, where he continues to work, write stories, and play guitar in a dance band.

More details on Shane's work and blog can be found on his website at www.shanejoseph.com

After the Flood

A dystopian novel of hope

Shane Joseph

Reading and Book Club Guide

The following reader and book club guide is intended to help you find interesting approaches to reading and discussing *After the Flood*. We hope this enhances your enjoyment and appreciation of the book – Hidden Brook Press

Questions and Topics for Discussion

1) This book has been called "*Noah's Ark* meets *Samson & Delilah* at *Camelot* in the *Brave New World*." What aspects of these classic stories are present in this novel?

2) In his Author's Note, Joseph disclaims that this is a work of science fiction. Would you agree? If not, why?

3) The ideologies of Humanitarianism and Capitalism are portrayed as forms of Fundamentalism, and David tries to forge a Middle Way between them. Discuss other forms of extreme attitudes in society today that could be classified as Fundamentalist. Based on your discussion, would you say that North America is tipping towards, or away from, Fundamentalism?

4) David is the reluctant hero while his father, Samson, believes in getting things done regardless of the consequences. How likely is David, as a passive hero, to solve Tolemac's problems compared to a swashbuckling, action-hero figure?

5) The children of Tolemac see ghosts. Is that something to be expected in people after a cataclysm of this proportion?

6) There is no real evidence of whether Delia committed murder. What is your opinion?

7) Why does Kamala get sick after Samson's trial?

8) Sean and Leo are victims of their respective societies. One self-destructs in a heroic act while the other is saved through his teacher's belief in him. How do we reach out to victims in society today? Are there more Seans or more Leos in our world?

9) The main story takes place in 2046, yet the technology appears antiquated for that time. Do you think that we will be further ahead technologically in the mid-21st century, even if we have to re-build should a massive flood destroy most of our known world? What are the bases of your projections?

10) An aircraft being deliberately flown into a building is considered the act of a madman in our post-9/11 world. In this book, it is an act of desperation, to dislodge duplicitous politicians from positions of power. What other parallels to present times are drawn in this book?

11) In the end, *After the Flood* offers no solutions to mankind, other than to propose taking a serious step from extreme rigidity towards openness and tolerance for the other side. Is this "Middle Way" a prescription for the "1000 years of peace" to come, or is this approach also fraught with risk of failure, and why?

12) How would Hanna and Joshua's generation govern this new world, given that they understand the art of collaboration and are not wedded to either Humanitarianism or Capitalism? Or would they too be consumed by these ideologies as they approach adulthood?

The author, Shane Joseph, is happy to talk, read or discuss *After the Flood* with book clubs, reading groups and schools who are interested in reading this book. He can be contacted at shane@shanejoseph.com or by visiting his website at www.shanejoseph.com.

**Other Hidden Brook Press books
by Shane Joseph**

— *Fringe Dwellers* – ISBN – 978-1-897475-44-7 - *Second Edition* – Collection of short stories

— *Changing Ways* – ISBN - 978-1897475-22-5 – anthology of short stories includes Shane Joseph's work – "Between Floors" – *p. 14* and "Revelations in Chile - Three Stages of Career Change" – *p. 149*

— *Spilling to the Sky* – ISBN - 978-1-897475-41-6 – anthology of poetry and short stories includes Shane Joseph's short story – "The Deer Hunt"